Print ISBN: 979-8-35092-9-263
eBook ISBN: 979-8-35092-9-270

JUPITER
CONTACT

DAVID PANKEY

ONE
THE MEET

J ON GALLOCK THREW A STICK on the small campfire and leaned back
against a tree. He had finished his second day backpacking in the Pecos
wilderness and he felt surprisingly good, although a little stiff. *Not too bad
for a guy hitting fifty this year,* he thought. Dinner was done, and dessert
was a generous shot of scotch, a little luxury he allowed himself on the trail.

Jon was a fit man with thick black hair going to salt and pepper. He
stood slightly over six feet and slightly under two hundred pounds. An
engineer by training, he was quickly drawn to the dark side—the business
side—and picked up an MBA. He quickly advanced into management due
to his people skills and analytical abilities. After three high-tech companies
in the last ten years, he needed this break before deciding if he wanted to
jump into another early-stage company. Divorced long ago, his one marriage had been a five-year, slow-motion train wreck.

A stick cracking made Jon look up from pouring the scotch. "Hello
the fire," said a voice as a man walked to the campsite. Except, this was no
man. This was an android.

The android, obviously a robot with roughly human shape, was about
Jon's height and composed mostly of what appeared a slick rubber or neo-
prene skin. The face and joints were metallic. "May I join you?" he (it?)
asked. "I promise not to put you on the spot by asking for your leader."

"Uh..., sure, pull up a log." Jon gestured at a nearby fallen, broken tree
which he had tried unsuccessfully to move earlier. No hallucinogenic
mushrooms in the area, he thought, and no way a person was actually
inside of that getup.

The android casually pulled, one-handed, the far end of the heavy tree
trunk closer, then the other end, took a seat, and rubbed his hands together

and extended his palms towards the fire. "The night air gets nippy at this altitude, don't you think?" he asked.

Alien, Jon thought. The strength, balance, and fluidity exhibited by the entity did not exist in current robotics. Nor was such sophisticated technology likely to develop anytime soon. This was so far advanced, the android was surely alien technology. *Shit, shit, shit.*

A short awkward silence ensued. Jon broke the ice.

"You're obviously not from around here," Jon said. "Will you tell me about yourself?"

"Of course," said the android. "Call me Robert. That's not really my name you understand, but simply a convenient label to make you feel more comfortable. I am not alive or even sentient by your standards. I have a high degree of what you call artificial intelligence. I am linked to my controller, who is a sentient being, who you may also consider Robert. I function as a telepresence—his eyes and ears in this environment. The construct before you has the knowledge and ability to carry on this conversation, and act independently, within certain bounds. Occasionally the sentient, Robert may give me advice or directions."

"I'm Jon Gallock," replied Jon.

"The sentient race that sent me, the device before you, you may call the Chait."

"Why send you?" asked Jon. "Why not come in person?"

The android leaned forward and casually poked at the fire with a stick. "Do you think the fire needs more wood?" he asked. "Here, let me get some." Arising, he broke a dead tree limb over his knee and carefully added two sticks to the fire. "That's better," he said.

Jon sipped his scotch. The display of robotics, as well as artificial intelligence, was mind-blowing. The android, or a remote controller, had accurately assessed the fire, poked the half-burned sticks into a better configuration, and then added a reasonable amount of wood to the right spot. The casual way the visitor expertly assumed ownership of Jon's fire subtly altered the relationship between them. *I wonder*, Jon thought, *if he is stalling for time while waiting for guidance to answer the question.*

The android answered indirectly. "The Chait did not originate in this solar system. An exploration vessel is in orbit around Jupiter. The ship is on a long-term voyage of exploration and study. We have been here, in your solar system, observing humanity, for a number of years. The work is interesting as we find humans engaging to study. The human race is extremely interesting and not a little appalling. Our instruments easily pick up your news and entertainment broadcasts. We also have sensors which monitor all human electronic communications. As you might expect, we initially had some difficulty in determining the difference between fact and fiction. We still struggle to determine the difference while watching your evening news.

"There could be many reasons we don't want to land in person," said the android, getting back to Jon's question. "Perhaps the atmosphere or gravity does not agree with us. Local molds, fungi, bacteria, or viruses may be deadly. Perhaps we are concerned with the legalities. Obviously, the Chait don't have official papers and might be treated as illegal aliens wherever they landed."

"Yes," said the android, "that was a play on words."

Robert continued. "Being nonhuman, we might lack basic rights, and could be treated like a chicken, or chimpanzee. So, the danger of being eaten, or confined in a zoo, might be a consideration. I imagine authoring a paper on the first dissection of an intelligent alien species would be a feather in the cap of a CDC or NIH researcher.

"Think about the furor any public appearance would cause," continued the android in his pleasant, accent-free colloquial American English. "Even if we could walk upon the Earth's surface, would we want to do so? A public landing of a large spacecraft carrying aliens would cause widespread political and religious upheaval."

"But you have so much to offer humanity," replied Jon. "Given your obviously advanced technology you could cure this world's ills. I imagine you could end disease, hunger, wars, provide clean, cheap power. Why not? And why won't you appear in, er, person?"

"Before I blurt out an answer, let us talk through the possible ramifications a little more," said Robert. "Why don't you refresh your scotch and light your cigar? We may be awhile."

As Jon pulled his aluminum cigar carrier from his backpack, he wondered how Robert knew they were there. *Were his senses that keen? Did he have a sense of smell acute enough to detect the well-packed stogies? If so, how had he obtained the knowledge to differentiate among various slightly different tobacco odors—cigars or cigarettes, pipe tobacco or dip? How did the android determine the brown liquor was scotch? Did he observe me packing for the trip? Did he possess X-ray vision? Can he read my thoughts?*

With Jon once more seated before the fire, Robert continued, "For example, consider your belief systems, including religions. Many are fundamentally irrational and ignore inconvenient, though incontrovertible facts. You have religions which believe one benign entity created the entire universe, while others believe the Earth rests on the back of a giant turtle. Consider Christians and Muslims for example. Not only have the respective followers killed the other since their institutions were formed, they also enthusiastically murder those of the same faith over minor doctrinal differences. Shia or Sunni? Protestant or Catholic? Some percentage of humanity reacts to otherness, with fear and revulsion. That certainly won't be less when the stranger is a hideous bug-eyed alien monster as well.

"Religion is only one belief system. There are many others. Some are harmless, like truly believing the Cubs win the series this year; others are not.

"At one level your political systems are based on belief. However, the leaders and organizers are more interested in the power and material gains. Those leaders will look at the existence of intelligent alien life from a transactional view. 'Does this change in events improve my personal position relative to others, or not? If not, I will oppose the change in any way I can.'

"Any technical advances we may introduce will have a disproportionate impact. Many winners, but always a few losers. And some of those potential losers have nuclear weapons. Clean, cheap power hurts the big-energy producers such as your America, Russia, and the medieval Persian Gulf states. Few of those nations' governing class will be happy with universal access to clean, cheap power.

"Revolutions tend not to occur when things are terrible; they happen when times are improving. Ironically, many of your governments would fall if the lives of their subjects improved. Most governments will not welcome advanced technology which improves the lives of their masses.

"Your planet contains eight billion people. Should we come to the Earth, some percentage of those people will hate and fear us. Furthermore, any technology we introduce will, at least in the short term, cause a furor as well.

"Our studies indicate physically landing on your planet and sharing meaningful knowledge, by which I mean transferring powerful, revolutionary technology, would likely trigger nuclear war. Transferring technology less potent may or may not improve people's lives. However, such a course is not very interesting to us."

After a pause, Jon's curiosity got the best of him. "People have been reporting unidentified flying objects for decades. How long have you been here?"

"A Chait craft is not detectable by your technology," said Robert shortly. "Whatever you believe you are seeing is not us."

"Are you implying we are detecting someone else, other aliens?"

"What I said was you can't detect us," replied Robert, even more curtly. "Unless we choose to allow it."

"Why did you choose to meet me specifically?"

"Why not?" replied the android. "It's not as if others on your planet are more experienced or better qualified to speak with us. For me this is quite an enjoyable novelty. For you, well, no one will ever believe you, so relax."

"There are conspiracy theorists," Jon mentions too casually, "who believe space aliens have been abducting humans for study."

"No, Jon," replied Robert, again shortly, "we have not and will not abduct humans against their will. Such acts would violate our ethics. We prefer to study you from a distance."

Jon backed off. Obviously, the aliens were prickly on matters regarding their activities.

After a pause, while Robert poked the fire with a stick, the being returned to the subject of human belief systems.

"As I was saying," Robert concluded, "given human nature, and cultural filters, we see no path forward to help your species in any material way, much less transfer significant technology, without triggering wars that set you back a thousand years."

The silence between them stretched a full minute. Somewhere in the woods an owl hooted. Then Jon leaned forward. "I know a way," he said. They spoke until dawn. Jon went home, put his affairs in order, and was not seen for two years.

TWO
THE TEAM

Tom Corker was Vice President of Operations for a manufacturer of small jet aircraft based on recently unclassified cruise missile technology. The first planes were just coming off the line. Tom was a serious stocky middle-aged man with endless energy. He was the third Operations VP in the company's short existence.

After ten hours of meetings, he was clearing his desk before heading home. Another hour of emails would have to wait until after dinner. Included in the stack of snail mail was an express package. Small, but definitely more than paper inside. The return address was nonsense, but not unusual for vendors who used a logistics service. The package was addressed to him and titled "VP." So, the sender had some legitimate information about him. *Oh well*, he thought, if the package was an attention-grabbing trinket from a salesman, he would pitch the thing into the donation box. Using a small folding knife, he opened the package. *Mother of God! Krugerrands, ten of them. At the current price for gold these would buy a small car.*

Rummaging further disclosed plane tickets, several documents, and a note: "Tom, long time no see. I've been traveling—still traveling—but I've got a new startup. Great market. I'm building a team, and best of all, I've got funding. I need you. Plan on a three-day weekend to hear me out. Someone will pick you up at the airport. Sorry if this sounds high-handed. All I ask is you hear the pitch. Call or text the number below. I'm out of the country a lot so you may have difficulty getting through." The handwritten note was signed by Jon Gallock.

Tom's cellphone chirped. He looked at the caller's name and answered. "Jon," he said, "great timing; I was just reading your note. I was amazed. When did you learn to write?"

"I kept the note short," said Jon. "I didn't want your lips to get tired." Ritual insults completed, the two got down to business.

"Gold certainly grabs one's attention," said Tom, "and so does a business-class seat. Since you're spending lavishly on recruiting, you're either well-funded or desperate."

"Both," replied Jon. "This is the biggest elephant I've ever seen. I have a pile of funding. The investors are patient, the technology is unbelievably mature and the IP—intellectual property—is well protected. But management-wise I'm starting from scratch here. I need to get the band back together. For the most part I'm targeting people you know; however, the names are confidential for now, for obvious reasons. What's your situation?"

High-tech early-stage companies are usually funded by deep-pocketed Venture Capital partnerships. The VCs, as they are called, exist in an ecosystem separate from the rest of the economy. The language differs, the management, financing, legal, accounting, human resources, insurance, banking, taxes, and so on are all specialized. Landlords may even cut the rent for a piece of the action. Average tenure is short. People move around a lot and their reputations follow.

Success in an early-stage company has a large degree of randomness. An average person fortunate enough to get in early at the right company can become a multimillionaire almost overnight from stock options. On the other hand, a hugely competent person working seventy-five hours a week for a poorly conceived dog of a company gets only his salary. In between are the companies which average managers will ruin or great managers will make successful. Given the physical concentration of these companies in Silicon Valley, south of San Francisco, one quickly learns who the truly talented people are.

Tom knew Jon's reputation as a serious player, a go-to guy. He wouldn't have called if he couldn't offer a seriously lucrative opportunity. The defining factor would be Tom's situation.

"Well," said Tom. "Only a few of my options have vested. If I left now, I'd be leaving money on the table. I don't want that. You'd have to make me whole." Tom knew, of course, that Jon knew most of this from public and personal sources. He would have checked before calling. Still, Tom had to start building a basis for making the best deal possible. All was negotiable. "Personally, I still I have plenty of gas in the tank. Moving on would depend on the opportunity, and the people involved. At this stage in my career, I don't have the patience to deal with prima donnas."

"This sounds doable from my end," said Jon. "I'm building the management team differently than usual. I'll have six to eight people, some of who you know, at the meeting. You will have an opportunity to evaluate those you don't know. At the end of the weekend folks will know if this is a group they can work with or not. I want to make the pitch to the prospective management team collectively, get feedback, and then get to yes, conditional on employment contracts spelling out the details. If we have any holes after the initial weekend, we'll fill them as we go." Tom noted the use of "we."

"There is a very generic nondisclosure agreement and a tax form in the package I sent you," said Jon. "I need the signed NDA back before the meeting, and yes, you must pay taxes on the Krugerrands. You keep the coins if you come on board or not." After discussing the logistics of the next meeting, they wound up the call.

"I'll have someone pick you up at the airport," said Jon. "I'll tell them to look for the fat, bald guy."

"Thank God you won't be driving," responded Tom.

After he hung up, Tom realized Jon never discussed his position or duties. *Damn, Gallock was good.*

The temperature is a hundred and one degrees in the shade, and there wasn't any. *I know Jon doesn't like resorts but this is ridiculous*, mused Tracey. *Not a lot of distractions here. I expect this trip is strictly business.* She did a slow circle, seeing no trees higher than her chin for miles. Only a long low ranch house which appeared a century old. The weathered adobe structure was the former Kite ranch house, now a rustic corporate retreat located an hour south of Albuquerque.

"How close are we to the White Sands Missile Range?" Tracey asked.

"Less than a mile in that direction," Jon answered while gesturing easterly. "The Range is highly restricted. Don't hike too far in that direction or you may wake up in Guantanamo Bay. The Trinity site, where the first atomic bomb was tested, is only a few miles south and east of here. You probably know the range is larger than some eastern states and operates a boatload of black projects. However, that's not related to what we're doing here. We will have our privacy though.

"Come on, let's get inside where it's cool," Jon continued. "Everyone is here except Tom. He'll arrive in a couple hours. Shirley will pick him up at the airport. We'll have drinks, then dinner, and then I'll brief everyone on the opportunity. You'll be amazed. You'll have all day tomorrow to grill me."

The sun was low on the horizon when Shirley returned with Tom in tow. "I found him, no problem," she said. Handshakes were exchanged. "The caterer will deliver the food in thirty minutes. Let's grab a drink before dinner."

Tracey and Shirley gravitated to a corner and started to catch up. The two hadn't seen each other for a couple years. After a few minutes Shirley changed the subject. "Jon's looking really good," she said.

"I'll say," responded Tracey. "He's always kept in good shape. He doesn't look like he's lost weight but he's tighter and fitter now. He's invested some major sweat equity in that bod. He sure doesn't look like a guy working a lot of overtime to get a short-staffed venture off the ground. I wonder how he manages that."

After dinner Jon tapped a spoon against his wine glass to gain everyone's attention. "Some of you know each other; however, there are gaps. Let's go around the room and introduce yourself, and give a very short bio, please." He motioned to his left.

"I'm Bill Hathcock," the tall, lanky man said. "I have a PhD in Optics and worked ten years for a National Lab. I have been CEO at two startups, one successful and one spectacularly not." The group chuckled. All had heard of the crash and burn of a hundred million investor dollars.

The next man stood up. "I'm Tom Corker, an engineer, and I run operations for high-tech manufacturers. I'm currently in aerospace."

The others followed. Tracey Irby was a slim runner. Her background was corporate attorney. Bob Irons was tough wiry man who had been CFO for several companies. Shirley Ishida was an outgoing curvy woman, obviously of Japanese descent. She had a Stanford MBA and a background in human resources and administration. Randy Irwin was a rarity in that he smoked, heavily. He had put in his twenty years at the National Security Agency (NSA) and become a technical security consultant. He projected a nervous air.

All had experience in early-stage high-tech companies. Each was extremely smart, exceptionally skilled, and proficient at juggling a variety of responsibilities. None had the "not my job" mentality. Most importantly, all had thick skin and performed well under pressure.

"Ok, Jon, you've bribed us with gold to be here. It's time to drop the mysterious act and tell us what's up," Tracey said. The others nodded in agreement.

"The sun is down," Jon noted. "The temperature comes down quick here in the high desert. The air will be comfortable outside. Let's move to the west porch and I'll tell you why you're here."

Oh, no, thought Tracey. *He's luring us outside where he can light up a cigar.*

Outside, due to the high altitude and extremely dry atmosphere, the temperature had already fallen by twenty degrees and the night air was cool.

"Okay," said Jon once everyone was situated. Fortunately, he had no cigar. He pointed to the western sky. "Focus about forty-five degrees off the horizon." After several seconds passed, a ripple appeared in the night sky which coalesced to a small dot. The dot was roughly circular and appeared the size of a small coin held at arm's length. The distortion rapidly swept nearer and grew larger until… something… materialized in the sandy area fifty feet from where they stood.

At first one could see through the object to the night sky beyond. It appeared as if one was looking through a gentle waterfall. The object grew opaque, and a sleek craft of some sort took shape. There were no wings or visible means of propulsion. The object appeared more as a fat, elongated saucer than an aircraft. Short, tapered blisters grew from each side.

From their angle it almost appeared like … a chiclet. A door opened and a ramp extended.

Jon's audience froze, except for Shirley, who took a step back and fell on her ass.

"It's a spaceship," Jon explained unnecessarily. "Mankind is no longer alone," he said in a deep, portentous voice and then hummed a few bars from *The Twilight Zone* theme as he helped Shirley to her feet. "Please, come aboard and I'll explain."

Jon went first and the others followed. The door shut silently behind them. The group found themselves in a wide cabin with high-backed comfortable chairs. There were flat screens embedded in the walls which showed the corresponding landscape outside. There was a tiny bar at one end. The fit, finish, and fashion of the décor seemed like those of an expensive business jet.

No alien technology was visible.

"Why is the landscape receding?" Bob asked.

"We've taken off," Jon answered. "We'll be in orbit in a few minutes and you'll get a view that only astronauts, aliens, and myself have seen before. I'll explain the opportunity while we orbit. We'll return to the ranch house well before daylight.

"Let's get the big question out of the way first. No, there are no aliens aboard and you will not meet one on the flight. For reasons I'll get into later, the Chait are reticent about meeting humans in person.

"This craft is remotely operated, or flies itself. I'm not sure which."

The group was uncharacteristically quiet. Randy broke the ice. "The screens could be a recording, but I don't see the point. Let's assume we really are in flight. Why is there no feeling of acceleration?" he asked, pointing at a view screen. "Do you really expect to return to where we took off? There are multiple air force bases in the state and they've all scrambled fighters by now. The state has more classified facilities, restricted airspace, and associated security than any place on the planet. You couldn't pick a tougher place to make a secret landing if you tried."

"To answer your last question first," Jon said, "the location was chosen partly to make your very point. This flight will not come to the attention of anyone in the government. The technology to operate an aircraft in this location, bracketed by air force bases, undetected, should grab your attention."

Jon continued. "Surely you noticed the lack of prop wash and blowing sand when the craft landed. The same technology that operates the reactionless drive allows for internal gravity compensation. The passengers feel no acceleration.

"The power plant in this vessel is sufficient to operate continuously without refueling. We will take off, orbit for a bit, and land without topping off any tanks."

Bill broke in. "Yes, I'm tentatively convinced this craft was built by intelligent life from another planet. I see evidence of multiple technologies which are simply too advanced, and too mature to originate from Earth. However, you've spoken of the technology several times but nothing of the alien beings. Is the technology the reason we are here? Why else would you recruit this particular group of people? Is the purpose of this venture simply to commercialize alien tech?"

Jon smiled. He had won a bet with himself that Bill, who lived and breathed licensing of intellectual property, would see that before the others.

"To a large extent, yes, at least at first," Jon said. "I've obtained an exclusive license."

"The government will classify everything and slap us with a gag order," said Randy, shaking his head.

"The Russians and Chinese will go ballistic, literally, if they see the United States acquiring advanced alien tech," said Tracey.

"The United Nations will lobby for free open-source access. For the good of all mankind, you understand, and the media will get behind the idea and push it hard. We'll be demonized," said Bob.

"The Europeans won't stand for a private group monopolizing alien tech," said Bill.

"Religious fundamentalists will go berserk," said Tom, a devout Catholic.

"What about the aliens?" wailed Shirley. "We've been contacted by other intelligent life from outer space! That's much more impactful than a freaking advanced engine for airplanes or whatever. When do we meet the aliens?"

"And what do they want in return?" added Bob.

"You've all brought up real issues," said Jon, "which we can manage. We'll be in orbit in a couple minutes, and then do a call with the aliens, the Chait. I suggest we take a few minutes now and enjoy the view." The screens now showed a circular, startling bright blue Earth.

Jon's cellphone buzzed. He answered and said, "Let me put you on speaker." He did so and laid his phone on the bar. He said, "Folks, let me introduce you to a representative of the Chait. For ease in communicating, he has asked we address him as Robert."

The group looked at Jon in various degrees of incredulity. *For Christ's sake*, their expressions said, *we do this on a cellphone?*

"Hello, people," said Robert breezily. "I apologize for doing this over cellphone. I'm not comfortable sharing visuals of our species. I'm afraid I'm also going to disappoint you by sharing no specific information about our species.

"We have been observing mankind for years now and find you fascinating. However, you are stuck on this one planet with, metaphorically speaking, all your eggs in one basket. Your cultures, your civilization, and your species are one disaster away from extinction. A disaster could come from anywhere, a nuclear war, a plague, climate change, a large meteor impact—the list is lengthy. In the fullness of time a disaster will eventually occur. It's inevitable and will happen sooner rather than later.

"Our civilization is thousands of years more advanced than yours. We can offer much, and the disparity in our technical base is such that any effort costs us almost nothing. Nothing but our time, which we freely give.

"We would willingly share advanced technology up to a level enabling practical interplanetary, or even interstellar, flight. However, we believe such a course could easily do more harm than good. Widespread open release of developed technology would upset the status quo. Even if we released for example, space flight technology, publicly, available for free to one and all, would your large political entities such as the USA, or Russia, or China allow one or more of the others to win the race to the stars? Of course not.

"You are like crabs trapped in a pot. If one starts to climb out the others drag him back down.

"And we don't consider the United Nations a viable neutral third party. Even if the bureaucracy wasn't rife with corruption, the institution lacks the practical skills and political clout to distribute and manage the technology release. Besides, none of your powerful states will ever cede large amounts of powers to the UN, or allow them sway over their internal policies. Such a course was proposed once for atomic energy and went nowhere."

Robert went on. "However, we have studied the matter for years, and in consultation with Jon, who has very good ideas and insight, have developed a plan that seems very promising. Jon will explain the details to you. Each of you, should you agree to join in this enterprise, has been assigned a personal Chait liaison who will call you three days from now. You may quiz them at length. Your representative will be available to you, within limits, anytime of the day or night for the duration of your employment. However, they will not divulge any information about our species. I suggest you save their number in your contacts."

No shit, everyone thought.

"Jon has our complete confidence," Robert concluded. "You will work for him, not me, not your Chait liaison. Have a great day."

As Robert abruptly hung up, Shirley spoke first. "A phone call? Really? We fly to orbit on an alien spaceship for a fucking phone call?"

"That's the purpose of a phone," replied Jon lightly, "to communicate when you can't be there in person. Especially if one is not a person."

Shirley was still fuming. "The voice sounded like a real estate salesman from California. Good grammar, no accent. 'Have a great day,'" she finished in a mocking tone.

"The Chait are obviously very intelligent and have gone to a great deal of effort to learn the English language so well," said Tracey. "That has a lot of implications. Do they speak other languages also?"

"Assuming you sign on, all your questions will be answered," Jon replied.

"Before I ask you to commit to this enterprise, I have to impress on you the pressure you'll be under. Word of our actions will eventually get out. Government intelligence agencies will put you under surveillance. Some percentage of religious fundamentalists will believe we are doing the work of the devil. A percentage of the business community will hate us for threatening their rice bowl. A similar percentage will become livid for us not moving fast enough. Terminally ill people will appear at your door begging for a miracle cure. Your personal security will be a big concern. We will take steps to ensure your safety, however, you have to understand there will be personal risk.

"On the plus side you will become insanely rich. You will also receive benefits that few people on the planet will ever know. As I said, we already have the initial funding. We'll need more; of course, that's always the case." Jon walked behind the bar and pulled out two aluminum briefcases, obviously heavy. He flipped them open and gold sparkled in the light.

The others understood. A startup company was always in fund-raising mode.

"Now," said Jon. "Let me tell you about Full Medical."

THREE
GRUBBING FOR DOLLARS

"THIS," JON SAID TO BILL, "is a Fab." Before them sat a box of nondescript dull metal the size of a delivery van. The location was an old warehouse in a rundown section of Phoenix, Arizona.

"I assume you don't mean a semiconductor fabrication plant," said Bill. "Those are the size of a city block and cost billions of dollars."

"Actually," Jon said, "This device can fabricate chips as well as many other things. The Chait have banned the use of this technology on the planet, with this one exception. This is the only unit they have allowed or are likely to allow in the future. This is for our use only. We cannot reproduce, license, or sell this particular piece of technology."

"What can it do?" asked Bill.

"This device can quickly fabricate almost anything," said Jon. "You only have to load the right ingredients and specify the output. For example, you could load a bar of silver and shortly afterwards get a teapot, coins, or spoons. Anything made from silver can be Fab'd. Of course, the process is not limited to one element. If you desire a complete semiconductor chip, simply load silica sand, trace metals, several chemicals and shazam, fully assembled, packaged functional computer chips come out a few minutes later. In fact, if you load the right materials, the Fab will put out complete devices, for example, cellphones, within minutes.

"The user interface is a powerful AI, so designing your desired output is very easy," Jon concluded.

"That's..., that's...," Bill was at a loss for words. "That's unbelievable. How does it do that? What's the secret sauce?"

"The alien tech inside," answered Jon, "can quickly disassociate material down to the component atoms. The various atoms are sorted, and the bonds rebuilt in the configuration required for the end product. The process occurs quickly. The Chait have not been forthcoming in describing the technology. However, I suspect the machine generates a field, or probably multiple fields, that manipulates the different chemical, and, to an extent, atomic bonds of matter."

"I've forgotten much of my chemistry," admitted Bill. "I do know atoms can share electrons in various configurations, and a lot of energy is required to change those. Where does this thing get its power?"

"It doesn't take as much power as you might think," Jon responded. "Sure, breaking bonds takes energy, however, the Chait tech has clever ways of shortcutting the process. The Fab also harvests and stores energy released during electron bonding. I believe the fields inside absorb everything— electromagnetic energy, gravity, even the weak interaction at subatomic levels—and stores it in an advanced battery."

"Sorry I asked," said Bill. "Let's put aside the energy question for now. Besides making teaspoons and computer chips, what other capabilities does the Fab have?

"Well," said Jon. "You can put in a jug of crude oil and get out a jug of refined gasoline. Both liquids are composed of hydrocarbons. The hydrogen and carbon chains simply have different arrangements, and lengths. You can load the Fab with an entire barrel of oil and receive an output of multiple plastic jugs containing gasoline. Or you can put in a bale of shredded plastic and get out a single plastic jug containing gasoline, or any liquid petroleum product."

Jon continued, "You can put in ore from a mine and a few minutes later, out pop separate marbles of whatever minerals exist in the ore, all separated and concentrated. You can even put in a log and get out paper. The Fab is very flexible."

"Yeah, I'd call a combination of semiconductor Fab, refinery, smelter, lumber mill, and assembly line flexible," Bill said dryly.

"This will produce samples of the tech you are trying to license," Jon said. "Better batteries, magnets, chips, advanced materials, and the medical items. Licensing tech that exists in a physical functioning form is a lot easier than pushing vaporware.

"As an added benefit the Fab is very clean and green. The device has zero emissions, and no waste stream. Too bad we can't publicize anything about the unit."

"I imagine you'll be dealing with large companies, and they don't move fast. I expect virtually no licensing income the first six months. I don't plan to bring in investors yet, and I want to demonstrate progress to the Chait. So, we need some immediate income. In addition to product samples, you need to use this baby here"—Jon patted the Fab on the side—"to make us some money."

"I'm not breaking the law," Bill began heatedly.

"No, no, no," said Jon, laughing. "I don't mean physically print money. Although we could do that easily enough, as well as baseball cards and other collectibles which would be authentic down to the molecular level. No, I mean produce small high-value items that we can sell quickly and anonymously.

"Tom has started hiring. A couple of people are scheduled to be here tomorrow. The logistics of getting products out the door, and billed and collected, is his bailiwick. He will coordinate with Bob's finance people. You won't have to get involved in that side of the operation. We have a hole in that we don't have a sales guy yet. I'm working on that—got a great prospect. In the meantime, work something out with Tom.

"While speaking with Tom you need to rope in Randy and re-review what information the new hires can access," cautioned Jon. "We're ramping up hiring and it's important to get the information silos right.

"Call Mango, your Chait rep," Jon suggested. For reasons unknown, the Chait, other than Robert, went by names of various fruits and berries. Shirley joked the Chait must be limited to thirty-one individuals. "He can give you a full rundown of what the Fab is capable of, and the limitations.

"One last thing. A safety tip. If the device heats up significantly, or that light in the corner starts to flash, drop everything and run. The AI is constantly scanning for threats. Any attempt to dismantle, or examine, or steal the device will trigger a catastrophic meltdown. The intense heat will take the entire building with the Fab. The Chait do not want this technology to fall into the hands of Earthlings. Good luck."

After Jon left, Bill stared at the Fab a few minutes. *I wonder what the device can do with carbon*, he mused, *or beryl?*

FOUR
THE SCIENCE PROJECT

"PROFESSOR BREWER?" A VOICE INTRUDED.

Paul R. Brewer, Professor of Exobiology and Planetary Science, suppressed a sigh. He had posted his office hours and disliked seeing students even on a good day. This was after hours, and not a good day. The visitor may just as well have the words "grad student" stamped on his forehead but didn't look familiar. "May I help you?" he asked resignedly.

The visitor shut the office door, sat down, and handed over a business card. "Call me Phil. I'd like to hire you to do a consulting project. The subject matter is in your field. This has a short fuse. We need the completed work product ninety days from now. I realize this is short notice and will pay accordingly—one hundred thousand dollars for the work."

Paul, taken aback, sat up straighter and looked at the card, which read, "Phillip Sandilands, Project Manager, XSolarian Inc." with a cell number and email. He looked at his visitor closer. He appeared in his mid-twenties, dressed somewhere between grad student and business casual. He did not look like a man to pass out large contracts.

"Why me, and what's the project?" Paul asked.

Phil replied, "You're an authority in the field of the geophysics and ecology of extrasolar planets. My company requires an objective rating system, a model, to apply to exoplanets to rate and rank in order of desirability for human habitation. The rating system should take the relative factors like atmosphere, gravity, temperature, water, and so forth, and factor them so as to get a ranking relative to Earth. Before you interject, yes, I'm well aware that no habitable exoplanet has yet been detected. This is a speculative science project needed to support one of our contracts."

Phil opened his briefcase, pulled out a small object, and waved the thumb drive towards Paul. "The details are in here; the contract with scope, schedule, fee, deliverables, nondisclosure agreement, terms and conditions, tax form, and so forth." He passed over a folder of paperwork with a check on top. "We will pay half up front, the other half on acceptance of the finished study. I think that's more than fair."

"Aaaah...," Paul floundered for second while he gathered his thoughts. *No need to run this through the university. The grants administration group would take a big cut, bitch about ownership of the intellectual property, pick at the contract language, blow the schedule, and generally screw things up as they usually did. Grad students could chimp out most of the work quickly for almost nothing. Best of all, no one could ever say the work product was bad. The deliverable would be as untestable and unverifiable as a climate change model. No risk.* He looked at the check, then at Phil. "It's not signed," he observed.

"Sign the contract, and the tax form, and then I'll sign the check," Phil replied. "Please initial each page."

Paul flipped through the contract for a minute and grunted "ok" and signed the documents. Phil endorsed the check and they exchanged documents. Phil passed over the drive, and the pair shook hands.

"I'll be in touch regularly to check progress," Phil said and left.

That went smoother than the first time, Phil thought to himself as he left the building. His instructions were clear. 'Dealing with academics is a crapshoot. Half will do great work, the other half will prove useless. We have a schedule to keep and plenty of budget, so get three academics on contract and hopefully one delivers a usable product. Sign 'em up quick and ride them hard.' The first prof was a dickhead. This one seemed better. One to go. He'd have to slim down his course load next semester to get this finished, but the coin these guys were paying would carry him through the whole school year. If this went well maybe XSolarian would have another project for him next summer.

What a great job.

FIVE
GRUBBING FOR DOLLARS AGAIN

"So, THIS IS THE PLACE," Joel Zimmerman remarked to his Uncle Daniel. "The New York City Diamond District." The cab had just dropped them on West 47th street between 5th and 6th Avenues.

"Yeah," said Daniel. "Remember what I told you. Gem merchants are always a target. Never take a cab directly to or from your hotel and here. Don't even ask the doorman for a ride to Saks. It's too close. The Schwarzer's look to rob people like us walking over, I tell you."

"Yes, Uncle," said Joel, who had heard this several times already.

"When we get inside let me do the talking. Bringing your source to the shop is just not done. You being my nephew won't count for squat. He'll suck up to you and try to cut me out of loop. That's how it's done, I tell you."

"Yes, Uncle," said Joel. "I won't cut you out of the loop. I know very little of the diamond market. I'm happy to pay your commission than try to deal direct. Even if I found someone to work with, they'd skin me alive. You're family. I trust you to take care of me."

"Of course, I'll take good care of you," said Uncle Daniel, radiating complete sincerity and honesty. "You're family. Now, explain to me one last time how a bigshot lawyer like you comes by a sack of ice. The whole situation is very odd, I tell you."

"Like I said, Uncle," Joel replied, "I got a call from a guy I went to law school with. He knew I'm an Ashkenazi Jew and had relatives in the business. He's got a corporate job doing intellectual property and contract law with some company I've never heard of. Next thing I know I'm talking to a corporate big shot who is the sales VP, an Aussie, who's asking if I can move the stones. This is not part of their core business. It's a sideline—peanuts to them. They stumbled across the supply. The company pays me a good commission."

Once inside, the firm's owner, Bernie Sonsini, met them with effusive greetings. "Daniel," he said, "I haven't seen you in a couple years. You look good. And you brought your nephew; what a fine young man. Let's go in the back, get coffee, and see what you brought today."

After coffee, chocolate, and getting caught up on family news, Uncle Daniel got down to business.

"I tell you, I got a rare treat for you, Bernie," Daniel said as he pulled an elaborate pouched money belt from under his vest. He opened a pouch and spilled the contents on the velvet desk pad. "Canaries!"

Joel had learned that fine light-yellow diamonds were often referred to as canaries, for obvious reasons. Although found in many places, virtually all gem grade stones of this color came from South Africa. Those mines were drying up and dealers were rarely able to source quality uncut stock anymore.

Bernie pulled a lamp over while a loupe appeared in his other hand. He examined the stones for a few minutes. "Fine looking stones," he said. "What's their provenance?"

"We got no documentation," replied Daniel. "But these ain't no African blood stones, I tell you. We both know stones of this size, quality, and color only come from one place, South Africa."

"Unless the color is artificial," Bernie retorted.

"Which you can test for," Daniel countered.

While the old men bargained, Joel mentally reviewed his schedule. Another stop today with Uncle Daniel, and another tomorrow. Next week was the International Emerald Symposium in Miami. Before he took this job, he'd no idea emeralds were simply beryl with some trace contaminants. He would like to stay over in Miami for the weekend. He'd have to check with the knuckle-draggers before changing his schedule. The client insisted on two bodyguards whenever he carried product. For all his caution, Uncle Daniel had not noticed the discreet escorts. One was drinking coffee at the deli across the street while the other played tourist on the sidewalk. The stones today were only samples and not hugely valuable. However, this was a good test run for Joel and the security team.

At this point the negotiations had progressed to excited arm waving and were being conducted in loud Yiddish. Joel broke in. "Did Uncle Daniel mention this is a steady supply? I'd like to do shipments every month, if you can handle that."

"How many carats are we talking about?" asked Bernie.

Joel mentally relaxed. Bernie was hooked. Closing the sale was all downhill from here.

What a great job.

SIX
THE RECRUITERS

THE CRIPPLES, AS THEY CALLED themselves, met in a room at the recreation center. Denver had great rec centers. The room was used for meetings, usually AA sessions, or other types of counseling. The room was half empty of furniture which was convenient, as those meeting tonight were in wheelchairs. Two of those present played in the center's wheelchair basketball league and had suggested the meeting venue. The others didn't care as long as the place was easily accessible.

Although a diverse group, they would have rolled their eyes if anyone made such a remark in their presence. Being Black or White or Hispanic, or man or woman, or enlisted or officer, or any other artificial distinction no longer mattered. None had legs, except for Jose, who was paralyzed from the waist down.

Their ages ranged from thirty-five to forty-five. None had close family members. None had served in the same unit. The loose group had met one another in the hospital, or rehab. Or counseling. All were discharged from the military and classified one hundred percent disabled. They were waiting for staff sergeant George Wilmes (Retired).

"What's he selling?" asked Jose.

"He said he's not asking for one penny," John said, "You know that. He spent a fair amount of time talking to each of us, so I expect this is important to him. We were in rehab together. We all know him, and he's not here to screw us."

"I expect you're right," said Jerry. "He's traveled to be here and that's tough to do in a chair."

"He said he got new legs," said Jeraldeane. "The VA won't pay for new, uncertified equipment. Anything really cutting edge has to come from your own pocket. If you can afford them, and can tough out the therapy, the new models are a lot better. Not as hard on the stump, I hear."

"Whatever you can afford, you're still a gimp with crutches," said Dave. "Big deal."

The door opened and George Wilmes walked in. Walked. On two legs. He looked like a fit, prosperous businessman on his way to the country club. He was dressed in a sport shirt and knit slacks. He wore loafers on each foot. His movements were sure and natural.

He had two feet, which was not the case when last seen.

Jaws dropped. Jeraldeane said, "George, it's great to see you. Don't take this wrong, but would you please take off your pants?"

George disrobed down to a pair of Speedos. He jumped up and down and did a couple jumping jacks. His legs and feet were perfect. No trace of any injury or operation remained. Not even a scar. He looked each in the eye as he said, "I have my legs, and I have my health back. I feel one hundred percent. It's as if I was never injured. I thank God every day for my recovery." The others understood only too well the health hazards of living in a chair.

George continued. "Interested?"

"Who do I have to kill?" asked Jerry.

"What about me?" demanded Jose. "I've got legs, but I'm paralyzed."

"Of course," said George. "Otherwise, I wouldn't have asked you here tonight."

"I'm sure new legs like yours are not covered at the damned VA," said Dave. "And if the VA did cover the cost, I'll wait years on a list before any operation. So, how much did you pay?"

"On one hand they cost you nothing," said George as he dressed. "On the other hand, everything."

Anna got the chocolate chip cookies from the refrigerator and laid several on a plate. The simple actions were difficult to do, with her walker and the tremors in her hands. The water in the teapot was hot. It was almost three pm. She had been surprised when Alice called and asked to visit. Alice had transferred to assisted living a year ago, and then to the medical section at another facility. Once that happened, no one ever came back.

The climate made Tucson popular for retirees. The Elana Gallegos Retirement Community was on the high end of nursing homes in the area. No urine-soaked diapers or diarrhea odors in the hall like the Medicaid facilities. Those here were fortunate enough to afford the move-in fee and eye-watering monthly rate. The individual apartments were comfortable and roomy. The staff was plentiful, cheerful, and attentive. The dining room, library, and other common areas were more like a cruise ship than an apartment building.

"Old age is not for sissies" was not a joke in these halls. The average resident stayed four years before moving to assisted living, or straight to hospice to die.

Let's see, she thought. Alice left and went into assisted living shortly after Jeff, Anna's husband for sixty-five years, passed away. That was over a year ago. *Alice must be ninety now. I wonder where she's been, and what's worth traveling to see someone you only knew casually. Not everyone our age still thinks and speaks clearly,* she thought proudly. *Maybe she just wants to talk with someone relevant.*

Someone knocked on the door. Anna slowly made her way to the front and opened the door to greet her guest. After a moment she said, "You're not Alice."

The lady at the door appeared middle aged, had glossy black hair, was healthy, straight, and well-dressed. She looked like one of the doctors. She laughed. "Actually, I am. Just not the one you expected. May I come in?"

"Oh, certainly; pardon my manners," said Anna. "Come on in. I get so few visitors nowadays. I've managed to outlive my husband and friends. Tea?"

Once Anna poured the tea, they each both had a sip and a nibble. Anna said, "You certainly gave me pause for a moment. I see the resemblance now. You must be Alice's daughter. I didn't know she had a daughter. She never mentioned you."

"You're close," said Alice. "I see your tremors are really mild today. Are you still using the propranolol or are you on a different prescription?"

Anna had a delightful visit. Alice knew all the long-term residents' names and history. She was especially well informed on everyone's ailments. The strokes, and heart attacks. Elaine, who had COPD and was down to five per cent of lung capacity and seventy-two pounds by the time she passed. Edna, who had dementia and regularly escaped from the memory care wing, who roamed the halls asking if anyone had seen her husband—who had died years before. Sarah, who was paralyzed by a stroke and remained in hospice unable to speak. Anna tactfully did not mention Mary across the hall who was convinced that Anna, and several others, were stealing from her apartment when she went for meals. Margaret had recently broken a hip and moved temporarily to assisted living. Anna and Alice both knew the statistics; at Margaret's age half of those who suffered a broken hip were gone within a year. They went through the residents— those who could no longer walk, talk, see, or hear, on dialysis, suffered crippling arthritis, and worse.

"You must speak with your mother often," said Anna. "How is she?"

Alice put down her cup and looked intently at Anna. "I think you've realized I'm not the daughter," she said. "Look closely, Anna. This is me, Alice. I've been taking the cure."

"You can't be Alice," Anna replied shakily. "She's almost ninety now. What cure do you mean? A cure for what?"

"A cure for old age," replied Alice. "A cure for everything"

Both sat back in their chairs and regarded the other. Then Alice leaned forward. "Would you like to hear more?"

Something faintly distorted the night sky. The distortion grew larger and solidified. A large streamlined craft appeared. An alien spaceship landed in a remote clearing in central Wisconsin.

A large cargo hatch opened and a ramp descended. The only lights were a dim red glow. The half dozen waiting vans and ambulances started their engines and drove closer using only their parking lights. Slowly, painfully, the seventeen waiting passengers exited the vehicles and boarded the spaceship. They came from nursing homes, hospital wards, and VFW halls. They came by wheelchair, by gurney, and by stretcher. Most of those able to walk used walkers or four-footed canes. Only one, a young man dying from cancer, paused and turned around for a last look before entering the alien ship.

The helpful attendants assisted the immigrants up the ramp, and into their waiting beds. The beds were comfortably padded and had thick sides a foot high. Those requiring oxygen were hooked up to the ship's supply system. There was surprisingly little fuss. Maybe not too surprising, given the immigrants were sedated beforehand.

It is difficult for a responsible adult to disappear without a trace. The federal government expects to see tax returns filed, Social Security checks cashed, and medical care charged against the appropriate social programs. Nursing homes will follow up on any resident transfer—that's quite rare. Friends, family, and neighbors will check in on you, and alert the authorities if something seems amiss. Needy heirs will grow impatient.

Still, a successful disappearance can happen. Especially when a large expert organization manages the process.

Finding qualified immigrants was an arduous task. The recruiters preferred motivated candidates. Which was the easy part. A pending death was sufficient motivation for most.

Successful candidates shared a common culture, and personal values. They were required to speak fluent English. One had to be intelligent, preferably well-educated, or trained in certain desirable fields. Successful candidates possessed a strong sense of civic responsibility, and understood the value of deferred gratification.

Hardcore leftists were blacklisted as counterproductive to the new society.

There were many other selection factors—men or women, young or old. However, the recruiters ignored one's race, religion, or nationality. Candidates' attributes were evaluated through the lens of the needs of a frontier society, and the need for a homogeneous culture.

The night before, the ship had landed at a different location a thousand miles away. There, tens of thousands of pounds of supplies were loaded. The destination colony grew enough food to be self-supporting but was missing certain staples, such as dairy products, condiments, and specialty items. Comfort rations were also needed. Primarily alcohol and tobacco, coffee and tea, marijuana, and cocaine. Like a sixteenth-century Portuguese caravel, the ship also carried large quantities of spices.

Once loaded, and the passengers resting comfortably, the hatch closed and the vehicles outside began to leave. The vehicles would stagger their departures so as not to draw attention.

Each passenger had a flat screen to watch the view as the Earth receded. As they quickly fell asleep, the lids closed and the sarcophagi latched tightly shut. A thick oxygenated, medicated foam filled each container as palliative treatment began.

"On the whole, the group appears pretty darn stable," said one attendant to the other. "Except for number twelve. Her pulse is thready and her blood pressure is all over the map."

"Thank you, Mister Obvious," joked the other attendant. "Do you plan to watch those dials closely? It's not like we can actually do anything." She was right, of course. No matter. Death was not possible while in a Chait sarcophagus.

SEVEN
THE TRADER

J ON AND BOB MET THE securities dealer at a restaurant overlooking the beach. Ceiling fans and a soft sea breeze kept the patio cool. At this hour there were few customers; however, the group used the table farthest from the others.

Jon and Bob arrived in Basseterre the night before on the company's Dassault Falcon 8. The city was the capital of the tiny island country of Saint Kitts and Nevis. The beaches were beautiful; however, the attraction was the strength and privacy of the Nevis limited liability companies (LLCs). Nevis was an offshore business haven whose secrecy put Switzerland to shame.

The meeting with the attorney earlier in the day to review the arrangements proved satisfactory. The pair was now meeting with Douglas Schar, a former high-powered securities dealer, who retired early for health reasons. He had been on the beach for two years.

Doug was amped. "Your intelligent trading program is the real deal," he enthused. "Your million-dollar initial cash investment grew to four in less than a month. That wasn't due to luck. If word of this trading program ever got out, securities traders everywhere will be out of a job."

"We plan to put another ten million in immediately," said Jon. "Can you explain in more detail for me the trading structure you and Bob have worked out?"

"Sure," said Doug. "I still have a peanut-size operation in Manhattan. There are only two guys, and an admin, working out of a storefront. However, we have bank accounts, the necessary securities licenses, trading software, relationships, and the rest of the infrastructure necessary to operate a brokerage. We'll move to a bigger place and hire more guys. You've already set up LLCs here, in Nevis. Conceptually, one of those LLCs is the client. The investment adviser, via another LLC, is your program. Every day the investment advisor sends instructions to the brokerage to buy or sell on your account. I'll answer any questions that come up.

"Those LLCs are only the first layer," Doug continued. "You want to keep this very quiet, and pay no taxes if possible. The process gets complicated. Let's walk through the rest of the shells."

Once Doug finished, Jon ordered a round of beers while Bob called the attorney to confirm dinner arrangements for the four.

"You've given me my life back," said Doug. "Look at me now"—he raised his arms and held his hands out—"I swim every day in the ocean. I'm up to a mile now. The money I make from this is simply gravy. I can't tell you how much what you've done means to me. I do have a question though. Who developed your trading program? It's odd working strictly through the internet. Sometimes I can't tell where the program ends and the person on the other end begins."

Later that night, after dinner, and after the others had left, Jon and Bob enjoyed a cigar in a sheltered spot away from the ocean breeze. "So," began Bob, "Given the Chait trading program can take a million dollars and run it up to a billion within months, why have we been grubbing for dollars other ways? And why bother to invest another ten million? The program will earn more than that in short order."

Jon smiled and blew a perfect smoke ring. "For a number of reasons," he said.

Bob knew how Jon managed people. Jon believed a manager should never do anything for a good reason. A dozen times at a prior venture Bob had heard some variation of 'You don't do stuff because it's a good idea. You do stuff because that action is important, and urgent, and it's more important and more urgent than the other stuff on your plate. You're not paid to be busy. You're paid to be effective.'

"The additional ten million shows Doug our commitment to this," Jon replied. "Also, he would smell a rat if we limited our investment to only one million. If we appear committed, Doug is motivated, which is important.

"The ten million is the last cash advance we'll ever have to make. The investment program can increase the investment by a factor of five every month. In a blindingly short time, the initial investment will reach the point of throwing off a billion every month.

"When the existence of the Chait becomes public, we need a plausible explanation of our funding source," Jon explained. "The explanation is licensing income. That revenue base provides us a reasonable cover. Licensing is a believable explanation of our funding.

"However, we need an ocean of money for the next stage, and technology licensing won't generate enough. That's why we need the trading program. However, if word of the trading program ever got out, worldwide financial markets would crash, and the blowback on us would be massive. That blowback would jeopardize our entire plan. The end result would not be as disastrous as leaking the capabilities of Full Medical, but almost. The Chait trading program has to remain secret forever.

"With licensing, and the trading program now in place, we can wind down the other money-grubbing activities. Those are small potatoes and have become a potential liability."

Bob was in the Inner Circle and knew much of the capabilities of the Chait. Not only did the aliens possess powerful artificial intelligence but their computer and sensor technology were also unbelievably advanced. The combination of the three allowed them to record and analyze, not only every electronic communication and stored file on Earth, the Chait also tracked most in-person interactions in real time. Cellphones, computers, automobiles, automated vacuum cleaners, and other electronic devices rarely turn off-and-on with mechanical switches. The switching is done in software. And software is easily corrupted. Informed people know a cellphone is never really off until the battery is pulled.

The world's largest social media companies combined, on steroids, did not begin to compare to the breadth and depth of the Chait intelligence apparatus. The knowledge accumulated by the world's spy agencies, banks, tax authorities, credit card companies, and internet retailers were not a pimple on a fly on an elephant's ass compared to the Chait database. Amazingly, their powerful AI analyzed all interactions relating to XSolarian anywhere in the world, in real time.

The trading program's power came as much from insider knowledge as from lightning quick and deep insight of market trends.

"At least insider trading is generally not criminal outside the US," Bob noted. "I hope Jamocha keeps Tracey and her people up to date on the fine print."

"Agreed," replied Jon. He continued. "Another reason for our commercial activities is plausible cover while we create the various worldwide legal entities we need, get relationships in place with the banks, law firms, and politicians. We now have large, powerful customers who will go to bat for us. Most importantly though, we've learned to work as a team. Take this trip for example. What we are doing is as much legal as financial; however, Tracey is comfortable with the two of us finalizing the arrangements. That level of trust and coordination is critical going forward.

"In any event," Jon concluded, "we'll get a heads-up should anything start to leak." Bob nodded in agreement. The Chait, or their powerful AI, were fluent in every language on Earth.

EIGHT
THE BUSINESS REVIEW

"THANK YOU ALL FOR BEING here," said Jon. "With our enhancements there's little need to meet in person. However, a face-to-face helps keep us connected. Let's keep this short and simple. We're not doing a dog-and-pony show for the investors, or to impress the boss. We're here to get up to speed on what the others are doing, identify any issues and how to address them, and adjust course if necessary. I've asked you to limit the visuals to three or four slides each. Please keep your presentation no longer than thirty minutes, and we'll spend the rest of our time planet-planning the next three or four months."

The Inner Circle had received enhancements from the Chait. These allowed them to communicate with the others, or even compose and view documents, or video, or cruise the internet, using only the brain. The person one called, or the images they viewed, appeared before the eyes as if an exceptionally advanced hologram. One could focus through the image and continue to walk, or even drive at the same time. To "speak" subvocally took practice but at this point was routine for the users.

Enhanced communication was only the tip of the iceberg.

Despite the long hours, everyone looked good. Remarkably good, considering their grueling schedules. Tom had lost weight, and Randy gained some. Both looked better for the changes. Tracey remained lean and fit. Bob and Shirley both looked like they had been exercising. Bill appeared more energetic than ever. The new Sales VP appeared carved from stone.

The executives had large staffs now. Each, except Jon, had an executive assistant and a deputy to deal with the inevitable administrivia. None of the staff were ever invited to senior management meetings. Only those of the Inner Circle attended.

"You've all spoken with Quinn at length." said Jon. "Some of you haven't met him yet. Please take the opportunity to get better acquainted while we're here."

Quinn Andreas was Australian. After college he played professional rugby for several years before getting a graduate degree at Oxford. He'd worked for several multinational companies based in Europe. He still looked like he could step onto a pitch and play.

Bill went first. "For background," he began and gestured towards Quinn, "we have picked four basic technologies and are targeting only the three largest players in those respective markets. We want to sign up two of the three in each market in hopes competition will keep them honest. To be blunt, we prefer that the players hate each other." The others nodded.

"To ensure competition, and for other strategic reasons, those players are distributed internationally. For example, GE, Siemens, and Philips dominate medical technology. Both Siemens and Philips are European, so I'll sign up only one of the two. That's good for GE; they will get a contract. We are working on several deals with GE. The big news is—fingers crossed—we're scheduled to close with Siemens on the MRI technology next week. The terms are eight million up front, and a fixed annual royalty going forward, or a percentage of sales, whichever is greater. Thank you, Tom, and your hobbits, for providing the working prototypes and detailed technical specs. Without those, we never would have closed the sales."

Tom had hired a dozen capable and energetic men and women to handle the myriad of operational chores that had arisen. None appeared to have defined responsibilities; however, everything was getting done. The others called them Tom's hobbits.

"The room temperature superconductor will be the most successful long-term revenue stream. The product is not wholly resistance free, but the alloy gets you most of the way there, and notably, without the need for expensive cooling systems. The product beats all other competing technologies handily. We're branding it as a megaconductor rather than superconductor. It has much less resistance than copper, and the alloy is mostly aluminum, so you get the weight advantages desired for transmission lines. Ten percent of all electricity generated worldwide is lost during transmission. Within a few years all transmission lines will use our product. The savings from reduced electrical losses will run tens of billions of dollars a year.

"Generating equipment, electric motors, batteries, anything that uses electricity will become smaller, lighter, and cheaper. Electric cars are about to take a great leap forward. This will also revolutionize the semiconductor chip industry."

No slides were projected on the wall. The enhancements made the material visible inside the eyes. Individuals could zoom in or out individually.

"Strategically," Bill continued, "we are avoiding China. Negotiating with a Chinese company is a time-suck with little potential payback. Although the country has the second largest economy in the world, it's effectively closed to us. Chinese companies don't pay for intellectual property. Eventually they will steal the technology from one of our clients. I'm not just bitching. Technology theft is communist China's government policy. Don't get me wrong. Chinese companies will engage with us. Negotiations will take forever, and at the end of the day we probably won't get paid. In the unlikely event we actually do get paid, the timeline is just too long.

"We're not avoiding Asia altogether. We are actively engaging South Korean and Japanese companies.

"Which leads to my last strategic point," Bill continued. "Per Jon's direction, we front-load the royalties as much as possible. We will give up a relatively greater future revenue stream in order to get something, quicker. Case in point is the battery technology we rolled out two months ago. The product is cheaper, lighter, and the energy density is twice that of lithium storage. Within a few years this will totally replace lithium batteries. We could have got a lot more cash long-term but settled for a big up-front payment and a relatively small ongoing royalty."

The meeting progressed. An outsider would have found the details odd. Tracey and Bob had created more national, and international, shell companies than the company had employees. The largest department was easily Randy's security group, which, in addition to IT administration, included hackers, detectives, retired spies, and paramilitary people. Randy was also responsible for managing the bodyguards. Nobody reported against their budget—there wasn't one. Bob prepared a one-page rolling summary for Jon every two months for use as a guideline. The responsibilities of each area oozed over to several others. The company didn't even have a formal headquarters. Shirley arranged to rent offices on all three coasts. In each case the company took an entire floor and hardened the physical security.

Near the end of the fixed agenda, Tom said, "We could easily pull in a lot more cash with less effort by licensing the power generation technology used by the Fab, or the spacecraft. Heck, we could make billions by using Fabs to replace high-tech manufacturing worldwide."

"We've had this conversation before," replied Jon. "The Chait have placed an embargo on Fab technology. We've been moving really fast, and I haven't taken the time I should have to expand on the rationale regarding what technology is available now, and what is scheduled for release in the future. If you haven't already, please discuss this with your Chait rep. They can tell you the what. I will clarify the why in the near future, I promise.

"Our cash is growing faster than our staffing," continued Jon. "It's time to begin planning the next phase. To do that we are going to hire people with a different skill set."

NINE
THE MINER

WHAT DIMWITS, THOUGHT MIKE SIPLE to himself. *I wonder who's dumber, the lady here before me, or Fred, the extraction manager.*

Mike, formerly of Clearwater Florida, was twenty-four years old. A couple of years in the army and a couple of years in college didn't agree with him, or do much for him. He tested in the top five percent in both his college entrance exams and the military's ASVAB. His friends and co-workers agreed he was one competent dude. However, he was rarely interested or engaged in much of anything. He drifted through life.

A case of acute lymphoblastic leukemia sentenced him to an early death. When the recruiter came calling, he agreed. Sure, why not. He was dying, so why not sit—well, lie—for a few short tests, and a couple interviews while in bed. He had no ties. His dad died years ago in an auto accident; his mom had remarried and moved—he hadn't seen her in years. His girlfriend was no prize and dropped him like a hot rock once he got sick.

Mike regained consciousness after only a week in the tank. "Leukemia is an easy fix," the med tech explained. "You're young, and generally healthy, only a case of the one disease, and the side effects of the godawful chemo treatments. Most of the tank treatment was removing the microscopic cataracts caused by the steroids. Well, that, and giving you the enhancements. The leukemia was easy. You also received a number of small fixes. You had two cavities which we fixed. You also had a small imbalance in your brain chemistry. You may find it easier to concentrate now. You'll need a couple weeks of rehab to get your strength back, and you'll be good to go."

The gravity felt about the same, but the fresh air was magical. This planet, Ouranos, was eerily Earth-like. Most of the plants and animals were recognizable, or at least looked familiar. However, some of the plants and animals didn't exist on Earth, not even in *National Geographic Specials.*

Mike felt fine in a few days but spent a month getting acclimated in the town of Shoreside. All new recruits were processed at Shoreside. Deep, wide tunnels had been driven into the low hills for safekeeping of the rejuvenation tanks. Some of the old codgers spent six months in a tank to get back to a young healthy baseline.

Even though the town overlooked the ocean bay, the air didn't feel as sticky as Florida. A steady ocean breeze kept the climate comfortable. From shore, the water was a brilliant iridescent blue. Once he got closer, he could see the water appeared abnormally clear.

The place was thick with birds. Each morning he was woken by the squawking of parrots. Clouds of seabirds patrolled the beaches. Flocks of colorful birds filled the skies at all times of the day.

After a few days lazing in the sun, Mike started to help in the kitchen, and the gardens. "Everybody works," he was told. "'Besides, it's good therapy while you get your strength back."

All routine chores were automated. Kitchen Patrol (KP) duties were light and not at all odious. The gardening seemed make-work to ensure Mike stayed active.

The food was extraordinary. Nothing was frozen or canned. Nothing was added. No sugar—fructose, dextrose, lactose, glucose, or sucrose. No preservatives either; no nitrates, sulfates, sodium benzoate, bromates, sorbates, tocopherols, or even salt. No artificial flavors, or food coloring. Everything was fresh. Storage was done in a stasis box which held the contents effectively frozen in time. All biological processes stopped inside the box.

Since the leukemia hit, Mike avoided artificial preservatives and religiously read packaging labels. Now, unless the food product was an expensive earth import, the food had no information labeling. As a bonus, food had never tasted this good.

He spent several hours each day training and taking classes. The level of technology and automation was beyond anything he'd ever seen. Many of the classes were tutorials on the capabilities and limits of technology. There were classes covering the government, such as it was, the planet's geography, and the local flora and fauna. The enhancements allowed him to sit outside, by himself, with a cool drink while participating in the classes.

He was cautioned not to swim in the ocean, except for one clearly marked beach. He was also told not to leave the well-marked perimeter of the town without a sidearm, a rifle, and an experienced resident with him. "Predators" was the terse explanation.

"The Deal" was explained in great detail. Every new recruit was given his life back. Most were quite aged. Their biological age was reset to twenty-five years. The first reset was on the house. Colonists had to earn subsequent rejuvenations. One could work ten years for The Project and earn a twenty-year reset. Mike judged most people planned to spend ten years working for The Project, ten years for themselves, and then repeat the process.

The pay sounded great. He wasn't sure since nothing was priced in currency, and there were no stores. The unit of exchange seemed complicated and was based on something called Fab minutes. Everyone he met sure seemed enthusiastic about the pay and benefits. Well, duh, the main benefit was a hugely extended lifespan. However, everyone also expected to get rich. Anybody who worked for The Project got land. You could also buy land. The Crown awarded special grants in certain cases. Those arrangements were complicated also.

The last week Mike went fishing.

The two men manning the boat gave what seemed an overly cautious safety briefing. "Don't ever put your hand in the water," one told him. "Don't even extend your arm over the side, without a gaff," the other said. "There are a hundred times the fish you ever saw in Florida, and two hundred times as many sharks. If you aren't careful, you'll find yourself missing a hand."

"We do only line fishing," the captain explained. "With a few exceptions, nets are not allowed."

The fishing was great. Mike had never seen such huge shoals of large fish before. The only bait was a brightly colored plastic ribbon attached to an otherwise bare hook. They were catching mostly striped bass. The fish ran ten to twenty kilos apiece, much bigger than Mike was used to. The inexperienced fish practically leapt on the hook. Late in the day he was reaching for the gaff to pull one in when something took the fish. Mike caught a millisecond flash of a giant mouth full of razor-like hooked teeth, and convulsively threw himself backwards. The other two laughed. "Tiger shark," one explained. "Big one." When Mike carefully reeled in his hook, only the head and small piece of the bass's body remained.

The fish were fileted and for the most part sent to the other towns on the regular cargo runs. Being from Florida, Mike knew how to clean and filet fish, which was much appreciated by the other two manning the boat.

Mike was considered a recruit until he had finished a probationary period, had met with, and sworn fealty to the king. Then his status became that of a subject. The whole setup sounded medieval; however, the others he spoke with liked the arrangement. "You're healthier, wealthier, and have a hell of a lot more freedom here than you did as a so-called citizen back home," another told him.

Mike estimated the total population was several thousand, scattered among four small towns. However, his initial assignment was not in town. He was scheduled to spend a month in the boonies.

His new hometown was a place in the North, well up in the mountains. The town was named Mountainside. He was flown up in a flying saucer, a no-shit flying saucer, with a half dozen other new recruits. Ok, the craft wasn't exactly a saucer, although everyone used the term. He felt as if he were on safari. From the saucer they saw huge herds of deer, elk, cattle, and other large animals Mike couldn't identify. There were no signs of civilization. Nothing. No fields, crops, roads, fences, powerlines, houses, or barns. No sign of man at all.

At Mountainside, Mike was partnered with a guide—a young woman! She gave a quick tour of the town, and then took him to his assigned company housing, a townhouse. The perky guide said the townhouse was a hundred square meters, which Mike had to convert in his head as a hair more than a thousand square feet. Everything was measured in the metric system. Mike groaned to himself. He would have to learn the dammed system.

The townhouse was luxurious. The interior was bright, open, and airy. The esthetics indicated the place was designed by a professional. The kitchen was minimalist with a wall of wood paneling concealing the pull-out storage cabinets. The beautiful stone floors had radiant heat, and the bathroom had several expensive touches.

"The place has two bedrooms," the guide explained. "You have a roommate, at least for the first year. He does the same kind of work as you, but with an opposing schedule. You'll rarely see him. You leave the day after tomorrow."

The guide also gave him a pep talk. "You are going to love it here," she chirped. "You don't see or hear stupid stuff all day every day like back home."

The entire civilization was starting from scratch. Building infrastructure was the primary activity. Infrastructure for the towns, industry, farming, and for The Project.

A modern civilization uses a hundred unique metals. Everything from antimony to zinc, copper tungsten, lead, nickel, titanium silver gold, and bauxite for aluminum. Many were found in association with others. Some tended to occur in isolation. Molybdenum was one of those. The mineral was primarily used to harden steel. Mike's job for the next month was extracting moly.

Mike was dropped high in the mountains with four HAL units, a small Fab, and supplies. HAL was an acronym for "Humanoid Automated Labor." The site had been worked previously, and there was a tiny living trailer on-site. The views of the surrounding mountains and the valley below were breathtaking. He was cautioned not to leave the warded perimeter without putting up a security drone, and carrying both a sidearm and a rifle.

"Be careful of the bears," Fred cautioned. "And the cougars, and the wolves."

"We practice campaign mining," Fred continued. "We mine a month at a shot, a couple times a year, until the requirement gets to a point where someone is needed full-time. The last person stayed four weeks and recovered enough moly to last us four months. We're going to run out in a couple of months and we're counting on you to get more ready."

The HAL units took some getting used to. The Androids were strongly built and over six feet tall. He'd seen them at Shoreside; however, the ones here were bigger. Their hands had five digits—three fingers with a thumb on each side. Their feet had five toes; however, three were in front and two in the rear of the foot. They were reasonably intelligent and exhibited basic common sense—more than the average teenager. The units worked day and night without rest. The battery technology was impressive. Once a week the units huddled by the Fab and recharged. Over a month each did the work of five strong men.

The HAL units tough, neoprene-like skin panels were colored, and each one differed for easy identification. After a basic course all subjects were issued a unit for their personal use. After a year of demonstrating that one could effectively utilize the unit, a second was issued. Although Mike wasn't qualified to own a unit yet, his boss had him supervising four. Go figure. The units Mike used were loaners, which the owners leased to The Project. He named his units Amos, Andy, Long John, and Captain Hook.

Mike thought the HAL acronym dumber than shit. He referred to his units as minions.

The Fab was a dull metallic cube about the size and shape of a delivery van. The device was used to separate the moly from the waste rock. One loaded a bucket of ore on one side, and a couple minutes later a small moly ingot, some tiny pellets of trace metals, and small briquettes of the waste rock came out the other side. The bucket was untouched. As Mike understood the process, energy fields inside the Fab disassociated the loaded material into the component atoms, which were then reconstituted per the operator's instructions. The unit could process four buckets, each about twenty liters, in each cycle.

The Fab was set up a hundred meters from the workings. The trailer where Mike was to live was another hundred meters further on.

The ground was rough and uneven. The minions went to work following the process setup by the prior manager. A couple of minions worked in the mine opening where the ore was located. They used hand tools and a small assembler/disassembler (A&D) to crumble the ore away. Another one lugged buckets from the work face over to the Fab, and helped load the unit. The last one unloaded the Fab output and threw the waste briquettes down the hill, the recovered moly in a heap nearby, and the marbles of trace minerals into a bucket.

What a flustercluck, Mike thought in disgust. The lady before him must've learned organization techniques by watching movies of the three stooges. Time for some changes.

Three weeks later his boss came for him. The saucer came down vertically on the freshly cleared and leveled landing pad. Fred got out, and, unexpectedly, Fred's boss, John Hayward, who ran operations. Well, actually, he ran the entire town.

"We're cutting your deployment short," said Fred. "You've done a great job. You've pulled three times the moly, and in less time than we planned." He paused and looked around. "You've made a lot of changes."

"No shit," said Mike. "Improving the output wasn't hard. The people before me implemented advanced alien technology on a level suitable for Nubian slaves in one of King Solomon's mines."

Fred immediately looked pissed. Hayward cut in to diffuse the situation. "Hey, we brought cold beer for the flight back." Beer was still imported from Earth, and expensive. "I'd appreciate it if you could walk us through the operation while the HAL units load the moly. We'll take the Fab, of course, but we'll leave the trailer. We need the lift capacity for the moly."

"First of all," Mike explained, "a minion ran the extra A&D over the working areas to get a smooth, even surface to walk on. By the way, the name sucks. I use the name 'Andy.' Get it? Then I reconfigured the Fab output to get pavers from the waste, instead of useless briquettes. The minions laid pavers in the muddy areas around the Fab, the trailer, and my new hut area. I reconfigured the Fab output again to get bricks—foamed with nitrogen for a reasonable R value—to build the larger quarters. The trailer is pretty damn cramped. I used one of the Andies to level the landing area so you're not sitting that expensive saucer down in a rock field. The Fab can oxidize moly in a controlled fashion, resulting in a bright color of your choice. Eye-searing yellow bricks seemed a good choice to ring the landing field.

"Anyway, to increase the output two things had to happen. First, the Fab had to be running, always, as close to one hundred percent of the time as possible. As soon as a load completed processing, a minion had to be standing ready to shove in the next. Every second the Fab wasn't operating was a second of output lost forever. So, the ore had to be waiting in queue, and a minion standing by ready to load at all times.

"Hauling a bucket or two at a time from the working face to the Fab was just moronic. I had the Fab make us more buckets, and several carts. Each cart hauls twelve buckets at a time. A minion then brought twelve buckets at a time instead of one or two. Once we got ahead of schedule, we cut a couple of tracks into the rock so the cart runs on slots. To me carving slots seemed easier than building rails. A minion just gives the loaded cart a push and it rolls all the way to the Fab. We built a table in front of the Fab so we can queue up a couple extra rows of buckets for faster loading. By then I'd freed up a minion to lay the pavers, and build the hut, and work on improvements—like the landing pad.

"Second, we could easily improve the richness of the oar being loaded into the Fab. I learned we can tune the Andy in a number of ways. So, I set up a process where a minion runs the Andy over the working face, and crumbles away not just the non-moly-bearing country rock but the poorer ore as well. The process is not perfect; however, instead of processing ore running around two percent moly, we load ore closer to a ten percent grade. Therefore, the Fab recovers five times as much moly in the same amount of processing time. This mountain contains about a hundred years' supply of ore. If need be, somebody can come back later and knock themselves out reprocessing the lower grade waste.

"The whole extraction process was designed by an idiot. We should be using a small dissembler to do the majority of ore enrichment, instead of the Fab. The Fabs, as I understand, are overbooked everywhere and the limiting factor on, well, almost everything. We should preprocess the ore, and then fly the Fab in for one single solitary week, instead of three or four. Oh, don't forget, my time is worth something.

"Automation would be a big help. There's a lot of other minor stuff—the size and shape of the buckets, the grain size of the ore, minimizing walking distance, a lot of stuff.

"Gee, if we used technology, the advanced super-duper alien stuff, I see where we could do a whole lot better. Using a million-dollar android to fill buckets with a shovel is not an efficient use of resources. You shouldn't have to send a dumb newbie like me out for a whole month with no booze, and no pussy.

"I even ran out of dip a week ago."

"That's all quite interesting," said John, amused with the brash kid. "You've obviously put a lot of thought into this," he said while looking downhill at Fred, who was overseeing the loading. "Tell me more on the flight back."

TEN
THE PROJECT MEETING

THE PARTICIPANTS CALLED THE SESSIONS the weekly prayer meeting. The group touched bases once a week and held a more elaborate review of The Project once a month. Present were John Hayward, the Mountainside manager; Dr. Valerie Atkinson, the Shoreside manager; Steve Kopec, the Rainy Town manager; and Juan Perez, who ran Amazon Cove. The four settlements were scattered a thousand kilometers along the east coast of the Poseidon Sea. Their enhancements made it seem as if they were sitting together in the same room. John ran the meeting.

"As usual, we start with the holy dogma," John joked. "Valerie, what is our project's mission?"

"Save humanity," she replied.

"Steve, what's our goal?" John asked.

"Build interstellar spacecraft," he replied.

"Juan, what's our vision?" John asked.

"Live long and prosper," Juan replied. He held up his right hand in a credible split-finger Vulcan greeting. He'd taped his fingers to keep them separated. The others laughed.

"I know the dogma seems a little bit hokey," said John. "But I feel the few seconds spent on recital gives us focus and keeps the meetings on track. Juan is the new guy, so let's go into a little more detail than usual for his benefit. Steve, you have been looking at our airlift practices and I believe you have a few suggestions."

"Yes, I do," Steve replied. "Everything moves by air. Outside of the settlements there are no roads, and we haven't developed any useful shipping capability by water. The fleet has three medium-weight saucers to move people and cargo. The bay has a carrying capacity of twenty thousand kilos—similar to a C130 cargo plane. We also have six smaller saucers which carry up to eight people and their luggage. In a pinch we can pull the seats and carry additional cargo.

"One of the three medium-weight saucers operates a set daily route. It stops at each of our four settlements, making deliveries and pickups at each stop. The other two do everything else, from moving small Fabs and raw materials among extraction sites to supplying the homesteads along the Osage and White River valleys.

"Our flight capacity is getting squeezed from either end," Steve continued. "Supplying the homesteads is time intensive. However, after the initial founding we don't deliver a lot of heavy cargo; we make a lot of visits. People get a few weeks off, they want to work the homestead, they need to get dropped off and picked up. The passengers bring a ton or so of food and supplies, and a couple HAL units, to carry back and forth. Or, they have to get home for a day or two to take care of some emergency. On the other end of the spectrum, we need to move bigger Fabs, and soon now, large spacecraft components. For that, as the saying goes, we're going to need a bigger boat. We'll need the ability to lift three or four times the capacity of our current saucers.

"Our pilots are run ragged. To get maximum utilization of the saucers, we've been flying around the clock in twelve-hour shifts. I suspect some sleep on the job. The pilots take off, turn on the autopilot, and nap en route to their next destination.

"I propose we build three drones. Two of them capable of delivering a loaded cargo container weighing four or five thousand kilos. Another one to ferry people, and light supplies. We have the technology for these to operate autonomously. Once people get comfortable flying in a pilotless aircraft, we'll evaluate building more. At the same time, I think we should start planning the build of the larger saucers. Each generation of Fab is larger than the next, and we need to transport bigger Fabs than we do now.

"Also, we've all agreed we're going to have to Fab individual components and assemble, rather than have a complete spacecraft appear out of one gigantic Fab."

"The thought of flying people in a drone gives me the willies," said Valerie. "Excepting people, why not move everything in a cargo container, carried by a drone? It seems silly to have a pilot sleeping in the cockpit while these intelligent semiautonomous saucers fly themselves. I can see you might need the human touch when exploring a new site, or flying people, but otherwise why not just shove everything in a can to move? You wouldn't even need an enclosed cargo bay. Maybe later, once we're comfortable, fly people in drones."

The root issue is the same every time, thought John to himself as the conversation continued. *We're all used to doing things the old way, and don't use the technology available as effectively as we could.* Most of the recruits were retreads, old coots like himself who had fifty or more years of hard-living stripped away. No matter if the person was a retread, or a first lifer recruit, they were limited by their imagination. Only a few were flexible in using the new tech efficiently.

A child could fly a saucer. *For Christ sakes*, he thought, *if one got in trouble, he only had to release the controls and the thing would simply stop and hover in midair. There was no need for highly trained pilots. An eight-hour familiarization course was more than sufficient.*

John redirected the conversation.

The group agreed on a training course. New flyers wouldn't solo until they had demonstrated a minimum level of proficiency. They agreed to build two smaller saucers, partly for additional availability, partly in fear the new flyers would crash one. The group also agreed to build the three drones, and to form a group to begin planning the larger saucer.

Humans didn't design saucers, as much as develop the requirements. The Chait AI provided the detailed designs. The design became more difficult when restricted by the available Fab size, and capacity. The Project would eventually build Fabs the size of a city block which could disgorge a complete spacecraft in one go.

Building that gigantic Fab would take years, and the colonization effort required several interstellar craft sooner. Besides, the Chait would eventually want their loaner interstellar ship back.

"Now, let's talk about Fab capacity," said John. The others seemed to sit up a little straighter. This was always a hot topic.

Half the internal area inside a Fab consisted of field generation equipment. Therefore, a Fab ten feet wide could only produce product approximately half that width. Creating a new, larger Fab was a lengthy process. The exterior panels had to be extremely tough, strong, and precisely made as they were integral to the internal processing. The first Fab produced panels which were then assembled together outside of the Fab. The field generation equipment was built one unit at a time and then moved to the larger Fab. The equipment was built up atom by atom, and required a variety of rare earth elements, superconductors, metallic hydrogen, and quasi-modal metals. Paradoxically, several of the required exotic materials did not occur naturally, and could only be made in a Fab. Given sufficient quantities of the right elements, a Fab could construct a clone, fifty percent larger, in two or three months.

Mountainside was located adjacent to a large low-grade iron deposit chock-full of trace minerals. Rainy Town was located near a large bauxite deposit, the precursor to aluminum. The deposit also contained a dozen trace minerals. Conventional mills typically did not recover most trace metals. A separate expensive mill circuit was generally required for each specific trace mineral, which was almost always too costly. However, a Fab recovered everything in one fell swoop.

Amazon Cove was established for the chemical industry. The town was near a large, shallow oil field whose hydrocarbons were slated for use as the basis for chemicals, plastics, carbon constructs, and much more.

Fab replication was done at Mountainside. Many of the required metals were available there. The rationale was that a modern society required lots of heavy metal—tractors, bulldozers, pipelines, planes, trains and automobiles, and most importantly interstellar spacecraft. Given the majority of the metals, and Fabs were there, Mountainside seemed destined to become the largest city on the planet. Obviously.

Not.

Now, as people began to understand the new technology, the need for metal would be in large part supplanted by carbon-based materials easily obtainable from hydrocarbons—oil. Carbon-based materials were endless and included carbon fiber, fullerenes, buckyballs, graphene, nanotubes, diamonds, and exotic materials previously unknown to humans.

Even clothing was Fab'd from a hydrocarbon feedstock. Modern clothing is made of one or more of dozens of artificial fibers sourced from hydrocarbons. Polyester, acrylic, nylon, spandex, and various microfibers were just the beginning. Any fabric for any specific purpose could be Fab'd to tightly engineered specifications. The warmest, softest fleece is produced from hydrocarbons. The artificial leather and furs from a Fab were indistinguishable from the real thing. For purposes of clothing there was no need for flocks of sheep, herds of cows, or fields of cotton.

The hardest material known to man is composed of carbon: nanocrystalline diamond. In a slightly different arrangement, carbon is the best possible conductor of heat. Carbon offers endless possibilities.

Fab programming did not allow construction of food, except aboard an interstellar craft. Which humans didn't have, yet.

Plastics, made from hydrocarbons, could replace metal, and wood, in many home and industrial applications.

The Chait power technology eliminated the need for burning hydrocarbons. Even so, the importance of hydrocarbons was going to overshadow metals.

Those running The Project now realized the interstellar craft and future saucers would be constructed primarily of carbon compounds. The structural component of the interstellar craft's shell was to be a carbon material a hundred times stronger than steel, yet lighter than aluminum. The structural material would be sandwiched with other layers that provided insulation, thermal conduction, and numerous field propagation layers. A sacrificial ablative layer would coat the exterior.

Very soon, The Project would formalize the location for spacecraft construction and systems integration. Amazon Cove was looking like a done deal. The body and structure of the craft would be made on-site of light, immensely strong carbon-based materials. The power, propulsion, and field generation units would be Fab'd at Mountainside and transported to Amazon Cove for final assembly. However, Amazon Cove was the least developed of all the locations. Not only were living conditions substandard, the site was also woefully short of Fabs.

"I've discussed this at the highest level," began John. "Amazon Cove is moving up in priority. The town gets the next two Fabs. The initial class of spacecraft will have a diameter four generations beyond the capacity of your largest Fab. Building up to a Fab of sufficient size will take a couple years. Until we get heavier capacity saucers, we will make Fab components at Mountainside and fly them down to Amazon Cove. We will ship everything—the exterior panels, field generation, and power components—separately. Up to now we've always shipped fully complete operational Fabs. This is a big change."

And Mountainside keeps control of the Fabs, the others thought.

I may have doomed Mountainside to be a backwater mining town, thought John.

ELEVEN
THE VINEYARD

T HE SAUCER OFFLOADED LIZ, HER companions, a six-meter cargo crate, and two HAL units, mid-morning. The saucer was hugely cool. The craft appeared as if a large airplane had been squished from either end, leaving a shorter, fatter, wider vehicle. Fat, stubby wings only a couple meters long protruded from each side and generated the propulsion fields. Landing was smooth as silk as the fields projected the equivalent of bubble wrap underneath and allowed the saucer to touch down gently. In flight, the same field projectors created phantom wings which mutated in real time for maximum lift and efficiency, allowing the saucer to fly far distances using little power.

"I'll see you in eight days," the pilot said cheerfully.

The homestead belonged to Elizabeth Neuwland. The crown established her land grant early in exchange for Liz's pledge to grow grapes and make wine. No vineyards existed on Ouranos, yet.

Those working on The Project were promised a hundred hectares of good land (approximately two hundred and fifty acres) for every year of service. However, the initial grant was predicated on the successful completion of the first two full years of service.

Crown Land available for homesteading was classified in three grades. Prime land was excellent farmland adjacent to year-round water. Good land was easily farmed, with accessible water, but might be hilly with intermittent seasonal streams and sloughs. Poor land was some combination of hilly, stony, desert, or swamp not readily amenable to development. A hectare grant of good land was equivalent to half a hectare of prime land, or two of poor land. Liz had four hundred hectares of good land, a small tongue of which fronted the Osage River.

"I still think you should have gone for the prime land," said Magnus Sahlin, Elizabeth's fiancé. It's not like you wouldn't have had enough, and there is no need to settle for second best."

Liz looked at Magnus affectionately. He was a twenty-seven-year-old Ontario, Canada, farm boy of Finnish descent. Liz was a woman of eighty-two. After her rejuvenation she looked, and felt, like a teenager again. When she decided to spend the next twenty years with Magnus, he had no chance. Seducing Magnus was like shooting fish in a barrel. She had him broken in and half trained in bed already.

Magnus was recruited from a hospital ward. He had lost both arms in a farming accident.

"Grapes grow best on south-facing hills," she explained. "The vines don't need the best soil either, not that the land here isn't good. The property is perfect for grapes. See the ridgeline in the distance?" she pointed uphill. "The slope gets steeper as you go up. My grant runs about halfway to the top. Nobody's going to want the steep part of the hill, meaning nobody's ever going to be pissing in our drainage. It's all ours." Well, hers.

Liz had been on-site most of the year with her HAL unit. She preferred the term peon and called hers Heckle. Magnus and Raimo had brought their peons for the week. Magnus was going to leave his with Liz when he went back to work. She was at the point now where she could use two peons effectively.

The other couple, Raimo and his girlfriend Anna, were just down for the week to enjoy their time off. Neither was eligible for a land grant yet. The pair planned to see what others were doing before planning their own place.

Liz and Magnus got the HAL units busy, launched a security drone, unloaded, settled in, and the group had lunch. In the afternoon they toured the property while Liz brought the others up to speed on her plans for the vineyard. Dinner that night was venison tenderloin medallions over an open fire, with roasted potatoes. Everybody on Ouranos ate a lot of potatoes.

Regardless of the security perimeter, all wore sidearms. The women carried theirs on the hip; the men were more comfortable with shoulder holsters.

The large carnivores on Ouranos considered the race of man an excellent snack. Men were soft and pink, with tiny, dull teeth. Men were slow, weak, and had no claws, hooves, or horns for defense.

"In the greenhouse are eight hundred seedlings ready to be put in the field," said Liz. "That's enough for one acre. Next year I'll be able to plant double that number. The vines will actually produce grapes next year, but it's not a good idea to let them fruit that soon. Good practice is to let the roots develop for another year. I'll prune most of them but let some go to get samples."

"One acre doesn't sound like much," said Anna. "Back home I'd drive by vineyards that that stretched a mile or more."

"Well, this is home now," said Liz shortly. Hearing others refer to Earth as home grated on her. "If we didn't have the peons for planting, you'd see how much an acre really is, after bending over to plant for a few days." Everyone groaned in mock pain. "But in a sense, you're correct, it's not a lot of grapes. In northern California, my old stomping grounds"—everybody groaned again—"you needed a minimum of forty acres of vine to have an economically sized operation. A lot of wealthy folks kept a second home in the country and grew a few acres of grapes, but the activity was just an expensive hobby.

"Furthermore," continued Liz pedantically while waving her finger in the air. "There're not a lot of people here to drink the wine. In a few years, when those vines are producing well, I might get several thousand bottles of wine from each acre. Unless the colony continues to grow, I might never need more than forty acres of vine. Unless the wine is consistently good, and everyone drinks a lot. My goal is to turn everyone into a wino!"

"How did you become such an enthusiast?" asked Raimo. "You seem to know a lot about making wine."

"I grew up in the business," replied Liz brightly. "My father owned a vineyard and ran a winery in northern California. After college I became a wine consultant and worked with a dozen different local vineyards."

She didn't tell them the rest. Her degrees in Enology and Viticulture. How she grew up in her father's vineyard. How she worked in the winery through high school and ran the whole operation during college. How the vineyard was her life. How her father remarried when her mother died. How her stepmother marginalized Liz and pushed her away from her father. How her stepmother spent all the money on gambling, televangelists, expensive clothes, and high living, leaving nothing for Liz when her father passed. How she spent the rest of her life as a paid consultant, a hired hand, instead of a respected owner.

By God, she'd be an owner now.

"Agriculture has become hugely mechanized," said Anna. "But I thought grapes still took a lot of manual labor. How much help do you expect from the peons?"

Conversations on Ouranos were sometimes difficult. Although everyone appeared twenty-five years old, most had experienced eighty or ninety years of life. Magnus was a youngster; the other three each had fifty years or more on him. He understood none of their cultural references. The rejuv's communicated with a tilt of the head, or a flick of the eyes, a single word, an inside joke, a casual wave of a finger. Magnus picked up and understood only half of what was going on around him, and was blissfully unaware of what he missed. Anna's question was a safe one.

"You're right," replied Liz. "On Earth the planting of the vines, the cultivating, and the picking is still done largely by hand. The peons are a godsend. You'll see tomorrow when we plant the seedlings. Peons learn quickly and have a surprisingly delicate touch when needed. They are capable of everything you or I can do by hand. You work with one on a delicate task, a task requiring some judgement and expertise, and peons pick up the skills almost instantly. After an hour or two working with me tomorrow, Heckle will finish the rest of the planting without us. When we put in the drip irrigation, I worked with Heckle on a couple rows and left him the rest. He finished the whole thing without any supervision the next day.

"The technology is going to help, but I'm not sure how much," continued Liz. "Maybe some different equipment to sort and de-stem, or crush the grapes, certainly better process controls. Maybe some automation in the processing and racking. The fermentation and the aging are done the same way as always. I've got a year to think things through.

"Once the vines come out, I'll train Heckle on proper pruning and cultivation. I could transfer his knowledge to a specially designed cart, with multiple arms, to cruise up and down the rows picking grapes at harvest time, and cultivating during the year. Right now, that'd be ridiculous; the cart would sit around unused most of the time."

HAL units were easily taught specialized skills. The units learned quickly, had excellent motor skills, and didn't forget a thing. A bricklayer could teach a unit to properly lay bricks in less than a day. Planning the job, picking the right mortar, mixing mortar correctly, and organizing the work took longer to learn. The human had to plan and organize the work for a while, but eventually the unit picked those skills as well.

Specialized knowledge taught to a HAL was considered personal property. A skill you taught your unit remained your property and could only be transferred to another HAL unit with the owner's permission. Given permission, skills were transferable among units in a split second. A lucrative, active market for blue-collar trade skills had sprung up.

Liz knew more about grapes and wine than the ten next most competent people on the planet combined. She was the receptacle of two thousand years of the art and science of growing grapes and making wine. She vowed to never share her knowledge in any way. She'd hold her skills close, forever.

"Ironically, the first use I made of the technology was to address a major problem, which is not a big deal in northern California. Critters. Every critter in existence loves grapes. I've tested everything around my gardens. The Wards keep the four-footed variety out, and the drones are working against the birds."

Wards were a simple two-meter pole with a bulbous top. The top emitted noise at subsonic frequencies that repelled animals. The devices were tuned so as not to affect humans.

"The aging barrels are a great example in figuring out the technology. Wine must be aged in wood, preferably oak, not just any oak, the right oak. The oak trees in this area are perfect to make into casks. The forest is old growth, which helps the wood quality. I'll need a couple dozen aging barrels for the first acre of harvest. Can a peon be trained to turn an oak tree into barrels? Is it sensible, or even possible, to throw a log in a Fab and have a barrel pop out?

"I can't complain about the deal with the Crown," Liz continued. "The grant included land, and the specialized equipment I need to get started. We can live easily with Magnus employed by The Project, but I've struggled getting the vineyard started with just me and one peon. We each get another peon in a couple months, which gets us over the hump. I'll keep two here, we'll lease the other two back to The Project."

Later that night after a bout between the sheets, Anna and Raimo lay cuddling. "Poor Magnus," whispered Anna. "She's going to eat him alive."

"Nah," said Raimo. "Not all of him. She'll save his bones and grind them up for fertilizer."

"Be serious," she said and pinched him. He pinched her back and one thing led to another, and Magnus was forgotten.

TWELVE
THE CONVERSATION

"**W**HY ARE YOU HELPING US," asked Tracey, "and why won't you show yourselves?"

Tracey was nestled in the soft, firm leather of her chauffeur-driven Rolls-Royce Cullinan SUV. The length and height of the seat were tailored perfectly to her legs. Her feet were flat on the floor and her back was firmly against the gently heated upper seat. Her hand was wrapped around a cut crystal cocktail glass of well-aged Calvados. The car ran with the eerie silence that was the trademark of the brand. Outside a beautiful view of the Pacific Coast Highway scrolled by.

Not really.

She was in a hotel room. For relaxation she had chosen a total immersion virtual-reality simulation via her enhancements. The car, the drive, the taste of the brandy, and the heft of the glass existed only in her mind's eye. She was able to choose the car and the rest of the simulation in seconds. The technology filled in the details. The view and other sensory inputs were razor sharp, yet silky smooth.

The effect was totally lifelike, and not a little scary. Her mind was no longer her own. What if she got hacked? What if the Chait made choices for her? Would she even know? What if a large consumer company ever got a hold of the technology? Would she overnight start thinking seafood tasted great, or come home from the store with the wrong toothpaste?

One day she came out to a gigantic baked-on bird splat dead center on the driver's side windshield of her car. She used her enhancements to edit the sight away while she drove. A week later someone remarked on the mess—she had forgotten it was there. The ugly splat was still invisible to her.

Both Jon and the Chait had assured the team of bright red lines around the control and functionality of the enhancements. Still, she wondered...

"As I, and the other representatives, have said before," said Jamocha, her Chait rep, "we are helping because we find the human race interesting, and believe the universe is a better place with you than without. Given what we personally know of the universe, your planet, and your species, the probability of the human race becoming extinct, on Earth, approaches unity. All your eggs are in one basket, and you are not watching it carefully. The basket is going to drop."

"Are you referring to climate change?" asked Tracey.

"Asking such a question does not become you," chided Jamocha. "An answer to such a nonspecific question would be meaningless. Why don't you try again, and be more specific."

"Sorry," replied Tracey. "Does Chait science indicate man-made carbon dioxide and other greenhouse gases are going to affect our planet's atmosphere in such a way to materially change the climate?"

"Much better," replied Jamocha. "No, there is no indication the relatively small amount of carbon you emit will change your planet's climate materially. Also, there is no reason a small change in the atmosphere's CO_2 would increase randomness of weather. Robert had this conversation with Jon the day they first met. Your climate constantly changes, as does weather, regardless of your emissions. However, your species is eventually doomed. If a plague doesn't get you, nuclear war, a killer asteroid, the next ice age, or one of your goofy belief systems is bound to do the job. It's just a matter of when."

At least Jamocha didn't mention the possibility of unfriendly space aliens ending humanity.

"Which disaster appears more likely?" asked Tracey.

The Chait actually sighed. "You seem to be channeling Shirley today," he replied snidely. "No matter, I'm fine with playing twenty questions. All the possible disasters have a high probability of occurrence on a long enough timeline. Would you perhaps be interested in which one is likely to occur first?"

"Jamocha, quit being a dick," said Tracey. "Yes, please tell me which worldwide disaster your science predicts will likely happen first, and in what time frame."

"There's a seventy-five percent chance that plague, or nuclear war, or more likely a combination of both, will end your modern civilization within thirty years," said Jamocha. "Should the Chait transfer significant bioscience knowledge, what you call Full Medical, or interplanetary level technology, or above, a global nuclear war will occur within five years.

"The natural sciences have a significant degree of randomness," said Jamocha. "Still, we have a pretty big baseline of planetary observations to work with. The next ice age will begin anytime in the next thousand years. More likely sooner, rather than later. And the ice age will destroy your civilization. Again, the event will definitely happen, the only question is when. That randomness thing, you know."

"Why don't you directly intervene?" asked Tracey. "Obviously you could end the threat of war, and cure any plague."

"Why would we?" replied Jamocha. "All the ills you perceive in your society are in fact caused by your society. Earth's affairs are not our problem. Direct intervention would make your problems, our problems. Kind of like 'you break it, you bought it.' Besides, most people like the way things run. The Chinese like to dominate Asia. Russia likes to dominate Europe who enjoys the cheap imported energy. The United States likes to throw their weight around, and nations enjoy the foreign aid, and defense assistance. Unless the great nations actively interfere in our plans, why should we meddle in theirs?"

"What makes the human race worth saving?" asked Tracey. "You are investing a lot of time and effort in this project."

"We don't talk about ourselves," responded Jamocha. "Our motivations are our own. And you can't know if this project is a significant effort for us or not."

The usual dead end. Tracey tried another tack. "Tell me about Ouranos."

"Of course," replied Jamocha. "You've read specifics on the planet itself, so I'll skip the detail there. Suffice to say it's Earth-like, a hair cooler, slightly less dramatic seasonal changes, and flora and fauna which, for the most part, are similar to Earth."

"As I understand it," Tracey interrupted, "the flora and fauna for the most part are exactly those found on Earth. Please do NOT skip those details. Explain."

Jamocha seemingly surrendered. "During your last period of heavy glaciation, it became apparent your planet's atmosphere is reaching the end of its current stage. Your current oxygen–nitrogen atmosphere is simply one stage of several in your planet's history. It's due for another change, and soon. When that happens nothing will survive, except certain bacteria, perhaps.

"We seeded Ouranos with life from Earth ten thousand years ago. The planet had a very simple ecology. We started with Earth algae and grasses, then small herbivores and aquatic life, and eventually worked our way up to apex predators. The process wasn't as difficult as you might think. The native ecology of Ouranos never had a chance against the more highly evolved and competitive Earth life. And we were patient; we let things take their natural course, with occasional corrections in the schedule of introducing the higher-level organisms."

Despite anticipating the answer, Tracey was chilled. The aliens had watched over Earth for ten thousand years.

"But not people?" asked Tracey. "Why not people?"

"We won't make choices for an intelligent being," replied Jamocha seriously. "An intelligent, naked aborigine who's never seen technology more advanced than a sharp stick doesn't have capacity to make an ethical choice. By ethical, I mean for the Chait. We transplanted no people to Ouranos. No *Homo sapiens*, no Neanderthals, no Denisovans, and no Aborigines. In fact, no Hominidae, alive at the time, at all. No chimps, monkeys, gorillas, orangutans, or the like. Those species are too closely related to you. For similar reasons we never transported whales, or dolphins. Earth's aquatic mammals are too close to attaining intelligent self-aware status.

"Now, however, humanity has technology. Rudimentary technology, but advanced enough that one can extrapolate and make informed choices. What we offer is no longer seen as simply magic. You can make decisions which we can ethically choose to act upon."

How screwy, thought Tracey. *Save the really smart, and really dumb species, but let the others go extinct. Alien ethics.*

"So, we have graduated from jailbait and moved up the scale to dumbass," Tracey snorted. "But you can accept and act upon our decisions now. You can get in bed with us and it's all good."

"Not well put, but yes," replied Jamocha. "We can ethically agree to Jon's plan. Remarkably, it's almost entirely his plan. We are assisting him to establish the Kingdom of Ouranos. The people on Ouranos have a higher level of technology—much higher—than granted the rest of humanity. The starships of Ouranos will carry mankind to the stars.

"There are fundamental, existential differences between Ouranos and your existing nation-states. Ouranos shares no territorial borders with belligerent neighbors. The kingdom does not have the power to bomb their opponents back to the stone age, or vice versa. There are no blood feuds spanning generations. No treaty entanglements, no favors owed. Jon is starting from a clean sheet."

"This seems a very colonialist way of planning the future," replied Tracey slowly. "Advanced starships from Ouranos transport colonists to faraway lands. In a hundred years will the people of Ouranos trade trinkets for the treasure of the simple natives?" she asked mockingly.

"What treasure?" asked Jamocha amusedly. "Precious gems, or metals perhaps? Land? Steal their cows, or maybe their women? Slaves? With the technology base of Ouranos, and an entire planet to expand into, none of that makes any sense. The people of Ouranos will have unlimited clean power, vast resources, and the HAL units to provide cheap labor. Maybe in a hundred years trading for luxuries, perhaps unique liquor or spices, will develop to a point where the colonies feel exploited. Getting cheated on the price of booze is surely a small price to pay for saving the entire human race.

"Once human colonies have been established on several planets, the odds of humanity going extinct drop dramatically. We expect Ouranos to assist these colonies for the foreseeable future; however, that's not essential. One would prefer these colonies to have a large well-established population capable of maintaining an advanced technology base; however, frankly, maintaining a civilization is a nice-to-have. As long as a minimum breeding base survives the early years, the rough years, a new culture will eventually grow and flourish. The universe is patient. Ten thousand years is nothing.

"What else can I tell you about Ouranos?" asked Jamocha.

"Nothing else now," replied Tracey, who had a million questions. "I'm a little overwhelmed. I need time to process what you've told me. Do you have any advice, for me, personally?"

"I do," replied Jamocha. "When you emigrate to Ouranos please don't establish or encourage any belief system involving human sacrifice, cannibalism, or the mass burning of your food, shelter, and belongings. When human civilizations fall, they usually do it to themselves."

"Oooh kaaaay," said Tracey bemusedly. The Chait rarely cracked an outright joke. Surely it was a joke. "I think I can commit to avoiding those practices. Thanks for the advice."

"You're welcome," concluded Jamocha. "Enjoy your Calvados!"

THIRTEEN
THE DIPLOMAT

T HE GROUP MET AT A shady table near the hotel swimming pool for coffee. Adrian arrived a few minutes early and requested table settings for four. After ordering two pots of coffee—one regular, the other decaf—hot water, and a tea caddy of assorted blends, he instructed the waitress to charge any subsequent order from the table to his room. Finally, he tipped her well, cash in advance.

Adrian Kelly was a fine figure of a man. Although pushing seventy, he stood a straight, broad-shouldered six and a half feet tall. He had a full head of thick grey hair and a genial disposition.

Shortly after the coffee and tea were delivered the others arrived. Adrian shook hands with the group while Shirley made the introductions.

While being aware of the probable benefits, both Tracey and Jon had reservations about hiring a retired diplomat, a career federal employee.

The first hour was spent going through Adrian's background. Jon and Tracey were interested in everything. Adrian was quizzed about his time at the east coast prep school, the Ivy League degrees, his ten years as a banker, his twenty years with the state department, and the project management work he'd been doing since he left government service. The interviewers even seemed interested in the summers he spent at his uncle's ranch in South Dakota.

"I've often been drawn into project management," Adrian said. "The bank sent me to Europe and a year later they did an acquisition. I got roped into integration of their back-office systems. I didn't do any technical work; my job was getting the group, who came from several different countries, working together as a team and moving in the right direction. The bank project got me interested in diplomacy. In the state department, I worked mostly on the diplomatic side at embassies overseas. I spent my last ten years since leaving the foreign service managing systems implementations for international banks and insurance companies. I found the secret of success is getting groups of people, with different interests and backgrounds, to agree on the requirements and keeping the implementation teams working in the right direction. Implementation of large projects is actually similar to diplomacy. I am good with people and leave the technical side to the experts."

Adrian continued. "The work XSolarian does is immensely exciting. I believe I could help with your mission. This is a lot more fun than time at home mowing the yard and writing pissy letters to the editor."

Jon sensed that Tracey was sold, as was he. The guy actually listened. When he spoke, it wasn't just to hear himself speak. "Should you come on board," he told Adrian, "You'll be under a lot of pressure, and have a significant amount of travel. Do you believe you can balance that with your wife's health issues?"

Shirley stirred but did not say anything. Like any human resources director, she was uncomfortable when EEOC rules regarding interviewing were broken, even if the employee would be hired by a foreign corporation with no such requirements.

"Yes, I can," said Adrian. "And, as I told Shirley, I will commit for a minimum of two years. We've got great health insurance and family support. We have relatives nearby, and a live-in housekeeper. My wife is tired of having me underfoot."

"That's great to hear," said Tracey. "I understand federal employees, even retired ones, have wonderful health insurance. Even so, you will find ours better."

FOURTEEN
THE REVEAL

"GREAT JOB, CASEY," SAID JON. "It looks like a good audience."
The press conference was being held outside on a small grassy venue overlooking the ocean. The location was well north of Honolulu, north of Pearl Harbor. The weather, not surprisingly, was perfect. A cool, gentle ocean breeze kept the bright sun at bay.

Kailani Caitlyn Tanaka went by Casey (KC) to her friends. Her business persona was Tiger. She was a stunningly attractive young woman of mixed Hawaiian, Japanese, and European ancestry who ran a small marketing and event planning company in Honolulu. She simply oozed energy, intelligence, and capability. Both Bill and Shirley urged Jon to hire her full-time. After meeting her, Jon agreed. He wanted her. He was waiting until after the event to make a pitch. The event promised to be legendary.

"Enticing the media people took some doing," said Casey. "Asking the press to travel more than ten minutes is a reach. Lazy bums," she said with a laugh. "I bribed them with a monster buffet and free booze. Thanks for the great budget! We have two camera crews from the TV stations, a couple radio stations, the newspaper, and a stringer for Associated Press. Several science-oriented bloggers came for the drinks, but you won't get much circulation from them. The only politician or government representative I could get was a guy from the state economic development department. You've been very mysterious and I couldn't get their interest without more facts," she said looking at him, her eyes questioning.

"You've done a great job," said Jon. "Why don't you go up front now and get everyone's attention. Give me a sixty-second intro. I'll take it from there."

Once Jon had the microphone, he scanned the crowd. His practice was to look an individual in the eye for a sentence for two, and then on to another.

"Thank you for coming," he began. "XSolarian burst on the world scene eighteen months ago. Since then, we have licensed highly advanced technology in a number of fields. Many of you are familiar with the great new batteries improving lives worldwide. However, we also have other technologies in the pipeline...." Jon droned on. He had coordinated the timing closely with Robert. The speech had to last six minutes.

"And how, you ask, is it possible for one company to have made such strides in so many fields in such a short time?" Jon asked rhetorically. Behind him the ocean began to swirl. A gleaming, streamlined shape began to rise from the water. People pointed, and one of the TV cameras swung over. "Ladies and gentlemen, mankind is no longer alone. There are other intelligent species out there. We are members of an interstellar community, and it is time to take our place at the table."

The craft was fully out of the water now, and slowly drifted shoreward, and gently touched down behind Jon. Half the audience fled. The other half gaped at the strange craft and held their phones at arm's length, filming, but appearing as if they were warding off evil with a talisman. The TV people hunkered down as the camera crews inched forward.

"Please, come aboard for a tour," said Jon, gesturing towards the hatch which had opened on the side. "This will be something to tell your grandkids."

Jon subtly nudged Casey ahead. As a recruiting pitch, this was one for the ages, and he did not want her to slip away. Several of Tom's hobbits were similarly shepherding the TV people forward.

A dozen of the media ended up boarding. The craft took an hour to circle Oahu. Robert spoke with the screens showing only a visual of Jupiter. The alien expressed his people's peaceful intentions, their intent to remain at a distance, and their respect for the cultures and peoples of Earth. Robert stressed the Chait were only visiting and expected to leave in five to ten years. Questions were answered, for the most part, by reiterating what he had already said.

The only intelligent question regarded the lack of time lag in the transmissions. The reply "we have more advanced communications" was accepted without follow-up. There was no other mention of advanced technology. After Robert signed off, the screens switched to scenes of the coastline rolling slowly past.

The TV people were enraged by the lack of visuals. Jon spent the remainder of the flight giving unsatisfactory answers to endless questions. No one was interested in hearing about technology improving the lot of humanity.

No, he had not met a Chait in the flesh.

No, he did not know where the aliens originated.

No, he had no idea why he was the one contacted. However, he thought an English speaker was a logical choice for first contact.

No, he did not know if others were in contact with the Chait.

No, he did not know why they refused to show themselves.

No, he did know the "real" reason why the aliens would not come to Earth. He referred back to Robert's statement how the great majority of the solar system, outside of the sun, consisted of Jupiter and its satellites.

No, he did not know what powered the craft.

No, he could not explain the engines, or source of power.

No, the aliens were not hiding in a cabin somewhere aboard. The craft was unmanned, or rather un-aliened, and was remotely operated.

No, this was not a hoax.

No, the Chait had not discussed their view of civil rights with him.

Yes, of course, you are welcome to try communicating directly. Just beam a signal towards Jupiter and see if you get a response.

No, the aliens claim no knowledge of abductions, cattle mutilation, flying saucer sightings, or ancient astronauts.

Towards the end, the questions became more pointed. The press was starting to think the affair was a hoax. That line of questioning ended when the screens showed Diamond Head grow larger.

"We've landed," said Jon. "We're in Kapiolani Park." The location was on the outskirts of Honolulu, near most of the media studios, miles from where the craft took off. "Please disembark quickly. We have shuttles waiting. We can take you straight to your studios if you wish, or back where we started." A combination of fear and eagerness to get the story broadcast stampeded most out the hatch. Two diehards with the science fiction blog were physically hustled out afterwards.

"Please stay," Jon said to Casey. "I expect the park will quickly be flooded with law enforcement and the military. Our freedom is why we didn't land in the Diamond Head crater—too easy to close the access tunnel road and hold everyone. We're going somewhere else."

FIFTEEN
THE SHITSTORM

THE EVENT WAS A MEDIA sensation and dominated the airwaves for weeks. The alien craft had not been stealth'd, and the leisurely flight circumnavigating Oahu at low altitude was filmed by thousands of tourists, many armed with professional grade cameras. A news helicopter filmed much of the flight live. Somehow, film from a navy fighter leaked out, which clearly showed the spacecraft from above with easily identifiable landmarks in the background.

Jon and the team went to ground at "undisclosed locations." Jon was the public face and did multiple interviews each day. The interviews were always online and routed through a different path each time. The torturous path might wind through servers in Uzbekistan, the Ukraine, and Panama. The path routed through the anonymous TOR site multiple times.

Initial interviews at major networks were unsatisfactory. The typical interview consisted of the news reader giving a short monologue and then asking 'isn't that right?' The networks resisted live interviews of more than a few seconds, and the taped sessions were always deeply edited. After one circuit with the major networks, Jon dropped them and went to mostly radio, internet, podcasts, and print media. The company maintained no social media accounts yet. Those were considered too easily hacked, and censored.

Jon did international interviews daily. The event was less of a sensation in other countries. Most considered the event simply another UFO hoax.

The most effective and well-received interviews were the scripted sessions where Jon pretended to read, and answer questions from the audience. He hated to communicate that way but found it difficult to elicit intelligent questions.

The message Jon pushed in the interviews was 'The Chait are orbiting Jupiter. The planet is very far away and the aliens show no interest in coming here. The Earth is a fraction of one percent of the solar system. The alien's interest in Jupiter seems understandable as the gas giant made up three quarters of the mass of the entire solar system, excepting the sun. The aliens are far away, appear friendly, and want to talk. What's the harm?' At that point Jon's message would become inspirational, invoking the wonder and potential of other intelligent life.

Within days the location of the XSolarian offices became known, and the sites were besieged by the media, federal agents, and cranks. To no avail. Company staff had been forewarned, and told to take time off, or work from home. Twice daily a lawyer would appear and warn off the most aggressive visitors.

Company executives carried specially Fab'd phones which were untraceable. Their laptops and internet applications were encrypted beyond the ability of even the NSA to track or crack. Those of the Inner Circle communicated via their enhancements.

The various agencies of the federal government went silent except to issue bland press releases saying the matter was under investigation. The FAA (Federal Aviation Administration) didn't get the word in time and issued a statement indicating the Agency's intent to cite the pilot, and the owner/operator of the aircraft seen over Oahu for a slew of infractions, including flying an unlicensed aircraft type. The media quickly blew the FAA statement out of proportion as a formal statement from the US government acknowledging the existence of UFOs, UAPs, and extraterrestrials.

Behind the scenes, however, the whole of the world's intelligence apparatus searched for all possible information on Jon Gallock, and, eventually, the other company executives. Hawaii was a popular destination.

Germany sent investigators from the Federal Intelligence Service (BND), Military Counterintelligence (BfV) Office for Information Technology in the Security Sector (ZITiS), and the Federal Office for Information Security (BSI) to Oahu. The two ZITiS agents were more techies than secret agents and came home after two days suffering with severe sunburns.

Russia sent agents from the FSB (formerly KGB), the SVR, and the GRU.

The Russian FSB leaned on the Syrian GIB to send a snatch team to take, not an XSolarian person—they were deemed too public—but a journalist who made the flight. The Russians didn't care which one. The FSB directors wanted one from the flight they could take, question at length, and disappear. The Syrians sent a team of four, traveling in pairs to avoid suspicion. Both pairs were arrested by local police while changing planes, at different airports, after they popped up on the no-fly and terrorist watch lists.

Documents proving that the GIB deputy who organized the operation was on the Mossad payroll were sent anonymously to his superiors, who had him unceremoniously shot in the back of the head and fed his corpse to pigs. The senior FSB man who initiated the operation had tapes of him severely criticizing the FSB Minister, and President of Russia, sent from a phantom email account to an aide of the president. After a short investigation the FSB man was taken to a dank basement and hung on a meat hook until he died two days later.

Randy, working with the Chait, had no need to manufacture the documentation. All the damning evidence was real. The plot to kidnap a journalist was abandoned.

China sent no one to Hawaii as their intelligence agencies had plenty of feet on the ground already.

In all, twenty-two foreign countries, including most of the America's NATO partners, eventually sent agents to Hawaii, or later, to the areas around the XSolarian offices inside the continental United States.

In the United States alone, seventeen intelligence agencies with a combined annual budget exceeding a hundred billion dollars mobilized. The FBI, CIA, NSA, CGI, DIA, DEA, DHS, the DOE Office of Counterintelligence, MIA, NGA, NRO, OIA, ONI, ODNI, INR, ISR, and INSCOM, each ginned up a rationale why this matter required immediate priority attention. None cooperated in the slightest with the others, except the justice department, which created a dedicated team to quickly

rubber-stamp all subpoena, warrant, wiretap, injunction, and FISA surveillance requests.

The federal intelligence agencies mobilized hundreds of subcontractors
as well.

Mostly out of curiosity, sometime in anticipation of requests for information from further up the food chain, the IRS began audits on all company
employees, and all the shell companies they could locate. The Department
of Labor gave the company formal notice of an audit of their EEOC compliance, another for their affirmative action plan, yet another regarding their
compliance with the Fair Labor Standards Act (FLSA), and also a notice
to audit the compliance of the company's 401(k) plan under the Employee
Retirement Income Security Act (ERISA). Both the Occupational Safety
and Health Administration (OSHA) and the Environmental Protection
Agency (EPA) showed up at the company offices unannounced to review
the workplace compliance with their respective standards.

The Census Bureau, under the Department of Commerce, quickly fired
off numerous questions regarding the most recently submitted mandatory
Annual Business Survey and other required reports, helpfully noting the
penalties for not reporting, late reporting, and most significantly, false
reporting. The Treasury Department demanded complete transaction
history from the banks on all company and employee accounts.

The special weapons and tactics (SWAT) team belonging to, oddly, the
US Department of Education got as far as the airport on their way to the
XSolarian Houston office before being ordered to stand down. The overex-
cited commander was disciplined, lightly. The Agency later issued a press
release in which they strenuously denied even having a special weapons
and tactics team. "We have a diverse team of dedicated well-trained professionals who use special weapons and tactics," the press release explained.

In every case the federal regulator was met at the office door by a pair
of lawyers who carefully and ostentatiously recorded all details of the
request, the name and title of the requestor, the reason for the request,
and the person's supervisor, and any other pertinent detail. The XSolarian
attorneys went to court and protested each request, the short notice, and
the ambiguous wording in the regulator's documents. All encounters were

recorded with full color visual and high-definition audio. In all cases the company, through the attorneys, declined to cooperate. Some of the agencies backed down; most did not. Court fights began.

At Jon's insistence, over the howling objections of his attorneys, the battles were made personal. Ethics complaints were filed against opposing attorneys. Randy's group investigated the various federal employees behind the frivolous actions. Dirt accumulated; a married man's afternoon visits with his girlfriend (on federal time), drunk driving, wife-beating, gambling, pederasty, expense-report fraud, coming in late and leaving early, and so on.

On several occasions the inquisitors had embarrassed themselves in the initial recording. Any videos showing curses, threats, and grossly rude behavior were released to the media with the names and agency of the offenders. Their supervisors' names and contact information were helpfully included as well.

Three weeks into the onslaught, Jon met, virtually via enhancements, with several of the team to review the legal battles.

"The Department of Education has their own fucking SWAT team. Is this for real?" asked Shirley while waving a piece of paper with the news report.

"Absolutely," replied Randy. "The DOE team has been reported to exercise no-knock warrants and kick down doors at four in morning to arrest people suspected of student loan fraud."

"All federal agencies have their own SWAT team," added Bob. "The teams use military grade weapons, machine guns, night vision gear, body armor, fifty caliber sniper rifles, the works. Every time the public has an ammo shortage, the stories come out about the hundreds of thousands of rounds bought by the Railroad Retirement Agency, or the Small Business Administration, or NASA, or some other agency."

"Bullshit!" said Shirley. "You guys are just screwing with me."

"No," said Jon. "It's all true. Over a hundred agencies have SWAT teams, and masses of armed agents. About two hundred thousand Federal agents carry guns on a daily basis, which is more shooters than the US Army and Marine Corp combined. We have one of the world's largest militaries, but only ten percent actually carry guns; the other ninety are the logistics tail. So, yes, the agencies field more armed men than the military. You need to read more 'angry white man' internet. You'd be better informed."

Shirley glared at the three of them and changed the subject. "I'm not comfortable with our aggressive, combative response to government inquiries," she said.

Bob nodded in support. "You know my philosophy on audits," he said to Jon." Give them what they ask for. Don't piss them off. Manage the process. Respond quickly with a detailed and well-organized response. The auditors will finish sooner and get out of your hair earlier."

Tracey was cool and analytical as always. "As a practical matter, I don't know how long we can keep this up. The legal bills are astronomical, and growing. I've asked for weekly billings to try and keep up. Some of our lawyers—solid guys—are saying this is counterproductive."

"They're assholes," retorted Casey. "They should burn in hell for eternity."

Casey's rant broke the tension. Everyone laughed.

"I assume you are referring to the government people," Jon teased Casey. "Not our guys.

"We are not pushing back against these actions to make ourselves feel good," said Jon as he headed for the coffee pot. "Lawsuits are rarely good business, and neither is 'getting' the other guy just because he's screwing with you. You simply disengage, get over it, and move on." Jon filled his cup. Via their enhancements the others could smell the coffee.

"Now, Bob," Jon continued, "I agree with your approach to managing audits. However, these are not audits or inspections to satisfy a valid regulatory requirement. These are demands which are illegal, malicious harassment. In all cases, every single one, these actions have been initiated outside of normal channels. Remember, when a regulatory agency writes a rule, the effect is if a law has passed in Congress. Anytime an agency works outside of their own rules, or published processes and procedures, they are acting illegally, by their own definition. News flash: the agencies don't really care about inspecting our fire extinguishers.

"And Shirley," Jon continued. "I agree the great majority, probably something like ninety-nine percent, of government employees are honest people simply trying to do their job. We are not retaliating against those people. Either the guy at our door, or the one who sent the notice, or his supervisor, or the upper-level manager who instructed the supervisor, is doing this to us on purpose. Just because they can. In all cases, every single one, we know that's a fact. A well-documented fact."

Casey had been read into the Inner Circle and knew the surveillance and analysis capabilities the Chait had made available to them. She was pulsing with youth and vitality and of no danger of dying anytime soon. However, the attraction of being young and beautiful, forever, had her hooked.

"So, the people we go after are not the ninety-nine percent who simply want to do their jobs and go home. We're only retaliating against the bad guys, and by going after, I mean ruining them. I want them ruined, personally, professionally, and financially. My preference is those responsible be in rags, begging on the sidewalk outside their former office with a sign around their neck saying, 'I illegally harassed a taxpayer.'"

"Don't candy-coat it, Jon," said Shirley. "We're all grown-ups here. Tell us how you really feel."

Jon ignored her and continued. "When World War I was not going well for the French, it is said several regiments mutinied, disobeyed their legal orders. Those units were pulled out of the line and decimated. Meaning, every tenth man was executed, stood against a wall, and shot. Most were fine soldiers. However, that was beside the point. The lesson was 'pour encourager les autres.' To encourage the others. That's why we're doing this. So, the next guy will think twice before initiating an action simply to satisfy his personal curiosity. We're not monsters, and we're not targeting innocent people.

"We're not going after them out of malice, or simple self-defense. We have to clear our path of the worst of the obstruction in order to execute on our next phase. We will fail unless we nip this in the bud. I am not exaggerating when I say the fate of the human race depends on our success.

"If we can't quickly and expeditiously get OSHA out of our hair, how in God's sake do you expect to hold out against the KGB?

"Speaking of the KGB, or more properly, FSB, remember, any overt actions from intelligence agencies to kidnap, or coerce our people will be met with deadly force—all the way up the chain to the person who gave the order. We limited our response in the journalist's case because the operation did not involve our employees; but it came damn close. Randy and I agreed a response was necessary.

"In the US we have four separate branches of government to deal with: the executive, Congress, the intelligence agencies, and the regulatory agencies which write and enforce their own laws. The Supreme Court doesn't count. The president and her staff spent a week not believing in the event, a week going 'duh,' and are just now starting to ask questions. The White House hasn't yet decided to give us a hard time. We all know the wheels in motion to blunt political problems with Congress. For now, we just watch the intelligence agencies closely."

Jon finished his rant. "The ball is in Randy's court now," he said.

Randy nodded and said, "I'm on it."

SIXTEEN:
THE LOBBYIST

THE FAVORITE PART OF CHRISTIAAN Wardell's day was opening the door to his oversized closet in the morning. The rich aroma of polished leather, silk, and wool washed over him. He dressed in silk underwear, argyle socks with wee Scottie dogs embroidered upon them, a snowy white linen shirt, and a Tom Ford suit. This was Wednesday, which meant Italian accessories, so he went with his favorite Panerai watch, a Ferragamo tie, and bespoke handstitched leather shoes to complete the outfit. After admiring himself in the mirror, he went back to the closet and grabbed one of a dozen identical black leather attaché cases. The security goon met Christiaan in the building's lobby and handed him a perfectly prepared cup of coffee.

The two arrived at the bank fifteen minutes after it opened. As usual the manager was waiting. The manager ushered the pair into a private room. "I'll be right back," said the manager. Two minutes later he reappeared pushing a small cart. "Here is the five hundred thousand dollars you requested for today," the manager said. "Correct?"

"Yes, that's correct," replied Christiaan. After a quick recount, he signed the receipt. He also took a photograph of the receipt using his cellphone. "I'll need twice this tomorrow, a full million," he said while shuffling the bundled bills into the attaché. "Will that be a problem?"

"No problem at all," replied the manager. "And, as always, take care with that briefcase."

Christiaan ordered the attaché cases ten at a time.

A few minutes later Christiaan was in the Hart building facing the sweet young thing who guarded the office of today's senator. "Is Dankworth around?" he asked brusquely. Dankworth was the senator's chief of staff. "He's expecting me."

After a short wait Christiaan was ushered into the chief of staff's presence. "I'm so sorry," said Dankworth. "Something's come up, and we won't have much time."

"No problem," said Christiaan. "This will only take a minute. I represent a political action committee which appreciates the senator's views on a number of issues." He placed the attaché case on the desk, popped the latches, and spun the open briefcase around. "Particularly his sensible views on the opportunities offered by peaceful contact with intelligent beings from other planets. The PAC I represent is considering a donation to the senator's reelection campaign." He was always careful with his wording.

Dankworth was visibly torn between grabbing the attaché case of cash and recoiling in horror. Federal law outlawed receipt of a donation while in a federal building. He explained the problem to Christiaan. "Let me have somebody drive you over to the campaign offices. I'll call and let them know you're coming."

Christiaan found it hilarious the way they were always in a fever to get him out of the building.

"I think it would be great if you drove over with me," replied Christiaan. "The trip will give us time to get acquainted. You can introduce me to your folks over there, and I'd love to have a few minutes to tell you more about our views, and the resources we have to offer. For example, I can supply glossy color handouts, and lots of background information on the E-Ts not yet available to the general public.

"I will also appreciate your help to ensure I get receipts from the appropriate entities," Christiaan continued. "Obviously, I want to do this legally, totally above-board. I'm sure you can recommend the correct PACs, Hybrid PACs, Super PACs, party committees, 501s, NGOs, nonprofits, law firms, consultants, and think tanks to funnel the funds in such a way to maximize the benefit to your senator."

Dankworth caved.

Christiaan had this down to a routine. He visited a different congressman each day, five days a week. The visits were his only job. First the bank, then the senate building, then the campaign staff in some cheap office space thirty minutes away. The donation was followed by either coffee or lunch with the congressman's chief of staff, and a meeting with the big guy in a few days. He was religious in squeezing in a trip to the gym, or a long swim in the afternoon. Between swimming and his early morning run he remained slim and fit despite two restaurant meals a day with senators and their key staff. An executive of the client and a full partner of his firm would accompany him to the meeting with the senator, where he would hand off the relationship.

Christiaan was finished with the House until the next election cycle. There were so many—and they changed so often—he only targeted leadership, and those on key committees.

He was lobbying from both ends. The senate leadership, and those on key committees, particularly the chairmen, were a priority to visit. On the other end were the nobodies from poor states who couldn't raise the cash their party demanded for membership on good committees. God bless the poor states. Those senators required a lot less effort and money to get their ear. His directions were clear. "We want quality, which is expensive. We also want quantity, which in most cases is surprisingly inexpensive. The party affiliation doesn't matter."

He always left the attaché case. For some reason lower rung political staffers seemed absurdly pleased with the small gift.

The donations were perfectly legal.

What a great job.

SEVENTEEN
THE INCIDENT

SECURITY WAS TIGHT WHEN JON traveled. A percentage of the world harbored homicidal thoughts towards him and the aliens. Even a small percentage of eight billion people meant tens of millions of potential deadly threats.

Jon traveled exclusively by private jet. Sometimes he took the company plane, other times he flew on a leased bizjet. Quite often he left in a different plane, from a different airport, from his arrival. The bodyguards preferred to avoid public transportation, so Jon was chauffeured in a rental car with heavily tinted windows. Security protocols meant he never sat in the same seat twice in a row. No hotel was ever booked in his name, except as a decoy. XSolarian staff routinely double-booked hotels, and a bodyguard checked in at the last moment. Standard practice was to never stay in the same hotel twice.

Jon's protection detail was headed by a former secret service supervisor. However, the actual bodyguards were young, large, street toughs with military experience. The men in Jon's detail had just enough polish to be unobtrusive, but the mindset to escalate quickly to physical confrontation if needed.

In-person meetings incurred risk. Designating a time and a meeting place in advance gave others notice of your whereabouts that particular day. Accordingly, Jon scheduled his meetings with as little advance notice as possible.

The corporate jet was also a risk. There are relatively few business jets in the aviation world, and the eye-catching craft always attract notice. The planes were kept guarded and searched before Jon boarded.

On a routine trip Jon was whisked from a jet directly to a waiting car, then directly to a hotel, or the meeting venue. On average he would eat one meal a day on the plane, snacks in a meeting, and dinner in the back room of a restaurant. Finding a place and time to exercise was difficult. He barely saw the light of day. Fortunately, his enhancements kept him fit.

The Chait maintained real-time surveillance on all aspects of Jon's travel. From the mechanic who worked on the plane, to the rental car agent, to every cellphone along every street of Jon's route, and of course the hotel, and the government and business moguls he met with. All communication anywhere near Jon was monitored and analyzed. If known, his security practices would have been envied by pampered politicians worldwide.

Still, spontaneous acts do occur.

Jon was in Berlin. He and the security detail entered a side door of the hotel and were taking a short cut through the spacious bar on their way to the elevators when his enhancements pinged.

"Jon," said Vanilla, the Chait rep who worked with Randy on security matters, "heads up. A particularly nasty group of German anarchists are meeting here before disrupting a lecture at the university. You've been spotted. The table at the balcony corner is talking by phone to another group coming in the far door. Both groups are coming after you."

One would expect a bodyguard to detect an imminent threat before the principal. However, neither of the two bodyguards had enhancements. Jon was two seconds quicker. He instantly pinged Gavin, who was leading, fifteen feet ahead, via his earbud. Gavin was six foot two and weighed two hundred and thirty rock hard pounds. Gavin had done one short hitch in the Marines, and afterwards supported himself as an auto mechanic while training and competing as an MMA fighter. A friend who worked security for XSolarian had recommended him, and he'd quickly shown an aptitude for the work.

"Gavin," Jon pinged, "intercept that group; they're coming after us. There's four more on the balcony." Jon triggered his enhanced combat mode. As the improved adrenal cocktail hit his bloodstream, everything slowed, his senses expanded, and his movements became more fluid. He had the illusion of his teeth sharpening and his ears growing hairy points. The fight instinct instantly became paramount.

"Newt," he continued, pinging the bodyguard bringing up the rear, "cover me. I'm zigging to the right." He quickly nipped under the balcony and picked up his pace, trying to get past the stairs before those from above came down.

The anarchists were intense skinny young men dressed in urban chic—black hoodies. Their modus operandi was to taunt until they provoked a reaction. The one in the lead had his cell to his ear, was raising his arm to point at Jon, and had his mouth open shouting, "Nazi alien collaborator!"

Gavin required no provocation. He took one long step forward and hammered the young man in the lead to the floor, breaking his jaw. His footwork and timing were perfectly synced to swivel his hips and deliver another crushing blow to the second man a heartbeat later. The third he snatched from the floor by his shirt and crotch and flung into the remaining anarchist, sending both to the floor.

Gavin could easily bench-press twice the body weight of any of his opponents. It was no contest.

Jon meanwhile failed to get past the stairs before the first group reached the bottom. Again, one paused to taunt. Again, the pause was a mistake as Jon blasted him with a forearm across the face. Another grabbed for his shirt. Jon pinned the man's palm against his chest and dropped to a knee while jerking his upper body forward, breaking the man's wrist. Jon then grabbed the opponent's hair and for good measure kneed him twice, quickly, in the face. The sounds of bones breaking were heard clearly through the room.

Newt, a former full-time British football hooligan, caught up and shoved Jon towards the elevators. He grabbed a half-full long-neck beer bottle from a table and briskly smacked his palm over the mouth, blowing the bottom from the bottle. He waved the jagged bottle at the demoralized group still standing. "Fun's over, boys. Take your mates to the hospital, and back to Mum's basement with ye."

Jon and his security detail met Bruce, the detail supervisor, coming down the hall as they left the scene. At a motion from Jon, Bruce slid his Taser back under his coat. "Skip the elevators," said Bruce. "I've called the car. Elvis is leaving the building."

Later, decompressing at a bar near the airport while waiting for the pilot to preflight the plane, Jon conferenced with Randy and Vanilla. Newt was showing Gavin the bottle trick at a trash can near the door, while Bruce burned up his phone arranging for a replacement team. Standard operating procedure would send the dynamic duo on vacation to Aruba for a couple weeks while things quieted down. A well-paid vacation.

"What the fuck, Vanilla!" exclaimed Jon. "What happened to my overwatch?"

"This was a spontaneous act," replied Vanilla. "We cannot anticipate those. We can only judge from what a person says, writes, or actually does. We can't read minds. Remember, at any time, a seemingly indifferent waitress might recognize your face and decide to drop soup in your lap.

"The anarchists planned to crash a lecture at the university and were meeting beforehand in the hotel bar. Outside of a narrow range of self-interests, the people in the group dislike almost everything. These people don't hate you, or the Chair, more than a hundred other people, groups, or institutions. You just happened to show up at the wrong place at the wrong time."

Jon was still pissed. "Well, going forward, don't route me past a group of new-age thugs drinking heavily while planning their next riot. What were such lowlifes doing in a five-star hotel anyway? The beer costs a hell of a lot more than any university dive."

"Looks can be deceiving," replied Vanilla. "Most of the group come from affluent backgrounds. One of them had a gift card; they met there to drink the funds."

"Randy, what are the next steps?" asked Jon, unnecessarily.

"The boys done good," began Randy. "Nobody got killed or seriously injured, and they got you out quick. Gavin and Newt now get a couple of weeks off, in a sunny clime, before going back to work. Other than a couple of the wannabe urban thugs, no one recognized you. Should anybody ask, we will be noncommittal. Following our standard operating procedure, we will ruin the lives of those involved. Kudos to Vanilla and his people, aah, his whatever's, for their help. The social media of the individuals involved are already filled with taboo beliefs, as well as the magic words guaranteed to send the Bundespolizei into a frenzy. Here's to Section 130 of the German penal code." Each raised a glass. A virtual glass in Randy's case.

Randy continued, "Anonymous emails with evidence of voluminous criminal acts, screwing their sister, snitching to the police, cheating on their skanks, are circulating to the right people as we speak. These incidents actually occurred. As usual, we didn't have to fabricate anything.

"Finally, these cretins are going to have a lot of trouble with their credit cards, banking, and email for, well, forever," Randy finished.

"Is the group directly supported by any 'socially aware' organization?" asked Jon dangerously.

"No," replied Randy, "just the usual generous German social net for those who don't work. However, the owner of a large German media company supports a defense fund for exactly this kind of people. The fund pays bail—in the rare cases bail is required—and supplies legal representation for those arrested for assault or vandalism while rioting for the 'right' causes. Almost all the individuals involved in your incident have been beneficiaries of this fund, some on multiple occasions."

"Really?" responded Jon. "Close enough. I'm still irate. Ruin him too. While you're at it, do whoever runs the legal fund. And whoever organized the operation to begin with, if that's yet another party. Those encouraging social disorder should get some of their own. And they should get it good and hard.

"In the back of their minds people should have this visceral feeling it's bad juju to screw with us, or our people. Nothing concrete, nothing in the press. Just the feeling you get when you see a rattlesnake. An urban legend, that's no myth. Treat this as an opportunity to reinforce that perception."

"Your will be done," said Randy in a tone mimicking a court flunky in an old movie.

"Also, I want you to replace Bruce," he told Randy. "Let me finish, please," he said when Randy started to object.

"We both know Bruce has run dignitary protection teams for the secret service," Jon continued. "Never for the president or the vice president.

He's managed protection for smaller fish. I don't believe he has the right reflexes. When the situation blew up, his first impulse was to pull his Taser, not his sidearm."

"I've done a quick review of the incident," said Randy. "I believe Bruce made the appropriate choice."

Bruce was not in the Inner Circle and was unaware of the enhanced conversation. To the others, Jon appeared to be eying the pretty waitress while listening to his phone.

"Yes, I agree with your assessment," said Jon, which surprised Randy. "In this particular situation Bruce appeared to have acted appropriately. However, a Taser will always be his first choice. Bruce is more concerned about lawyers, cellphone videos, the media, or being arrested than shooting someone. News flash: when a security alert goes to those around the president, his detail doesn't pull Tasers, they pull submachine guns.

"Put him in charge of the advance team. He's a great advance man," Jon continued. "The best you have. Tell him so when you lateral him over to his new duties."

Randy brightened. "That's a great idea. He'll actually like the change. I'll tell him."

"Finally," Jon continued, "I'm still not convinced this was spontaneous. Was somebody probing our security? Vanilla, do a deep dive on everyone in or around the restaurant that night. Do the same for the urban warriors. Go back a month and analyze everybody's contacts; keep surveillance active over the next couple months. Professionals may be involved, and limiting their interactions to strictly verbal contacts, away from phones, or with their cells in a faraday box—though you'll see them dropping out of service. Maybe someone's starting to suspect the Chait capabilities.

"We will do what you ask," promised Vanilla. "We will be very thorough."

EIGHTEEN
THE REGULATOR

R ON GREEN HAD A COMFORTABLE job. The position paid well, the benefits were great, and he didn't have to work very hard. He rarely saw his boss. Best of all, he could indulge himself from time to time and bully powerless business owners. Ron had been a bully since third grade. He did workplace inspections for OSHA.

The high point of his career was when he closed a minor league ballpark and stranded four thousand people in line. The stadium was brand new, and the game was the team's first in the new venue. But the mirrors in the men's bathroom were an inch lower than code, and contractors couldn't get them rehung before game time.

When his supervisor tried to put a disciplinary notice in his file, Ron fought the action successfully. The lawyer provided by the union pointed out the law was the law and Ron, though perhaps overzealous, acted in the finest tradition of the agency. When the manager the next level up tried to fire him, Ron got a paid six-month vacation, a promotion, and the posting of his choice. The union had great lawyers. He chose San Diego and never regretted the move.

Ron and his buddy Julio were on their way to the XSolarian office. Julio was an inspector for the local fire department. "Thanks for coming," said Ron. "I'm really curious to see what's in there. Everyone says it's space aliens. My sister's kids want pictures. Did you get the inspection notice mailed?"

"Not until this morning," replied Julio. "It's not really fair to show up before the recipient has a chance to receive the notice. "

"That's okay," said Ron. "I'm from the federal government. These assholes have been jerking me around for two weeks. Our judge gave me a warrant yesterday. This is legal. An inspection notice from the fire department is just icing on the cake."

One of Julio's guys met them at the building. "The offices still look closed," he said. "The doors are locked, and nobody answers the bell. A guy who looks like a lawyer was around for a bit, but he's gone now."

"Okay, fine," said Ron. "The super is supposed to meet us with a key. In fact, here he is now."

The four of them rode the elevator, which stopped on the second floor. "That's strange," said the building manager. "The elevator requires a key to reach the third floor. I didn't authorize that. I've never allowed a key in the elevator." The group took the fire stairs to the third floor. The manager's key did not fit the office door lock. "Tenants are free to change their locks, of course," said the manager. "However, they're required to put a request in to maintenance, who calls a locksmith. I should have a copy."

"Fine damn building manager you are," grated Ron, getting right in his face. "If we had a fire, or another emergency, people would die, and it would be your goddam fault. You don't even know what mod's these tenants made, or if they meet code. The building owners will be pissed at you when I start writing citations." Ron ragged on him awhile before turning to Julio.

"Call your guys," Ron said to Julio. "Have them bring a crowbar, saws, and jaws, and we'll force the damn lock open."

"No way, no how," replied Julio forcefully. "I'm not a Fed. There's no emergency. If I break a door down, I lose my job and my pension. You're on your own here. You're the one with a warrant. Once you open the door, I'll be glad to do an inspection, but I ain't touching that door."

Ron went back and forth with Julio for a minute but knew he couldn't bully him. He called a contractor the agency kept on purchase order. The guy took an hour to get there. When he showed up, he had a large, powerful circular saw with a diamond-edged blade. The bolt was surprisingly tough.

"You're paying for the damage," complained the manager. Ron ignored the jerk.

"Looks like we were lucky," the contractor said. "See, the other dead-bolts weren't thrown. The door is lined with steel, and has bolts, like one would see on a safe. I've never seen a setup like this. If the last person out had thrown all the locks, it would have taken hours to get in."

Inside was a comfortable, nicer-than-average but plain-vanilla place of business. There was a reception desk, a couple of bullpens, a copy room, a break room, a server room, bathrooms, some small offices, and several large comfortable offices. The suite was unoccupied; no one was there. Nothing out of the ordinary. No space aliens.

"Well, damn," said Ron after a few minutes. "Not much here."

"I'm outta here," said Julio. "This was a bad idea."

Ron spent an hour doing a detailed inspection. Given the damage he caused, he had to come up with a list of violations as long as his arm. In a couple of places, the hallway did not quite meet the minimum width. *The moldings on the corners always get them*, Ron thought with satisfaction. Safety goggles in the janitorial closet were the wrong type, and a couple of the fire extinguishers were mounted incorrectly. The hot water in the break room was too hot. The bathroom hardware didn't meet the latest ADA requirements. The list grew.

Some of the infractions may well have been grandfathered in, and no issue. Ron didn't bother to check the code; he would cite XSolarian and let them argue with the agency, and their landlord. He left in a bad mood, closing the door behind him the best he could.

When Ron got home, late, his clothes and tools lay scattered in the front yard. *What the hell?* His wife met him at the door. "You bastard," she hissed. "You scum-sucking, low-life, fat-assed, lying goddam bastard. Do not set foot in this house. I'm filing for divorce. I got a lawyer, and he's on his way over here now."

"How could you?" she continued. "It's one thing to cheat on me. It's another to make a porno film and post the video online. Somebody, probably your slut, your crack-whore slut, sent the recording to everyone in my mahjong group, my bridge club, my book club. I'm humiliated.

"You've beaten and abused me," she screamed. "I covered for your ass all these years. Now you're going to get what's coming to you. I saved all the police reports, all the hospital reports, all the X-rays, painkiller prescriptions, everything! I'm going to get the house, the car, the bank account, your precious boat, and your fucking retirement. You raise one objection and I take everything to the police. They'll throw your fat ass in jail. You understand me?!"

"Now, honey," he said. "Calm down."

That was a mistake. Her bulging eyes grew flat and hard. She spun and raced to the fireplace across the room, scrambling for the poker. Ron ran to the car, chucked his armload of clothes in, and shut and locked the doors. She came racing out with the fireplace poker. As he backed out the driveway, she beat the shit out of the whole side of the car.

"What the hell!" he repeated to himself as he drove away. "We fooled around a little bit filming with our phones, but I didn't post anything online. And that cunt Janealle'a is too fucking stupid to know how."

When Ron got to work the next day, he found a note from his manager on his desk. 'See me immediately,' said the handwritten note on the yellow sticky. When Ron entered his manager's office, he was told, "You're an hour late. Sit down."

"Did you see the news last night?" his manager asked. He was pissed.

The HR being was with him. It was of indeterminate age, sex, and race. Its skull was shaved and bare except for a purple skullcap tattooed on the khaki skin.

As Ron sat down, the manager spun the computer display around and a video from the ten o'clock news played. The images were apparently security camera footage from the XSolarian office. Ron didn't remember seeing cameras. The bold chryon at the bottom of the screen was 'GOVERNMENT THUGS BREAK INTO OFFICE.' The tightly focused video showed Ron visibly angry with Julio and the building manager. The video was unflattering. On screen his eyes looked piggy, and his mouth mean. Other footage showed Ron swaggering through the office, poking through desk drawers, and once taking a candy bar.

"You're suspended for two weeks." the manager said. "We don't do this kind of thing anymore. And we sure as hell don't get caught on camera. Leave now, and we'll talk next week."

The nightly that night showed the state's junior US senator harshly disparaging the agency. On all four networks.

The next morning Ron was called in to explain the porno movie to his manager. The HR being was extremely unhappy with the misogynistic statements Ron used in the video and vowed legal action.

The next week, local law enforcement showed up to ask about the evidence they had received, regarding bribery and extortion.

The following week the FBI showed up asking similar questions.

The week after that, Ron received notice of an IRS audit. The agency was interested to see if he had declared the bribes and extortion on his tax return. They were also curious about his boat.

Ron was ruined.

NINETEEN
THE PRESIDENT'S STAFF MEETING

T HE PRESIDENT, AND HER POLITICAL advisors, including the National
Security Advisor, met in the Oval Office. Nobody from Defense or
the Intelligence Agencies were present. Neither was a science advisor. The
post was vacant.

"What does the polling show?" asked the president of the United
States, Elaine Rosa Hildreth Natal. She was a slightly heavy sixty-year-old
Californian lesbian of Hispanic appearance.

"Mixed," replied her chief political advisor of many years. "The largest
bloc doesn't know, or doesn't care, about the existence of intelligent extraterrestrials." The White House had banned the use of the word "alien" in
any executive branch communications years before as inappropriate and
inflammatory. "The second largest bloc is cautious and apprehensive, followed by the group who is optimistic this is a good thing. About five percent of the sample is strongly favorable about this; however, seven percent
indicate strong, really strong, feelings of fear and anxiety."

"So, there's no indication of a parade forming, that we need to get in
front of, correct?" asked the chief of staff.

"That's correct," replied chief political advisor. "Also, the media is in
a holding pattern. The editors want indications from us before pushing a
narrative. They don't yet know which way to lean."

"What's the view overseas?" the president asked, looking at her
National Security Advisor. The NSA was a lawyer who had worked as an
international business consultant before bundling contributions from
ex-pats, and foreign interests for the president's campaign. His role in the
meeting was insight into the politics of Russia, China, and Europe. Nobody
else mattered.

"The Russians are dubious. They think the event may be a hoax. They are suspicious that any civilian, defense, or intelligence evidence of the Oahu event may have been fed to them as a ploy. However, products using the new tech this guy Gallock is touting, like better batteries, are actually being sold to consumers in Russia. Their intelligence agencies are chasing leads hard to find the origin of the technology. The FSB doesn't believe tech so sophisticated just sprung into existence from someone's garage. Regardless of the tech's origin, they won't be left out.

"The Chinese are dubious, but less so. The new tech is not being licensed to them, and China doesn't import many manufactured goods. The government feels stiffed. Their agencies, and their large industrial concerns, want to know the source, and don't care if the origin is extraterrestrial or not.

"On the other hand, the Europeans are optimistic about this being real. The continent has a big green influence in their politics and they eat shit like this up. So, generally—each European country is different, of course—the politicians are opining of the real possibility of a positive encounter."

The president nodded and raised one finger. "Here's what we are going to do. The public tends to stay with the party in power in times of crisis. This isn't a crisis, yet. However, we must lay the groundwork to manufacture one, if that's the direction I decide to pivot. Our current message is, we are investigating Mister Gallock's claims. If true, we will approach this with an abundance of caution to assure the safety of citizens, and so forth.

"Also, have DARPA evaluate the technology XSolarian has licensed to see how advanced the science really is. And have the FBI and the IRS develop files on the company, and Gallock, if they haven't already. I want dirt for leverage.

"Finally, get someone from the staff—not Defense or Intelligence—give Gallock a friendly, I repeat friendly, call to chat about this. I don't want to dignify this with a subpoena yet. The science advisor post is vacant; however, make sure our caller is somebody possessing a PhD."

The remaining meeting was a lengthy discussion of managing the press.

The discussion was finishing up when the president said, "One last thing. Has anyone got a report indicating the extraterrestrials are real or not?"

The NSA shook his head. "Nothing concrete. While the craft which circled Oahu was definitely real, with technology no one on Earth can duplicate, we haven't confirmed the existence or location of actual, living extraterrestrials. We've turned a number of telescopes—even the James Webb—and sensor arrays towards Jupiter but haven't identified any vessel. Several ham radio operators claim to get responses, but we are unable to backtrack the source.

"The Oahu UFO went straight up to a hundred thousand feet and simply disappeared. Our Space Force can locate and track an object the size of a pack of cigarettes at a thousand miles, but not this thing."

"Well, find them," the president said. "We need to know details before the Chinese." They didn't really *need* to know, of course. Like most issues, the matter was likely to blow over in a couple weeks.

TWENTY
THE WEEKLY GIG

CASEY WAS ABLE TO ARRANGE a media avenue which worked for Jon. He was now a regular Friday-night guest on the most widely watched largest cable channel in the country. The host threw a couple of open-ended softballs and then allowed Jon to talk uninterrupted. The show's producer was happy to coordinate on time requirements. Some weeks Jon needed more time than others.

The segments were quickly available via YouTube. The soundtracks were translated into a dozen languages and became immensely popular. The previous week Jon had hinted a big announcement was forthcoming.

"In your talks with the Chait, have they mentioned other intelligent extraterrestrial species?" the host asked.

"No, Trudy, they haven't," responded Jon. "However, in their travels, in this arm of the Milky Way galaxy alone, the Chait have identified ninety-four planets which appear well-suited for human life."

"Let me make sure I'm hearing this straight," the host replied. "The aliens have identified ninety-four Earth-like planets, without intelligent life. And, in this arm of the Milky Way galaxy, means, relatively speaking, fairly close. Is that correct?"

"Yes, that's absolutely correct," said Jon. "More importantly, they're willing to help us, in a limited way, colonize one or more of those planets. As we've discussed before, the Chait are extremely cautious about releasing technology to us. I've had a number of frank discussions with their spokesperson Robert, and the Chait believe they've found a way to make interstellar travel available to the human race, while keeping adequate safeguards on the technology."

"Obviously," said Trudy, "the key help we need is transport. The ability for interstellar flight. Are they releasing that technology to humans?"

"I'm afraid not," replied Jon. "The Chait are keeping interstellar flight technology restricted. Obviously, we require that capability, or assistance from the Chait to colonize another planet. However, the Chait will assist in developing our ability to lift heavy payloads into Earth's orbit. Much heavier payloads than we currently launch.

"Allow me to summarize. We would build craft using Chait designs and carefully tailored technology capable of lifting our people and supplies into orbit. Non-Earth craft would then deliver the people and supplies to a far-off planet, and presumably supply landing craft at the other end.

"Their propulsion systems use physics we don't understand," continued Jon. "The Chait travel to distant stars in only a couple days. So, interstellar travel is not a big deal for them."

"One might think the aliens don't trust us," needled Trudy.

"The Chait are proceeding with caution," replied Jon. "You wouldn't let a six-year-old handle a chainsaw. Especially amongst a group of six-year-olds that fight a lot. However, I imagine some of the reasons are simply practical. The propulsion system may use power sources unknown to us. I imagine many of the related technologies are unknown to us also. Even with a great deal of technical assistance there's no way any government, or private enterprise, could develop, build, and integrate multiple new technologies into a spacecraft in any reasonable time frame. Remember, the Chait are leaving in a few years."

"But isn't that exactly what you're proposing for the new heavy payload craft?" retorted Trudy. "An entirely new spacecraft, with entirely new engines and propulsion technology?"

"No, not really," replied Jon. "The design and construction of a craft capable of lifting cargo into orbit is an order of magnitude less complex than an interstellar craft. Obviously, we already have technology to launch loads into orbit. Somebody puts up a satellite almost every week. So, that part is relatively simple.

"What's not simple is putting large, heavy cargo into high orbit, on a regular basis. The Chait have agreed to help by supplying advanced propulsion and power technology. I assume they will deliver sealed units that can be easily installed during ship construction.

"I have one last thing I want to get to before we run out of time," said Jon.

"Certainly," replied Trudy. "This is amazing news, and I don't want our viewers to miss a thing."

"I have been informed the Chait will soon contact the secretaries of state, or persons in an equivalent position, of the largest, most influential countries in the world. Although lacking any diplomatic status, the Chait feel the time has come to establish formal communication channels with Earth's governments.

"I can't speak definitively for the Chait," continued Jon. "However, I've been told calls are planned for next week, and the subject will include what we've talked about tonight.

"All this talk of spacecraft presumes we are actually interested in going there. To the stars."

TWENTY-ONE
THE SITUATION ROOM

T HE PRESIDENT AND HER STAFF gathered in the situation room thirty minutes before the scheduled call. Defense and Intelligence were included this time. She made crystal clear the meeting would use the protocol developed for communicating with a neutral but unfriendly power. Other than herself and the secretary of state, no one was to speak unless directly asked to do so by the president. The secretary would be carrying the conversation, leaving the president to disavow any statement she felt necessary.

Her instructions to the secretary were clear and concise. "We don't want to look like fools if this is an elaborate hoax. Don't recognize them formally. Make no promises. Give as little information as possible. Ask lots of questions. Make them commit to do certain things for us. Do not let the Chait dominate the conversation. Take a hard line."

The secretary, a former senator, was a longtime political hack with few interpersonal skills, a former senator. This position was payback for his role in getting the president elected. He had never held a diplomatic position before. He understood well who would be held the fool should this call go poorly.

Thirty seconds before the call was to begin, the screens in the room snapped to life. The master sergeant in charge of the hardware made an exaggerated shrug with his palms out in the universal 'I didn't do it' position.

"Please accept my sincere apologies for breaking in like that," came the butter-smooth voice of Robert from the speakers. "No harm done, and the trick helps establish my bona fides." The screens showed a now familiar close-up of Jupiter.

"Thank you for meeting with me on such short notice," he continued. "I don't see Jon Gallock. Is he there?" Robert had suggested Jon be present for the call.

"No, I'm afraid he does not have the necessary security clearances for this meeting," replied the secretary. "Furthermore, you must understand this meeting is classified under our laws. No information exchanged here may be reproduced or transmitted to any third party without our written permission. Is that clear?"

"It is a pleasure to meet you, Mister Secretary," said Robert, ignoring the secretary's question. "And you as well, Madam President. I understand your election was a historic event. Please accept my sincere, if somewhat belated, congratulations."

"Thank you," the president replied simply. She did not want to be drawn into the conversation.

"Why have you been dealing with private individuals and commercial enterprises rather than doing so properly, through our United Nations?" demanded the secretary. "Surely you realize that was not the appropriate route."

"As to your first statement," began Robert, "I'm pleased to see you recognize us as beings analogous to people. One would not threaten a chicken or chimpanzee with penalties under your laws. Although, based on our understanding, which may be incorrect, this type of thing must be adjudicated by your Supreme Court more than once to have any significant legal effect.

"As to your question; we have followed local law and custom as best we could," continued Robert. "In most of your political jurisdictions corporations enjoy similar rights and privileges as a live human being. One cannot buy or sell property, hire employees, remit taxes, pay bills, or contribute to politicians without bank accounts and tax identification numbers. We obviously cannot do so as private individuals, so we use corporations. The individuals you refer to are employees, and representatives of these corporations.

"You mentioned *your* United Nations. Our understanding is the institution is simply another corporation, originally founded, and still owned

I believe, by a consortium of French banks. The original entity now has subsidiary corporations throughout your world. We have followed the UN's example.

"Your UN only deals with recognized sovereign states. Among the UN's criteria are a defined physical territory, and the existence of people. Those criteria are challenging for the Chait to satisfy. In some cases, we've seen your UN deal with an organization recognized by several sovereign states. The OAS—Organization of American States—for example. However, again, we are not a recognized sovereign state by the UN, though three of your nation-states have recognized us without prompting."

The secretary of state was clueless. He also knew nothing of the legal underpinnings of the UN. Nobody had told him that Burundi, Panama, and Saint Kitts and Nevis had formally recognized the Chait.

"Mister Secretary," asked Robert pleasantly, "do you wish to end this call and have us pursue a route through the UN?"

"Of course not," the secretary replied. "What's done is done and now we need to move forward." In a matter of sixty seconds the secretary had managed to look like an ass, recognize the Chait as an intelligent species, and insult them. Not a good start.

"Are you interested in a planet to colonize?" Robert asked. Those in the situation room were thunderstruck. They had expected an hour of quibbling over ground rules, embassies, rules of engagement, and gestures of goodwill. All those things customary to begin a diplomatic process. Not this.

"The existence of those planets has not been verified, nor has your right to offer them," replied the secretary carefully.

Robert ignored the secretary and pressed on breezily. "We plan a tour in a couple weeks and will invite a dozen or so people from several different nation-states. The details will be announced on a website, which will take applications from those interested in making the trip. For reasons I'm sure you all understand, we will not be including individuals with a military, intelligence, or purely political background.

"To familiarize your people with our existence, we plan to fly one of our craft low and slow over areas it can be widely seen." Population centers, in other words. "This will happen worldwide. The craft is nonthreatening in appearance. Please do not shoot at our spacecraft, or even approach too closely."

"You can't do that," protested the secretary. "You will create a worldwide panic and endanger our citizens!"

"From our perspective," replied Robert, "your species' greatest fear is the unknown. A leisurely fly-by will confirm our existence, and end the rumors. The craft will slowly float by, and then leave, which will reassure most people. We will appear no more threatening than a hot air balloon.

"Our colonization offer is being made to several other of your nation-states. As a practical matter, the offer is limited to those large and prosperous enough to take advantage. The effort will involve considerable expense on your part. This program is still under development; however, we will publish a list of those offered, and additional details before the month is out. Let me stress, this is only an offer. You don't have to accept.

"We will shortly send a simple one page 'notice of interest' document which you should sign and return if you are interested in being considered for the program.

"I see we're out of time. Thank you all for taking the effort to be here today. Again, congratulations on your election, Madame President. Goodbye." Jupiter disappeared from the screens.

TWENTY-TWO
THE BOYS OVER A BEER

B OB AND QUINN WERE RELAXING over a beer. An attentive waitress had brought Quinn a small bag of shaved ice, which he held on his left cheek.

Quinn had been on board for two months when Bob appeared at the door and plopped himself down in Quinn's office. "I heard you do karate. What level?"

Regular exercise is a challenge for business executives who travel a lot. Bob and Quinn each knew of congenial dojos in cities they often visited.

Eventually Bob invited Quinn to Friday night sparring with the advanced belts. "I go about once a month. It's for the old guys, I mean the more mature black belts," he said. "You're not there yet, but it's not a problem. I'll get you in." Quinn, a former professional athlete, was taller, fitter, and noticeably more muscular than Bob. No matter. Bob beat on him like a drum every time.

After sparring, several of them usually went out for beer and wings. Only Bob and Quinn went this time.

"You're about a year ahead of me in taking the cure," began Quinn. "Have you noticed a change in your reflexes? You seem very fast, very smooth. Do you swear you aren't using your enhancements?"

Quinn had never seen a person combining such an utter lack of ego and supreme self-confidence as Bob. The old guys at the sparring sessions—some were pushing fifty—had those qualities as well. Quinn was disconcerted at first when such a retiring personality spoke with such clear, concise confidence. Now, however, Quinn realized why Bob felt no need to emote swagger.

Bob knew karateka everywhere. Both he and Quinn were in Stuttgart tonight. Bob was a card-carrying member of the German Shotokan association.

"Nope, no enhancements. Only training and experience," replied Bob. "I started doing this in high school. By the time I graduated from college, I had my black belt and was nationally ranked. I was lucky to go to a couple dojos with great instructors, and extremely gifted students. So, I had to keep up. I learned good technique. Over time you develop technique and muscle memory and whittle away extraneous motions so you get to the point of attack faster. You're a relative newbie. However, you're a much better athlete than I'll ever be. You got great legs, powerful, fast. We're just doing light sparring, tag-you're-it kind of stuff. If we were going full contact, you'd whip my ass."

"So, what changes have you seen?" asked Quinn, unconvinced of his chances of kicking Bob's ass. He steered the subject back on path. "I haven't noticed much yet, except my energy is better. A lot better."

"Well," replied Bob, "that sounds similar to what the others say. I assume you've discussed this with your Chait rep, Orange, and Doctor Marra?" Bob asked. Quinn nodded.

"I know there are alternate treatments, some of which are embargoed here on Earth," said Bob, subtly shifting the subject. "I believe we on the management team are starting from a similar spot and receiving similar treatments. The process will take several more years, but eventually, physically, you'll be twenty-five years old again. Just think of it! Being young again with what you know now. You'll be living every man's dream.

"I don't know exactly what you were told," Bob continued. "I'll tell you my understanding; you let me know where we differ. Ok?"

A general rule of corporate life is the CFO knows everything. Another rule is he keeps his mouth shut. However, to those with a need to know, he always tells the truth, and nothing but the truth. However, the whole truth may depend on the listeners' need to know. So, Quinn listened very carefully.

"From a simplistic point of view, all that happens is you get scanned every couple months, take a couple daily pills, eat well, and drink lots of water," began Bob. "And magically, your body begins to change.

"Everything can't happen at once," said Bob. "Your body doesn't have the resources. Certain things are done first, other things happen slowly in background over time, and the process is repetitive. Your body's functions and mechanical structure are brought to some baseline, perhaps that of a healthy forty or fifty-year-old. Then another pass that knocks off maybe ten more years, then another, and so forth."

"Initially though," Bob continued, "one is stabilized. Any life-threating health issue is addressed first. Any blocked coronary artery is cleared, any crippling arthritis, or missing cartilage repaired or regrown. Any incipient aneurysms are fixed. Cancers are excised, and any dangerously low liver or kidney function are addressed, and so on.

"In addition to those, let's call them mechanical fixes, the body is cleansed of infection. The body is continually battling bacteria, viruses, mold, fungus, phages, cancers, cysts, parasites, and God knows what else. I believe that's a major reason we are feeling the extra energy—simply being free of low-level infections, and inflammation.

"After a month of beginning treatment, your body tissues are carrying a pound or two of nanites, which are doing most of the repair work. In the long term, however, the strategy is to get your body systems performing optimally, like in a young person. At that point the body heals itself.

"At this time a virus, or actually a retrovirus, I believe, begins to insert repairs to damaged DNA. While this is happening, at least two more parallel repair processes are underway as a low-level background activity. Do you, at least vaguely, know what telomeres are?" Bob asked.

"I think so," Quinn replied. "Telomeres are structures on the end of our chromosomes designed to keep the cell from fraying during division. Like that thingy on the end of your shoelace. Over one's life, telomeres degrade, and shorten, allowing errors to creep in during cell division. The result is our body breaks down and ages."

Everyone on Full Medical had developed a keen interest in biology and the processes of aging. Lacking formal medical education, they rarely got things exactly right.

"Exactly my understanding," said Bob. "From day one our treatment starts repairing the telomeres. That in itself slows aging appreciably. Later in the treatment a process kicks in which will, as I understand it, 'tag' damaged cells, even those with restored telomeres, for treatment by certain of the retroviruses. Depending on the cell, and other factors, the virus will either repair the DNA or simply prevent that specific cell from renewing. Over time the damaged cells die off and are not replaced. Only the healthy cells divide and reproduce. We grow younger.

"The second thing is the nanites shift from the gross mechanical repairs to finer repairs of specific systems in the body. Not everything is worked on at once. Remember the strategy: help the body to help self. If your body doesn't have the proper nutrients, you won't be healthy. So, the digestive system is usually repaired first. Next up are the immune and endocrine systems. The two work hand-in-hand to keep the body healthy.

"From there the treatment will start to vary among individuals. For some it may be the respiratory system, where on another the higher priority is the circulatory system, the heart, and arteries. For women at, or near, menopause, the hormones and reproductive system are a big deal. Women have a raft of issues around their reproductive system that cause problems later in life.

"For many, at least at first, the little things matter most. If you've been constipated for years, or plagued with hemorrhoids, then work on that excretory system! An enlarged prostrate, tinnitus, missing teeth, poor vision, diabetes, postnasal drip, a slipped disk, a bum knee, all need fixing before your heart, lungs, and muscles are upgraded to run a marathon. All the unpleasant crap your grandparents bitch about gets fixed."

"By God," exclaimed Quinn, "my bridge—I wear a partial bridge—has been feeling off. I lost three teeth in a match with the All Blacks. I wonder if I have teeth coming in!"

"Probably so," replied Bob. "If I were you, I'd see Doctor Marra right away. I've found it's better to see her sooner, rather than later. If she tells me to come back for my next scan, and treatment in two or three months, I schedule for six or eight weeks out.

"Teeth are prioritized. Generally, however, bones take the longest," Bob finished. "Unless one has osteoporosis, bones are generally a minor issue. However, the skin, which your body totally replaces every thirty days, is not repaired. Or the hair," he said rubbing his thinning pate. "For security reasons we can't have those on Full Medical start looking remarkably younger. That would let the cat out of the bag and we'd be screwed. Worldwide riots would ensue and all of us would disappear into government labs for the rest of our lives. So, all your warts, and hard-earned scars, stay until you leave."

"Fuck me!" exclaimed Quinn, the continental sophistication slipping away. "I can't wait. When I was twenty-five, I could run through walls. Literally. I did so once on a bet. I wish I could jump into a tank and do this tomorrow."

"Nope," replied Bob, dryly. "Not unless you go to Ouranos."

TWENTY-THREE
THE STAFF MEETING

T HE INNER CIRCLE RARELY MET in person. There was hardly a need. Their phones were never out of the service area, never dropped a call, and never needed charging. The mic was so good one only had to whisper, and the audio went straight to your ear. The devices were un-hackable.

Of course, those in the Inner Circle rarely bothered with phones. Jon, and the others communicated via their enhancements.

Each had an office, of course, but traveled so much the space was rarely used. More commonly one would camp out in a conference room, or coffee shop. The company largely ran on coffee.

The company's systems, especially email, were heavily encrypted.

Today, however, the group met in person.

"What's the excitement outside?" asked Jon, standing, and looking through the heavily shaded glass at the street below.

Randy, who was listening to his phone, held up one finger for a couple of seconds, said "gotcha," and then hung up. "Apparently a car with a couple of French DGSE agents had a fender bender with the Japanese PSIA people."

"Are we absolutely sure we're secure?" asked Tracey. "This is turning into a circus."

The security of interacting with those outside the Inner Circle, and outside the company, was Randy's concern. Randy looked at Jon, who nodded, and said, "Let's take a couple minutes and review the precautions."

"Among ourselves you should use your enhancements as much as possible," Randy began. "This room is cloaked. Our conversation is completely immune from snooping. Our meeting today is absolutely secure.

"All our communication and information technology, both hardware and software use Chait technology," said Randy. "Not only is the programming language unique, the coding is done on a language not found on Earth. The coding may as well be in Egyptian hieroglyphics, except much more obscure."

"I don't type in hieroglyphics," said Tracey wryly. "I type in plain old English, which appears on my screen. Is anyone out there reading what I see on my screen?"

"Nope," replied Randy. "Absolutely not. The Chait technology makes 256-bit encryption look flimsy in comparison. Not even the NSA can read our email, or internal documents.

"I believe you all know the Chait phones are not really cellphones," Randy continued. "The devices don't route through any cellular network. The phones supplied by the Chait communicate directly with each other, and don't utilize any detectable RF spectrum. The technology is BFM."

Seeing blank looks from several, Randy elaborated. "BFM is a technical term used by geeks—Black Fucking Magic."

Randy continued. "We don't want others to know our full capabilities, so outside our impermeable shell is a totally plausible but fake environment using normal commercial hardware and software so those folks out there"—he waved a hand towards the window—"have something to scratch at."

"Lastly," Randy concluded, "we run an active counterintelligence program. The Chait do the heavy lifting for us. Our friends see, hear, and listen to everything on the planet. Absolutely everything. Obviously, they use an immense degree of automation coupled with hugely powerful artificial intelligence. For example, their systems know who we are, obviously, however, they also monitor our relatives, friends, family, former co-workers, neighbors, doctors, accountants, and lawyers. Whenever anyone in the world touches anything related to those people, the Chait system knows in real time. The Chait know which person is looking at your sister's tax return, who they work for, and where that tax return was emailed. The circle expands to whoever reads the email, and to whoever acts on the matter. Same with the people going through your trash, or hacking your sweetie's home computer. The Chait know."

"So far, the agencies are just observing, and gathering data. However, their agents have dozens of draft warrant requests, subpoenas, and national security declarations in queue ready to go. When the intelligence agencies decide to put the screws to people close to us, or when a snatch team gets dispatched, we'll get warning and take appropriate action," Randy finished.

"Ok," said Jon, "on that cheery note, let's get started. Most of you know what I'm going to say, but that's true of most meetings. Seriously, we're going to go through a lot of changes this next month and I want everybody on the same page. This is likely the last time we meet in person for quite a while.

"First, the Chait flybys have been extremely well-received. The bright flashing colors and loud, cheerful music have given somewhat of a circus aspect to the events. The press coverage has been immense, and quite positive.

"Several nations, primarily China and Russia, issued flat statements of their intent to shoot down any unknown aircraft. They didn't actually do so. The craft appeared over Moscow shortly before dawn one day and flew a large slow circle around the heart of the city for several hours. The Russians held their fire for fear of damaging the Kremlin. When leaving, the Chait craft went straight up to a hundred thousand feet and then simply disappeared. Similar flybys were done over several major Chinese cities. The governments in both countries have tried to demonize the Chait, with little success.

"The appearances in Europe, the US, and elsewhere took on a party atmosphere. An impromptu carnival broke out in Rio.

"Second," Jon continued, "the Inner Circle must move out of the US, to Europe. We're sitting ducks here. In Europe one can easily move across several national boundaries in one day. The multiple jurisdictions make interagency coordination more difficult for the intelligence agencies. Moving to Europe will also reduce the attention paid to our friends and family in the US.

"We now have reasonable cover from Congress, and the regulatory agencies. The White House has her thumb up her ass and doesn't know which way to move. However, the intelligence agencies are ungovernable and that's why we have to stay nimble."

"Can't we, ahem, lobby the people in the White House directly?" asked Tom.

"Not effectively, no," replied Jon. "Our assessment is those in the White House don't meet the definition of an honest politician. A dishonest politician gladly takes your money, but won't stay bought. And, of course, nobody in the White House can control the intelligence agencies.

"The president herself is a creature of the west coast tech industries. With the coming of Chait technology, that's like being backed by the buggy whip and horseshoe industries in the year nineteen hundred. The tech industries are putting a lot of pressure on her to either ban, overregulate, or monopolize any new technologies. She doesn't know which way to jump.

"Also," said Jon, getting back on track, "I'm confirming the money-grubbing activities have stopped—except for the trading program. We needed the cash early on, but not so much now. Those activities are now just a distraction—with downside, if word gets out.

"Next, Bob is preparing an initial public offering for the licensing subsidiaries. Counting only existing agreements, the margin baked into next year's plan is on the order of a hundred million dollars. Given the XSolarian group's cash flow and growth potential, we should be able to raise something north of a billion dollars, while keeping majority control of the companies. In essence, we are just pulling the next ten years of expected cash margin forward. This is a huge subject involving multiple subsidiaries, and possibly multiple exchanges in different countries. Neither Bob nor I am getting into details today. However, you should know those subsidiaries will need mostly new upper management. Until you hear different, assume those new hires are not of the Inner Circle.

"Finally, the Friday night YouTube show, and podcast, has been a huge success. Casey is now a big star." The others hooted and clapped. Casey stuck her tongue out at Jon.

"I am making the big announcement on Friday's show," Jon continued. "Adrian has handed off his lobbying work and will earn his paycheck another way." Adrian Kelly smiled broadly. He was now in the Inner Circle. "Once the announcement goes out, Adrian is going to be one busy guy."

The meeting lasted another hour. Jon didn't say much more; he'd already gotten his message across. When the meeting broke up, Shirley motioned him to the side. "Are you sleeping with Casey?" she demanded.

"Not yet," Jon replied blandly.

"Goddammit, Jon, you have to be careful about this," exploded Shirley. "There are laws covering this, which I don't have to quote to you. And don't give me crap about different laws govern an entity incorporated on the isle of Malta, or Panama. This kind of thing is always a bad idea. Obviously, she's your protégé. Everybody's aware of the relationship between the two of you. She's way too junior for most of these meetings. She has a vague title. For Christ's sake, Jon, one joke is she sleeps on a mat at the foot of your bed.

"I'm not just worried about you," she continued, "I'm concerned for her. An affair with you can end several ways, most of them badly."

"I hear what you're saying," replied Jon. "Look, Casey ran her own company. She has tons of ability. She just needs more seasoning. I'm moving her up as fast as she can absorb the necessary background. You have to admit she's a natural in the public eye. She's becoming a celebrity. In six more months, everyone here today will see her as an equal. As far as our relationship, well, I'll be careful."

Shirley rolled her eyes in disgust and stomped out.

TWENTY-FOUR
THE NEW WEEKLY GIG

I N THE MONTH AFTER JON revealed the existence of habitable planets, and the Chait's willingness to help a human colonization effort, a lot had happened. The alien spacecraft flybys were witnessed by a billion people. The talk shows went crazy with speculation. A tour of alien planets was announced and the website took ten million applications the first week. And Casey now hosted her own weekly show and podcast, *The Tiger Tanaka Friday ET Update*. The show instantly became the most highly watched half-hour segment on any broadcast, or cable media. The show had only one sponsor and was more of an infomercial than journalism.

Jon loved doing the show on Friday night. The politicians and their staffs had to work weekends to prepare a coherent position and response by Monday morning.

"Aloha," said Casey. "Welcome to the *Tiger Tanaka ET Update*. We have a great show tonight, and a lot of ground to cover. So, let's just jump right in. Here's our first guest for tonight. I'm sure you know Jon Gallock."

The screen blinked and then showed a close-up shot of Jon sitting behind an imposing desk. "I've been told," he began, "the Chait held calls this week with the leaders of approximately a dozen national governments. In those calls the Chait continued to express their peaceful intentions, and indicated a willingness to help humans colonize other planets.

"Tonight, I reveal which nations will receive the opportunity to colonize another planet. The Chait have their reasons why these nations were chosen. They obviously chose nations based in part on their ability to support such a program. By support I mean financial, technical, and industrial capacity. The Chait may also have political reasons for their choices.

"I have in my hand"—he lifted a sheet of paper—"the text of the actual formal offer which goes out Monday to the respective secretaries of state, or equivalent position, of those countries. The document is only two pages long, with simple and easily understood text. The offer must be signed and returned, unchanged and unedited, within thirty days."

Thousands of government employees, from half the countries on the planet, immediately accessed the XSolarian website in hopes of finding the notice, in order to send to, and suck up to, the boss. Tens of thousands of journalists also hit the website, as did hundreds of thousands of students, and millions of the merely curious.

"There are no strings attached," Jon continued. "The offer makes no demands on any of these nations to clean up their act. There are no demands for social or political change.

" This is an offer only. Each nation is free to accept, or decline, as they choose.

"To be clear, and I understand there was some confusion on this point, each of these nations will be offered a separate planet. They need not share a planet."

The president of the United States, watching from her private quarters, almost fell out of her chair. The White House staff had assured her the offer was for one planet, shared by all. This changed everything, politically. She picked up the phone and started making calls.

"Here, now, are the countries chosen," continued Jon. "I'm going to present them in order of gross domestic product, GDP. First up, no surprise, the United States of America. The land of the free and the home of the brave. The US has the largest GDP, and great financial and technical resources. Although fifty trillion plus in debt, the government still has the ability to spend hundreds of billions of dollars on a whim. Their manufacturing ability is in decline, but still among world leaders.

"Next is the People's Republic of China. Their GDP is growing the fastest among developed nations, and the Chinese are expected to eventually surpass the US. China has immense financial, technical, and manufacturing capability. They are tied with India for the most populous nation on Earth—home to approximately one point five of the world's eight billion people.

"Third was unexpected, at least to me," Jon continued. "The Commonwealth of Nations, originally the British Commonwealth. The Commonwealth has expanded over time. The entity is not just the United Kingdom of England, Scotland, Ireland, and Wales. This is the greater entity which includes, Canada, Australia, New Zealand, South Africa, India, Pakistan, and a number of East African, and Caribbean countries. This diverse collection of countries has a collective population in excess of two billion people. In large part, the citizens share a common language, and recognition of the crown. As a whole, the organization has tremendous industrial capacity.

"Next is Japan. This relatively small island nation has a distinct, unique culture, and is an economic and industrial powerhouse. The remaking of this country after World War II was a model for many developing Asian nations.

"Fifth on the list is Germany. This country has been the economic and industrial engine powering Europe for fifty years. One might speculate the Chait do not consider the European Union a unified entity.

"The sixth and final spot on the list is Russia. The Russian economy is not in the world's top ten. For example, Germany's GDP is twice the size of Russia's. Even Italy has a bigger economy. Their financial resources are not on par with the other countries on this list. Russia does have good technical resources, but not a lot of quality manufacturing capacity. However, the Russian state possess a million-man military, thousands of nuclear weapons, and intercontinental ballistic missiles. I suspect the country was chosen for political reasons.

"Let the whining commence," quipped Jon. "Actually, I believe the Chait did a solid job with these selections. The selected nations include half the world's population. Most of the major continents are included. Only South America seems to have been left out. One can make a good case for Brazil, I imagine. Participation from Africa, via the Commonwealth, is light."

The screen flashed briefly to Casey. "That's earthshaking news. I can't begin to image what this means to people around the globe." The screen flashed again, splitting into four panes.

"Joining Jon and I tonight are Richard Jesinskis, the former Secretary of State of the United Kingdom; Doctor Marcelle Aufort, the popular author and poly sci professor from Stanford; and the XSolarian vice president of government affairs, Doctor Adrian Kelly," said Casey.

The outside guests had been handpicked and coached carefully.

"Minister Jesinskis," continued Casey with a laugh and a smile, "can you briefly, very briefly—without sucking the air from the room and losing us a million viewers—explain the difference between Britain, the United Kingdom, and the Commonwealth?"

"It's difficult to explain concisely, but I'll give it a go," he replied. "Britain, or Great Britain is physically composed of two large islands and many smaller ones. Politically, the United Kingdom includes England, Scotland, Wales, and North Ireland. The UK, as we call it, does not include the Republic of Ireland. The head of state is the queen.

"The Commonwealth of Nations, formerly the British Commonwealth, currently includes fifty-five nations, including those mentioned by Mister Gallock, and consists mostly of former British colonies, or possessions which maintain ties through the Commonwealth Charter, which defines basic human rights, rule of law, and democratic values. The Commonwealth encompasses about a quarter of the globe, and the world's people.

"This is a loose association, and any major effort to coordinate a large expensive project, quickly will prove challenging. One also has to wonder how much flexibility the Chait will allow the Commonwealth to add or remove participating states under this offer," Jesinskis concluded.

"Thank you, Minister Jesinskis, for that great explanation" Casey said brightly. "Even us Yanks could follow along.

"Now," said Casey as the camera cut to another guest, "I'd like to ask Doctor Aufort his views on Russia. Doctor Aufort, I realize you received this document shortly before airtime and haven't had much of a chance to analyze the document. However, I'd like to hear your initial impressions on why the Chait would include Russia. Economically and population-wise the country appears marginal, and the government certainly doesn't share the values of the Western democracies."

"Well Tiger," began Aufort, "we have Central and South American banana republics, bloody tribal warlords in Africa, unending conflict in the Middle East theocracies, and brutal despots in the 'Stans on one hand, and reasonably enlightened Western democracies on the other. From five hundred million miles away, Russia may appear reasonably mainstream and middle-of-the-road to the Chait.

"That aside, from a political viewpoint, Russia simply must be included. The country is frenemies with China with whom they share a border, and Europe depends on Russia for half their total energy needs. The Russian Bear can make a great deal of mischief and spoil things for all, if so inclined. The offer to Russia appears a smart political protection payoff."

The discussion ping-ponged around for several minutes on political matters, and possible reactions from those counties left out. Jon deferred mostly to Adrian.

"Now, for our favorite part of the show—questions from the audience!" announced Casey enthusiastically. Ten people were screened before finding one person suitable to air for ten seconds. Most stuttered, looked at the ground, said 'like, you know' every sentence, picked their nose, were unattractive, poorly groomed, dumber than dirt, spoke poor English, cursed, had crossed eyes, chewed gum, or were one of a hundred other varieties of not quite right. Anyone televised had to look like the average Joe on the street but not drive away viewers. Teams of assistants had been working with a half dozen callers—video callers—since the show started. The pool of tonight's callers was not deep.

The screen blinked again. Now the split-screen view showed Casey on one side and Jon on the other. "Our first caller is Daryl, from Miami, Florida. Daryl, this is Tiger Tanaka; what's your question?"

"Yeah, Tiger, thanks. Uh, Mister Gallock, who gets which planet? Does the country get to, like, you know, just pick one, or is one just issued to them? Will the US of A know if we're getting, like, you know, the Okefenokee Swamp, or frozen Fargo North Dakota?" Daryl mercifully finished.

"Great question," said Jon. "The short answer is, the day after the deadline, after everyone has returned their signed document confirming their desire to own a planet, a lottery is held. The five least desirable planets on the list, plus one other, are excluded from consideration, leaving eighty-eight possibilities. A numbered ball is pulled from a container and that's the planet the country receives. Think of a TV game show, except for a lot higher stakes.

"Earth itself has a great many different ecological zones. The whole planet is not the Okefenokee Swamp, or frozen North Dakota. Even a planet seeming only marginally habitable will have large areas well suited for human populations. It doesn't really matter which planet one draws; all have vast areas of really good, desirable land.

"The process of rating and ranking habitable planet is complex, and quite interesting. The planets identified by the Chait have been analyzed and ranked using the Sandilands–Brewer Exoplanet Assessment Model."

A thousand miles away Professor Brewer spewed his gin and tonic out his nose. "Sandilands! That smarmy little turd!" he shouted at the screen. "Who the hell does he think he is putting his name on my work! The bastard doesn't know planetary ecology from a hole in the ground. I'll sue his ass till he bleeds!"

Jon continued, "Tomorrow, we will release a short description, approximately ten pages, of each planet. We will also distribute an abstract describing the model, and the various factors and weightings used to rate the exoplanets. We will also post videos, something like thirty minutes on each one. Those will also be on the website."

Minions of the political class would now have to spend their entire weekend analyzing an opaque computer model and nine hundred pages of planet descriptions.

"Don't get hung up on the relative ratings. Remember, we're talking about an entire planet. As Daryl astutely alluded to a minute ago, big differences occur between one point and another, even on the same continent. Any one of these planets is a prize beyond measure."

"Okay, next question," chirped Casey. "We have Onge from Paris, France. What's your question, Onge?"

The screen flicked to an image of a stylish young lady much more presentable than Daryl. She appeared to be a student. In a cute French accent, she asked, "What happens to these colonies when the Chait leave?

Supposedly the mysterious aliens are only here for another few years, and, oh, they don't trust us with interstellar flight. Nobody's mentioned that. So do we just say to the colonists, 'goodbye, good luck, hope to see you in a thousand years?"

"Another great question," replied Jon. "Thank you, Onge. The point you raise was the biggest issue which we had to overcome before the Chait could make this offer. Transporting people to an undeveloped world and then abandoning them would be cruel and inhumane. That's not going to happen.

"The Chait have always maintained that any release of interstellar travel technology to Earth is unsafe, and unwise. However, they have agreed to release the technology to an organization of private individuals who are not of Earth, and who are not affiliated in any way, shape, or form, with any government, nation, state, or private organization on Earth.

"A human colony was formed, and has operated for several years, on a distant planet. The Chait provided the necessary transport. Using Chait technology those colonists will build and operate starships. Construction has already begun. Those starships will pick up the colonists and their supplies from Earth orbit, or somewhere in the solar system, and transport them to, and from, their destination.

"The colony has been recruiting for years, and in many countries. The people in this colony are all volunteers. The colonists have renounced all earthly ties, and once the starships start flying, will never return to their birth planet again. In fact, they are forbidden to do so. Currently, fewer than a dozen people are allowed to travel to and from the colony. I'm one of them. I leave, forever, with the first human-built and crewed starship.

"The colony planet is named Ouranos. The Chait granted me ownership as compensation for facilitating first contact with their race.

"Next question."

TWENTY-FIVE
MOUNTAINSIDE

U NLESS YOU COUNTED THE NEWBIES still in a tank at Shoreside, the Mountainside settlement was the largest on Ouranos. The town was in a high valley, in a setting rivaling the Austrian Alps for natural beauty. A small river divided the valley almost exactly in two. Neat houses, set well back from the water, ran alongside a rough road on one side of the river.

Following the road out of town, and uphill, for a kilometer one started to pass the large metal-sided warehouses and workshops. Further on one came to the mine workings, followed by Fabs and more warehouses co-located with the Fabs. The structures grew in size as one continued along the road. Like a nautilus outgrowing a shell, each Fab was noticeably larger than the one preceding. Each Fab was located in a nondescript metal building with a steeply pitched roof. Two raw material staging warehouses, each offset slightly, fed the Fab. At the rear was another warehouse to hold the finished goods.

Two landing fields for the saucers were located a prudent distance away, and a third smaller saucer pad was located at the edge of town.

The whole area swarmed with workers, autonomous vehicles, and HAL units.

Eons before, a gigantic intrusion from deep within the planet's crust pushed upward. Kilometers short of the surface, the plume stalled. There, the intrusion cooked for millions of years, braised in metal-rich fluids. Eventually, the magma cooled and hardened. Over the ages, tectonics and weathering exposed the huge metal-rich intrusion, and the surrounding altered country rock. The deposit was not especially rich in iron; however, the ore had an unusual number of trace metals, notably, rare earth elements, needed for the colony to thrive.

Almost a hundred different metallic minerals are needed to run a modern society. Those not found at Mountainside were obtained from Rainy Town, or one of a dozen remote sites which had no permanent residents.

The ore was mined, transported to a Fab, and reduced to the component metals. Waste was used for pavers, or building bricks. The metals were stored in large warehouses until needed. When an order, for example a tractor, was scheduled, the necessary materials were pulled, transported, and queued in a warehouse adjacent to the Fab.

In theory a Fab could manufacture a tractor in a single cycle. In practice it was more time effective to prepare major subsystems separately. After each subsystem was Fab'd, they were transported to an assembly building. Tractor components were parsed into five separate production runs, which were then assembled by automatons, or in yet another Fab cycle.

Of course, a tractor on Ouranos was a lot different than one on Earth. These tractors ran on electricity. Sealed power plants smaller than a conventional diesel engine converted mass to energy without emissions, heat, or waste. The small power plant ran practically nonstop feeding a battery. The alien battery technology featured power densities a thousand times that of terrestrial technology.

After assembly, the tractor either went into a warehouse if they were building ahead, or if filling a pending order, the tractor would be moved to yet another warehouse where the large shipping cans were packed with everything one needed to establish a remote holding.

Hence the hustle and bustle.

Today a small crowd had gathered to watch the first Class III saucer come out of assembly. The sleek craft had three times the capacity of the existing saucers.

"Beautiful bird," said Juan Perez. "However, saucers should be Fab'd at Amazon Cove. The body is mostly composed of carbon constructs."

John Hayward smiled. "If we'd moved saucer construction to Amazon Cove, we wouldn't be looking at this beautiful bird for another six months," he replied. "Analysis indicated the quicker path was to bring the carbon feedstock here than to move bigger Fabs to Amazon Cove. Besides, by weight, the metallic components, the power plants, field generators, lift units, and batteries weigh a lot more than the carbon shell."

Juan was still pouting. John threw him a bone.

"The assembly of the interstellar craft is still planned to occur at Amazon Cove," said John. "Once Fabs of sufficient size and capability are established there, one has to believe the saucers, and the interstellar craft, will be Fab'd there as well. We're not going to locate our primary spaceport up here in the mountains. In fact, the first scheduled load of this new saucer is large Fab components to your place."

Juan emitted a noncommittal grunt. He was still unhappy.

Juan better pull his head out of his ass, thought John. *Schedule is the number one priority. Being bull headed, and stinky while lobbying for a suboptimal solution which benefits only his team, will get him squashed like a bug.*

Several pilots were watching the saucer float out of the huge assembly building. All three were grinning ear to ear. The pilots had flown a smaller saucer in a training mode that, supposedly, mimicked the feel and flight characteristics of the larger craft. Over the next several days they would verify the actual flight performance against the specs. Nobody expected major problems. This was Chait technology.

One of the pilots strode over where the two managers were talking and introduced himself. "I'm Ken Edson," he said. "I'm one of the pilots assigned to this. At least until I begin prepping for the *Argo*." The three exchanged handshakes.

Both Juan and John were familiar with Ken's resume. He was a high-value recruit penciled in as the lead captain in the first interstellar craft built on Ouranos. The *Argo*.

The naming of the first interstellar craft was a source of entertainment and good-natured rivalry for months. The initial favorite, "Enterprise" soon fell behind the more aptly named "Mayflower." However, many felt the Mayflower was too White-Anglo-Saxon-Protestant (WASP) centric. "Argo" was a classic compromise. The crew would be called Argonauts. In deference to the large Enterprise contingent, no crew member would wear a red uniform.

"The assembly process is sure different than terrestrial tech," continued Ken. "I've toured the Boeing line. Their Everitt location is the finest aircraft assembly plant in the world. But this"—he gestured—"is so much faster and efficient. The automation is mind boggling. No people!"

The Chait technology was indeed mind boggling. A modern aircraft contains miles of electrical wiring. The Chait technology used almost none. Everything, even most power, was transmitted with wireless tech, which greatly reduced the assembly complexity. Only the engines and field generators required a direct physical power hookup. There was no rat's nest of wires behind the instrument panel. A Chait-designed craft also contained no rivets, nuts, bolts, welds, fuel lines, hydraulics, or windows. All joining was done with an Andy unit which melted components together at the molecular level. The process left no seams. HAL units, and other specialized automated equipment, swarmed over the craft during assembly. The automated assembly units worked around the clock without human supervision, breaks, grievances, or errors.

"Yes, robots don't waste a second," replied John. "Their flexibility is also a good thing because the program's requirements tend to change. A year or two from now a saucer that size will emerge complete, in one go, from one gigantic Fab. No assembly required. So, the need for these robots will change overnight.

"We can't wait for a gigantic Fab. Work on the next Class III saucer starts tomorrow. The build begins on the *Argo* in a couple months. I imagine you are jazzed about piloting an interstellar flight."

"Oh, yeah," exclaimed Ken. "Every flyer dreams of becoming an astronaut. Flying interstellar as an Argonaut is even beyond that. I imagine The Project will build three to five vessels of the class. In the near term I don't see how we could crew more than that. Deck officers with the right skill set are thin on the ground, even on Earth."

Ken was a graduate of the prestigious United States Merchant Marine Academy. He worked diligently through the ranks and earned his master's license by his early thirties. He captained expensive liquefied natural gas (LNG) tankers all over the world. Early in his career the love of his life turned down his marriage proposal. Two months away at a time was a deal breaker. Once he got over her, Ken got a slot flying F-16 fighters for the Arizona Air National Guard to keep busy in his off time. He gave the Guard thirty days a year. He earned big bucks, drove fast cars, and slept with many beautiful women. He hunted big game in Africa, drank expensive bourbon, and kept a condo on Maui.

The accident occurred when a buddy flew him and another in a small plane to a ski resort in Colorado. A deer darted underneath a split second before landing, flipping the plane. His two friends walked away unscathed. Ken was left a quadriplegic.

The recruiters kept an eye on quadriplegic wards. They didn't have ask Ken twice about emigrating. He was motivated.

Juan had a brother who worked on ships, so he was familiar with the industry. He had perused Ken's resume with interest. A ship's captain with a Master Unlimited License who also flew high performance jets. Really? Few on Earth had those qualifications, much less on Ouranos. His resume fit the command needs of a crewed interstellar craft like a glove.

"For now, we're going to focus on putting the new saucer through its paces," said Ken. "Tell your guys at the launch party tonight the job they did was outstanding."

"You're invited; tell them yourself," said John, smiling. "At least if you don't bend the new saucer on the maiden flight this afternoon."

TWENTY-SIX
THE FARMER

BLUE DINGMAN WAS A FARMER, and a good one at that. He'd started slowing down in his sixties and spent most of his seventies in the rocking chair, enjoying the grandkids. His body began failing at an increasing rate in his eighties. By then his wife was gone, and the kids had moved out of state, taking the grandkids with them.

When the recruiters offered him the deal, "hell, yes," he agreed. The most onerous condition was banishment from the planet, forever. Blue didn't care. For him, planet Earth had narrowed down to a narrow bed in a nursing home. He didn't even have pictures on the walls.

He'd been a hell-raiser in his youth and worked a dozen different occupations before settling down with the wife. Like most farmers, he could thread a pipe, drill a well, and wire a barn for electricity.

Blue never had to start a farm from scratch before. He loved to build things, and was looking forward to the challenge. Here, the equipment didn't exist, the land was difficult to get to and had never been plowed. Should he get a crop in, he had nowhere to store the grain and no mills to process the wheat into flour. This was a lot more satisfying than his paid job—putting up warehouses at Mountainside.

Not a day passed without Blue missing his wife.

A lifelong farmer received special treatment on Ouranos. Blue had a unique dispensation to homestead outside of the two river valleys open for settlement. He was a hundred kilometers north, and east of Mountainside. He was into the flat grasslands of the interior. The weather, humidity, and soil were perfect for grain.

When news of his homestead got out, he was deluged with lobbying. The guys wanted barley for beer, and the ladies wanted wheat for bread. He planted wheat.

When he first went to work at Mountainside, a co-worker clued him in on the menu. "The food is great, but a little monotonous. Today is wild game day. For breakfast we have black bear sausage, hash browns, and eggs. For lunch the cafeteria is serving elk burger on a potato bread bun, with French fries. Dinner tonight is venison steak, baked potato, and green beans. Most days we have beef on the menu; however, even cows are wild game, and tough. So, the beef is usually ground or stewed. We get fish on Fridays."

"So, it's potatoes for breakfast, lunch, and dinner," Blue said resignedly. He was not a potato fan.

"Yep, that's pretty much the menu every day," the co-worker replied. "The homesteads are starting to produce beans and fresh vegetables. The vegetables are tasty, tasty. Shoreside sends us plenty of fruit and fish, but the potato is the primary source of carbs. I don't know why."

Blue knew why. Cheap carbohydrates. Potatoes were easy to grow, harvest, store, and process. An acre provided enough calories to support fifteen people for a year. An acre of wheat or barley was harder to plant, harvest, and process, and would only produce enough calories to sustain two or three people. Wheat was for rich people. Corn was better than wheat, although not as calorie-intensive as potatoes. However, corn was lacking in vitamins and nutrients. Poor people ate potatoes. Lots of potatoes. Blue could fix that.

Blue had planted an acre of spring wheat. One miserable acre. He did the planting as a trial run to test out the equipment, see how the wheat fared, and establish farming practices. If things went well, he'd harvest a lot more seed. He'd put in a winter wheat crop after harvest. In the spring he'd expand the wheat field, and maybe add a field of barley. He was thinking he could easily do ten acres of wheat in the spring and prepare enough land to plant twenty-five acres in the fall. He planned to work up to a thousand acres in five years.

The first batch of seed was imported from Earth, and therefore expensive. Blue was planning to use most of the first crop as seed for the following planting. This was not an ideal way to farm, but that's what he had to work with.

Harvested wheat required a lot of processing before one saw a loaf of bread. Blue was in discussions with two different people trying to hammer out a reasonable deal for processing. Blue wanted to farm, not run a mill.

The grassland was like nothing Blue had ever seen. The native tall-grasses were over two meters high, and so thick a man could hardly push his way through. The prairie teemed with birds. Herds of bovines, followed by the inevitable predators, would periodically migrate through and thin the grass.

Clearing land was a snap. The terrain was flat as a table. When wind, weather, and season were right, he simply set fires and let them burn. Thousands of hectares burned; nobody complained. He felt bad at first about burning so much land just to get his tiny plot started. Upon reflection, he realized natural fires, usually caused by lightning, were common. The prairie ecosystem evolved with fire as a constant companion. The fires were not hot enough to destroy all seeds; the prairie would sprout anew in the spring. Except on Blue's land.

When the fires cooled, his hand (he called his HAL units field hands, or just hands for short) ran an Andy unit over the land and broke down the fibrous root systems to powder. No tough sod busting required. The Andy unit was also tuned to recognize the native seeds, and diced them as well. The end result was a loamy, well-fertilized soil awaiting planting.

Today he would begin to grow his barn. He had a lot of equipment and was going to get more. Farm equipment was made to suffer outside in the elements. However, he wanted to store anything with an engine inside. The equipment stayed in better shape and was easier to work on.

The Project's standard work schedule was four weeks on, four weeks off. The arrangements included a round trip to your homestead, if you had one.

Blue adjusted his shoulder holster as soon as he stepped out of the saucer. You couldn't be too careful.

The saucer pilot was unhappy and didn't help with the unloading. "It's a long way out, and back just for your postage stamp plot here," he bitched. "I better get more than a case of crappy wheat beer out of this."

Actually, pal, Blue thought to himself, *you won't.* He had other plans for the wheat.

The pilot, Gerry Bass, was grossly overqualified for an airborne bus driver. He'd done seventy missions over Vietnam, led a fighter squadron, and later commanded a large air force base. After retiring from the air force, he ran a good size company. The rumor mill had him tapped to fly the first starship, or maybe even run the entire program. He was chapped over his current assignment and eager to move on. He felt his current job beneath him. Not an uncommon attitude among the retreads, although most handled their demotions better than Gerry. Tough. Flying beat rotting in a nursing home any day.

Blue had two field hands helping him today. His own unit, Tonto, and the loaner he called Kemosabe.

Conventional construction materials were not readily available. There were no trees within sight. The closest stone was an outcrop five kilometers away. The soil wouldn't work for adobe. He didn't even have a hill to burrow into. He flew in several shed kits and constructed them on-site. A small camping trailer was flown in on a separate trip.

His field hand spent a week digging out the stone and carting gravel to the homestead. The field hands laid the gravel in trenches around the exterior. Blue then ran his Andy unit around the perimeter, which melted the gravel to a hard, solid exterior footing.

On the previous trip, the field hand had rototilled hardening enzyme into the area surveyed for the building's interior, and pounded the dirt hard and flat. In several months the enzymes would transform the dirt into a rock-hard floor.

Now, under his direction, the two hands unrolled a giant tent-like structure and secured the perimeter to the footing. The task took most of the day.

To begin, Blue blew air into the building cavity to get the membrane inflated. He then prepared the first feeding circuit for the relatively thin outer layer. The circuit consisted of a large air blower, and a device which stripped away the oxygen and trace gases from the air, leaving a carbon dioxide and nitrogen mix. The stripper had the appearance of a thick air filter. A second device then cracked the carbon dioxide molecules and stripped away the resulting oxygen. What was left were carbon atoms in a nitrogen carrier. As the mix continued through plastic ducts into the outer membrane structure, a catalyst was added, and the temperature and humidity of the mix was adjusted precisely. Within twenty-four hours the catalyst and carbon atoms turned the original carbon filaments inside the outer membrane into a lightweight web stronger than steel.

At that point a second circuit added a different catalyst, and a specific, tailored hydrocarbon was introduced into the mix in order to increase the number and thickness of the filaments. After the structure got a good start from the two barrels of hydrocarbons delivered to the site, air blowers from both circuits would continue to run for another month, stripping carbon from the air and delivering into the outer membrane. When finished, the structure would resemble a large Quonset hut with walls a hundred and fifty millimeters thick.

The end result would be a tough, strong, and well-insulated structure analogous to an eggshell. Other than the footings, the only materials used were hydrocarbons, transformed at Amazon Cove into the membrane structure, catalysts, feedstock, and enzymes. The equipment was Fab'd at Mountainside and was reusable many times. The operations people urged him to test the process, loaned the equipment, and cut him a sweet deal. All the materials and equipment were delivered in a single load.

The atmosphere on Ouranos was similar to that of an earlier Earth. However, carbon dioxide was several times the level found on today's Earth. Similar construction would have taken a year on Earth.

Looking good, thought Blue. *Assuming no tornadoes, the structure will be finished when I come back in a month. Then, I'll put in the lights, doors, power unit, and get the structure usable. I'll want to do a house and a couple more sheds next time out. I'd better work up a requisition tonight.*

In a couple days, after I check the wheat, the wards, and the barn, I'll go hunting. I'd like to get two on this trip. The dominant plains animal on this continent were aurochs, giant bovines half again the size of today's Earth cattle. The aurochs died out hundreds of years ago on Earth. Their existence here—in fact, the existence of the entire ecosphere—was a mystery. The great majority of the flora and fauna appeared to mirror Earth's. Blue hadn't heard any reasonable explanation yet.

Among his many skills, Blue was an expert butcher. Aurochs were tasty, and the kitchen paid a premium when he brought one back. Still, an aurochs was so huge, butchering one took him an entire day. He wasn't set up to grind hamburger, make sausage, or cure meats yet. That would have to wait until he got a proper kitchen set up. For now, he would stick with the basic cuts and make any scraps into stew meat. He'd brought several of the stasis units. Any food product put in a stasis container stayed fresh forever. The effect was as if all cellular processes were suspended. Blue didn't know how the container worked; however, he preferred the device over a refrigerator or freezer.

The tender shoots emerging in the burned area would attract grazers, including aurochs. The increased visibility would make hunting in the burn a hell of a lot safer than the tallgrass. Hunting aurochs was dangerous. Not only would the herd bulls stomp you to paste if offered the chance but there were also the great cats to worry about.

The great carnivores who died out a thousand years ago on Earth flourished on Ouranos. In the area of Blue's farm were saber-toothed tigers the size of Earth lions. The giant cats roamed in mated pairs. There were also plains lions, half again the size of their modern African cousin. The plains lions lived in prides of ten to twelve animals. Fortunately, the packs of gigantic dire wolves stayed closer to the mountains and rarely got this far into the plains.

The scent of blood and sight of gathering vultures meant one must quickly ward and move any downed aurochs. Field-dressing an animal without a second hunter standing guard was dangerous. The wards, drones, and field hands helped but didn't entirely eliminate the danger from the hungry cats.

Carnivores on Ouranos had no fear of man.

Blue thought the threat of nearby cats an opportunity. If successful in bagging an aurochs, he planned to watch the gut pile by drone and return once a cat was attracted. He wanted a lion skin rug.

While reading equipment specs through his enhancements that night, Blue learned he could tune a stasis box to let the contents degrade in a controlled manner. In addition to ripening fruit, one could age meat as if the cut was hanging in a well-controlled cooler. He could get the equivalent of thirty days aging in a week, and then stop once the meat was perfect. *USDA choice, here we come,* he exulted. *I wonder if the kitchen people know about this?* Wild game, being so lean, was often tough—unless stewed, or prepared exactly right. Properly aged meat was much more tender. *Maybe I could brand my meat and charge more for the product. "Blue's Better Beef" had a nice ring.* Food for thought.

His thoughts went back to the wheat. *I can't wait to see the look in Jean's eyes when I show up with a loaf of fresh-baked crusty bread. She'll drop to her knees and give me a blowjob right on the spot. I better get far enough inside I can close the door. That would be embarrassing out in the open. Shoot, half the ladies here crave bread as bad as Jean! Screw barley for brewing beer; I'm growing wheat for making flour, and delivering every single bag personally. In some ways it's a shame though. In ten years, I may be known as the man responsible for bringing the fat ass to Ouranos.*

TWENTY-SEVEN
THE RANCHER

JAMES HARRIS, AND HIS WIFE-TO-BE Susanne Russell were showing James' brother Edwin, and his girlfriend Jo-Ellen, the ranch. Rather, where the ranch would be. There wasn't much there yet.

The group all worked at Amazon Cove. The brothers were born in Oklahoma and knew their way around drill rigs and pipelines. Even with advanced technology you still had to put a hole in the ground, pump, transport, and store the oil. All of which required practical experience, which the brothers had in spades.

Siblings were rare on Ouranos. The brothers had been burned in a fire—James terribly so. Most of his extremities burned away, along with other, horrible damage. Edwin was burned in the same incident, though not as severely. Unfortunately, Edwin did not handle painkillers well and became a hopeless down-and-out fentanyl addict. When James was approached with "the deal," he insisted Edwin be included as well.

The Project's townhouses were ok. Most people built a proper house as soon as they could. Given the explosive population growth, contractors had long waiting lists. Many people acquired a lot in town and started building themselves. However, the Harris brothers did not want neighbors and spent their time off starting a ranch well away from anyone else. The men wanted buy-in from the ladies. Suzy appeared sold; Jo-Ellen was not.

"The flunkies are cutting stone for the house walls at a quarry about a kilometer over that way," said James, waving vaguely to his right. "The house will go up quick once the materials are ready. The milking shed will go there next to the barn. The tool shed and holding pens over there," he said, pointing.

"The technology is unbelievable," he continued. "With a cargo container of equipment, I can build almost everything—the barn, outbuildings, and a house, from materials found on the property. With power from the tractor, flunkies, an Andy, and hand tools, I'll have the house ready in a few months. The appliances came with the Homestead starter kit. The rest of the buildings will go up after the house is finished. Of course, the barn is the first thing we did.

"The flunkies cut timber, sawed out planks and beams using a specialized Andy. After the wood dried for a season, the pair put up a simple pole barn. I did have to buy nails.

"The foundation is in for the house. The flunkies spent the last week cutting the stone for the walls. Tomorrow they'll start carting the blocks over. The day after, we start putting up the walls. I'm not an expert, but the country rock appears limestone. I do know about stone floors. I've found a great quality travertine deposit back in the hills. I had travertine floors back on Earth and loved them. I'll quarry my own stone for the floors. I may even start selling fancy floor stone to others in town.

"I wanted a slate roof. They last a hundred years, as I intend to do. Unfortunately, there is no suitable deposit nearby, so I'm going with copper sheathing. I had to buy the copper, however it's dirt cheap.

"The timber is superb. I'll have the most beautiful ceiling beams you ever saw. I'll run a Texas porch on two sides of the house.

"The Andy cuts and joins everything you can think of. I even used the thing to make stone water and sewage pipes. We cut a small trough in the rock, filled it with sand, and ran the programmed Andy down the length. A minute later we had a hard-walled pipe full of sand, which we simply pour out. There were stretches coming down from the water tank where we cut pipes in situ, about eighteen inches down. Every ten feet I'd cut a plug, suck out the sand, and re-cap the rock. I'll have to use copper pipes in the house; the stone is too heavy and cumbersome to use inside.

"I'm planning to make a large, grand house. Something only a cattle baron, oil millionaire, or politician could afford back on Earth.

"When the house is livable, we'll start on Edwin's. I've got a beautiful spot picked out about a kilometer away. If he wants the place."

"I'm sure the place will be fine and dandy a couple years from now, once you get it built and all," said Jo-Ellen too sweetly. "But doesn't a ranch need cows?" Jo-Ellen was a country girl, but all the years of college and later, city living, left her aware of certain drawbacks involved in ranching.

"How funny," retorted James. "The cattle are grazing. I haven't got them trained yet to come when I call. The herd will perform for you the next time you visit. They will fetch, and roll over on command too."

"Both of them?" she shot back.

Everyone laughed, but a bit weakly. Fortunately, the ladies got along. James was working on Edwin to go in with him on the ranch. Edwin was almost convinced; Jo-Ellen was holding him back.

The group retired to Adirondack style chairs under a shady tree for cool drinks and to hear out James.

"It's true I only have a handful of milk cows," he said. "Obviously, I had to import the breed, and shipping cost a grotesque amount of money. I got the best dairy cows money can buy. Jersey's. Only one's being milked right now."

The others nodded. Transport from Earth was extremely expensive. No sense in skimping on the cargo quality.

"However, I do have two excellent bulls. I plan to also breed them to the wild cattle to supplement the dairy herd. People are sorely missing dairy products. Milk, cheese, and butter are all in high demand, which translates to high prices—"

Suzy cut in. "Which means we will operate a dairy as well. We'd like to make everything, even cheese."

"How the heck is that going to work?" asked Jo-Ellen. Edwin wasn't going to turn down his brother. Or even negotiate the deal very hard. She was stuck playing the evil witch. Damn if she was going to restart her life over as a young lass to wear muddy boots, and milk cows on a remote ranch. "Somebody must be here all day, every day, to milk, feed, and shovel shit. That won't fly with the four of us working full-time jobs. We're fifty kilometers away from town, with no roads. I don't think any of us is looking to break contract. I'm know I'm not risking my next re-life."

James leaned back and smiled broadly. "A HAL flunky, of course. Feeding, and shoveling manure, is simple manual labor. I've also taught

Fuck-up and Fuck-off—pardon my French—to milk." James's HAL units were named after two grad student interns he had the misfortune of working with years earlier.

The others looked dubious.

"Think about it," he continued, "nobody's milked by hand for years. Even Daddy used machinery. Only a few things still involve the human touch. Even those can be done by a HAL. I'll show you in the morning. Truth be told, it was as much training the cow as the flunky. That's why I haven't trained the herd to fetch, and roll over yet," he teased Jo-Ellen. "Been busy teaching both parties to milk."

She smiled thinly as the others laughed.

James got more serious. "There is plenty of good pasture. I've put up wards to protect the cattle. A flunky can move them to and from the barn for milking and grazing. I'll put in corn to supplement the diet and keep them fat. We'll store the milk in a stasis container, and transport it to town once a week. The dairy will be in town. We need human hands for the dairy, so we have to locate it in town, or at least nearby. People are funny about flunkies preparing food, and there are regulations on what is allowed. The regulations don't directly address a dairy. We'll push hard on the grey areas.

"We've all worked in a dairy." Sure, if driving a forklift on the dock counted. "We'll pick up what we need to know real fast.

"I also plan to collect wild cattle and contain them in several large pastures using wards. Their fields will have graze and natural water sources, so we'll ignore them until fall. Then we let them loose in a cornfield for a month before butchering. There ain't no slaughterhouses established yet. However, I know a good butcher.

"Of course, I'll separate some young stock to benefit from our bulls."

His audience was doubtful of breeding a domestic Jersey bull to a wild longhorn. James pressed on.

"I've discussed this with folks further up the totem pole. The Crown will grant us a limited license to herd and harvest wild cattle on Royal land.

"Anybody else will have to breed wild cattle for fifty years to even get close to my Jersey stock. I'll never sell a bull. Once we get established, we can freeze out any competition. We'll have the dairy herd, and the only dairy in existence. We'll get rich!

"This location is on the saucer route between Amazon Cove and Shoreside. The stasis containers will ship to town easy-peasy.

"It seems half the women on the planet are pregnant," said James, while looking at Suzy. She blushed. "To bottle-feed, they'll have to buy our milk."

Oh, hell, thought Jo-Ellen. *I'd better think of something fast. I'm not going to ranch, especially out here, and I don't want to lose Edwin. James has something up his sleeve. A guy who built a ten-million-a-year oil-field servicing business is no dummy. He's too smart to think he can get rich price-gouging women with infants in arm. That's a good way to end up swinging from a short rope tied to a tall tree.*

Then, the reason came to her. Simple, debt capacity. He didn't know enough to get subsidies from the Crown when he brought in the small—well, tiny—dairy herd. *He's overextended and needs cheap financing from us to finance the dairy. A person's ability to borrow was their most valuable possession. That rat-bastard. He plans to get rich and pay his friends and family back a few percent in interest.*

"Here's what I'll agree to," Jo-Ellen said. "Edwin and I will finance, own, and operate the dairy. Obviously, the facility needs to be in town, which will be Amazon Cove. I already have land there, and I know a couple granola types who would be interested in making cheese and yogurt. They really miss their yogurt.

"Now, you'll sell us the milk at a fair price. You hear me, James? A fair price. If you try to screw your friends and family, I swear I'll buy goat's milk instead, and watch you slaughter your dairy herd for dog food.

"Does that sound good to you Edwin?" she asked. He nodded vigorously.

Jo-Ellen and James hammered out the details and bullied the other two into agreement. Jo-Ellen would provide financing and would own the dairy. Edwin would kick in some funds and contribute his time (which would keep him in town), and the efforts of a flunky at a rock bottom rate. Jo-Ellen would retain rights to any skills learned by the flunky.

James tried tweaking the deal a couple times, but Jo-Ellen held firm. "Stick to ranching," she told him. "Don't be distracted by the dairy. You'll be busy for years building your herd and the dairy will be a sideline the whole time. Properly finished beef will sell like hotcakes, now, today."

James eventually came around, and the group relaxed.

That night Jo-Ellen found herself humming a tune while helping Suzy clean up the kitchen in the cramped trailer. The men were by the campfire, each smoking a rare cigarette, and spitting.

"You seem in a good mood," remarked Suzy.

"Life is good," Jo-Ellen replied. A small dairy herd didn't require a lot of land. She figured in a few years she and Edwin would have the entire herd of Jerseys on a hundred hectares on the edge of town, and the dairy. She'd manage the dairy and Edwin would look after the cows. Why in hell put the cows in the middle of nowhere and transport the milk? Dumb.

She would also look into the process of making baby formula. Her grandmother may have used cow's milk, but powdered formula caught on for good reasons.

James seemed happy to raise beef and play cowboy in the middle of nowhere. Jo-Ellen and Edwin would have a great life, in town. Granted, the town wasn't much yet, but the place was poised to grow.

"Gotta hand it to you," said Edwin to James. "She took the bait. Hook, line, and sinker."

"Yup," said James, spitting into the fire. "If we made the proposal flat out, she would have dismissed it out of hand. She had to think of the idea on her own. This way she's married to the idea and committed to make the dairy work out.

"Like I'd ever want to own a dairy," James continued. "The work is endless, way more than you'd think. I'd get sucked in and end up spending my time working indoors. Can you see me in a beard bag wearing a silly little paper hat making cheese? No. Thank. You. The flunky will do the milking, I'll send the containers to town, and that's it. Done.

"This way everyone's happy," James concluded. "I'll be able to spend my off-shift time out here, outside, running cattle, and growing a little corn. I'll stay busy building my place, and not worry over spilt milk."

TWENTY-EIGHT
THE PLANNER

ANNA MEDLOCK WAS THE MOST popular girl in town, if not the entire world. Anna was attractive, but not stunning. Her personality was outgoing, but not outrageously so. She wasn't promiscuous. Nevertheless, a steady stream of flowers, cards, candy, and little gifts arrived like clockwork. Everyone said hello on the street, and if she accepted all her invitations, she could have her choice of dinner companion every night.

Anna planned Fab production in Mountainside. If you wanted something Fab'd, you had to go through Anna. On her office wall was the parable For Want of a Nail: 'For want of a nail the shoe was lost. For want of a shoe the horse was lost. For want of a horse the rider was lost. For want of a rider the message was lost. For want of a message the battle was lost. For want of a battle the kingdom was lost.'

Her job was to maximize Fab output while satisfying a mass of mutually exclusive goals and objectives. She thought of the constraints as the sides to a box. The king had decreed that half of Fab output was to benefit his people, the other half was for The Project. Ok, fine. Another major constraint was Fab capacity would grow by a factor of three every year. Ok, plan for more Fabs, and bigger Fabs. The need for raw materials grew accordingly.

The Fabs, and the products they manufactured, required certain raw materials. Their largest Fab could put forth a complete saucer—a small one so far—in a single cycle. To do so required dozens of different minerals and carbon inputs be in queue, ready to load, when the Fab opened up.

Raw material planning was less controversial. Anna had an assistant who finally had that side under control. Anna spent most of her workday planning Fab output. To special-order an item, one submitted an online request. If the estimated delivery date was unsatisfactory, call Anna. If you didn't like the cut of the clothes in your wardrobe, you ordered something different. If the priority was deemed low, call Anna. In fact, for anything not kept in a warehouse, you put in a requisition, hoped for the best, and called Anna with any problems.

Adele Krieger got on Anna's good side, and did quite well. "Look," Adele explained, "personal hygiene and grooming products are for the most part the same base goo. You shampoo and condition your hair with goo while in the shower. You wash your face with goo. You shave your legs, brush your teeth, and rub goo in your pits to keep the odor down. I've been working with the Fab AI for weeks and learned how to get all those products without doing dozens of small custom runs. We can take one barrel of hydrocarbons—oil—and process once into four different feedstocks. Then we make a second pass with those four feed stocks and make a hundred plastic bottles or tubes of each of the hundred different products I've identified. Boom, done! Enough toothpaste, shaving cream, soap, and hair products to last the whole town for months. The output is all premium first-rate copies of designer products. You, Anna, will no longer have to deal with fifty custom requests every month. Since the Fab processing time is a whole lot less, the product is less expensive to make.

"People are not happy with the standard-issue products. Do this for me, and I'll stock and resell the products. People will get excellent products at a lower price, with no lead time. You'll be happy, they'll be happy, and I'll make a bundle. Sound good?"

Adele got her products and one of a thousand details became less annoying for Anna.

One by one Anna organized the recurring items. The HAL units were created four at a time in one dedicated Fab. Homesteader starter kits became standardized, and prepacked in cargo crates. One crate held everything needed to equip a new home—appliances, kitchen, bathrooms, plumbing, electrical, and numerous household goods. Another crate held items for gardening—even a small tractor. Six containers would hold everything a homestead needed.

Artificial fabrics were made in one pass through the Fab; clothing was prepared in a separate run. The separate passes were vastly more efficient in Fab time than attempting to do everything in one cycle. A warehouse held dozens of fabrics in various styles and colors. People placed orders online, and once every week or two, a Fab would be loaded with the right fabrics. Finished clothes, curtains, and bedding came out shortly afterwards.

As the Fab complex at Mountainside grew, Anna was able to dedicate a Fab to custom orders, and charged accordingly.

Now, Anna was planning the production of a starship.

A traditional aerospace executive would have been incredulous. The planning committee consisted of only five people: Anna; the Mountainside and Amazon Cove managers, John Hayward and Juan Perez, respectively; and the pilots Gerry Bass and Ken Edson. None of the group had training or experience in aerospace engineering, or manufacturing.

The group included a sixth member. Not a person, but a Chait AI. The AI provided several different base starship designs based on the preliminary mission requirements. There was no hundred-man engineering team calculating trade-offs among power, weight, capability, and a myriad of other factors. There were no quality, safety, or finance people cluttering the agenda.

"How do we know these figures are correct?" asked Gerry, waving a large sheet of actual paper in the air. "Let's take for example, a sixty-day oxygen reserve. How do we know that's a good number? What are the assumptions, the constraints? How do we know sixty days is the number we truly need? Are we cutting it too close, or taking way more than we need—with the resulting weight penalty? In fact, how do we know the air plant itself works as advertised?"

"All good, legitimate questions," replied John, who chaired the group. "And one might have similar questions for every line on this summary spec. How do we know? Taking the question literally, there's several possible answers.

"We might find a dozen engineers, spend a week or two getting them up to speed, and ask them to verify the numbers. Or we miraculously find one exactly perfect person, a former submarine officer, or somebody with relevant experience in the space program, and ask them the question. A qualified person will tell us if our planned oxygen reserve equates to sixty days of breathing, or not. However, that person couldn't tell us the tradeoff between a single tank, or multiple tanks, or the proper locations to minimize risk from micrometeorite punctures. They could offer informed opinions on the adequacy of the environmental system, but at the end of the day it's only an informed opinion.

"We either trust the AI or have a hundred engineers spend years verifying figures in the spec. Of course, we don't have a hundred qualified engineers, and we don't have a year of slack in the schedule to poke at the design."

John continued, "The way we are going to proceed is to trust the AI, but verify. Gerry, you're the overall project manager, and oversee the construction. I'd like you to get a small group, no more than three or four people, and have them poke at the design, verify as much as feasible, but do so in parallel with the construction. If a fatal flaw emerges, which is unlikely, we'll retrofit before launch."

Gerry nodded. His reflexes, developed over forty years of working for large organizations, had triggered his burst of cover-your-ass.

John continued, "Even though it flies, His Lord's Vessel, the *Argo*, is more of a ship than a plane. The crew must perform for weeks at a time. The circumstances are totally different than a long shift in a cockpit. As a former ship's captain, Ken is well-qualified to ensure the working and living arrangements allow the bridge crew to operate at a high level of performance for extended periods of time. The crew needs a comfortable environment, good food, clean clothes, and all the things necessary to keep the stress down. Please go over to those parts of the design closely. I know you and Gerry are more interested in flight characteristics, and how many Gs you can pull in a turn than living conditions for the crew." The flyers smiled. "But you're not just pilots anymore."

John changed the subject. "We need to understand the schedule constraints, if any, to make an effective plan." This time John was the one waving a large sheet of paper. "So, Anna, please educate us."

"We now have advanced to a Fab large enough to produce a saucer in a single run," she began. "However, the power units and field generators are so time-intensive, we still produce those separately, and then install once the saucer comes out. That's a much more efficient use of Fab time.

"However, the *Argo* is much bigger than even our largest saucer. For this vessel we plan on making the metallic components at Mountainside, and then ship to Amazon Cove for assembly. The major components are the power units, batteries, field generators, and all the electronics used for command, control, and navigation.

"The fuselage and wing blisters are primarily carbon constructs, and will be Fab'd at the large unit now coming online at the Cove. Even so, the fuselage will be built in segments, and joined by specialized Andy's. The joining is a lengthy process; the fuselage is a sandwich of dozens of layers. Each joining must be perfect, down to the molecular level." The others nodded; none of this was news to them. "The fuselage and wing blisters also have a large requirement for more than a dozen different metals, either to dope the carbon or provide exotic alloys for specific layers.

"So, when I schedule the material requirements, I get this result." A schedule, splotched with red, appeared in front of their eyes. "Don't panic, the schedule is not as bad as it first appears. I've spoken to the new extraction manager, Mike Siple— he's a godsend, by the way—and most of these can easily be squeezed from the current supply base." The display twitched, and most of the red went away. "The three remaining problem children are Hafnium, Boron, and Niobium. Each of these will require a new extraction site, and six to eight weeks of mining to pull what we need for the *Argo*. Of course, extraction will take another six to eight weeks for each additional vessel afterwards."

The entire planet had been surveyed in depth by the Chait long before man came. The size and richness of every significant ore deposit was known, and mapped. The Chait database was available to the colony. No prospecting was required. One simply looked up the required mineral and planned accordingly. In a sense the depth of knowledge seemed a shame. No prospectors with mules were needed. The romance was gone from the industry.

"I don't have insight into the hydrocarbon supply, I'm not supplied with the Amazon Cove production schedule, just a yes or no when I ask for quantity or delivery dates. Those lines are marked in yellow for now."

Juan was defensive. "If you'd asked, we would have supplied you the data. Besides, the ship will be built here. I run everything here. I'll be planning the schedule for the Fabs here, at Amazon Cove. It's you who needs to give me the schedule information for the other components."

John could have throttled the jerk. This was a responsibility issue for the two of them to work out between them. Juan had no business dumping on Anna. He could see Gerry spooling up as well. Ken was enjoying the show.

"Well, Juan, I'm glad you brought the subject up," said John calmly. "Hold that thought. I see Gerry has something to say."

"I've only been program manager for ten days," began Gerry. "That's outrageous. Somebody should have been working this for the last year. We've lost a year. We can't make that up."

"That's an overly dramatic view of the state of affairs," retorted Juan. "The group has a good handle on the supply chain, the Fabs are consistent in operations, and we've assembled saucers—if not spacecraft—before. We've managed to get along just fine."

"Not totally correct," replied Gerry briskly. "So far, the people involved in this project have approached the activity as if manufacturing a hammer. Where are the staff? The pilots and crew? Where's the ground support? What about housing? The assembly building will be immense, a couple hundred meters on a side. I don't see one sitting out there. I also don't see a paved apron leading from the Fab to the assembly site, or from assembly to any pad. The existing saucer pads are inadequate and I haven't heard of plans to upgrade, or make a new dedicated pad for the *Argo*. Assembly will require a swarm of specialized devices from floaters to move components, to customized Andy and HAL units. None of which yet exist."

Ken spoke for the first time. "No shit. I need to identify the pilot candidates, and get a flight simulator online as soon as possible."

Gerry's polished executive persona was coming out. He spoke crisply in a nonconfrontational tone. "Obviously Anna does a tremendous job in managing the Fabs; however, that's all she does. She doesn't have responsibility for the program's facility requirements at Amazon Cove." Anna was nodding in agreement.

"As I've said, I've only been on the job a short time," continued Gerry. "Most of which I just mentioned is on me now to make happen. I'd appreciate it, Juan, if you'd bring me and the group up to speed on the status of the ancillary structures and the project pre-work accomplished, here at Amazon Cove."

Juan blustered and cast blame on Anna and everyone else. He deflected, denied, and waved his arms a lot. Obviously, nothing was being done.

John wrapped things up. "Good meeting." From his view the meeting went great. Juan was toast. "Gerry, I'm really glad to see you onboard. The obvious next step is a deep dive into the technical and operational requirements of the entire project. We need to better understand the requirements before spending time on the schedule. Juan, I'd like you to deputize someone with project management experience to work with Gerry and Ken on this. Anna, I have the same request for you. However, please stay involved. You are the best we have at this, and we need all the help we can get.

"Now that Gerry's on board, please go to him rather than me with any issues. He's running the show now," John concluded.

Nothing more was said of Juan managing the great Fab at Amazon Cove.

John dropped by, bearing coffee, and spoke with Anna afterwards. He was grooming her for larger roles and actively asked for her opinion. Partly to test her judgement, partly to make her feel valued, but mostly because she was thoughtful and gave great input.

John thought Anna would be a good town manager to succeed him, once the interstellar craft were built and flying. Once the great vessels were active, the king would be conferring patents of nobility on key people. Those titles would come with thousands of hectares of land, Fab access, HAL allotments, and certain rights to govern subjects. John planned on being the Duke of Mountainside.

TWENTY-NINE
MEETING IN THE OVAL OFFICE

T HEY MET IN THE OVAL Office. The president, her chief political advisor, chief of staff, and the National Security Advisor. And Jon Gallock.

"At last we meet, Mister Gallock," said the president. "You're a hard man to get ahold of." The president and her staff pretended the meeting was informal. Everyone sat on sofas around a coffee table.

Jon did not apologize. "I get a lot of prank calls," replied Jon. "And the gentleman who eventually left a message didn't seem credible. I had my staff google his name and apparently, he's a world authority on soybeans. I couldn't imagine why I should talk to him."

The president's staff rarely needed more than a few hours to locate and pull somebody in for a meeting. The aides tried for two weeks before corralling Gallock. The president's earlier request to have a PhD contact him had been passed down three levels to a twenty-something staffer who found a former professor of agriculture on the national security staff. Jon blew him off.

An attractive man, the president thought. Good shoulders, in good shape, good hair. He seemed quite comfortable in the intimidating surroundings of the Oval Office. So much so he brought no functionaries with him. He came alone.

If only she knew.

"Mister Gallock, the president said, "I have asked the FBI to open an investigation into you, and your associates, for kidnapping, grand larceny, smuggling, conspiracy, and whatever else the agency deems appropriate. Spiriting our citizens away in the dark of night, in secret, is outrageous, and I will not tolerate your actions.

"Furthermore, we are classifying all Chait technology based on the threat it poses to the national security of the country," she continued. "You personally, and the companies you represent, will immediately cease and desist from disseminating any and all such technology, and turn over all related documentation to the FBI. You may not retain any documentation. Should you fail to comply, you'll be prosecuted and sent to federal prison. Is that clear, Mister Gallock?"

"She's bluffing," said a voice in Jon's head. "She's spoken to no one but her political staff over this. Other than drafts prepared back in the beginning by the various intelligence agencies, nobody's pushed a pencil on this subject. Nobody in the White House has drafted anything, there's no executive order being prepared, no FBI warrants, nothing. And, of course, the patents are filed, publicly, in half the developed countries on the planet."

Jon reached into his inside coat pocket and pulled out a small leather case. He extracted a business card and wrote a name on the back. "Please send all formal notices to our company attorney," he requested, "not to me. My personal attorney is with the same firm; I've written his name here." He slid the business card across the table to the president. "See that he's notified for anything meant for me, personally. For convenience, please send two hard copies of each notice. You should also beam copies to Jupiter, to the Chait directly."

"Neither the agency nor myself work for you, Mister Gallock," the president said tartly.

"Actually," interrupted Jon, "you do. I'm a United States citizen and a taxpayer. At least for several more years. Every person in this room works for me. You said so yourself, loudly and proudly, multiple times during your campaign."

Great, she thought. *One of those.*

The president began her lecture. "The average US citizen has received nothing from your association with the Chait, Mister Gallock. Oh, a few, a very few, might have a better battery in their leaf blower, or a computer chip in their car that's not distinguishable, to them, from one they had five years ago. As a citizen you've done nothing for your country with your relationship with the extraterrestrials. You, and the people that work for you, may call yourselves Americans, but pass off advanced technology to everybody else on the planet, in many cases to unfriendly regimes. You've personally benefited by this chance relationship to the tune of millions and millions of dollars, while your government, and your fellow citizens, have received virtually nothing. The people know this, and I'll make sure they don't forget."

Jon was unruffled. "What would you have me hog for our country, and keep from the rest of humanity? The flavor of the week with the flying monkeys of the press is clean, cheap power. Let's take that as an example. We, the human race, already have technology for multiple sources of clean, cheap power. The technologies are simply stifled, taxed, demonized, and regulated by the government to the point of being useless.

"China or India can build a power plant in four years. The US can't build the same plant in twelve years due to federal regulatory red tape. So, if a hypothetical source of power is kept solely for the benefit of America, the US citizen will see no benefit for twelve years, everybody on the planet is unhappy with the US, and you've alienated the aliens. Sounds like a lose-lose-lose proposition to me.

"And best of luck in classifying Chait technology. I imagine that will prove a challenge. Of course, if you're successful the aliens will simply find another middleman, a foreign middleman, and offer a similar deal. I wonder if the voters will forgive or forget that.

"I appreciate the situation you're in, Madam President. Keeping to the same example of clean, cheap power, should a magical power plant technology appear, something better than a more complicated way to boil water, much of the world will see the benefit years before any Americans. That's our fault. Everything from power plant components to computer chips aren't built much here anymore. We've driven most manufacturing to Asia. The benefit of Chait technology will happen there first. Much of the world is set to improve faster than we do. Unless the political climate changes, the US will actually become poorer—not in absolute terms but relative to other countries. That's on you, and your administration.

"Ironically, developing countries will receive the benefit of advanced technologies before more mature states, such as America. The new megaconductor technology is already rolling out in the Chinese and Indian power grids as they add capacity. Payback for European, or North

American companies to retrofit, though quite lucrative, is much slower. Cellphone proliferation is a great example. Many third world countries never put in phone lines; they went straight from nothing to cellular."

"Mister Gallock," the president said, "you will play ball with us or life will become difficult."

"I love my country," said Jon. "I consider myself a patriot. However, I've already prepared the paperwork to formally renounce my citizenship. I haven't filed yet. Yes, I'm aware the government will take about half my property when I do so. I'd rather that happen later rather than sooner. I want to see this affair through to a successful conclusion. However, I'm mentally prepared for any eventuality.

"No hard feelings though," continued Jon. "I mean that sincerely. Whatever happens, XSolarian will follow through with a planned ten-million-dollar contribution to the Banana Slug Foundation."

The president had taken the political construct of a supposedly-but-not-really arm's-length nonprofit to another level. These nonprofits used funds extorted from "donors" to employ friends, family, staff, and other associates in between political jobs, into well-paying, lightly taxing positions. Her alma mater had several associated educational foundations, one named after the school's mascot. The president's pet nonprofit was a subsidiary of the university's foundation, which added a level of opacity, and tax leverage, to the activities. The practice had been subsequently legislated out of existence, except for a couple existing entities which were grandfathered in.

"How are we doing?" subvocalized Jon through his enhancements once he was in the car.

"You seem to have bought some time," the voice in his head, Robert, replied. "The meeting purpose was to put you on a leash, and gain control over your relationship with the Chait. The president and her staff don't see how your success will help them in the next election. However, your activities are mildly popular with the public, so they are cautious about coming down on you too hard, yet. The group is still talking; however, no one is mentioning a follow-through on the threats. The ten million dollars allowed them to save face. The president believes she scared you out of the funds."

"Have I bought any goodwill?" asked Jon.

"Not really," Robert replied. "The foundation will keep the money, of course, but don't expect any favors. The president will be mildly embarrassed for a few days when word gets out, but that's never been a significant problem in the past.

"My assessment," Robert continued, "is the administration will come down hard one way or another, a full court press as you would say, about ninety days before the election. The lack of consideration for the health and prosperity of the subject population is quite remarkable. All potential material benefits are ignored, while only political ramifications affecting a handful of people are ever discussed, or considered.

"Four chances out of five, the administration will come down against us, and you. I'll let you know when the president decides to take concrete action," Robert finished.

The enhancements worked great, allowing Jon and his people to communicate invisibly among themselves, and the Chait. Listening in on the president while she discussed matters with her staff was another huge benefit of Chait technology.

"This is why I detest what our Republic has become," said Jon. "Politicians seeking power for its own sake. A hundred bureaucracies, with the power to write their own laws, employ their own judges and maintain their own police forces. And poorly informed citizens pay for everything.

"I'll never allow this on Ouranos. I'm eternally grateful to you for granting me the planet. As it's my property, I'll never allow grasping busybodies to write laws putting strings on me, and expect me to fund their fantasies."

I'll have to actively manage the executive branch for a while, thought Jon as he headed to the airport. *I'll use the age-old carrot and a stick technique, and repeat regularly.*

THIRTY
THE CRUISE

JON AND CASEY WERE ABOARD a Chait spacecraft, headed to Hephaestus for a photo op with the tourists. This was Casey's first interstellar trip. Travel time was two days out, and two back. They had the craft to themselves.

They had wild-animal sex three times a day.

The Inner Circle spent a lot of time flying. On this trip Jon filed a flight plan to the island of St Helena, but deplaned from the corporate jet in Windhoek, Namibia. A driver met them and took them ten kilometers into the desert where the Chait spacecraft picked them up.

"Do you think anyone knows we've left?" Casey asked Jon. Governments around the globe kept them under intensive watch.

"Probably," he said. "But we can't make life easy for them. Three different navies have diverted detachments to St Helena in hopes of grabbing a Chait saucer. Every intelligence agency in the world is tracking us. We can't get complacent and fall into a routine, especially when getting a lift. A lot of people would love to shoot down, and loot, a Chait spaceship. Besides, a visit to Namibia is always nice."

With enhancements the Inner Circle could work efficiently from anywhere in the solar system. After several virtual meetings Casey asked Jon's advice on how far to go using the functionality.

"The functionality is up to you," he said. "We each have different wants and needs. I've advised everyone to load an unarmed combat ghost into primary. Other than that, it's your personal preference."

Enhancements came with different physical skill sets organized into distinct and separate overlays, called ghosts. Over a hundred separate ghosts were available. These came as simple as touch typing, to as complex as basketball or motocross racing. The motor skills were the level of a Division I college athlete. Skills ranged from tennis or swimming to more serious activities such as evasive driving, piloting an aircraft, or gun fighting.

All these skills were available, in background, to pull and apply as needed. One could also run one or more in primary mode.

Unless one ran a ghost in primary mode, the usefulness was limited. A swimmer with excellent strokes and perfect flip turns will fade fast unless his physical condition is already good. A concert pianist who hasn't played in a couple years can still play well, but quickly turns ragged. One needs muscle to have great muscle memory. When a program was run in primary, the body actually developed the muscles used in the particular skill. You could run more than one program in primary; however, the necessary muscles developed much slower if more than one or two ghosts were selected.

With muscle memory came the vocabulary, and knowledge of the skill. One "just knew" the rules around the associated scoring, tactics, and strategy once the ghost was loaded.

Now, on a long private trip, Jon and Casey had time to get to know each other better.

"Maybe you'd like to become a left-handed player," Jon joked. Casey had lettered for the University of Hawaii tennis team and still played regularly. "If you knew any deaf people, you could learn to sign—ASL. How about juggling? Let's see, you're from Hawaii, so maybe hula dancing? How about the horizontal mamba—not that you need to improve in bed. Ouch!" Casey slugged him on the shoulder.

"I'm serious," she said. "Which ghosts do you run in primary?"

"The unarmed combat ghost, of course," he replied. "I've enriched my version towards grappling as it complements my body type. Tennis, since we've started spending time together—it's for self-defense when I'm playing against you. Although, we only play once a month. Ouch!

"I've also cobbled together skills related to interpersonal observation," continued Jon more seriously. "The skills are more mental than physical—although I've improved my hearing, eyesight, and memory. I have the observational skills of an elite bodyguard, someone who watches over the president, or the King of England. I can assess a person's shoes, jewelry, haircut, posture, fingernails, a million things, in a split second to determine friend or foe, or even their profession. I've found this quite useful in high-level meetings. I read most people like a book. I'm to the point I see and interpret minute changes in pupil dilation, pulse, respiration, even body odor. I can even tell when pundits lie on TV—my keen senses detect their lips moving. Ouch! Quit doing that!

"Reading body language is a related skill. The ability allows me to tell when a person is nervous, uncomfortable, deceptive, or about to slug my shoulder.

"The interpersonal skills even include medical knowledge," Jon continued. "Just by looking at a person on the street an experienced doctor can detect telltale signs of illnesses or injury. A doc can sit on a park bench and watch them walk by; 'that guy has heart trouble, the next one has the beginning of osteoporosis, her thyroid is out of whack, wonder where he caught malaria.' A chiropractor notices a hip or shoulder a fraction of an inch out of whack, and even knows what injury led to the misalignment

"Another example is drug abusers. A cocaine user has different signs than a heroin addict, which is different than meth, which is different than alcohol, which is different than pot, which differs from Benadryl abuse. I have all those observational skills, and the knowledge to interpret what I'm seeing, and more.

"I can lip-read, even foreign languages if I have loaded them beforehand. Which I do before meetings with those who don't speak English or learned it as a second language.

"When I enter a high-level meeting, I might as well be negotiating with children. Even with experienced politicians or businessmen the tells are obvious. The scary part is the Chait almost certainly read people better than me, better than any of us.

"Hey, I ghost-play the guitar. I've run the program in primary a month now. Look here." He held out his hand, palm up and fingers slightly curled. She took his hand and looked intently. She gently rubbed his fingertips and looked him in the face quizzically. She had the darkest eyes, the whitest teeth, and the most amazing skin he'd ever seen. *Oh boy*, he thought. *I got it bad.*

"I've grown calluses on my fingertips without touching a string," Jon said. "Just to play for a pretty lady named Kailani Caitlyn Tanaka by a campfire under an alien moon." The lovers smooched. Pulse and respiration rose.

When they came up for air, Casey was still processing the implications of enhancements. "It pisses me off that a person can download a ghost and play competitive tennis the next day," she complained. "I worked my ass off for ten years to get to this level, and now any yay-hoo can play in a day. Even though the newbie is only capable in short bursts, it's still scary. I'm creeped out. The things which make us who we are, are copied and passed out like candy."

"That's exactly the reason we keep this a deep, dark secret," replied Jon. "If word of this ever got out, the public backlash would be uncontrollable.

"Only those of the Inner Circle have the ability to run ghosts," Jon continued. "Enhancements for others, even on Ouranos, include only the communication, memory, and query abilities. The knowledge base available for query is huge and includes the one percent of internet content that's actually useful.

"I've asked Robert the origin of these skill sets a number of times. Some of the knowledge could have come from books, like the theory of musical scales, or how to score bowling. However, the muscle memory has to somehow be downloaded straight from an individual. Robert doesn't ever give a straight answer. I doubt Robert's people take a highly skilled person, put him in a blender, and extract the good stuff. Can the Chait possibly read brain, muscle, and nerve activity at a distance? Or do they kidnap trained people, run the specimens through some type of recorder, and let them loose the next morning reeking of alcohol? Do the Chait employ human agents unknown to you or I? I just don't know.

"What I do know," said Jon with a smirk, "quantitatively, thanks to my enhancements, is my adrenaline and semen levels have risen to a level acceptable for another round. What do you say, babe?"

THIRTY-ONE
THE TOURISTS

"BEFORE THE CLOSING CEREMONY," THE scoutmaster said, "Mike Morris, our Senior Patrol Leader, is going to speak for a few minutes about his recent trip."

Mike, a seventeen-year-old high school senior and eagle scout candidate for troop 582, stepped forward. "For those living under a rock and haven't heard, I, and eleven others, were selected to tour habitable planets on a Chait spacecraft. I got back four days ago.

"I was told to be at the airport at six am on the day of departure. A couple of guys picked me up in a private jet. We flew to Canada, then Paris, then doubled back to Ireland. I heard, but can't confirm, there were threats against the Chait spacecraft, so the XSolarian people shuffled us tourists around a few times before boarding in Ireland.

"A dozen of us made the trip. Everyone spoke English. I think everybody was a student, mostly college students. I don't know about the others, but I was selected because I'm awesome." Good-natured jeers, and one inappropriate comment came from the assembled group. "Bite me, Dombrowski," Mike retorted cheerfully.

"There was me and two others from the US," Mike continued. "There were three from Europe, two Chinese, two Japanese, and a lady from Lithuania. The lady from Lithuania clearly did not consider herself either European, or Russian. She was hot.

"Three supposed tour guides"—Mike made air quotes with his fingers—"came with us, two men and a woman. All three were really buff and had scars. Whenever you'd ask for something, one would point and grunt 'get it yourself.' Whenever we landed, all three would gear up with body armor and guns, and two would go out first to clear the area. The so-called 'tour guides' were twitchy the entire time, even on ship. It's obvious they were really bodyguards.

"We never saw any Chait. A pilot would speak to us in perfect English. I don't know if he was in an area sealed off from the rest of us, or if the craft was a drone, piloted remotely. The Chait said to call him Pom, short for pomegranate. I don't know why. I was really disappointed to not see a Chait—and Pom rarely spoke.

"Inside, the spacecraft was a cross between a fancy cruise ship and the bizjet I flew in on. The interior was really nice, but small. There was a common room about twenty by thirty, and a second smaller room for eating. We had small cabins with bunk beds and slept two to a cabin. I roomed with a guy from Germany named Wit. He was pretty cool.

"We had boxed meals. Really first-rate stuff, like something you'd get from a sit-down restaurant. You selected from a menu, and a few minutes later the light would blink, you'd open the door, and your food was ready. It was like the world's best vending machine.

"We visited four planets. Travel time was about two days each time. Somebody was lazy and named the planets after Greek or Roman gods. No cool names like in *Star Wars*, or *Star Trek*, no Sigma Draconis IV, or anything like that.

"We visited Attis, Caerus, Hephaestus, and Pontus. I posted pictures on my Facebook page, but I've heard a lot of people are blocked. So, Mister Heller is going to put them up on the troop page. I'll also do a full hour's talk with slides next week. Specs for the exoplanets are on the XSolarian website. Mister Heller is going to put copies of these four on the troop site also.

"The view coming in each time was unbelievable. The ship would orbit a few times to give us a good look. Surprisingly, the colors were similar to Earth. The oceans were blue, the deserts brown, and vegetated areas were green. The plants were usually green; some of them had color, but you didn't see like a purple tree.

"I am absolutely positive, no doubt, that we landed on a different planet each time. On Pontus you could tell the gravity was a bit less; on Caerus your weight felt a tiny bit heavier. The other two felt pretty much like here.

But not the air. The air always tasted and smelled different, super fresh and clean. Of course, the plants and animals were noticeably different each time.

"We always wore long pants and long-sleeve shirts. The Chait say the plant life wasn't generally poisonous, but we wanted to play it safe and avoid the local version of poison ivy.

"On Attis, the plant life was very simple. The vegetation seemed mostly different types of ferns, with moss underfoot. The tallest plant was maybe twenty feet high. The only animal life we saw was something that flew. The creature looked like a cross between a big bug and a small bird. Pom told us most animal life was in the oceans.

"Pontus, at least where we landed, had thick jungle and the most wildlife. The critters usually had four legs and two arms, and spent all day and night eating each other. The tour guides were really nervous. The ship landed in the open, and the guides sent up a couple of drones which patrolled the whole time. I took some truly gruesome pictures, even grosser than the ones shown in drivers' ed.

"I wanted to kill something and eat it, just to say I did. However, the tour guides wouldn't let me.

"On each planet we would spend part of a day at one location, and then move many miles away. Sometimes we would move three or four times.

"On each planet there was a stone marker saying 'Gallock Was Here.' We actually met him, on Hephaestus! He was there with Tiger Tanaka. They had flown in on another ship, just to check on us and see how things were going. He wasn't a serious hard ass like you see on TV. He brought a guitar and played that night at the campfire. Seeing him play was way cool, not something you think about watching him speak in public.

"I was voted best singing voice. Who cares about Grammy Awards? I was voted best voice on the entire freaking planet! Everyone was voted something; best storyteller, best juggler, best joke, or something. It was almost like one of our Troop campouts. We carved everyone's name and a date into a rocky outcrop before we left.

"I planted a troop 582 flag, and left a troop pin cubed in Lucite, on each planet. Be sure to rub that in every other troop's nose at the next Jamboree."

Mike held up a clenched fist, on which glittered a large, gaudy ring. "See the gems?" he asked. "There's four stones, one from each planet I walked upon. Earth doesn't count. The ring is mostly platinum, which came from Caerus. The gemstones are unique to each of the four planets. We, well actually the ship, made these on the way back. A couple of the girls did the design—one of the Japanese was an art student—and the ship fabricated them overnight. One for each of us. I also got this NASA patch"—he pointed to his sash—"which means I'm an astronaut; I've flown in outer space. I'm even more awesome now than when I left."

More hoots from the crowd.

"See this other patch?" he pointed at his sash again. "The same girl who did the rings designed these beforehand and took them on the trip. This designates an astronaut who's made an interstellar flight. Nobody, not a single person, at NASA, SpaceX, or Roscosmos has one of these puppies!"

Cheers from the scouts.

"Tiger recorded interviews with each of us. You'll see my smiling face on her show this Friday. Eat your hearts out. In person she's beyond hot."

A buzz rose from the crowd of assembled teenage boys. Years before, the national organization surrendered to the social warriors, resulting in the admittance of young women, homosexuals, and transgenders. Total membership fell by half. One-hundred-plus years of history down the drain.

However, troop 582 still consisted of only red-blooded young men.

"Jon said – we're best buds now, I call him Jon – he's actually visited every single planet on the habitable list, and left markers. I have this great picture. I'm leaning casually on a chest-high stone 'Gallock Was Here' marker with Jon on one side, Tiger on the other—she's rubbing up against me—and two alien spaceships looming in the background." More teenage moans. "There's even a moon overhead, which looks way different than ours. That picture is going on the cover of my book. My mom already hired a lawyer, an agent, and a ghostwriter. I'm gonna make a million bucks. My agent is already talking about a movie.

"I'm going to buy a brand-new Corvette and hire Dombrowski to wash it," Mike needled. "What's that? Don't be too quick to turn down a job offer,

Dombrowski. After you flunk out of State, you won't be qualified to do anything else. Not that any employer cares if you graduate—it's State. I'll sit in a lawn chair with a cold drink and tell you what you're doing wrong, and make you wash it again a couple times."

The scoutmaster stepped in before things got out of hand. Part of scouting was to teach self-confidence and leadership skills. Mike had great skills, and was certainly comfortable speaking to a group. Unknown to him, communication skills were the primary reason he was chosen. The scoutmaster and Gallock went back a long way, and when Jon asked to interview recent Eagles, and current candidates, he'd quickly agreed.

Mike was a great Senior Patrol Leader. He kept the younger scouts interested and amused, and the older scouts in line without resorting to a knuckle sandwich. Most of his theatrics was to pump up the troop. The young men would leave tonight feeling ten feet tall.

"We're devoting all of next meeting to Mike's trip," he told the assembled group. "Please hold your questions until then. Now, clasp hands with the people next to you and let's do the closing ceremony."

THIRTY-TWO
THE CHAEBOL

THEY FLEW TO SINGAPORE ON separate aircraft and landed at separate airports. Jon and a young employee who spoke Korean flew in on the company's Falcon and landed at Seletar. Bill and Tom flew into Changi in a leased Gulfstream. Jon wanted options in case they had to leave in a hurry.

Jon gave the necessary background information via enhancements during flight. "Koreans are not the stereotype inscrutable Orientals," he said. "Koreans can go off on you. We don't want to do this meeting in Seoul. The South Korean government is incensed at being left out of the exoplanet draw. There's not much of a dividing line between the chaebols and the government. If the meeting went poorly, we could find ourselves surrounded by a thousand angry demonstrators, and no police, when we tried to leave.

"A dozen large family-owned industrial groups called chaebol dominate the economy, and the government.

"The country is technically still at war with North Korea. No peace treaty was ever signed, only a temporary armistice. Their entire population has grown up during a time of war. The despot to the north has nuclear weapons, and one of the largest active militaries in the world.

"South Korea has one of the most highly developed economies in the world. There is a stretch of coastline where, at least at one time, the world's largest shipyard sits next to the world's largest steel mill, which sits next to the world's largest auto plant, and more.

"The purpose of this trip is, first, defuse their anger. We don't want them as an active opponent. Secondly, we want to take advantage of their industrial capabilities. I'm hoping we can kill these two birds with one stone. Finally, we can play them off against other nations. South Korea doesn't have many international obligations.

"The big guys, the senior executives, rarely travel. Once a year, however, an important regional, economic conference is held in Singapore. CEOs of two of the big four, and another of the number six or seventh largest chaebol, will attend the conference. We're going to try to hold an impromptu meeting," Jon concluded.

"I'm dubious," Bill replied. "Guys at this level, especially Asians, have their next twelve months scheduled out in fifteen-minute increments. I bet these guys even have their bathroom breaks on the calendar. How do you plan to get their attention? Land a Chait spacecraft on the hotel roof?"

Jon grinned. With his enhancements Bill and Tom could see Jon's face as if he was sitting three feet away. "Pretty much," Jon replied. "The Chait will do a slow goodwill fly-by this morning. I'll send a text, with help from our friends, to the three senior chaebol executives, and their deputies. Once they see the others have been invited, none will dare not show. I'm asking for a late lunchtime meeting at the Marina Bay Sands.

"Now," Jon continued, "let's go over how I'd like to choreograph this meeting."

All three chaebol executives showed up. Choi Hong-keun of the industrial giant best known in the west for cars, Park Jung-tai's chaebol was known for electronics, and Park Jung-soo whose company's industrial activities were generally unknown to those in the west. Each brought only two functionaries. Two was a lot by Western standards, not so by Asian. One of the functionaries would interpret. None would trust the other's interpreter. A deputy minister of trade also showed up, uninvited and unannounced. Robert informed the group the young man was well connected, and more senior than his age indicated. He was allowed to stay.

Jon skipped the customary lengthy introductions, and gifts. The only appropriate gift would be an alien trinket, which would just piss them off. Bill had worked in Asia and was aware of the customs and manners appropriate to this level of meeting and tried to coach Jon, who didn't care. Only a child or an idiot takes offense at an unintended slight. Everyone in the room was a grown up.

Bill did have three useful tidbits of advice. 'Don't apologize, don't explain, and show respect to the oldest guy across the table.'

"Gentlemen," Jon began, "thank you for fitting us into your schedule today." He waited for his interpreter to translate. The young XSolarian interpreter was terrified. The chaebol interpreters whispered in their masters' ears, confirming the translation. Of course, their enhancements also gave the Americans an accurate representation of what was said.

"The company I represent, XSolarian, is forming a company to manufacture spacecraft," Jon said, skipping the preliminaries. "Our senior vice president, Tom Corker, will manage this enterprise." He motioned to Tom sitting on his right. "We require contractors to manufacture components. I will announce this new enterprise to the public in several weeks. We desire Korean companies in the contractor base. We prefer South Korea speak with one voice. If you are interested, please have an appropriate person contact Tom in the near future to discuss the many details."

Consternation ensued. One executive blinked twice. Another licked his lips. The third shifted his shoulders. The three looked among each other and by an invisible, nonverbal calculus selected the youngest to speak. The youngest was fifty-five years old.

"You award planets on whims, to gangsters and financial speculators, to fornicators of swine, but not to South Korea? But you need us to make the ships to take you there? But we are not worthy of the knowledge? Are we your beast of burden?" the Korean ranted behind a cloud of halitosis.

Jon made a small gesture. "We are in early times. I offer the opportunity to participate, to improve your position, and be present for the end game. But, of course, you must do as you see best."

The Korean continued his rant. "You do not lower yourself to touch our soil; you must accost us here. You surround us on all sides with your whores. You shower others with gifts but leave us paupers. You use us as pawns in your nuclear games with China, and Russia."

The guy had a point. All around them, Japan, China, and Russia, each were tapped for a planet. On the other hand, Korean industry had done well—better than most—in licensing Chait technology.

Jon had considered stringing them along with vague promises of a planet sometime, later, maybe, in the future. He'd decided to hold on to that card for now. The offer might prove more useful later.

"As I said," Jon replied coolly, "you will do as you see fit. Again, I thank you for taking time out of your busy schedule to meet with us. Please convey my deepest regards to your father," Jon said, addressing the youngest executive. He said a sincere farewell, separately to the senior executives, and the ministry of trade representative. "We would stay longer," he said. "However, we have many meetings such as this, scheduled this week," he said pointedly. The executives glowered at him.

The ministry of trade representative unexpectedly spoke up. "Thank you for thinking of us, Mister Gallock. A representative of our ministry will contact Mister Corker later this week." His English was perfect.

In the elevator, Tom subvocalized to the others, "Do you think they're going to bite?"

"They have to," Jon replied silently. "It's simple realpolitik. South Korea can't afford to be left out."

Their junior interpreter wondered why the big bosses seemed so relaxed and satisfied when the meeting went so hideously awful.

THIRTY-THREE
HEAVY LIFTING

CASEY'S SMILING FACE FILLED THE screen. "Aloha, folks; welcome to the *Tiger Tanaka Friday ET Update.* Our guest tonight is Jon Gallock, the CEO of XSolarian, with, once more, big news!"

The screen split, showing Casey on one side, Jon on the other. "Thank you, Tiger," he said. "Before getting to my announcement, I am going to give you a plug, and remind your viewers the exoplanet lottery will be shown here next week."

Social media was full of derisive comments and humorous memes about Tiger pretending to interview her rumored boyfriend in what was actually an infomercial. Nevertheless, this was fresh information straight from the horse's mouth. The ratings were huge.

"There are reports China is protesting the lottery," said Casey. "Is that true?"

"The reports are true," replied Jon. "The Chinese government has publicly objected to the entire concept of a lottery. China wants the exoplanet of their choice. They also don't like anything about the lottery, who runs it, the format, and pretty much all the rules, everything. Of course, if one was allowed to select from the list, you'd have the exact same issues. Who chooses first? Who goes last?"

"How are the concerns of the Chinese government being addressed?" Casey asked seriously.

"They're not," replied Jon. "The lottery will go on as scheduled. If China doesn't like their draw, they can decline the exoplanet, and remove themselves from consideration." In other words, they could pound sand.

"I can't imagine passing on a planet would be a popular choice with Chinese citizens," said Casey. "I guess we'll find out next week. What do you have for us tonight, Jon?"

"We recently announced the existence of a human colony, Ouranos, where the process of building interstellar spacecraft has begun. The Chait are not going to release that technology to the humans on Earth.

"The Chait do not trust the human race to act wisely. One intemperate player can spoil things for all. Look at our own government, for example, which consists of three separate branches, designed to limit the others. The founders understood the nature of man and designed a structure which addressed their concerns. No wonder the Chait have concerns as well.

"The Chait have placed a restriction on interstellar craft, those operated by humans from Ouranos, to approach no closer than an orbit around Earth's moon. The distance is approximately a quarter of a million miles away. The issue now facing the countries on Earth is to deliver the colonists, their materials, supplies, and equipment into lunar orbit."

"How is delivery a problem?" asked Casey. "A half-dozen private companies already provide launch capability. SpaceX alone makes a launch, or more, every week. And, most of the countries receiving a colony planet have some kind of space program."

"Tiger," Jon replied, "launch capability is a big problem. Putting a payload into orbit is one thing; putting a payload into lunar orbit is an order of magnitude more difficult. Although a number of space programs, both private and government, could in theory put material into lunar orbit, the capacity per flight is limited to something in the tens of thousands of pounds. And such a flight is still a big dang deal.

"Once the colonization program begins, there will be an immediate need for regular flights, at least weekly, with a capacity in the hundreds of thousands of pounds per flight. Think about it, six colonies each needing periodic resupply and support lights. Assuming each colony is visited once every six weeks, we need a weekly flight to the Moon."

"I realize this is breaking news, but Jon, is there a plan to address this need for heavy lifting?" asked Casey.

"Yes, Tiger, and it's quite exciting," Jon replied. "The Chait have decided to release some advanced interplanetary-level technology, with restrictions."

In an earlier show Jon had described what he saw as three levels of alien technology. The lowest level was a planetary level of technology. This was the tech level being released to Earth. This was technology humans could reasonably be expected to develop on their own, in the next twenty or thirty years. From the Chait point of view, there was little risk in releasing these technologies.

The next level up was described as interplanetary tech. This level was embargoed and not generally available to Earth. This tech was perhaps a hundred years advanced from today, and a level that a species which has expanded inside their home own solar system might reasonably possess.

Yet another level advanced was described as interstellar technology. At a minimum, this was what the Chait possessed. The aliens obviously had the ability to travel and communicate faster than light. Anything beyond that was unknown. The Chait held such knowledge very close. Jon and the Inner Circle knew the aliens possessed, at a minimum, advanced biotech, field technology, sensing, robotics, and powerful artificial intelligence.

Of course, the Chait could be even more advanced than an interstellar civilization. Jon suspected intergalactic technology. Maybe the race didn't even originate in the Milky Way. Interdimensional tech? Time travel?

Speculating about the Chait was the biggest theme ever on social media.

"So," asked Casey, "how exactly are the Chait going to help us with the heavy lifting? And what are the restrictions?"

"The first is a propulsion system," replied Jon. "We've all seen, either in person or on a screen, the Chait spacecraft floating along, with no billowing flames underneath, no visible engine of any kind. The propulsion appears to be antigravity. The big brains may tell us the physics are different; however, for all practical purposes, yes, it's antigravity.

"The second technology is the power source. The Chait spaceship obviously has some highly efficient power source inside, to power the antigravity. We require the power source as well."

"That is game-changing news!" exclaimed Casey. "I've always been appalled by all the chemicals a rocket launch spews into our atmosphere. A single launch today uses the equivalent of a half million tanks of gas for your car. Much of the exhaust is injected into the upper atmosphere where it lingers longer and has a greater effect than a surface emission. The exhaust includes not just carbon, but a whole bunch of crap that's a lot worse for the environment. It seems a launch happens, somewhere, almost every day."

Casey continued. "Does this mean we finally get flying cars!?"

"I suspected someone would eventually ask about flying cars," laughed Jon. "But no, Tiger, we don't get flying cars. This technology will be released to only one company, for only one purpose: lifting heavy loads into lunar orbit to support the colonies."

Jon continued. "I am announcing the formation of a new company—Isabella—to incorporate Chait technology into terrestrial built launch vehicles in order to develop the heavy-lift capability this planet requires for a successful colonization effort. This program will be massively expensive and involve most of the industrialized nations on Earth. We are operating on a tight schedule. We don't know when the Chait plan to leave. They're operating on their schedule, not ours. The Chait originally said they would be around for five to ten years. Time has passed since then. They could depart in as little as three or four years. We must have these craft operational before the earliest of the time range."

Casey commented, "The choice of the name Isabella seems obvious. The queen who financed Christopher Columbus's voyages to what the Europeans eventually called the new world." Jon was nodding. "I know everything involved in spaceflight is extremely costly. So, when you say 'massively expensive,' I assume you mean even by aerospace standards." Jon nodded again. "So how much money are you talking about?"

"The development of the Space Shuttle is probably the closest comparison we have," Jon replied. "In today's dollars the cost was north of fifty billion dollars. After development, individual shuttles cost billions each to build. The development of nuclear submarines by the US government is another good data point. The initial costs were well in excess of ten billion dollars. Each submarine has an individual build cost in the billions.

"SpaceX put about ten billion into their development initially, and continues to invest. Which is a fraction of what a government program costs, and an anomaly.

"Based on the data points we have, a WAG, a wild-ass guess, of the cost, to design, develop, and build five to ten heavy-lift craft, within three years, is a hundred billion dollars."

"Good Lord!" exclaimed Casey. "That's a ton of money—where is it coming from?"

"The short answer," explained Jon, "is from any investor we can find. Private investor, that is. We're not going to accept direct investment from government. The time, effort, and strings attached take any direct government funding off the table. XSolarian will put every nickel the company has into the new venture. But our investment is just a drop in the bucket. I will personally lobby the world's tech titans for investment, starting with those already involved in aerospace. A politician once said, 'A billion here, a billion there, and pretty soon it adds up to real money.' Eventually the company will sell shares on the public market."

Now, Jon turned the interview over to Tom, who explained in very broad terms how Isabella would operate. Although Tom had a certain gruff charm, he was not a natural in front of the camera. Jon and Casey coached him up as best they could. "I know quality standards and IT infrastructure are important; however, if you mention them on my show I will shoot your dog," Casey vowed.

Isabella would be the spacecraft's integrator. The major subsystems would be supplied by multiple subcontractors. In industry, key components are commonly second-sourced. That is, a primary supplier with the lion's share of a specific component is backed up by a secondary supplier. Should problems arise with the primary supplier, the ratio flips. In this case, partly to spread the work around, mostly to insulate the project from political pressure, the plan called for three suppliers for each component. In this way no two governments could conspire to withhold delivery. Collusion was exponentially more difficult with three governments in cahoots, than two. This was also why the South Koreans suppliers were important. The chaebols were immune to outside pressure, and everybody hated them.

Normally, triple sourcing was unheard of. The strategy was too costly and difficult to implement and effectively manage. However, Isabella would have the Chait helping.

This was where the rubber would meet the road. This was the heart of the plan Jon sold to the Chait years before. Bribe the important players with a planet and give them incentive to work together to get colonies established. He could not let any government inside the effort; however, the lucky six had a vested interest—an entire planet—in seeing the plan through to fruition. Except for "that one guy."

In any endeavor undertaken in the history of humanity, there was always that one guy. That one guy who worked tirelessly to ruin the project, from either malice or stupidity, to spoil everything for everyone. Jon did not know, yet, who it would be—the leaders of Russia, China, or the US—or how he would deal with him. However, that one guy would not be around to see their colony planted.

THIRTY-FOUR
THE DRAGON

THE FOOD, THOUGH LIGHT, WAS exquisite. The drinks, though small, were rare and expensive. Their informal dinner finished, the most powerful politicians in China settled into comfortable chairs and began the discussion.

"I want to impress upon you," said the general secretary and president of the People's Republic of China, Xi Zheng, "this is an informal meeting, merely to discuss the boundaries of the possible."

The others nodded. Of course not. At their level nothing was informal.

The general secretary, and the others in the room, were frustrated with the United States and their allies stymieing China's policies. The culprits were the US, Japan, South Korea, the ASEAN countries, and of course Australia, who was waging yet another trade war with China.

"Minister," Xi asked of Guo Keqiang, the defense minister, "please summarize the ability of our military forces relative to the Americans."

"In a war of conventional weapons, within our sphere of influence, we have absolute superiority," Guo replied confidently. "From Siberia south, including Australia, we are preeminent. We also have absolute superiority in the Indian Ocean all the way to the east coast of Africa. Our navy is larger than the Americans', our weapons are more advanced, and our ships more modern. In the last ten years we have closed the gap in equipment, training, and readiness.

"Australia will side with the Americans in any open conflict. We really don't care. We will largely ignore the Aussies. Their military is small, and their ability to project power northward into Southeast Asia is insignificant. China is their most important customer. We buy their coal, iron ore, natural gas, and other commodities. Both the military and the Australian political leadership prefer to avoid hostilities altogether, or end them quickly should war break out.

"In any nuclear war the winner is uncertain. Most likely, he who strikes first, wins. Should we foresee a strategic, nuclear war with the Americans, I suggest, respectfully, we consider plan Primrose."

However tactfully Guo mentioned plan Primrose, he was taking a risk. An earlier defense minister had received a personal call from an unstable American military chief of staff. The American general believed his president was a Russian spy, and assured his Chinese counterpart he, and a cabal of officers under his leadership, would sabotage any order to launch intercontinental ballistic missiles (ICBMs) armed with thermonuclear warheads against China. Given an ICBM flight time of less than thirty minutes, any delay in launching a counterstrike was fatal. China would be able to kill American ICBMs on the ground, before launch could occur. The rogue American general unilaterally ended the sixty-year-old doctrine of mutually assured destruction (MAD). The sabotage was seen as a golden first-strike opportunity by the Chinese defense minister.

The minister lobbied so forcefully for so long, for plan Primrose, a first strike designed to decapitate the American government, he was relieved and retired.

"Minister," Xi asked of Li Jinping, the state security—spy—minister, "what would be the likely reaction of the aliens should open conflict break out between us and the Americans?"

"We simply don't know," replied Li. "Nobody knows. I realize this is not a useful answer; let me expand on what we do know." Everyone settled back and listened carefully. Li was notoriously opaque.

"The aliens obviously have a lot of resources," Li began. "We know of multiple spacecraft designed and built for human use. There are the two seen on Hephaestus, used by Gallock, and the tourists. Those craft appear different than the original ship seen circling the Hawaii island of Oahu. So, three separate ships, that we know of, are modified for human use. There is at least one more craft still performing fly-bys around the world. We suspect the XSolarian people have several small craft at their disposal. Certainly, the aliens have more ships for their own use.

"The miraculous technologies the Americans have received from the Chait and introduced to the world mean nothing. For an advanced species that's the equivalent of one of us giving some bare-assed native a disc containing technical information which we copied from somebody else. What the Chait gave the human race cost them, in their terms, virtually nothing.

"The aliens appear quite interested in Jupiter. We don't know why.

"We have no details regarding this supposed colony of Ouranos.

"Apparently, the aliens have invested very little, except time, in the Americans. A small investment is easy to abandon. The aliens show no interest in Earth politics. I see no evidence they would intervene should we go to war with America. I believe our chances of success would be improved by a lightning strike, and the aliens presented with a fait accompli."

Another pause while they digested Li's words.

"Comrade Wang," asked Xi, "what are your thoughts regarding the geopolitical situation?"

"First of all," replied Wang, "I am not your comrade." The others acknowledged his attempt at humor. Slang of the day used "comrade" as an appellation for a homosexual lover.

Wang Zhanshu was a powerful member of the politburo and a member of its Standing Committee.

"The situation we face is analogous to Japan's at the inception of the Second World War," Wang began. "We require certain raw materials, which the Americans keep from us. Coal, oil, natural gas, iron ore, all lie within our sphere of influence. Some of the world's greatest oil fields, natural gas fields, and mineral deposits are, geographically speaking, relatively nearby, and owned by small, weak countries. Should the American influence wane, we would have no need for adventures in Africa, or poorly considered investments in South or Central America. We could better employ those resources closer to home.

"We can use a reliable combination of hard and soft power to pick these small countries off one at a time. We talk, talk, talk in the UN, and the Americans will dither, bluster, announce sanctions—but take no military action.

"This astonishing appearance of aliens has roiled the waters. Among those receiving a planet—an entire planet!—Germany and Japan we can ignore. Nothing those countries say or do is important to China.

"The United Kingdom is also of little concern. Their military force is primarily in the Atlantic. Should we focus on Southeast Asia, our only concern is Australia. Any conflict with India can be deferred until we consolidate our gains in Southeast Asia. Our navy and our air force can certainly keep Indian forces bottled up in the Indian Ocean.

"As this century progresses, it has become evident that Russia is a natural ally. The Russians have few ambitions in the Pacific. Let Russia play their games with NATO, and the US in the Atlantic, and they will happily leave Southeast Asia and the Pacific to us."

Again, a pause while the old men sipped their tea and digested the words.

"My dear Zhou," said Xi, "do you have any thoughts?"

Zhou Yang was retired. He had been a member of the Politburo Standing Committee along with Xi and Wang. He was easily the oldest in the room, and Xi's longtime mentor.

"I am grateful for the frank words and carefully considered thoughts from all of you," said Zhou. "You have spent a great deal of time and effort studying the Americans, and the aliens. My knowledge on these matters is insignificant compared to the rest of you. I will do my best to clarify and summarize what I believe has already been said."

Zhou held up a nicotine-stained bony, wrinkled, palsied forefinger. "First, we will receive a planet within a few days. A staggering treasure! However, we have no way of getting there. We cannot even see the planet's star in the night sky."

Another finger. "Our ambitions are being unfairly thwarted by the Americans. We are confident of winning any military conflict; however, we don't know how the aliens would react to a war. Would they rescind their offer? No war is likely to help us with the aliens.

"Third, we believe we can ally, at a minimum, with Russia, to gain control over the program to build heavy-lift orbital craft.

"Fourth, the technology to build interplanetary spacecraft, if held by China alone, would make us immensely rich, and powerful. Conversely, we would suffer greatly if another had a monopoly on the knowledge. Possession of the technology is a two-edged sword. We cannot allow others to monopolize this technology."

Zhou held up his hand, fingers, and thumb outstretched. "Fifth, until China controls the alien technology, we are entirely dependent on others if we ever plan to leave the solar system, or to establish colonies.

"When one goes fishing to feed his family, one wants to catch a big fish. He must really try hard to catch a big fish. However, he must come home with something, even a little fish." He closed his fingers into a fist.

"So, my question to you, old friend," said Zhou to Xi, "do you want a planet, or this planet?"

THIRTY-FIVE
TALKING HEADS

THE SHOW WAS THE HIGHEST rated Network weekend talk show on TV. Network ratings were a big deal before cable, and the internet. The statistic still meant quite a bit. The longtime host was a former comedian who wasn't that funny. However, he had a pleasant engaging personality and drew more from his guests than they intended to give. Tonight's topic was the Chait.

The host, and his guests, sat in comfortable chairs around a low circular coffee table. "Tonight, we welcome Stuart Abrams, the well-known author, pundit, and all-around gadfly." As he spoke, he motioned to his right at a poorly groomed, tall, thin young man. Unmentioned was his PhD in physics, another in biology, and a master's degree in political science.

"And on my left," the host continued, "is Doctor Jerry Patterson, retired NASA scientist and well-known intellectual on all things regarding our extraterrestrial visitors." Dr. Patterson was a stocky middle-aged man with good "Dennis the Menace" hair. He did have a PhD in electrical engineering, however his career at NASA was in the public affairs department.

"Doctor Patterson," the host asked, "what is likely the most impactful technology that we, here on Earth, are likely to benefit from?"

"Well, as you know," Patterson began, "we face an existential problem in climate change. Our planet is being poisoned by the burning of fossil fuels. Unless we act in a very short time, a few short years, we will incur catastrophic consequences. Clean, cheap unlimited power from safe and reliable fusion reactors is the answer. The best scientists in the United States, Europe, and around the world have been working on this for decades. The Chait advanced material technologies will make this a reality." He droned on for a minute until interrupted by a rude noise.

"Yes, Mister Abrams?" the host asked. "Did you have a comment?"

"Yes," Abrams replied. "Given my two PhDs, I should be addressed as doctor. Technically, since I have two PhDs I should be addressed as 'doctor doctor,' however that sounds too much like an old Monty Python skit. Just doctor is fine." He glared at the host.

"My apologies," said the host. "Please continue, Doctor Abrams." Mission accomplished. Abrams was volatile; you just had to light his fuse.

"First of all," Abrams began, "obtaining useful power from fusion is a fantasy. Fusion research is welfare for PhDs. Many of you watching tonight have a gas hot water heater. Take a look, you'll see a big tank with a tiny burner about the size of a dinner plate. The burner is constructed of ten cents of tin, and lasts thirty years without maintenance. A coal plant, a nuclear plant, and a fusion plant—if there ever is one—make electricity by boiling water. That's right, those plants are just bigger honking tanks with larger, more expensive burners, requiring a lot of maintenance. The water is flashed into steam, which expands over a thousand times in volume and drives a turbine, which powers an electrical generator. Even with fusion, you still need the entire generating plant. You've only replaced the burner.

"Replacing a hundred-million-dollar coal furnace, or a billion-dollar nuclear furnace, with a ten-billion-dollar fusion furnace—if one ever exists—will not get you clean, cheap power."

"I disagree," responded Patterson, shaking his head. "When one factors in the associated environmental costs, fusion promises to be much more economic than the alternatives. Burning coal has huge environmental costs, and nuclear waste is highly dangerous, lasts thousands of years, and requires extremely expensive remediation and long-term storage."

Abrams gave an exaggerated eye roll. "What horseshit. The French, those world-renowned French engineers, designed cheap effective nuclear waste storage about nineteen sixty. I don't know about you, but I wasn't born yet. Current reactor design is vastly improved since the nineteen sixties. I know my car sure improved over my parents' ride. Current nuclear designs can actually use the waste from the earlier plants as fuel.

"And burning coal is actually beneficial for the environment. The sulfur and other by-products provide nutrients for plants, and we need more CO_2, not less. The molecule is a nutrient required for plant life. You know, the plants that provide the oxygen, which gives you and me, and our kids, life. The CO_2 in the atmosphere is near the lowest it's been in a warm period in the last hundred million years. Plant life evolved in a time when CO_2 was ten times that of today's atmosphere."

"I certainly don't want to live downwind from a coal-fired plant," retorted Patterson. "Or anywhere near a nuclear plant."

Abrams cut in. "Yeah, but do you disagree with any of my facts? I don't think so, because they're, you know, facts."

Patterson didn't know much about pollution from coal, other than CO_2, so he backtracked. "Worldwide scientific consensus is CO_2 and climate change are existential threats to humanity."

Abrams cut in again. "Climate change, what hooey. This vague, mysterious, unknown, unknowable effect, an untestable theory to rebrand global warming—that isn't happening. Bullshit. We can debate that for a while if you'd like. You might be more comfortable, since climate change doesn't involve any facts. Here's a thought: look up the definition of a cult in the dictionary. Then look in the mirror."

The host decided to refocus the conversation towards the Chait. Another climate change show would crater his ratings. "What have the Chait said about CO_2, climate change, and related matters? Doctor Patterson?"

"The Chait haven't been very forthcoming," replied Patterson. He was happy as a clam. He had accomplished what he wanted. Like most retired federal public affairs people, he had a consulting contract with his former agency to "socialize, publicize, and educate the public" on the dangers of carbon, and climate change. He was paid a flat ten thousand a month, with no set duties. However, the contract witch asked for quarterly reports with specifics of his activities. Two minutes on prime time would more than satisfy her this quarter.

"Zip, zero, nada," replied Abrams.

"So, who are the Chait, where are they from, why are they here? And why are they so shy? Thoughts, Doctor Abrams?" asked the host.

"I've thought about the Chait a great deal," began Abrams. He was pissed at Patterson. They'd been invited on national TV, prime time, to talk about the Chait, and the idiot burned half their time bringing up climate change.

"Our tourists report the Chait can travel to distant stars in only a couple days. So, from the alien's viewpoint, the voyage here is not a major effort. I theorize their lack of personal interaction with humanity is due to the fact they have plenty of other species to talk to. For example, when you go on vacation to let's say somewhere in South America, do you consider a mere conversation with a native a significant event? Of course not, at least not a bigger deal than talking to somebody in Europe, or Asia. The language, and skin coloration, doesn't matter—he's just another person."

"The aliens have come all this way," the host interjected, "but not that last little bit, Jupiter to here, and they're not really talking too much."

"A slight correction," Abrams countered, "if I may. The Chait are not really talking much, to us.

"Outside of the Sun, Jupiter contains the vast majority of all matter in the solar system. Earth, though approximately twenty-five thousand miles in circumference, has a life zone only a couple miles thick. Our environment is less in comparison than the rind on an orange, or the skin on an apple. It's infinitesimal compared to the volume of the entire planet.

"Jupiter, however, is a gas planet. The ratio of planet to life zone is reversed. Excepting, perhaps, a small solid core, the entire volume is an atmosphere. The volume of Jupiter's atmosphere is thousand times that of the entire planet Earth. The Jovian gases are chock-full of chemicals, nutrients, trace elements, and electrical impulses. We think of life as carbon-based, and oxygen breathing. But life may come in many forms. You're much more likely to find intelligent life inside of Jupiter rather than here. I suspect the Chait are talking their heads off, but to somebody else."

Patterson felt the spotlight slipping away. "That's an interesting speculation," he said. "But purely speculation. In fact, NASA has studied Jupiter for decades and detected no signs of life. No emissions on any spectrum our scientists can measure, certainly no physical artifacts. All attempts to model life in other forms, including gaseous, have been unsuccessful. Science says intelligent life on Jupiter is highly unlikely."

Abrams grinned. "You probably heard the old joke. The one where a flying saucer comes to planet Earth looking for intelligent life and can't find any. We can't detect the frequencies the Chait use for communication either, can we? But the aliens communicate somehow.

"Here's a thought that's way out there. Maybe Jupiter does not contain intelligent life. Maybe Jupiter *is* the intelligent life. Maybe the entire planet is one brain, one body, one intelligent entity. Mind-blowing, eh?"

THIRTY-SIX
GOVERNMENT INTELLIGENCE

VLADIMIR SERGEEVICH, THE HEAD OF the primary Russian intelligence agency, the FSB, looked at his two subordinates without saying a word, for a full minute. His office was fifty feet on a side, and paneled in silk and gold leaf. A king, or the Pope, would not feel out of place. On his desk lay a single piece of paper, a thin report, and a thick report. He looked at Yuri. "Kustinavage?"

Yuri Shitikov, the FSB deputy director of field operations replied, "The debriefs went well. Jewa Kustinavage had Lithuanian parents; however, her childhood was unsettled, and she spent as much time with Russian relatives in Russia as she did in Lithuania. She considers herself Russian. I don't think anybody who matters was fooled. The American front for the aliens, Gallock, and the XSolarian people, knew her allegiances. Gallock's people would have received a briefing from the American intelligence services. To call our little Jewa Lithuanian was a polite fiction, a palatable cover story. According to the media no evil Russians were included on the exoplanet tour. Her selection was an unexpected accommodation from the Americans. Any accommodation is cause for suspicion."

Vladimir made a motion with his hand. Yuri skipped the history. "We have done three debriefs with her so far. Each session was two to three hours long. To maintain the Lithuania fiction, she is traveling and doing numerous interviews with the European press. This report"—he pointed at the thin report on Vladimir's desk—"is careful to partition her factual statements, from any conclusions."

Vladimir held up his hand. Yuri went quiet. Vladimir rotated his head a few degrees and looked at Ilya Boldyrev, his technical services deputy. Ilya began, "I have listened to recordings of the debriefs carefully, as well as reading the fine report prepared by Yuri's people." This was the reason

Vladimir had promoted Ilya to his current position. He always reviewed the source data rather than relying on summary reports prepared by others. However, his genius lay in boiling down complex material into a few salient bullet points, without losing important context. One page from Ilya was more useful than ten pages from anyone else.

Ilya continued, "I've also read transcripts of media interviews of the other tourists. I had to rely on transcripts as I don't speak the various languages used in the interviews. Nothing said by the others contradicts what Kustinavage has told us. Additional details of the trip and the exoplanets have come out, but nothing contradictory. Yuri's people should confirm these details in Jewa's later debriefs." Yuri grunted and shot a hard look at Ilya. The unspoken message was 'stay in your own lane, asshole.'

"Given our prior intelligence"—Ilya pointed at the thick report—"and what we've learned from Kustinavage"—Ilya pointed at the thin report—"I have prepared a list of what we know, and don't know, of the Chait." He pointed at the single page.

Vladimir extended his left arm, put his index finger down on the single page, and pulled it in front of him. He then looked at Ilya to continue.

Ilya quickly went through the bullet points without wasting time on the sources, or the reasoning.

The Chait undoubtedly existed.

The Chait had technology beyond any Earth government.

Their spacecraft possessed a sophisticated stealth ability.

The aliens had faster-than-light communication.

The alien spacecraft had the ability to travel much faster than the speed of light.

The exoplanets visited by the tourists existed. Analysis of photos of the night sky taken by the tourists was inconclusive in determining their actual location.

There was no evidence the aliens resided near Jupiter, or anywhere else.

At least three separate spacecraft had been seen by reliable observers.

No one knew if their spacecraft were manned, remotely operated, or highly automated—which would imply strong artificial intelligence.

The existence of a Mothership was unknown.

The primary interface between the Chait and the human race was Americans.

There was no evidence indicating the Chait known as Robert was their leader, or simply a spokesman.

Robert spoke a dozen languages, fluently and with colloquial grammar. Robert could be one or many different Chait. The language skills may or may not be machine generated.

The Chait were obsessive in concealing particulars regarding their race. There was much speculation, but no facts were known.

The lack of knowledge regarding Chait made their motivation being in our solar system, or interacting with humanity, unknown.

Their motivation in assisting humans and colonizing other planets was unknown.

Nothing was known of the alien's weapons capability.

Vladimir sat back one half an inch. Ilya paused from reviewing the list. Vlad put three fingers of each hand on the edge of his desk. He was not happy.

I can't take this to our president, or the politburo, Vladimir thought. *I'd look like a fool, which would be fatal. We have no actionable intelligence regarding the aliens. This report could as well come from a newspaper. We don't know who they are, what they want, or what capabilities they possess. A Russian sympathizer spent ten days on a Chait spacecraft and all we've learned is the food was good, and the chairs comfortable. We don't even know for sure if the fucking aliens are in bed with the Americans, or just using them as pawns. Visiting aliens from outer space had to contact somebody first. Americans seemed a reasonable choice.*

That only young, unsophisticated, and untrained civilian tourists were selected for the interstellar trip raised his suspicion that the Chait were hiding something about the craft used, or the planets visited.

To Ilya he said, "Split this into two separate lists, one consisting of what we know, and another of what we don't know. Give copies to only to Yuri and myself. Dismissed."

After Ilya departed, Vladimir said to Yuri, "Find an answer to every item on the do-not-know list. Also, in a month or two, after media attention has died down, bring Kustinavage in and dismantle her. We must know if she is an American plant. "

"You are dismissed," he finished.

He will fail, Vladimir thought to himself after Yuri departed, *which gives me cover to crucify him. Which will buy me six months reprieve from the jackals.* He had already decided to promote Krasnov into Yuri's position.

At least the GRU isn't doing any better, he thought. *Or the Chinese.*

General Dingbang of the People's Liberation Army considered the matter carefully before coming to a conclusion. He called his two key deputies in for a short meeting. The junior of the two, also a general, was then dispatched with orders for the General Staff Department. The aide went in person and met with General Jing and two of his key deputies. After the meeting ended General Jing discussed the matter privately with the two men and issued orders. Again, the junior aide was dispatched to the next level down. The process was repeated with the Second Department, and then the Winter Bureau.

Colonel Cheng Li Qing of the Winter Bureau and his key aide met with Major Deng Zhang Wei of Department 12. The colonel sat and spoke, and the major stood and listened.

"Do you understand your orders, Major?" asked the colonel.

"Yes, sir. I do," responded the major. He understood them perfectly, and didn't like them.

"Repeat them to me," asked the colonel.

The major began to sweat.

"Sir," began the major. "My orders have two parts. I am to take and exhaustively interrogate a senior XSolarian manager, but not Gallock. I will then disappear the manager. Second, I am to turn another executive, preferably Gallock, by any means necessary. Bribery is unlikely to work, so I should immediately begin developing a list of loved ones to take to provide the necessary leverage. Time is of the essence. I will report to only you, and do so daily, in person."

"That's correct," replied the colonel. "Use your best people on this. You are dismissed." He nodded to his aide, who saw the major to the door.

It's always a bad sign when serious orders come verbally, thought the major. The junior officer always gets the shaft when the situation goes badly. As he waited for the elevator, he called his secretary to tell the stupid cow to call people in for an emergency meeting. The elevator opened and the major, engrossed in his call, stepped in... to nothing. He fell seven stories to his death. The doors closed behind him. The stupid cow tried calling back. He didn't pick up.

The colonel and his aide left the office together shortly afterwards. Once in the elevator, the doors closed and went into free fall until the car hit the ground at the parking level several seconds later.

The investigators were puzzled, and could not explain why one of the three crushed bodies appeared under the wrecked elevator car, instead of inside.

The colonel who ran the Second Department was electrocuted in his hot tub. The junior aide inadvertently drove his late model BMW off a cliff.

General Jing was killed when a large truck broadsided his car. One witness, obviously confused, said both vehicles had a green light. His aide was stabbed to death by his mistress's jealous boyfriend who had discovered sexts on her phone.

General Dingbang of the PLA died of a heart attack despite his state-of-the-art pacemaker. His junior deputy was accidentally asphyxiated in his garage by car exhaust.

In a plane over the Pacific, Randy pinged Jon. "We've finished," he said. "The last one in the chain had his accident. The operation was a bright idea of General Dingbang. Nobody further up the food chain knew what he planned. The Chinese won't bother us in the short term."

THIRTY-SEVEN
THE LOTTERY

THE EXOPLANET LOTTERY WAS HELD at the Hyatt Regency Hotel in London. Adrian Kelly was the master of ceremonies. The secretaries of state, or equivalent, of the six recipients were invited. Each were allowed two aides and a couple security agents. The Secretary General of the United Nations was also invited. After much wrangling, the Commonwealth was represented by the Crown's Secretary of State. The event was televised live.

The Big Three—China, Russia, and the US—chose to send a deputy secretary. Even so, security was a nightmare.

The location was announced with only two days' notice so as to minimize the reaction time for the expected protesters. The short notice didn't work.

The exoplanet ranking system was proving unhelpful. In reality, since one was speaking of an entire planet, a ranking of, for example, thirty wasn't really much different than a ranking of twenty or forty. Already though, pundits were stoking the fires of envy and greed. The question posed was inevitably something along the lines of 'what if my country only gets a planet rated fifty, while some other country, who's obviously less deserving, gets the one rated thirty? The lottery is not fair.'

None of the participants trusted an electronic drawing. The lottery ball—the draw used actual physical balls—had the planet name printed on the side. The rotating contraption which blew the balls in a frenzy looked like something from a cheesy TV game show. The candidate exoplanets were listed on a large screen alphabetically rather than by number.

The Chinese had spent the week prior arguing the lottery was illegitimate and unfair. The US and Russia were noncommittal for their own reasons. Germany, Japan, and the Commonwealth were ecstatic.

Despite the short notice, the streets outside were thronged with pro-testers. The wildly different groups were well-organized using a variety of social media. London had a large population of Indians and Pakistanis—so much so that wits referred to the city as "Londonstan." Regardless of the fact that their home countries were also members of the Commonwealth, the immigrants were vociferously protesting for greater representation. The immigrants enjoyed assaulting the police.

The Pope issued a Papal Bull announcing Chait had no souls. Several Christian fundamentalist groups were protesting the Chait as "the devil's spawn" and vowed to burn Jon, and any other XSolarian employee they could get their hands on, at the stake. Other Christian groups were clam-oring for the aliens to take them to Heaven, presumably Ouranos.

The Greens always turned out for a good protest. This time the group was more violent than usual. Declaring that man had no right to despoil virgin planets, they emphasized their point by burning out small Pakistani shops and businesses.

Jews and Muslims marched separately, demanding their own planet. So did a dozen other tribal groups from Africa and the Americas. Any European nationalist group able to make the trip through the Chunnel in time showed up and protested. Lower Franconia was well represented. The tribes largely stuck to breaking windows.

Those protesting the new technologies were approximately equal to those who showed up to demand greater access to the advanced alien tech. Both groups tended to burn cars.

A thousand people with missing family members protested. The bereaved relatives believed the Chait or XSolarian had taken their loved one—usually a long-term homeless drug addict—against their will for horrible unspecified experiments.

There was a contingent of terminally ill demanding a cure. The pitiful group heard rumors the extra-terrestrials could heal them. If treatment involved kidnapping by godless devil's spawn, well, such a price was worth paying. The terminally ill did not have the energy to break things or fight.

Large numbers of soccer hooligans attended. The thugs didn't march against anything. They enjoyed putting boots to the protesters.

Inside the hotel, insulated from the throng outside, the lottery was about to begin. Jon and Adrian had discussed the drawing at length. The big question was, who would draw the ball? Having a representative of the lucky country make the draw was an idea dead on arrival. There was no controlling any scene one might choose to make.

If Jon or Adrian made the selection, somebody would accuse them of chicanery. Some lotteries pick a person from the audience to do the selection, usually a child. This live audience was small, and certainly included no children. Anybody, from any country could be construed as having an axe to grind. Jon didn't want to pick someone at random and then endure some long political rant. Adrian flirted with the idea of having a member of the British royal family make the draw, but no, he would be seen as favoring the Commonwealth.

"Screw it," said Jon. "You run the show, Adrian, and I'll do the draw. For the next few years, I'll be kicking people in the nuts to keep the heavy-lift program on schedule. I might as well start practicing my bigfoot routine now."

The show began. Robert, against the now-familiar backdrop of Jupiter, started with a few minutes of complimenting each of the nations involved, though fortunately not all fifty-odd Commonwealth members individually, and expressing his wishes of a successful colonization program by the peoples of Earth.

Adrian Kelly spoke reverently of the historic occasion, and how honored he was by his selection as Master of Ceremonies of the show. He briefly explained the process and logistics of the draw and turned the microphone over to Jon to make the first selection.

Each draw was a two-step process. First, from a clear Lucite container, Jon opened a gate which allowed the swirling air to push a ball into the exit port. Jon then closed the gate, removed the ball from the exit port, and read the small letters. He held the ball at head height, with his arm outstretched, and said, "The first selection is the Republic of Germany." The portly German minister for foreign affairs leapt to his feet and pumped both fists skyward in exultation. He then exchanged backslaps, handshakes, fist bumps, and high fives with the dignitaries around him.

The unaffected joy of the otherwise staid German minister brought laughter to the crowd, and the serious atmosphere in the room evaporated, leaving anticipation in its wake.

Once the impromptu celebration settled down, Jon turned to a larger clear Lucite container and repeated the process. "The planet is Pricus," he announced. He handed the ball to Adrian, who placed both spheres into a clear display case aligned so that the writing was clearly visible.

The applause was down a notch. Pricus was considered the fifty-ninth best planet for human habitation of the eighty-eight possibilities. In other words, well into the bottom half. The air was a little thin. At sea level the atmosphere was equivalent to three thousand feet on Earth. The ecology was simple. The limited plants and animals were edible by terrestrial mammals, barely. Still, Pricus on average was more livable than several Earth continents.

Adrian walked the beaming German foreign affairs minister to the next room, where a podium and microphone awaited. The broadcast filled the gap in activity with a video of the planet supplied by XSolarian. The minister's speech was aimed at the home crowd. He said the word "lebensraum" a lot.

The second pick was Russia. The planet draw came up with Caerus, one of the planets visited by the tourists. Caerus was considered the forty-fourth best planet—exactly average. The flora and fauna were edible and the planet had abundant metals.

The Commonwealth picked third. The planet was Triton, ranked seventy of the eighty-eight. The existing life was not edible, and the planet had a pronounced axial tilt which exacerbated the seasons. Still, the simple ecology could be easily overrun by Earth flora and fauna.

The Chinese were fourth. They drew a nice planet—Nereus, rated twenty-five. The existing plant and animal life was edible. The Chinese deputy minister began a lengthy vitriolic denunciation of the Chait, XSolarian, Jon Gallock, and the lottery process, in Cantonese. After a couple minutes, security forcibly ejected the deputy minister, his aides, and the Chinese security team from the room. Away from the cameras the entire delegation, excepting the deputy minister, were repeatedly tased, and then ejected from the building.

The deputy minister was allowed to speak in the second room to his heart's content. He delivered a three-hour monologue which nobody broadcast. He never directly declined the gift of a planet.

The Chinese later filed a formal complaint with the British government regarding the roughing up of their delegation. The Brits only shrugged. Neither XSolarian nor the Chait were recognized diplomatic entities, so there was no one to receive a formal complaint.

The United States drew fifth. The nation was rewarded with Hermes, which was rated fifty-two. The planet had a simple ecology with limited plant and animal life. On the plus side, some of the flora and fauna were edible. As the Chinese deputy minister was monopolizing the mic in the next room, Jon allowed the American deputy secretary to use his. She went on too long about respecting the local ecology, and the environmental care the US would lavish on the planet. The American deputy secretary pledged not to exploit the planet in any way. Eventually one of Jon's security team in the back of his room opened his coat and, hidden from all but those facing the back of the room, fondled his taser. Her aide got the point and assisted Jon in peeling the mic away.

Last up were the Japanese. The delegation was a little down at being the last drawn. The Japanese were all smiles when the ball for Aeolus was picked. The planet was rated number twelve—the best draw of the night. The planet was temperate, and had no primary continents but dozens of large islands. The flora and fauna were similar to Earth's. So similar, the primary danger would be local carnivores which had no fear of man.

Adrian ended the broadcast by noting each of the countries had thirty days to formally accept their gift, or not. Should anyone decline, there were no plans to fill any resulting vacancy. He then announced the formation of Isabella.

The riots outside continued until dawn.

THIRTY-EIGHT
TROUBLE

"**J**ON, ADRIAN, RANDY, ARE WE good to go?" Tracey pinged the group.
"Yes," the others replied. Jon was on the company plane with several
employees not of the Inner Circle. He was pretending to read reports.
Adrian was lounging in the back of the hotel's coffee shop, pretending to
use his cellphone. Tracey was jogging. Randy was the only one in an office,
sitting in front of his wall of displays.

"You called the meeting," said Jon. "Fire away."

"Things are falling apart," began Tracey. "Every little issue which was
manageable, or just background noise, has become exponentially more
trouble since the lottery. Protesters are more aggressive, and more organized. Police support in the United States has evaporated and we've reached
the point employees can't go into the office. Europe is not much better.
I was physically attacked by a guy dressed as homeless while jogging in
Stuttgart three days ago. A pretty goddamn healthy-looking homeless
guy. My ape-who-shaves tossed the guy face first, over the rails, down the
subway stairs before he could do any damage. We may be safer in Europe
from our government, but not from the protesters. The European protesters
are really aggressive."

Jon broke in. "Randy," he asked, for the group's benefit, "did we follow
protocol on this? How could this have happened, and what actions have
we taken?"

Randy replied, "We knew about the protestors, of course. The entity
is an AstroTurf rent-a-protest group hired by a nonprofit, nonpolitical,
nongovernmental organization named EcoClimateHealth Foundation
(ECHF). The organization is funded by everybody's favorite stateless lefty
billionaire. He gets a tax deduction for paying protesters to throw dogshit at
people. The members were supposed to merely harass her. This particular

guy got carried away and spontaneously decided to throw Tracey into traffic. Nobody ordered him to do so.

"We've obtained a restraining order against the group. Tracey has filed a formal assault complaint with the police, and tomorrow we're filing a civil suit against the attacker and his employer. Our story is the guy who threw the protester down the stairs was simply a good Samaritan passing by. Other than the incident itself, recordings of Tracey and the bodyguard together no longer exist. The bodyguard has been replaced and sent out of the country.

"The attacker has multiple broken bones and will be in the hospital a while. His boss, the project manager at this shady group, is a real dumbo. We arranged his arrest yesterday for possessing a kilo of cocaine while driving a stolen car. We have a lawyer showering money on his gay lover, to file and support a lawsuit for his torn rectum. The person next level up, the guy running this organization, will soon receive a visit from the police regarding funds he embezzled over the years, plus the million euros he's stealing tomorrow.

"The shady billionaire is recovering from frostbite. He may lose a couple toes. His driver took a wrong turn down a closed, snowy Swiss mountain road, then his car died in a stretch with no cell coverage. Lastly, one hundred eighty million dollars of his Bitcoin stash has been hacked and stolen, ostensibly by a Ukrainian group.

"The Chait technology is simply tremendous. I wish I'd had this intelligence-gathering and action capability when I worked at the NSA," Randy concluded. "It will take ten more years before the US intelligence community has this ability."

"Thanks, Randy," said Jon. "Good job. And Tracey, you don't get a commission on the funds we took in," he joked.

"Ha ha," Tracey replied. "It's too late. The psychic income I got hearing my attacker's face hit the cold hard steps twelve feet down is all the bonus I need this quarter. Thanks, Randy. Now let me get onto the other concerns.

"We've been able to distract the press every week with another squirrel, but it's only a matter of time before the media gets traction with some sob story about somebody missing a family member.

"Within a month of formally accepting their free planet, the US government will issue arrest warrants for all of us. We know this for sure now. Yes, I'm aware we have plans to address the warrants; it's still extremely stressful for all of us. Actively supporting us will not give the current administration as many votes as demonizing us. The administration gets more press coverage smearing us than they would helping us, which translates into votes. Peace and prosperity don't even enter into the equation. Two years ago, I would not have believed such a thing. You've convinced me, Jon.

"All the great powers are scheming. To others, it appears China was rewarded for their bad behavior with a good draw. Both China and Russia believe they can throw their weight around more than usual pursuing their national goals. The two nations believe the US and Europe will take no decisive action against them out of fear of upsetting the alien applecart. They are probably right."

Tracey spoke to Randy and Adrian. "Guys, I'm carrying the ball here, and happy to do so, but please speak up if I don't get things exactly right. Adrian, can you please speak to the political side?"

Adrian spoke, "In the north of Europe, Russia is preparing to annex Estonia and Latvia. Similarly, in the south they are pressuring Georgia and Azerbaijan into stronger ties. The G2 supplied by the Chait confirm the leaders of Russia and China are, for the most part, cooperating with each other. The leadership of both countries hold regular calls which are quite cordial. For example, both sides are whitewashing over minor border issues, which used to receive a great deal of attention.

"China has become extremely aggressive in Southeast Asia. They are signing extremely one-sided trade deals, at the point of a gun. The People's Liberation Army has pre-positioned a lot of military resources, indicating a physical invasion of several small countries in the area is imminent. Their primary interest is oil, of course. The Chait have confirmed all this.

"Each of the big three plans to physically take control of the heavy lifters upon completion. The big three have already begun bullying the little three. For example, with China's tacit approval, North Korea is firing missiles over Japanese airspace again.

"Virtually every country in the world is lobbying the lucky six for a continent of their own. France and Italy are putting a huge amount of diplomatic pressure on Germany. Austria, a German-speaking country, is as well—and might have a shot. An oil-rich Sunni coalition is firming up and is expecting to buy in from somebody. Naturally their offer will be a 'buy in, or else' proposition.

"Even private factions want in. Every individual or family group with tens of billions of dollars is used to buying whatever they want. Some individuals, and now informal partnerships, are buying into key industries with plans to extort their way into a private colony. Several scum suckers are even hoping to buy rights to a continent, and then flip it down the road for a huge profit.

"I don't have to tell any of you how much pressure we're getting to expand the program to seven or eight or even twelve colonies.

"The wholehearted peaceful cooperation we counted on isn't happening," finished Adrian.

"Guys," responded Jon, "everything you've told me is true. I can't argue otherwise. However, I believe we are making progress towards our desired outcome. Take a step back and get some perspective. Sure, we are seeing an unprecedented level of governments plotting and scheming with each other. But one man's plotting and scheming is simply another man's working together."

"For God's sake, Jon," Tracey interrupted. "You can't be serious."

"I'm quite serious," Jon replied. "Let me continue. The relations between Russia and China are the best they've ever been. Neither of them is provoking the United States. The loose arrangement of the Commonwealth is being tested right now, but the odds are they come out of it more unified and stronger than ever. Germany and Japan are receiving a lot of pressure, well, tough cheese. The little guy always takes a beating. The United States, oddly enough, is sitting on the sidelines. Their foreign policy is impotent. I expect the US policy to become more active after election, but other than making our lives hell, the US is doing okay.

"Adrian, with his project management background, understands this better than most. Every large complex project goes through 'oh boy, things are going great' to 'oh shit, things are falling apart,' and oscillates through the stages several times.

"As far as private groups buying in, more power to them. If a consortium of uber rich want to shower money on a particular country in exchange for land, well, who's harmed?

"I encourage you to consult more with your Chait representatives. The Chait have complete, up-to-date intelligence on the international machinations and can assure you the situation is not out of control.

"Casey and Shirley are working a plan to address the unfounded charges of kidnapping. The matter is purely a media problem. Even the forthcoming arrest warrants are based on unsubstantiated media reports.

"We have a good chance to sabotage any legal action against the company, or us personally. If not, the legal issues will certainly go away after the election.

"The one existential threat we face is a major power grabbing control of the heavy lifters once they're ready to fly. Of course, we have plans which address the threat.

"Tracey, I believe you had one more thing, the internal issue?" asked Jon.

"We are starting to have internal issues regarding the policy barring serious leftists from Ouranos," Tracey said. "Yeah, I acknowledge you spoke at length with each of us before we signed on, and we went through every single family member, and identified those who weren't eligible. We all understood the conditions, and we all agreed. Now, however, several of us are facing the reality of a terminally ill loved one, and it's really hard to not help."

"Seeing a loved one slip away is the hardest thing a person ever has to face," replied Jon. "However, you can help—to a point. Each of us has tremendous financial resources, and can afford out of our own pocket the best care available on Earth. And everyone on this call agreed to the policy. The harsh reality is, everyone dies.

"Leftists turn whatever society they infest into hellholes. Communists, Socialists, Nazis, Anarchists, whatever flavor of leftist it may be, poisons society. The lefty groups follow a deliberate process to destroy productive society and herd the population into becoming wards of the state. Leftists have murdered hundreds of millions since the beginning of the twentieth century, and still deliberately keep billions in abject poverty today.

"With the exception of the Inner Circle, Full Medical is embargoed on Earth. For good reasons. The colonies do not get access either. The only people eligible are on Ouranos. And Ouranos does not, and will not, accept leftists.

"I'd like you to work with Shirley and the Chait on this. There is one possible work-around that I'm aware of, but it's far out there and has a serious drawback.

"You know this, but you need to hear the message again," Jon finished. "It's not a Democrat versus Republican thing. Hell, most of the Inner Circle vote Democrat. If we let committed leftists into Ouranos, the colony fails, and we fail in our mission, and our goal. The existence of humanity is at stake."

THIRTY-NINE
AMAZON COVE

A MAZON COVE WAS AN ESTUARY where the Amazon River emptied into the Poseidon Sea. The Cove was kilometers across at low tide and several times as large when the tide rolled in. The estuary was surrounded by fetid swamps.

The swamp was teeming with wildlife. Flocks of colorful birds found safety in the trees. Everything from fish to rodents to large cats, bears, and reptilian life lived in the swamp. The most dangerous was the alligator, which could grow four meters long and weigh up to four hundred kilos. Clouds of mosquitos hovered over the swamp most of the year. The Chait AI listed no poisonous snakes. No matter. Those who experienced swamps in a prior lifetime remained leery of snakes.

Solid ground eventually rose from the swamp. By the time one was ten kilometers from the estuary, the land rose free of the muck. The country was flat, humid, and thickly covered with weedy trees, and undergrowth.

What drew men here was the wealth under the land. For millennia men banded together to wrest wealth from the Earth. In this godforsaken place the draw was oil. A large, shallow field of good-quality oil was pooled kilometers under the estuary.

A random finger of land extended into the swamp surrounding the estuary. Although not high enough to be called a hill, the land stood several meters proud of the surrounding swamp. This was where the first drill pads were cleared, and the first well completed. The amount of oil pumped was ridiculously small by terrestrial standards. Tanker trucks hauled the crude to a small Fab complex and tank farm ten kilometers away. HAL units hacked out clearings in the forest. The better timber was used to construct rough dwellings for the workers. The town of Amazon Cove was born.

Neither the river, the estuary, nor the sea was visible from town.

Everyone involved initially begrudged the effort. The output was planned for use in making plastics, pharmaceuticals, and fertilizer. Ouranos had unlimited access to clean, cheap power. Hydrocarbons would never be burned to provide energy. The explosive growth in the use of hydrocarbon-derived products blindsided everyone.

Now, the site was gearing up for construction of His Majesty's Vessel (HMV) *Argo*. The Project required a dozen large buildings for material storage, assembly, and hangars. Wide, strong taxiways were needed to move first large subassemblies and later the completed vessels. The tank farm also needed expansion.

Manufactured items which could not be derived from hydrocarbon were laboriously flown in from Mountainside. Consequently, almost everything Fab'd on-site was some version of plastic or other carbon construct.

The current expansion required clearing large plots of forest. The scope of the work made HAL units using hand tools impractical. Heavy metal was needed.

"What the heck is that thing?" asked Adolphus (Duffy) Grant. His question was directed at the two roughnecks standing nearby.

"That, my friend, is a dozer, a piece of equipment used for clearing land," explained the larger of the two.

"That doesn't look like any bulldozer I've ever seen," remarked Duffy. "It flies."

The machine was roughly the size and shape of a locomotive. The body was smooth and tapered at each end. The machine was hovering a meter off the ground. As the group watched, the dozer rose higher and moved away at a sedate pace towards the edge of the clearing. Nearing the edge of the cleared field, the dozer rotated lengthways, and drifted over the forest at the height of the tallest trees. A dull roar began, and a cloud of leaves and twigs erupted underneath.

"What's it doing?" asked Duffy.

"The machine is loaded with tractor and repeller beam generators," replied the man. "The tractor beams pull everything but the largest trees out by the roots and hacks the debris into manageable lengths. The dozer then makes another pass and pulls the big trees out one at a time. The beams trim the logs for use as construction lumber. Then, it makes yet another pass to sweep up the clippings and dump them somewhere. Once the land is cleared, the dozer makes a number of passes to level and compact the soil.

"The operations people should prioritize the dozer to improve access to the well head. The road is god-awful and getting worse. The bosses need to maintain the road properly, or bite the bullet and put in a damn pipeline," concluded the man.

Duffy was noncommittal. His view was they should fly an automated tanker drone back and forth to the wells, and not dick around with a road, or a pipeline. A pipeline doomed them to eternal maintenance of the service road, and a tanker drone was cheaper than six kilometers of pipe. In fact, if he was in charge, he wouldn't have located anything here but a tank farm and loading facilities to fly the oil out. The place sucked.

Duffy went back to work. He was a builder and tasked with putting up housing for the influx of new workers. He needed to ponder how he could use the dozer. The fuckwit who ran Amazon Cove did not share information widely. Duffy had no idea the dozer was coming.

Unlike the other towns, Amazon Cove had no ready access to stone, or Fab waste pressed into blocks, to use as building materials. Initial housing was constructed of wood, or plastic panels. The esthetics of the initial plastic sucked—people called them playhouses. Eventually the homes improved with fancy wood grain floors and cabinets. Drapes and carpets helped as well.

Duffy was doing five houses of a new design. The first was ready to plant; he called the dwelling a treehouse. His HAL units—Butch and Sundance—had put up a three-bedroom, two-bath uninsulated wooden house. The walls were no more than a thin plank of unfinished wood – no insulation, and no vapor barrier. The construction was closer to a shack than a house. However, the inside was finished carefully, with attention to detail.

A meter-wide plant bed was prepared around the perimeter of the house. Several hundred pounds of a custom fertilizer was mixed into the bed, and a package of bioengineered seeds planted. When the seeds sprouted a week later, he was to spray the sides of the house with a dopant which attracted the tendrils, which grew with astonishing rapidity. A month later he was to spray the roof. Within several months the house should be covered in leafy vines. In the second stage, the leaves grew to the size and shape of an elephant's ear. At this point the interior was cool, and watertight. The third stage began after a year and saw a thick bark similar to balsa encase the entire house.

As a bonus the treehouse repelled insects, including mosquitos.

Duffy was skilled at construction and the related trades. However, he didn't play well with others, which was why he'd ended up working by himself and not on a team. Everyone was happier this way. He despised the HAL units at first. Once he saw their common sense and untiring way of working, he warmed up to the technology. HAL units were never late, never argued, never stole, and took no breaks for weed. Now, he loved his HAL units the way Earth children adored their phones.

Duffy was not enthused at the treehouses. If the plants grew as advertised, the dwellings would evolve into comfortable homes, in a hippie kind of way. However, the base construction took months and he, and two HAL units, could only work on a couple at a time. In a year he would have built five homes, capable of comfortably housing fifteen to twenty people. Big whoop. Where were the other two hundred new people supposed to live? Tents?

After some research Duffy spoke to the town manager and recommended trailers. "A six-meter-long trailer can be Fab'd easily," he told Juan, the manager. "A medium-sized Fab can make a trailer and everything inside the four walls in a single day. We'd need a hundred kilos of assorted metals from Mountainside for each trailer, but that's all. Everything else is derived here from hydrocarbons: the exterior, the interior, even the bedsheets and pillows."

Juan dismissively rejected the idea. "I'm not going to dedicate a Fab for months to build crappy trailers. Shortsighted solutions won't work. The town will continue to grow, and need permanent homes. We're on Ouranos, and I'm not going down in history as the guy who built the first trailer park."

"We need housing, quickly, boss," replied Duffy. "Unless you reconsider dormitories, or townhouses, I don't know a quicker way to get housing."

"Your job for the next year is to build treehouses," replied Juan tightly. "I'll worry about the overall housing picture."

Stupid, thought Duffy as he walked away. Townhouses were the obvious way to go for company housing, which was why the other sites built them. Every detached home required separate infrastructure, which took time. *Does he really think men with seventy or eighty years of life experience will live in tents for years? Or women? Ha! The jerk is ignoring the problem, and hoping it will go away.*

If Juan insisted on detached dwellings, trailers were the obvious solution, thought Duffy. Trailers can be moved, or stuffed back in a Fab and disassociated when no longer needed. Juan never consulted the AI. *The dumbass believes the biggest brain on the planet is just a souped-up search engine.*

Duffy had got off on the wrong foot with Juan from the first. At an early meeting Juan pretended to care and asked for recommendations to improve working conditions. Duffy jumped up and asked for ten thousand liters of mosquito spray, and a dedicated drone to treat a kilometer-sized circle around the town. The audience roared in approval. Juan took the suggestion under advisement, and nothing ever happened.

On the other hand, Duffy was proud of the fact he'd spoken to several people today, and didn't lose his temper, or get in an argument. His behavior was not typical of his last twenty years of life. Unknown to him at the time, an undiagnosed chemical imbalance had deeply affected his moods. He'd pushed away friends and family and worked as a one-man contractor until he almost died. His endocrine system was fixed during his re-life, and he was normal now. He was able to converse, or even flatly disagree, with people, without a violent argument.

The energy of a young man oozed through from pores. As soon as he received his land grant, Duffy spent a year building a house. The large, comfortable home overlooked the White River, and was located twenty kilometers outside of Shoreside. He didn't trust alien tech, and used the devices sparingly on his homestead. Any alien tech he did use had a low-tech backup. He put up a windmill and installed solar panels for electricity. He specified exact replicas of common Earth brands to avoid the alien tech, but admittedly had no way to know what was inside the electronic components.

He built an old-fashioned root cellar under the house. He put in a large vegetable garden and built up a year's supply of calories in beans, rice, pasta, and expensive imported olive oil. There was game in the hills and fish in the river, so he built a smokehouse. He laid in ten thousand rounds of ammunition. He acquired manual hand tools his grandfather would have recognized: braces, planes, and crosscut saws. Being nonstandard, the tools were expensive as hell. He even had a springhouse.

The weather near Shoreside was mild. For the inevitable cold snaps, he installed radiant heat under his floors. He used tubing and hot water rather than the commonly used electrical setup. He used a power unit to heat the water but had a high-efficiency wood-fed boiler as backup. He also installed a wood stove.

His neighbors thought he was eccentric when he built a game fence. The barrier was three meters high and constructed of heavy grided wire. The fence enclosed the five hectares containing his house, garden, and immediate surroundings. He characterized his caution as a belt and suspenders approach. One should use both. Just in case.

Duffy's view was the wards worked great, until the day they didn't.

HAL units did most of the physical work. In his prior life Duffy begrudged time spent designing a structure, and enjoyed the actual construction. Now, with reliable help, he happily spent time up front on designing, and teaching his units advanced skills.

Word got around of Duffy's building skills. A lot of people needed advice or help, or would just pay outright for Duffy to build them a house. Once his personal house was finished, he began taking jobs in town, working in his off hours. He quit leasing his HAL units to The Project and used them on his own jobs. He charged exorbitant rates which people seemed happy to pay. There wasn't much else to spend money on.

Duffy was philosophical about Juan's view on housing. Piss on him. Duffy would just punch the clock at work and concentrate his energy contracting on the side. He felt so young and vital that the nickname

"Duffy" no longer seemed to fit. Oh well, he sure as hell wasn't going to go by "Adolph."

FORTY
THE BANISHMENT

LYNN BYMAN WAS A JERK. A wanker. A dickhead. A tool. He had been born in South Africa, educated in Britain, and spent most of his life in Central and South America working as a civil engineer and surveyor. About the time age and his drinking habits caught up with him, he received a modest inheritance. He returned to South Africa to spend his last few years in a civilized country with good health care. He was recruited from a hospice in Johannesburg to go to Ouranos.

In spending his adult life working projects in undeveloped areas, Lynn had a minimal online presence. He participated in no social media and rarely used email. His boorish behavior in remote mining and construction camps rarely escalated to arrests, or court time, much less jail. He paid cash at the bars and whorehouses. He had no online record of bad behavior.

Lynn was a large, brawny man who liked to use his size to bully people. He was brutal to subordinates, and barely tolerated his superiors. However, he was good at his job and didn't mind the most taxing of work environments.

The recruiters were always looking for civil engineers. When a pair visited Lynn in the nursing home, he had a touch of dementia, the version which makes one rude and nasty. The dementia masked his basic personality and allowed him to pass muster during the recruiting process. The recruiting process also failed in that most of those who knew him well were in South America, not South Africa, which made his background check cumbersome. The checks were cut short. During his time in the rejuvenation tanks, the basic fixes to his biology were completed without issue. However, the problem with Lynn was not in his brain chemistry or hormones. The problem was his basic personality.

Once on Ouranos, and feeling his newfound youth, Lynn constantly got into fights, scrapes, and arguments in his off time. He acted as if he was still in a third world mining camp. Things came to a head when he brutally beat a woman who came home with him one night. Such behavior crossed a bright red line.

The skeletal justice system on Ouranos was part of civil administration. The system ran on a few basic principles, not a detailed judicial code. The system was centered around the victim, not the criminal. There were no criminal rehabilitation programs. The philosophy stressed compensating the victim over punishing the transgressor. However, the transgressor was indeed punished. For first offenses, such as fighting (usually after a few drinks), the sentence was light—a night in the pokey until one sobered up, payment for damages, and a fine. Second offences got one an unpleasant job for a week or two, payment of any associated expenses, and of course, a fine. Repeat offenders were treated much more harshly. The most severe penalty was banishment.

"Lynn, goddamn it," said Steve Kopec, the Rainy Town manager. "This time you've gone too far. There is no excuse for your behavior." Steve had listened to Joy Monsein's side of the story and viewed her ugly bruises. He also listened to the remote testimony of several people who had seen the two at the restaurant beforehand. "What do you have to say for yourself?"

"Bloody kaffir bitch," began Lynn aggressively. "She came home with me because she wanted to—and the others in the bar all testified in my favor. Once we got to my apartment she guzzled booze straight from the bottle, and got drunker than a striped-ass baboon. She started breaking shit, and then came after me with a knife. She's lucky I didn't hurt her worse."

Everything he said after her coming home with him were lies. Steve had medical reports downloaded from their enhancements; hers indicated only a modest amount of alcohol, while Lynn's showed he was extremely drunk. The apartment wasn't trashed. Lynn was unmarked. Joy had no violent history; Lynn did. In the end, a review of the evidence was just theater. In these cases, a direct replay from the enhancements of those involved was available to the judge via the AI. The AI Knew All.

Steve, as Rainy Town manager, served as judge, jury, and prosecutor. He hated this part of the job. Back on Earth even a peaceful community has one or two violent crimes per thousand every year. Ouranos was much more peaceful than most Earth communities; however, the society was not totally crime free.

"Lynn Byman, I find you guilty," said Steve formally. "I sentence you to one year of banishment. Because this is your first offense of this magnitude, the sentence is not with prejudice."

The accused was entitled to no representation.

Other than a small facility at each town designed to hold a couple offenders overnight (the drunk tank) there were no prisons on Ouranos. Lynn would be cast out of society and spend the next year on a small deserted island in a temperate clime. He would have cases of meals-ready-to-eat (MREs) to provide approximately half the sustenance needed during the sentence. His remaining food would be whatever he could catch or gather. He would be given a few hand tools, a modest amount of water, fishing line, and one change of clothes. He would have no human contact, and his enhancements would be disabled.

From the state's point of view banishment was beneficial to society. There were no prisons and no guards. There were no endless appeals requiring someone on a government payroll to read them, and respond to them. There were no criminal lawyers, and no defense attorneys.

Young men are responsible for virtually all petty and violent crime. Although not widely known, the primary reason for limiting rejuvenations to no younger than age twenty-five was to avoid the hormone overload and poor decision-making inherent in a young man's brain.

A banishment with prejudice meant one's youth was not completely restored at the next rejuvenation. Their biological age would not be rolled back to twenty-five but something older. For gross repeat offenders the ultimate prejudice was no rejuvenation at all.

"The income from the HAL unit you have leased to The Project is assigned to Miss Monsein, in compensation for her injuries, lost time at work, and medical costs," continued Steve. "Once those have been paid, including one hundred percent punitive damages, the income will revert to Rainy Town until your court costs, feeding, housing, and transportation costs are repaid. Again, the costs include a charge of one hundred percent punitive damages.

"Do you wish to appeal the ruling, or your sentence?" asked Steve. A miscreant could appeal any ruling to a tribunal consisting of the other three town managers. However, if one lost on appeal, the sentence was doubled. People thought the matter over very carefully before appealing.

Lynn cursed.

"Joy, do you find this sentence sufficient?" asked Steve. Within limits, the victim could petition for a heavier, but not more lenient, sentence.

"Yes, sir," she replied. "I suppose so. I hope he rots painfully for the entire year."

Two days later, Paul Gaztelumendi the Rainy Town constable, and Warren Ganley, the Shoreside constable who had come down to assist, stuffed a tranked Lynn into a packed saucer. The pair fastened the five-point harness and shackled his hands and feet. The flight took two hours. Once they reached the island, the saucer landed on a broad, firm beach and unloaded the supplies at the edge of the thin jungle.

Lynn was fully awake but his limbs remained rubbery. The constables helped him to the shade, removed the cuffs, and stepped back quickly. Lynn tried to rise and charge them but stumbled twice trying to get up.

"Good luck," said Paul. "I'll see you in a year."

"Hope you like fish," added Warren.

Upon departing, the constables cruised the island. The place was quite pretty—approximately ten kilometers in circumference and dominated by a central peak created by a dormant volcano. A couple of freshwater rivulets appeared near the base. The beach where the pair left Lynn featured a lagoon sheltered by a reef two hundred meters offshore. There was no other visible land within a hundred kilometers.

"Club Med it ain't," remarked Paul as the saucer headed for home. "He better ration his packaged food and keep his water jugs full."

Warren shrugged. "Stupidity is always a capital offense," he quoted loosely.

FORTY-ONE
THE REORGANIZATION

COLONEL DOUGLAS BICKEL, US ARMY Corp of Engineers PE (retired), blew into his new office. *Not too bad*, he thought while opening drawers and poking around. Too much paper, mostly trivia. Nothing on the walls here, or in the conference rooms either. He'd fix that.

In his prior life Doug built facilities all over the world for the US Army. After a career of living in third world hellholes he transferred to the Corp, and later retired and began work as a civilian employee, living in Portland, Oregon. He was on the doorstep of a nice restaurant when a mugger hit him in the head with a steel pipe, leaving him blind. He was fifty-eight years old when the recruiters came. He was divorced; his children, and grandchildren, rarely visited. He eagerly signed up for the deal.

Doug was replacing Juan Perez as the Amazon Cove town manager. Doug met, virtually, with the king and the three other town managers before assuming the role. He was given carte blanche by the king to fix the problems at Amazon Cove. He was later told such a meeting was unprecedented. He also went through a nonstandard rejuvenation. He spent a month in a tank to fix the neurological issue which caused his blindness. The tank also eliminated any minor health issues. He emerged five years younger than when he went in. He also received a treatment similar to one given to members of the Inner Circle and would continue to grow younger for years, or until he went back into a tank.

The entire Project was careening into a bottleneck caused by the lack of facilities in Amazon Cove. Infrastructure was so far behind, the town even lacked housing and utilities for the workers required to build the needed flight-related facilities.

Doug spent a week at each town getting to know the people and resources available. He was also given a deep dive into the capabilities of the available technology.

Juan was given a lateral move and assigned a strategic planning role to assess and tweak the land grant process. A wave of immigrants would soon be eligible for grants, and the king wished to review and perhaps overhaul the system.

Valerie, the Shoreside manager, gave her two cents worth to Doug privately. "It's the Peter Principal," she said. "You do a good job, which earns you a promotion. The process continues until one works himself into a position where he doesn't do a good job. People are rarely demoted and so they stay in a position over their heads for years. Juan has a wonderful resume and lots of abilities; however, he's not well suited to the job of town manager."

Valerie was a kind person.

This was Doug's first morning on the job. He had called an early staff meeting. The meeting was held in person. The town's management organization structure was unclear—one possible source of the poor performance—so Doug included a couple extra people in addition to the three who appeared to report directly to Juan. Not enough people was probably another reason for the lack of progress.

The others started to filter in at the meeting start time. The last arrived ten minutes after the scheduled start time. Another black mark in Doug's mind.

Doug introduced himself. He then picked up a meter stick and a permanent marker and started drawing a large chart on the wall. Not on a marker board but on the wall itself. "Here is our schedule to assemble the first interstellar spaceship built by the human race," began Doug. He wrote a date at the end of the horizontal axis. He then drew a thick black line from the meeting point of the two axes, upwards at a forty-five-degree angle, and a small star at the end. He turned back to his audience. "The king decreed the craft be available by this date. He commanded this several years ago. This is necessary to prevent nuclear war on Earth, extinction of the human race, and keep technology coming from the Chait. The technology that saved my life, your life, and keeps us young and healthy." He looked at each of them in turn. The small group shifted uneasily in their chairs.

Doug turned back to his chart and drew a second line, in red. This line only traveled half the distance of the first line, and ended halfway between the original schedule line and the horizontal axis. He labeled the end point with the current date. "Here is where we are now," he continued. "Half the schedule is gone; however, only one quarter of the work has been completed."

A thin-faced woman in the back began to speak. Doug cut her off. "Please hold your thoughts until I finish," he said briskly.

He then drew a dotted line from the line ending at the current date steeply upward, terminating at the original end date. He turned back to face the group. "Here is the schedule we now have to meet to launch His Lord's Vessel *Argo* at the given time.

"I want to spend an hour today with each of you, individually." He looked at the thin-faced woman. "Sharon, you first, please. The rest of you can go. We will hold a quick stand-up check-in every morning at this time. Thanks."

The chart was bullshit of course, but effective motivation. He would leave the writing on the wall for the remainder of The Project.

Doug was meeting with Duffy Grant. Duffy had just filled him in on the marching orders Juan had given him regarding the treehouses.

"I see," said Doug noncommittally. Juan had left a lot of cleanup to do behind him. There was no zoning, or master plan. Juan winged everything. Doug got to the point. "The town needs housing for fifty new Project people within sixty days, and another fifty beds the following month. And the people are going to keep coming. Everybody says you are the man when it comes to building housing. Give me some options."

The tree houses were never mentioned again. Ten years later the concept became quite popular.

"I could put up something like an army barrack," began Duffy. "You're familiar with those. The army figured this problem out a hundred years ago. Barracks can be ready in time to meet your schedule. I can even Fab Quonset hut components with snap-in panels to wall off semi-private rooms."

Doug shook his head. "Barracks won't be sufficient given the background of the people. Even hardship pay won't make barrack life palatable."

Duffy then explained his concept of Fabbing trailers. "Given the raw material and power unit support from Mountainside, I can put a trailer a day into service by dedicating one of the Fabs here," he said. The trailers are self-contained and require no facilitation as internal systems recycle sewage and grey water. I've specified a luxurious interior and I believe the living arrangements will satisfy most people. At least for a year. By dedicating a Fab for two months, you would have reasonable, though cramped, quarters for sixty people.

"I've already spoke with Anna. From a Fab planning perspective, she will support the idea, if you make the recommendation."

Doug was relieved but kept a poker face. From experience, he knew temporary housing tended to stick around forever. However, trailers could move overnight.

"What else?" he asked.

"Townhouses," replied Duffy. "As the other settlements have done, for good reasons. I can build a block of ten units in about three months. Each townhouse has two bedrooms, so you get nice housing for twenty single people. More, if they shack up.

"I'd need the dozer for a couple days to clear and prepare a strip of land. We have enzymes which can turn soil into a substitute for concrete, but the process takes too long. I'd need to bring in gravel to make footings. I've designed a single block stacked two units high by five long, which maximizes the use of the expensive foundation. The shared interior walls, floors, ceilings, and roof minimize construction time. The dwellings would be built from wood, which is readily available. I'd need a couple more HAL units and Fab time to make fine polymer-infused lumber products for floors, paneling, and exterior sheathing."

Doug was familiar with the housing concept Duffy described. Similar structures were used for officer quarters at army posts a hundred years ago. "Those might work in the longer term. Townhouses don't solve our current problem. Would a couple more guys help?" he asked. "I've got priority on recruits."

Duffy recoiled. "I don't work great with others. If you staff this up, I respectfully request you keep them away from me. Use the others on a parallel effort, please."

Doug wasn't going to run the place for Duffy's convenience. However, he recognized the man's value. Doug saw the opportunity to dump the issue on Duffy and motivate the man to run with it. Doug was already planning to assign several people to manage the completed housing, perform maintenance, and listen to the inevitable complaints from the residents.

"Any other ideas?" asked Doug.

"Sure," said Duffy, thinking fast. He had to sell an approach quickly or this hotshot would make his life miserable. "But the conditions get rougher. I can do a bunkhouse for a dozen people in a week or two. However, I already know bunkhouses aren't palatable."

Duffy leaned forward. "Boss, let me get a little more conceptual here. As the only starship base in existence, this town is going to boom in ways I can't imagine. Lots of people will come here on a permanent basis. Also, like any port city, we'll have a lot of transients. Portable housing trailers will always be needed somewhere. Give me a waiver to manage two more HAL units. I'll start a trailer park and the townhouses in parallel. Once the trailer Fab and placement is running smooth, I'll be happy to turn that activity over to somebody else. I'll put up one townhouse block after another and connect them with a breezeway. I'll get faster after I put in a couple. If we get some slack or more resources I can put in a pool, nice grounds, fruit trees, and flowers in the complex and make the grounds more attractive. Same with the trailer park. You'll need somebody else to manage the park and look after the upkeep. I wouldn't do well as a manager."

"Do it," said Doug. "Send me the requisitions, and I'll review and forward on with my approval. I'll start looking for someone suitable for you to hand off the trailer effort. I believe you'll reach that point within weeks."

Duffy grinned. "Great! The AI did the analyses for me, and I prepared the req's months ago. I'll send them over within the hour."

"Say, while you're being agreeable, may I make a request? It has to do with bug spray."

Doug Bickel and Gerry Bass stood in the morning sun and watched at a safe distance as the status lights flickered in the nearest field generator. "I don't want to jinx things, but this is great," said Gerry. "We could recover a big chunk of schedule if this works."

"Some elements of a redirected approach were obvious to me even on day one," mused Doug. "However, I'd been here a couple weeks and was shooting the breeze with a young guy, a first lifer, at lunch. He was visiting his girlfriend. This guy, Siple, was a real smart ass and remarked how he'd heard everything was fucked up down here."

"I've met the guy," said Gerry. "You're right. He's an ass."

"Yes, but he's a really smart, ass," quipped Doug. "We got to talking and he knew things I didn't about Chait technology, and how to effectively use the capabilities. Of course, I know a lot more about building, and engineering. We put our heads together and lunch ended up running three hours. He's spent a lot of time thinking on using the technology. To make a long story short, here we are."

Within days of taking over the management of Amazon Cove, Doug trashed the sketchy plans to upgrade facilities. Revised plans were drawn up to float the larger subassemblies of the *Argo* and related equipment. Project personnel working with a Fab AI were able to design a floater containing a power unit, batteries, and antigravity generators. A loaded Chait antigravity floater could almost be pulled along by a single HAL unit. The large trucks, trailers, and overbuilt taxiways were no longer needed. The assembly and hangar areas now had hard points sitting on deep pillars to support the *Argo*'s main subassemblies, and the ship itself once completed.

The surrounding taxiways, aprons, assembly, and hangar areas were now of much lighter construction than originally planned. The change in design allowed the thickness and overall mass of the load-bearing flat spaces to be cut by two-thirds, with a corresponding improvement in schedule. The construction method used a relatively thin layer of concrete poured over a much thicker layer of compacted dirt dosed with a hardening enzyme.

Doug now planned to entirely eliminate the need for a large assembly building.

"Get ready, here it comes," he told Gerry. Quantum field screen generators the size of a small washing machine were set at the corners of a square a hundred meters on a side. The units synced, and a silvery dome two hundred meters in diameter flickered into existence. The small crowd cheered and clapped their hands.

"Come on, let's go inside," said Doug. As the pair approached the dome a semicircular area thinned appreciably, and the two pushed on through with little effort. The dome thickened behind them.

"Very cool," said Gerry, looking around. "I'm massively impressed. Tell me more about the environmental controls."

"Sure," said Doug. "As you can see, it glows. We can have around-the-clock daylight or dim the brightness down to utter blackness if needed. The inside is shielded from weather. All rain, sleet, or snow slides right off the sides. We'll ring the dome with drainage tomorrow. The shield is semi-permeable and tuned to keep the interior at a comfortable working environment. The outside environment is warm right now, so the screen decreases the vibration of air molecules allowed through, reducing the temperature. We also have two air tunnels pumping in fresh, filtered, dehumidified air. In a couple days the Chait-designed air-handling equipment will have particulate matter in the inside air down to a level of a class one clean room."

"Not quite there yet, I see," said Gerry while waving away a large flying bug. The insect life had declined dramatically since the spraying program started. However, bugs remained a problem.

Doug laughed. "At shift change tonight we will clear everyone out, and the dome will do one gigantic bug zap. The first hour of the following shift will be housecleaning."

The two walked over and inspected the hard points and attached cradles. "Not only are the cradles strong enough to support the full weight of the craft," said Doug, "they are isolated from any vibration which might interfere with the assembly process.

"The pad to the south is curing. The second dome will go up there in a month. The third dome a month afterwards. I planned to erect permanent hangars at some point in the future. However, if this arrangement holds up, you may not ever need them.

"A Fab took only a single cycle of one day to pump out the field generators," gloated Doug. The entire setup came down from Mountainside on a single supply run, along with a bunch of other materials. This is a heck of a lot easier than traditional construction."

"This is goddamn amazing," exclaimed Gerry. "We've got a roof over our heads with power, light, heating, cooling—the whole shooting match. The first large fuselage subassemblies will come out of Fab next week. Are we ready to start joining?"

"That's a question for the assembly team," said Doug. "The building is ready. Oh, I'm going to put in a wash station to hose down any incoming vehicles, and equipment. And some porta-potties. But you can start working today."

"Yeah, I was asking about the building," replied Gerry. "I damn sure know the status of the other bits. The specialized Andy units are ready. So are the floaters, and other specialized automata to install the few items not already pre-built into the fuselage. Those items are sitting on a shelf ready to go."

Gerry looked straight up and slowly turned in a circle gazing at the dome high overhead.

"This is goddamn amazing," he repeated aloud to himself.

FORTY-TWO
THE *ARGO*

T HE *ARGO* WAS READY TO fly.

"Tell me, Gerry," asked Ken Edson. "Did you ever really believe the *Argo* would be ready on time?"

Gerry Bass, the program manager, had driven the teams hard. No one involved in building the *Argo* believed the starship would launch on schedule. No one, except Gerry.

"Of course, I did," replied Gerry. "The initial schedule appeared very challenging. I ran simulations on the AI over and over, and the scenarios appeared unbelievable. One night I drank too much while pondering the sky overhead and had an epiphany. After sobering up I ran simulations looking at certain details from different angles, and it popped right out."

"What popped right out?" asked Ken.

"My epiphany related to a test question I had in a chemistry class long ago," answered Gerry indirectly. "The question involved a mass of complicated information related to cell growth, nutrients, a starting point, and the fact the cell mass doubled every second. The question was, simplified for you here and now, 'If the cells fill the beaker in sixty seconds, how long does it take to fill half the beaker?'" He looked at Ken expectedly.

"I have no idea of course," answered Ken. "The answer would depend on all the complicated information I don't have."

"That's where you're wrong, bucko," said Gerry, punching him in the shoulder. The shoulder punch was a project norm inflicted on whoever said something dumb. "If the mass doubles every second, and the beaker is full in sixty seconds, it's half full in fifty-nine seconds. You can ignore the starting point and all the complicated stuff. Half the class missed the easiest question on the test."

"Ok, I missed the easy question also," said Ken unabashedly. "And your story relates to my question exactly how?"

"The technology we use here is unlike anything we grew up with," said Gerry. "We expect fairly gradual learning curves, and linear project progress towards the stated goal. For example, recruiting a person used to take weeks. The new hire might require weeks of training. Then they quit, or didn't work out, and you started over. That kind of slop was built into your schedule, maybe.

"The learning curves are different here. Now, we order a HAL unit and it arrives the next day. The units are synced up and trained the first minute on the job. Each does the work of five men. If the work is repetitive, we get specialized equipment which works even faster than a HAL unit. When I looked at the sims from that perspective the schedule made sense."

Gerry finished up. "Traditionally the last five percent of a complex project perversely soaks up twenty percent of the total effort, and schedule. Which is why almost no projects are ever finished on time. This technology enabled a paradigm shift. We swapped those stats and finished the last twenty percent of the build using only five percent of the schedule. Our learning curve increased at an increasing rate until the line was almost vertical."

The pair watched silently for a minute while the four Argonauts waved to the crowd before boarding the first interstellar craft built by man. The hatch shut behind them. The crowd moved off the saucer pad.

"I sure wish I was on it," said Ken wistfully.

"Me too," said Gerry. "But we're the big bosses. You're the operations manager, and I'm manager of the whole stinking Project. Sure, we're flight qualified, and will pilot a few runs. But not now, not here, not today."

Vickie Warren, the production manager, and Pat Palmer, the technical manager, joined the two men.

"Not making the maiden flight, I see," needled Vickie.

"Fuck you," Ken and Gerry replied in unison.

"Nobody twisted your arms," Vickie retorted. "You were the ones who selected the pilots for the initial flight." She turned to Pat. "This thing is going to fly, right?" she asked Pat playfully.

"The AI says it will," answered the double PhD in math and physics. "No human understands the math or physics well enough to answer your question definitively. We are in monkey see, monkey do, territory here."

The others winced and glanced around to see if anyone else had overheard. "Jesus, a little less plain English please," pleaded Ken.

"That hull is a sandwich of over fifty discreet layers," said Pat. "Shoot, the hull is closer to a computer chip than a structure. The equipment in the wing blisters generate permutations among one hundred and fifty-six separate, discrete quantum fields which propagate via those layers in various combinations depending on the requirements. I'll spare you the field nomenclature.

"In terrestrial science the big kahuna of physics is the Standard Model, which posits only twenty-four possible quantum fields. Obviously, Chait science goes deeper into the physical universe. The secret sauce in this ship is the use of Chait lattice quantum field theory."

Pedantically, Pat began ticking off points on his fingers. "First, antigravity. Then, a second, internal antigravity field to compensate for the first. If the *Argo* accelerates at a rate of a hundred gravities without internal compensation, the humans aboard would be reduced to a jelly on the rear of the interior shell."

"We don't want that," Vickie agreed, while making a face.

"With the internal antigravity compensation protecting the passengers, the *Argo* will be capable of ninety-degree turns while traveling thousands of kilometers per hour," continued Pat.

"The ship can generate numerous types of force screens. Those are useful in protecting against anything from bird strikes to directed energy weapons. The fields are strong enough to hold against even a nuclear explosion, within limits. Several of those fields can be tuned so as to absorb, or reflect, one hundred percent of light across a wide band of spectrums. Others can make the craft invisible to the human eye. Other fields will stealth the craft against all bands of radar, sonar, lidar, etc. Of course, the effect works the other way also—the craft has superb sensory capabilities. These fields can do a lot of other useful stuff as well.

"The captain will shout 'shields up!' quite often on the *Argo*." No one laughed. Everyone was nervous.

Pat plowed on. "The fields can interact to create a particular interference pattern instantly ejecting the craft from its point of existence in our universe. However, for this to function reliably the craft must be well clear of any gravity well. The fields are tuned in such a manner the craft reappears instantly in an entirely different point in our universe. Done correctly, the craft reappears in the exact point you specify. By instantly I mean as defined by quantum mechanics. Do you want to hear more detail on quantum measurement of time?" he asked hopefully.

The others hastily shook their heads and urged him to continue. The group already knew this by heart. The use of field technology was the reason the craft was so streamlined. There were no rocket exhausts, antennas, radiators, or weapon turrets to break the hull outline. Ken and Gerry were masking their nervousness by killing time before the launch.

"Just as well," said Pat morosely. "The Chait version of quantum field theory is vastly different than ours. The theory is melded with lattice theory as well. These two hugely difficult fields of Chait physics will take me years to understand—if ever.

"We have options regarding fields used for communication," continued Pat. "We use certain fields, unknown to current terrestrial physics, for our own communications. We use other fields to pick up communication methods used on Earth. We can generate both tractor and presser beams originating from any point on the exterior hull, directed in any direction, or angle. Other fields can create a directed high-energy pulse for offensive purposes originating at any point within a hundred meters of the ship. The beam propagates from empty space towards whatever target you've designated. Because the pulse originates in empty space, the cooling problems associated with terrestrial high-energy weapons are a nonissue. Any back blast is absorbed by certain fields and stuffed into buffer energy storage—the batteries.

"But wait! As the shysters on late night TV used to say, *there's more!* There are superconducting layers for thermal management which—"

Ken interrupted before Pat could continue. "But the *Argo* will fly. Right?"

Pat puffed out his cheeks and exhaled heavily. "I think so. We'll know for sure in sixty seconds." As one, the group turned to face the *Argo* and became quiet while their enhancements completed the countdown.

FORTY-THREE
ISABELLA

THE LAUNCHING OF ISABELLA WAS of a magnitude never before seen by investors. No one considered it practical, or even desirable, to raise one hundred billion dollars in one round. Jon floated twenty billion as an appropriate number for the first round. He priced the company obscenely high.

"Thirty percent ownership for twenty billion doesn't sound doable," Tom told Jon. "Right now, one's money buys thirty percent of a whole lot of nothing, except a verbal promise from the Chait to supply power, and engines, and of course design help with the heavy-lift craft. On second thought, thirty percent prices the entire company at sixty-seven billion dollars today, if I did my math correctly. Which is ridiculous."

"We should be advised by the largest investment banks in the world," said Bob. As the saying goes, 'A man has got to know his limitations,' and I'm over my head pricing something this size."

"Bob, we'll call Lemon in a minute," Jon replied. "We might only give up twenty percent for twenty billion. We can't fall into the trap of negotiating against ourselves. I'm sure the guy advising Peter Minuit on how to screw the Indians out of Manhattan Island was thinking they should offer more than twenty-four dollars' worth of beads and trinkets.

"Right now, today, Isabella is conflated with ownership of entire virgin planets. Also, a piece of Isabella is the only lever anyone has over ownership of this particular Chait technology. I'm going to set a minimum investment of a billion dollars. We can find twenty investors easily. I don't believe we'll even require twenty. Some will want to put in multiple billions. Look at our target list of probable investors. They're loaded. Let's ask Lemon about the various oil sheiks; the Sunnis could fund the entire project. The sheiks dream of a Sunni planet. However, this is a fat enough hog we have the luxury of picking and choosing the investors. We can be strategic—we *must* be strategic—in who we allow in.

"Each of the lucky six wants a seat at the table. We won't allow direct government investment; however, they are already lining up proxies. Do you think a Russian oligarch or Chinese tycoon will say no to their respective presidents? Of course not. Those guys know they'd fall out of a high window if they refused.

"The second-tier countries are also encouraging their local heavyweights to buy in. South Korea, via a chaebol, has already expressed interest. India, Brazil, and Mexico want in also."

"What great investors," grumbled Bob. "Russian oligarch gangsters, Chinese tech billionaires, cash-rich Arabs, drug cartels, dictatorships, and poor countries that can't even feed their people.

"I'm dubious," Bob continued. "Terms are more important than price. We're offering crappy terms. An investor might as well be a citizen on the street owning one share of a Mongolian company. The shareholder rights we contemplate granting are approximately zero."

"This is all mental masturbation until we get hard intelligence from Lemon," said Bill dismissively. "I will however bet each of you a nice dinner the round, whatever the amount we agree, will be over-subscribed."

No one took Bill up on the proposed bet.

The group called Lemon. Naturally the Chait already knew who was planning to invest, and the depth of their pockets. The appetite for investment was huge. Bob and Jon settled on a target of twenty percent ownership for forty billion dollars. The targets were fronts for the lucky six, Sunni oil families, and American tech billionaires. Jon planned to play them against each other. They would also allow a small number of second-tier countries to invest via proxies.

If successful, the money raise would value Isabella at two hundred billion dollars.

No arm-twisting would be needed.

"Well, that's a load off my mind," said Jon after Lemon left the meeting. "On to the next detail. We must maintain strict confidentiality during The

Project. The bank selection is critical. Who are you recommending for our primary bank?" he asked Bob.

"I disqualified most major banks immediately," replied Bob. "Banks operate only with permission of the local authorities. Regardless of banking laws when the local regulators or law enforcement come calling on a major issue, the banks roll right over. Any bank hosted by a member of the lucky six is out. That excludes the banking centers of New York, London, Toronto, and Frankfurt in the Western world. Ditto for Hong Kong or Shanghai."

Tom Interrupted. "How about Zurich?"

Bob shook his head. "When a matter rises to a level of concern to their national government, a Swiss bank is no more confidential than a hair salon. The fabled Swiss secrecy has been a myth for thirty years.

"In fact, with a few exceptions, no European based bank of any size is truly confidential. Brussels broke the EU banks years ago. The largest group still using the Swiss are African politicians. Nobody important cares about an African politician hiding money."

Tom was intrigued now. "Where do the South and Central American corrupticrats hide their money?"

"Surprisingly," answered Bob, "thieves from south of the border hide their money in the United States. Unless you antagonize an American law enforcement bureaucrat, the US has the strongest bank secrecy in the world. American banks tell every nosy government on the planet to pound sand, court order or not. Obviously, that's of no help in our situation.

"I've tentatively selected two banks. One is in Budapest, Hungary, the other is in Panama. Both are reasonably large and sophisticated, although admittedly second tier. However, the institutions are hard to muscle, and a key selling point is the management of these two specific banks speak no English. Which makes dealing with them, or spying on them, a royal pain in the ass. Not many CIA agents speak Hungarian.

"First item on my plate is hiring several senior managers and a couple dozen more employees to keep the gears turning," Bob concluded.

"Now, to the interesting part," Jon said. "Tom, you must hit the ground running. We've capitalized Isabella with a billion to get started. Can you spend that much in the next ninety days?" The others laughed.

"Actually, I probably will," answered Tom seriously. "We better have a second billion ready if the closing on the big bucks is delayed. I've hired a dozen senior guys and expect to have a hundred guys on board inside two months. Within a year we will hire a thousand people.

"It's easier to explain if I start from the desired end point and work backwards," Tom continued. "We want to do final assembly in a remote unaligned country, which is difficult to visit, or to influence. Each of the big three plan to seize and control the Chait technology. China's leader doesn't really care if their actions scuttle the colonization program. However, the factions within US and Russia want to have their cake and eat it to.

"For several months now, we have been working to, ah, influence key members of the Namibian government. This is a poor African coastal country, lightly populated, just up from South Africa on the Atlantic coast. The country is very desolate, mostly barren sand, and sparsely populated. Walvis Bay is a small port with deep-water facilities—well, deep enough—and an airport with a runway capable of handling commercial passenger jets. At one time the country was a Commonwealth member but withdrew a couple years ago.

"The remote location is difficult for the great powers to regularly patrol with naval units, or by air. Surveillance using feet on the ground is tough also. It's a small place. Any new face in town, especially a white one, sticks out like a whore in church. We've optioned a couple different properties ten miles out of town. We will put in a ten-foot-high security fence and tightly control the access.

"Namibia is a poor country, but surprisingly immune to pressure. They have made peace with South Africa, and their other neighbors ignore them. The government cares little about international banking regulations, or tax treaties, because they have no money. Namibia also doesn't care about trade agreements or sanctions, since they have no trade to speak of. You get my drift."

"How corrupt is the government?" asked Bill.

"Very," replied Tom briefly. "This is Africa. We can make corruption work for us. The country's largest revenue source is mining, diamonds particularly. There exists a well-developed black market for diamonds.

Suitcases of cash, or a fist full of diamonds, identical to Namibian sourced stones, go a long way towards buying goodwill. I've already Fab'd the diamonds."

Tracey had been silent until now. "We're getting pretty cavalier about buying people," she said. "This makes me personally and professionally uneasy. I'm an attorney, and an officer of the court. Have you even tried to do this aboveboard?"

"I've worked through the legal, ethical, and moral issues and am comfortable with what we do," replied Tom. "It's not just passing out cash—although, yes, we do that. I've engaged a high-powered local, Mister Muinjangue, to help us meet people and build genuine relationships. He's been in and out of senior-level government positions. He's a tribal elder, and what passes for a successful businessman in those parts. We've helped his daughter get a student visa and a scholarship to study in London. We've helped the president's nephew get out of a legal jam in the US. We've helped a general's mother get into an expensive Swiss clinic to treat her health issues. We plan to build water and wastewater treatment plants, a clinic, and a whole bunch of infrastructure.

"Namibia is similar to the US in that it's legal to give suitcases full of money to politicians. You just have to carefully follow the local legal rituals to stay out of trouble. Which we do. If you have reservations, send one of your staff, an adult please, down to review how we operate. That is your job," Tom said pointedly.

"I'll do that," replied Tracey tightly.

"Moving on," Tom continued briskly. "The second location is Hobart, Tasmania." A map of the far South Pacific flashed up. "Tasmania is a large island off the Southeast coast of Australia. Hobart is in the Southeast corner of the island. The town has a fair port and an airstrip, which has been recently upgraded. XSolarian has optioned a large suitable property on a nearby island. We'll have to barge building materials over from Hobart. We are also pursuing property adjacent to the airport. This is the far end of nowhere; however, the town and the facilities are much better than in Namibia. The Russian Pacific Fleet, or the Chinese, will have to travel thousands of miles to Australia and then circle the entire continent, which is about two thousand miles on a side to reach the place. The American Pacific Fleet will have a similar lengthy trip. Granted, Australia is a member of the Commonwealth, and included in the L6. However, in this case I believe the benefits outweighs the downside of the connection.

"The Aussies play things fairly straight. They're generally realists. Their economy runs on commodity exports. The permitting process for anything we want to do is rigorous, but straightforward and honest. We don't anticipate permitting problems.

"The Aussies export a lot of commodities to China, but have no issue waging a trade war with their largest customer. Surprisingly, the country's institutions even keep the American government at arm's length. The Australian government is not strong-armed by anyone.

"The construction of the heavy lifters will follow the Airbus production model. For those of you who don't know, Airbus is a European consortium to build large commercial aircraft. The only way for anybody in Europe to compete with Boeing was a group effort. Another view is Airbus was created in one of the largest corporate welfare projects in history. Different parts, subsystems, and systems of the plane are built in every political subdivision of the Economic Union. The parts ship to a couple locations for final assembly.

"We're following the Airbus model to build the heavy lifters. Components are sourced from every continent, and transported to Namibia and Hobart. Smaller components will come by Jet. The larger pieces by ocean cargo. The sensitive Chait components will come in last. The ships launch the second they are ready to fly. As we know, these designs don't require much infrastructure to land or take off.

"Now, let's talk about the design side, and the procurement processes," continued Tom. "We are going to follow designs mostly supplied by the Chait, using current terrestrial materials and manufacturing techniques. We will control any third-party contact with our friends carefully. For example, we won't allow real-time back-and-forth conversations. The engineers will submit their written questions in the afternoon and receive answers the following morning. As we know, the Chait are sensitive about revealing clues to their diurnal cycle, if any. The design centers are on different continents..."

It was a long afternoon.

FORTY-FOUR
ON THE RUN

NO HIGH-POWERED BUSINESS EXECUTIVE HAS much leisure time. Bill was no exception. He did email at five in the morning, and again at night before he went to bed. He exercised at lunch and ate a sandwich at his desk—or airline food. He had a nice house in a nice neighborhood, which he rarely got to enjoy. He had a pool service, a yard service, and a housekeeper who came in twice a week. The house was equipped with a sophisticated alarm system, and the security company cruised the house regularly.

Over thirty years of marriage Bill and his wife developed different interests and social circles. He only saw her six or eight times a year. She spent most of her time in Florida with her mother and two sisters, drinking fruity rum concoctions and painting seascapes.

Bill's primary leisure activity was working, well, pretending to work, in the backyard for an hour every weekend. He played music from his formative years and puttered around the yard while digesting the week that just ended and planning the one coming.

Today he had an actual job. With the coming of spring, it was time for the annual cleaning of the pool shed, something the pool boy or yard guy never managed to accomplish. Bill had forgotten and left his N95 mask in the garage, so he tugged the ratty long-sleeved Stanford T-shirt he wore for the occasion up over his mouth and nose and triggered the leaf blower.

An immense grey cloud of dirt, leaves, spiders, cockroaches, unidentified insect parts, powdered chlorine, lime, pool filter media, paint chips, pesticides, fungicides, herbicides, fertilizer, rat poison, mouse turds, snake scales, lizard skins, rodent hair, snail poison, ant poison, wasp nests, and charcoal dust billowed from the shed and drifted over the lawn furniture, pool, yard, apple trees, flower beds, and Bill. He kept the blower running until the air coming from the shed was clear. He then ran the leaf blower over the pool deck and lawn furniture, blowing the debris onto the lawn, or into the pool. The lawn was beautiful, something Bill attributed to the yearly dosing.

He was in his underwear, in the utility room, stuffing clothes into the washer when his enhancements pinged. It was Mango.

"Bill," he said (all Chait had male personas), "Code Red. The President is speaking to an aide who will shortly pass word to the justice department to initiate arrests of XSolarian executives. The FBI and network camera crews will arrive in the early dawn, but you must leave now, immediately, before the surveillance intensifies. Take evasion track A."

"Roger that," replied Bill. "I'm out of here in five." He called his bodyguard and told him to disappear and leave the country. He stuck his head under the kitchen faucet and roughly dried his hair with a kitchen dish towel while walking to the bedroom. He dressed quickly in casual clothes, bomber jacket, and hiking shoes. He grabbed his go-bag and was out the back door in six minutes.

He went to his side fence and pulled a couple of pickets to the side; they hung from the top rail by only a single nail. He slipped through the gap and pulled the pickets back into place. The neighbor's yard was terraced and he walked the length of the house, unseen from inside. He then went through a back gate to another neighbor's yard. The communal motorcycle was parked in the usual spot at the side of the house. The bike was built from several junkers as a shop project by the man of the house, his son, and two neighbor boys. Bill had kicked in cash for the tires. Half the young men in the neighborhood borrowed the bike at one time or another. It would not be missed for days.

He quickly secured his bag with a bungee cord, opened the fuel cock, shoved the bike down the inclined driveway, and popped the clutch. The engine sputtered twice and caught. Bill took a circuitous route to a main street and disappeared into the evening traffic.

The Inner Circle linked up the following morning. Jon, like most of the others, was in Switzerland. "Everybody disappeared cleanly," he said. "Bill was the only one in the US; the rest of us were fortunately here in Europe. The FBI will take several days to file for Economic Union arrest warrants and extradition requests good in all EU countries. Which is why we are initially in Switzerland—not an EU member. Once the justice department learns we are here, they will request extradition from the Swiss. Naturally we are throwing sand in the gears. The EU warrants are not a slam dunk either, and with luck will take a month or two to formalize. At that point the election is over and the current administration thrown out on their collective ass. The current administration is unpopular—historically unpopular.

"The specific charges, of which we have backdoor copies, don't matter. They are a pretext to whip up a hysterical media campaign to assist in getting out the vote. Here's an example: kidnapping, without a specific victim named. Most of the charges are national security related, and so heavily classified even we and our lawyers aren't allowed to see them. Of course, the juicier details have already been illegally leaked to east coast media cronies.

"With our resources we will muffle the media campaign, although we can't totally eliminate the propaganda.

"My personal favorite is income tax evasion. The FBI, oddly not the IRS, claims I did not report barter income of the value of the planet Ouranos on my income taxes. No specific value was named."

"Gee, Jon," Shirley asked, "how much is the planet worth? A hundred trillion dollars?" Everyone laughed.

"Actually," replied Jon. "I'm golden. My fee, and I have my paperwork, was for all the pre-work I did over a two-year period, while outside the United States. Off-planet actually, so any barter value is not taxable in the US or anywhere else!"

More laughter.

"We have lawyers and video teams camped out with your spouses, siblings, parents, and children. Please continue to urge them to congregate as much as possible. They'll be easier to cover if they stay together.

"You should continue to move regularly. Yes, we will get advance notice via our friends, but you can't make life easy for the snatch teams. The Feds know most of us are in Europe, just not exactly where. The FBI already has a team in the air. This is of such priority that the agents were allowed to use the director's personal plane. Guess what! The check engine light will come on shortly before the hallway point."

More laughter, but nervous this time.

"The FBI counterterrorism group is setting up an ad hoc command center in Brussels. They will hang around and physically kidnap and traffic you out of the country, even without a warrant, should the opportunity arise.

"We've already launched the counterattack. Few believe the administration will win reelection and retain power. We're going to make sure. Randy has details."

"Some of you are more squeamish than I," began Randy. "You can relax. Nothing we are using has been artificially manufactured, yet. Occasionally you read stories about computer graphics and how fraudulent video can be manufactured of such high quality one can't tell if they're real or not. That's hooey; you can always tell on close examination using the right analytical tools.

"Unless the video was prepared by the Chait.

"Our friends can manufacture a video of our political enemies eating babies for breakfast, and not even the CIA could detect it was fake. However, that's unnecessary. We have enough real evidence to publish.

"Half the voting public doesn't read. Any dirt must be live video with the face clearly visible and the voice of the miscreant distinctly heard. Second, nobody cares about corruption. A politician can spend an entire career on the public tit and end up with five houses, and ten million dollars in the bank, and nobody cares. It happens so routinely the voting public has become desensitized to simple corruption.

"Our data bank contains solid incontrovertible visual and audio proof of the current administration, the president on down, doing horrible things. As an aside, I find it depressing the current administration is probably no worse than any other.

"Censorship is a big problem. This close to the election, given the party in power, the mainstream news will report nothing detrimental about the ruling regime. All social media is being warned by the FBI to censor their platforms accordingly, or else. However, we're still blowing this out through a hundred thousand accounts in every existing social media platform. The censors can't get it all. We are also doing chain letters of internet memes which will continuously circulate. The videos themselves are circulated, not just a link to a server that can be neutralized.

"Due to our, ahem, influence, the government disinformation and censorship programs will not be as effective as our enemies hope."

Shirley broke in again—it was her role on the team. "Give us a juicy example," she demanded.

"Sure," said Randy. "We are already circulating a video of the president telling the attorney general to prepare warrants charging XSolarian company officers with kidnapping. The AG protests there is no hard evidence of XSolarian kidnapping anyone. The president replies: 'Since when has that been a problem? Just do it.' There's another great one of the president telling the FBI director to ruin a person's life. The best part is when the director says, 'Sure, we'll do him just like the others.'

"The FISA judges rarely bother going in to work. The clerical secretaries rubber-stamp most requests for warrants and subpoenas. We have the secretaries on video gossiping about their lazy bosses and making jokes as they process the requests. They actually use a real old-fashioned rubber stamp to apply the judge's signature before making a pdf of the approved warrant.

"The juiciest is a clear video of the vice president performing an unnatural sexual act, while on a phone call with a foreign leader. We also have several extremely explicit videos showing him having sex with clearly underage girls, and boys. The youngsters are obviously unhappy. A young boy is crying in one shot.

"Accumulating evidence is not hard. What is hard is finding a plausible scapegoat for the leak. We don't want people suspecting the Chait's full capabilities. Political people at this level are very careful about what they say, even behind closed doors. In most cases we get a twofer. Long-term trusted associates are framed, seen as turncoats, cast out, and punished. The hard feelings in turn lead to even more turmoil.

"For example, a certain longtime aide to the president was physically present in all the videos which feature her personally. He's finished now. He's pissed, and rightly so. The day he was canned he started hitting up publishers for an advance on a tell-all book. He wants to beat the rush.

"We are applying similar pressure to key owners, execs, and editors of the big media conglomerates. The industry ownership is highly concentrated. The majority of the companies are owned by a very few people. Those oligarchs will play ball with us, or go to jail when the compromising material on them is released. The media foot dragging and lack of cooperation will surprise the FBI.

"We are asking all the congressmen we support to make a stand. Correction, we're not really asking. For most, a stand consists of a disapproving noise when asked about the matter. Only a few will actively support the current administration's position. Those we will punish.

"We're flooding the system with cash. We've had commercials ready for months. The PACs we own will run these ads nonstop, in all the swing states, through the day after election day, just to be safe.

"Tens of thousands of credit cards will make anonymous contributions to the challenger this week. Again, there is a legal way to do this, and we follow the rules, mostly. Ironically, some of the dirt in our attack ads is exposing how foreign governments, enemies of our country, use this method to illegally fund the incumbent's campaign to the tune of tens of millions of dollars.

"Lastly, the usual 'midnight surprise' post-election is not going to happen. The counting is all electronic nowadays and state's results are easily manipulated. That ease of manipulation is now a two-edged sword. The magical appearance of a hundred thousand phantom votes for the incumbent, in multiple swing states in the middle of the night, will not happen this year."

The group looked distinctly queasy by this time. Randy attempted damage control. "Look," he said, "all the above, everything I mentioned, and a lot more, is already done by the other side. All we are doing, with the help from our friends, is leveling the playing field. If you believe what we are doing is wrong, I can show you a video of 'those people' casually doing awful, awful things. Anyone here want to view the vice president doing a ten-year-old boy?"

"So, why do I feel greasy?" asked Tracey. "My skin feels as if I just spent a twelve-hour shift as a fry cook. Anytime anything political comes up, I feel a need for a long hot shower using industrial grade cleanser. Saying 'those people' are worse does not make me feel better."

Jon stepped in before Randy made things worse. "Politics is not for the faint of heart. Or the queasy. The important thing is not to lose our focus, or our momentum. You have to keep a positive state of mind. Please speak with your friends and family regularly. Be careful to not make any comments about the weather or drop any other clues of your location. Remember, our phones cannot be traced. We are supplying lawyers and heavily armed security to keep your loved ones safe.

"This will all be over in a couple months," Jon continued. "We can push ahead with building our organization in Europe, and in Asia. Please do as much pre-work as efficient in the States, but don't waste your time in areas where you're not getting traction."

Quinn chimed in. "Thanks for the support. I never heard a bloody CEO say we are bringing lawyers, guns, and money to a fight." The tension in the (virtual) room lessened as the others smiled, except Tom, who didn't get the reference.

FORTY-FIVE
PERFORMING

THE ELECTION WAS OVER. THE incumbent lost thirty-eight states. The new president, King Colston, was a wealthy middle-aged business-man from a midwestern state. The media spent as much time crafting snarky jokes about his name as criticizing his policies. He was pro-business and pro-alien bug-eyed monster. Jon and his team accepted a dinner invitation at the White House.

Their legal difficulties dwindled away. An afternoon of interviews was held at the XSolarian east coast office involving Jon, his team, the justice department, and lots of lawyers. The charges were not dropped outright. The government attorneys would spend a year drafting and polishing memos recommending non-prosecution of the noncrimes. Maybe two years. The president was friendly and supportive but not stupid. He would hold on to this card for a while.

The media vilification had stopped. Instead, the media published a raft of articles incorporating a tone of gee-whiz, by golly, isn't this amazing, look at the possibilities from peaceful contact with another intelligent race.

Even Russia and China had pulled in their horns. Each government was going through a difficult time of attempted coups, aggressive political cabals, and citizen unrest. XSolarian assisted the opposition from behind the scenes.

Isabella had progressed to the point of issuing contracts.

Life was good.

"Leverage is a great thing," Jon remarked. He was having lunch with Randy and Bob in the back room of a Mexican restaurant in Houston.

"Give me a lever and a place to stand, and I will move the world," Bob volleyed back.

"Life would have been easier if we had figured this out a year or two earlier," Randy chipped in. "Old too soon, wise too late."

"That's it," said Jon. "You're cut off. Both of you. Once you start quoting philosophers, no more margaritas." The three continued to work on the chile relleno plates.

"Frankly, I'm embarrassed by how long I've taken to process and absorb the Chait capabilities available to us," said Randy. "Looking back, I feel stupid. Using the tools is still not automatic; I have to consciously think how best to use the capabilities." He used his napkin to wipe the sweat from his brow and took another sip of the margarita.

"Take the media, for example," continued Randy. "Who knew that only about ten people own and run everything in the entire country? Print and networks, both. And the whole industry is run out of three buildings in New York. We spent a year wrestling with a thousand-armed octopus, and all we had to do was influence those ten people."

"Cellphone videos are a wonderful thing," said Jon.

Randy was on a roll. "A new person in the White House, several dozen people axed and replaced at the federal agencies, and all of a sudden everything changes. Instead of a million people, literally, a million government employees, making us miserable, they're here to help. Instead of chasing after our stuff, and our people, the leaders of the Russian Empire are too busy stabbing each other in the back to bother us. Instead of strong-arming everybody in Southeast Asia, the Chinese commie leaders are scrambling to avoid being sent to a re-education camp, or thrown from a helicopter while en route."

"Video conferences are a wonderful thing also," said Bob. "As are not-so-confidential bank records."

"All those tools were available since day one," said Randy thoughtfully. "Again, it's taken a while to learn how to use them effectively. We had to integrate what we already knew, and we all have huge gaping holes in our knowledge base, with the dimly understood tools available from the Chait. Take social media as an example. We avoided those applications like the plague until we learned how to manipulate the platforms. Looking back, we were operating at a teenager level of knowledge."

"Teenager?" asked Bob.

"A teenager level of knowledge is when you're dumber than dirt, so dumb you don't even know it," replied Randy. "The next level up you're still dumber than dirt, but you're aware of your ignorance, and you know enough to ask the right questions. Which is where we are now.

"Using an integrated approach is what has turned things around," continued Randy. "It's not just the hammer, and not just truckloads of money. Our success is due to the personal touch. Do a few favors, provide a little access, tailor the approach to the individual, and people cooperate more fully."

"And if they don't, there's always the video with the German Shepherd," replied Bob.

That's not exactly my point," said Randy. "Earlier, when we neutralized a foe, he was disgraced and replaced, and we had to start over. Now we coexist, and our enemies just don't mess with us. The other thing working in our favor is the injection of FUD. The others knew the acronym well: fear, uncertainty, doubt.

"The situation with the Russian FSB is a great example of FUD. Sergeevich out, Boldyrev in, followed by six months of FUD. Now, he's out and Shitikov—there's an unfortunate name—is in. Now again, no work gets accomplished while all the bureaucrat cockroaches scuttle around assessing their standing, while maneuvering to find a safe spot."

"I don't follow your point," said Bob. "Which is it? We allow the foe to remain in place but under our influence, or publicly torpedo the guy in a way that maximizes FUD?"

"It's the tailored approach," reiterated Randy. "Whatever works in a particular situation. Look, whoever runs the FSB will always be after us, and after Chait technology. Whoever heads Russia will have those goals. The Russian parliament would have to completely turn over to get a more congenial regime. Even a hundred percent turnover would not guarantee a more favorable political environment. A new parliament might be even worse from our perspective.

"China is different. Zheng is barely holding on as president. The two most likely to prevail are conservative isolationists. Neither is enamored by the possibility of a planet which they, personally, will never see. Their new planet is like another space station, a shiny toy. The leadership-in-waiting would love to monopolize Chait technology, but won't risk being seen doing so at gunpoint. Same with the Chinese politburo, unless they see another great power maneuvering so first. The majority of the politburo is quite conservative. Unlike the situation with Russia, our lives will become easier once this particular Chinese president is gone.

"Unfortunately, both Russia, and the US will undoubtedly try to seize the technology, which means China must as well."

The conversation paused while the three wiped their plate with sopapillas and sipped their margaritas.

"That's enough politics," said Jon. "From a corporate point of view the situation appears manageable." He turned a basilisk eye on Randy. "You need to keep it that way—stay on top of the politics. Be proactive." Randy nodded.

"Let me give you a quick update on the tourist Jewa Kustinavage," said Randy. "As you know, our agents approached her with a plan to get her safely out of the country. She flatly refused the offer. She never believed Russian intelligence would harm her. Well, guess what? She was kidnapped and subjected to sixty days of chemically enhanced mentally dissociative interrogation. A month ago, she was found in an alley in Vilnius covered in needle tracks and addicted to heroin.

"She is not coherent yet. Through cutouts we are funding her stay in the finest mental institution we could find in Lithuania. Which is not very good. She is still accessible to the Russians, which is dangerous. We have plans to get her out of Europe, but her mental state precludes moving her. In lucid moments she is still uncooperative. Finally, she is still somewhat in the public eye, which, along with other factors, rules out immigration to Ouranos.

"We'll do what we can, but I believe she is doomed to an unhappy life. We have punished those involved, except Shitikov. We'll do him six months from now when the timing is right. We plan to kill two birds with one stone—Shitikov and another injection of FUD into the FSB."

"Damn," said Jon, shaking his head. He had personally approved the tourist selections. Her fate was on him. There was a brief moment of silence.

"Let's talk about Isabella now," said Jon, closing the sad subject of Jewa Kustinavage.

"Are you going to rope in Tom?" asked Bob. Rarely did the CFO question the CEO in public. It raised the danger of showing daylight between their views.

"No," replied Jon. "He's jammed. Of course, we're all jammed. But he, more than anybody. Since the money raise, I've spent a lot of time with him, Shirley, and Bill launching Isabella. I don't want us to retreat into our respective silos. So, I thought I would take a few minutes to sync up with you guys.

"We got a jump on recruiting before Isabella was even created. Even so, hiring staff is a quagmire. Tom has to interview three people, a couple times each, before hiring one. You know the statistics as well as I. Half the people you hire don't work out. We're trying to do better than half; however, it's unrealistic to believe we will do much better than everyone else in the history of the world. We have to build a multinational organization from scratch.

"The Chait could simply hand us a complete, finished launch vehicle design, but that's not what we want. We want a true multinational team involved with this. We want to spend scads of money and spread it far and wide. It's in our interest to get as many governments, and large corporations, as possible on board. A multinational team is ordinarily a recipe for disaster. A widely distributed effort would normally have a schedule much longer than a focused project team working out of a single location. We of course will have the Chait helping organize the infinite details. The Chait will provide an initial design which is seventy percent complete, which saves a ton of time and money.

"Given the schedule constraints, we have to begin construction at the final assembly locations before the final design is ready. Work has already started on the assembly and launch facilities, as well as placing orders for certain long lead materials."

Bob nodded. He watched over all major expenditures closely.

Jon continued. "The engineers will have to do a deep dive into the seventy percent design in order to complete the remaining effort. The deep dive will also aid in interacting effectively and knowledgably with the vendors when procuring the hardware.

"I'm sure you've heard the media rumors about using a terrestrial-designed chemical rocket for a first stage. The Chait never seriously considered the possibility. In addition to such rockets being difficult to design and assemble, the sheer number of launches with the resulting exhaust high into the atmosphere is a big environmental concern.

"So, the engines and power systems are one hundred percent Chait designs. The craft will carry cargo containers similar to those you see on container ships or rail cars."

"That's embarrassing," grimaced Bob. "I can hear the 'Spam in a can' jokes already. The design team needs to dress them up. I obviously need to stay more on top of the design, not just on the spending."

Jon nodded in agreement and continued. "When loaded, the heavy lifter will take off and land as an aircraft. The craft doesn't ascend vertically like a rocket. The beast actually flies. The aerodynamics aren't great—frankly, it flies like a pig. However, the design will get the job done. The stubby wings help more at landing than when ascending. Which is why the shape slightly resembles the old space shuttle.

"With constant acceleration the craft can reach the moon in a matter of hours—certainly less than a day. Once the proper lunar orbit is achieved, the cargo containers are released, and the heavy lifter returns to Earth. Once the terrestrial craft is sufficiently distant, the interstellar craft, built on Ouranos, will move in, pick up the container, and transport out of the system. The Chait will not allow a terrestrial craft anywhere near the interstellar transport."

"How about the return trip?" asked Randy. "I mean, people returning from the colonies?"

"Well, obviously, the intent is to build self-sustaining colonies," said Jon. "Over time this is a one-way trip for most. However, yes, within limits containers carrying people can return. There is a procedure to pick up containers from lunar orbit and return to Earth. The heavy lifter is designed to land while carrying full containers."

"Is there any access from the container into the interstellar craft?" asked Randy.

"Nope," said Jon. "We are not allowing passengers access to the crew at any time. The cargo bay has no direct access to the inside of the ship. The bay is kept in a vacuum. The only way to enter the interstellar craft from the bay is to leave the container and make your way to an airlock on the outer hull, which is locked from the inside. Those in the containers have no space suits. Shoot, the container doesn't even have an airlock. There is absolutely no danger of the passengers taking over the ship. The security is literally airtight.

"That's enough about the ship itself. Back to the design and build process. We have three primary design locations. It's best done in a single location. Unfortunately, the political factors take that option right off the table. The locations are Tsukuba, Japan; Cologne, Germany; and Houston, Texas. All three locations are aerospace centers for their respective countries, and good people are available. The sites are located approximately eight hours, or time zones apart.

"Each site will specialize in one or more subsystems; however, the bulk of the work is done as a single team working around the clock. The team in Houston will sync up with Germany early in the morning, work all day, and hand off to Tsukuba in the evening. Shared systems make this possible. Big multinationals have been doing this for years. Distributed teams are a bear to manage, but we have our friends to help. This is a change for us. Up till now we haven't had a lot of people in these locations. We are hiring a ton of people, quickly, but we have to keep security tight."

"We've got Houston covered," said Randy. "We've had offices in Texas since day one. We have a good core team in Germany, but we'll have to move people into Cologne and hire a lot more. Japan is where we're starting from scratch. I personally don't know any Japanese security contractors. Shirley has gotten each of us full-time recruiters, but hiring is a slow process, especially in Japan. Any native qualified for this work probably has former colleagues in the Japanese bureaucracies, which raises the risk of leaks. Security agencies are available for hire, but again I can't trust them not to speak to the bureaucracies. I'm also not going to hire Yakuza gangsters."

"Sitting here today, what's the plan?" asked Jon. "Things can change, but what do you see right now as the path forward?"

"I'll just buy a private security company in Japan, owned and operated by Japanese," replied Randy. "A Japanese company gives us a base which we can grow from, relatively quickly. Our friends have already identified a couple of good possibilities. Post-acquisition I'll purge the security risks, except for a couple to feed misinformation through. Our friends will help with oversight. I'll be flying to Japan next week to feel out the current owners. I'd like to take Tom with me. However, his schedule might not work. Either of you guys are welcome to come. You both carry more clout than me."

"I'll go," said Bob. "We recently set up the country organization there, and it's past time for me to go and scare the bejesus out of the new hires." The other two smiled.

"That's great," said Jon. "With the organization expanding exponentially, staying aligned is critical. Any new hire who doesn't get with the program should be shown the door sooner rather than later. The smartest guy, the hardest worker, the most knowledgeable IT geek holds everyone back if they insist on doing their own thing.

"The new hires aren't the only ones who have to get with the program," Jon continued. "Our existing staff must adjust as well. As we speak, Tom is making plans to put in massive systems to support the design, assembly, and operations, CAD systems, inventory, document control, bill of material, and God knows what else. He and his people have specific software, hardware, and operating environments in mind. Your security group, Randy, has to work with Tom, not at cross purposes, to get a safe and secure yet user-friendly and functional systems up and running. I'll be unhappy if I have to spend my time playing referee."

Jon looked at Bob. "Each of these locations will spend billions of dollars. In addition to the normal banking arrangements, be sure we have some black accounts set up and ready to go."

"I'll make sure everything is ready," said Bob. "Each location will manage lots of international subcontracting. In fact, people in the design centers will procure the production components for shipping to the assembly sites in Namibia and Tasmania. Do you have any update on that?"

"Yes," replied Jon. "The entire craft and the cargo containers—let's start calling them transport modules—are procured by the design centers. Those sites are where the project management and the procurement happen. As we speak, Houston is placing purchase orders for long lead items, or reserving capacity with key suppliers. The effort is limited given the state of the available design.

"The facilities for the assembly sites are sourced from the respective locations. The sites differ. Hobart isn't bad. However, Walvis Bay needs a ton of work, including buildings, docks, and a major upgrade to the airport. We even have to put in roads, power, water, and sewer—all the utilities. It's going to happen fast and end up rough around the edges. We'll use local contractors whenever feasible; however, the majority of the work will go to one of the big international firms who can throw a lot of resources at the job quickly.

"The overall project and supply chain processes are managed out of Houston. Shipping the massive components, either by air or sea, is complicated. We can find the right people there."

"The complexity is concerning," mused Bob. "Three design centers, two assembly sites—that's five purchasing centers which Tom and I have to manage coherently. Operationally, there are two big projects to facilitate the assembly sites. plus, the big kahuna—design and build of the heavy lifter. Don't forget we have to build the administrivia infrastructure, which includes the IT, and quality systems near and dear to Tom's heart. And git-er-done while half the world's intelligence agencies are trying to get their hooks into us. Did I miss anything? Pirates, perhaps?

"Have we made this too complex to work?" Bob finished. "I'd feel better with a solid contingency plan."

"I ask myself the same question in the middle of the night," replied Jon. "I always go back to the beginning. When we seemed to think more clearly, when we brainstormed this approach. This *is* the contingency plan. No single design center is mission critical. If we lose one, even two, we keep right on rolling. All the data is backed up and distributed across a half dozen countries. Same thing if we lose an assembly site. We've got another. On the other hand, if everything goes great, we'll be free to deemphasize several of the sites and double our efforts on the others."

"Here's a suggestion," said Randy. "Let's put a bizjet at each site. Staff will be traveling continuously; a company plane makes everyone more effective. A Falcon is overkill, and horrendously expensive. Honda makes a medium-range jet. The Japanese would be happy if we bought Honda's. Beware, I don't know enough about aircraft to make a specific recommendation. Just thinking out loud here."

"Do it," said Jon. "Delegate the plane selection to somebody knowledgeable. Let Tom and Bill know I green-lighted the idea."

Jon looked at the other two. "It's finally happening." He raised his glass containing the margarita dregs and waited a second for the others to follow. "Gentlemen, Ad Astra!"

FORTY-SIX
THE SITES

ISABELLA HAD TO CONSTRUCT INFRASTRUCTURE at the assembly sites before any work on the heavy lifters, nicknamed Arnold, could start. Each of the sites had unique challenges.

Walvis Bay was a small port town on the western shore of Namibia. There were no suburbs or surrounding hamlets. The next nearest port of any size was almost a thousand miles away. On one side was the ocean, on the other side was barren desert sand stretching hundreds of miles. Walvis Bay was one of the few ports on the coast of Southwest Africa. Even so, the shallow port required large ships to anchor a mile or more offshore. Only fishing ships or medium-sized tankers or cargo vessels could safely access the harbor.

Incongruously, a couple miles out of town was an actual international airport. Formerly a South African air force base before Namibia's independence, the airport was primarily used for refueling on long commercial African flights. Only the occasional passenger came for business reasons. The tourist trade was almost nonexistent.

Within a week of Isabella's launching and initial capitalization, the first of the construction crews arrived. The foremen reviewed the capabilities of the port and the airport. Engineers assessed the housing, roads, electricity generation, water and sewage capacity, the drinking establishments, and knocking shops. All were inadequate.

Palms were greased. Orders were placed. An additional hundred workers flew in. An old small cruise ship, meant to house western oilfield workers offshore Nigeria, was diverted to Walvis Bay. Unless sourced from Cape Town, anything coming by ship required a voyage of several weeks. As many materials and supplies as possible were sent by water from Cape Town. However, much was brought in by air. Fuel supplies were limited and so a small tanker of jet fuel was ordered. Eventually, an obsolete product tanker was permanently anchored offshore to store the large amounts of jet fuel, diesel, and gasoline required by The Project.

Given the remote location it was essential the site's airstrip was capable of handling large cargo planes. The largest cargo plane in the world, a Boeing 747, was needed to carry in the larger fuselage components of the heavy lifter. The runway was not designed for such. Even with a limited load, no version of the plane could squeak in. Smaller cargo jets swarmed the field day and night while the engineers and construction workers did as much pre-work as possible on lengthening the runway while awaiting delivery of large amounts of cement. A bulk carrier loaded with cement began plodding its way to the port.

Soon the airport, the assembly site, the docks, and the surrounding area teemed with hundreds of workers preparing to build the large assembly hangars and related facilities.

The challenges in preparing the assembly site at Hobart were completely different than at Walvis Bay. Hobart was a prosperous city of hundreds of thousands of people, and the capital of the state of Tasmania, Australia. The city had a sizable pool of trained workers. The international airport was capable of handling the largest of planes. The busy port had excellent facilities. By air, the town was scarcely an hour away from the millions of people in Melbourne and Sydney. The travel time by cargo ship from those metropolises was measured in days, not weeks.

The problem lay in the fact that Australia was a first world country. Australia, more than most civilized countries, loves rules and regulations. Work visas take months to obtain, if granted at all. The building and environmental permitting processes are arduous and lengthy. Import and export rules are strict. Taxes are numerous, and high. The workforce is highly unionized and militant.

Jon's people flooded Hobart with agents and cash well before the site was announced as one of the two assembly centers. Valuable land adjacent to the airport was purchased well ahead of time. A nearby island was also acquired, and the sheep relocated. The various groups of birdwatchers and environmental watchdogs were co-opted. Politicians from the local districts to the National Parliament, and every level in-between, were wined, dined, and given fat consulting contracts for community outreach. Approved environmental and construction permits began to appear.

The actual company behind The Project was not initially disclosed. A cover story was concocted, and a trail of breadcrumbs was left for the journalists to follow elsewhere. Nothing too hard. Apparently, a high-tech firm was developing a research center coupled with light manufacturing facilities for something cool, clean, cutting-edge, and lucrative. No smoke-stacks, strictly a white-collar kind of place. Just the kind of neighbor you'd like to see move to your town.

When Isabella announced Hobart as an assembly site, the local jour-nalists felt played. There were no hard feelings as journalists are routinely lied to and misled. Still, a full-court press was mounted to mollify the press and dispel any bad feelings.

Union leadership was given certain incentives to sell the project to their membership. Pay was generous; however, the company demanded round-the-clock work schedules, with proper compensation for night and weekend shifts. Of course.

Quinn Andreas was seconded to Isabella and made point man for The Project in Hobart.

"Why me?" he moaned when Jon told him his new assignment. "I'm not a bloody politician, or a construction manager. I know nothing of project management, or working with unions for that matter."

"You're Australian," explained Jon. "You don't need a work permit. You're the only one in the Inner Circle with those sterling qualifications. We can, and will, hire qualified people to get the work done. The country takes forever to grant work visas. Even for us. Your job is to sell the project. Keep the sea turtle guardians sweet, the whale watchers happy, the birders satisfied, and the unions mollified. Talk rugby or football to the politicians. Get a luxury box in Sydney, or Canberra, or both."

"Jon," grated Quinn, "a luxury box on the mainland won't help us in Tasmania. Tasmania is not New South Wales. They are different states."

"Sure, it will help," enthused Jon, "when you fly folks over for a game in the company plane. Everyone likes being treated like a big shot. Take them golfing, or fishing, or sponsor their kid's sports team. You'll feel like you never left sales.

"You'll be fine," continued Jon. "Isabella has already obtained the initial environmental permits. I suggest you hire a passel of recently retired regulatory agency people to keep things moving. Or their kids, wives, girlfriends, and mistresses."

"You don't understand," Quinn complained. "If I work in Australia, I have to pay income taxes!"

Quinn's bitching and Jon's pacification were pro forma. They both knew Quinn would do this for the next year, and even enjoy himself. Probably.

FORTY-SEVEN
THE BUILD

ISABELLA GREW EXPONENTIALLY. SPECIFICATIONS FOR the heavy lifter solidified. Bid packages were developed and circulated. Contracts were let. Quality came first, followed closely by schedule. Cost was a distant last when evaluating bids. Many of the contracts were cost plus, usually a license to print money.

At this point the great powers bought into the program. After all, the alien tech comprising the power and propulsion systems would not be released until the vehicle was otherwise ready to fly. Better to get behind the program and actively support the build than be obstructionist. Intelligence services wanted to keep abreast of the construction. Accordingly, the big three, and dozens of smaller nations, did their best to flood Isabella and the subcontractors with agents. The agencies attempted to suborn existing employees or, preferably, place their own people, which was more difficult. The professional agents tended to get hired in menial or low-level administrative roles, and not in positions of responsibility. Still, the agencies kept trying.

Randy and his team, with help from his friends, easily stayed on top of security. He actually preferred to have a few spies sprinkled throughout The Project. Following age-old tradecraft, the spies were allowed to collect and pass on voluminous amounts of verifiably authentic information of little value.

The low-level plants were generally excellent workers. Still, there were so many that regular weeding was required. The preferred method was to arrange for a spy from country X to stumble upon the spy from company Y. After the discovery came the same inevitable routine. The spy from company X would report his find and suspend all active clandestine activities until he heard back from his superiors several layers up. His superiors would invariably instruct the spy to focus on the other agent. Months would pass while Isabella's activities received little attention. Eventually country X would attempt to turn, rat out, or assassinate the spy from Company Y. When the dust settled, a spy from country Z would "accidently" discover the agent from country X, and the cycle would repeat. Nobody ever suspected Isabella's security organization.

When efforts to suborn employees escalated to murder, maiming, or similar strong-arm tactics, the party responsible, at all levels, met with fatal accidents. A particularly nasty case occurred at the Walvis Bay site. A Bulgarian freelance agent chopped off the hand of a purchasing clerk's child in a blackmail attempt to gain access to delivery schedules. Because he acted on his own, there were no clients to punish, only the freelance agent. The purchasing clerk was a local hire. Many laborers were of the same tribe and sub-tribe as the clerk. Word spread to the right ears, and the Bulgarian was taken, slow-roasted alive, and then ceremoniously eaten by a dozen laborers. Isabella was not implicated.

The thawing of relations between XSolarian, Isabella, and the great powers led to a larger involvement of companies based in those countries than originally planned. Russian suppliers had surprisingly good quality. American suppliers tended to perform well, even if their lead times were long. Bonuses were offered for early delivery. The Chinese suppliers initially proved difficult to manage.

Relatively few contracts went to Chinese companies. Of those, one fabricated cost charges, was caught, and their contract immediately terminated. The Chinese government arrested three company executives who may have been involved and shot them the following day. The performance of the remaining Chinese vendors, in fact all vendors, improved dramatically.

Parts and assemblies were sourced in dozens of countries. Quality titanium components were sourced from Russia, Inconel super alloy fittings from Germany, and highly engineered glass from Japan. Companies based in each of the lucky six nations received contracts. However, largesse was spread far and wide to reduce leverage of any one government or large aerospace contractor.

The biggest hurdle to overcome was blackmail from the private sector.

"Ok folks, let's get started. Bob, what's up?" asked Jon. Four of them were on the call. The CFO, Bob, representing security was Randy, and Bill as president of Isabella. Bill's initial responsibilities as head of licensing and intellectual property had dwindled. He became a key troubleshooter and moved into Isabella as soon as the corporation formed.

"Bill and I asked for this call as we are being blackmailed by parasitic bloodsucking financial consortiums," replied Bob. "Unless we take immediate, direct action, these pirates are going to significantly impact the schedule and cost of Arnold." The term "direct action" was a euphemism for ruining people. Which was why Randy was on the call.

It took a lot to get Bob riled. This was serious. "Please expand," said Jon.

"Imagine a fifty-million-dollar fighter jet sitting on the apron outside the end of the assembly line," began Bob. "Imagine an empty hole on the dashboard where a hundred-thousand-dollar box is supposed to fit. The plane can't fly, so it can't be sold without the black box. Imagine the supplier of the box is short one custom ASIC costing about a thousand bucks. The supplier can't ship and invoice the hundred-thousand-dollar box without the chip. The chip is already made, printed on a silicon wafer, and costs about a hundred bucks at that stage. However, the chip supplier can't get product packaged, tested, or qualified because the plastic used for the package is on back-order. However, ninety-five percent of that specific packaging compound used in the world comes from one factory in Japan. If you're on their shit list, you're screwed. Historically the company has been scrupulous in meeting their obligations, but not under the new regime. Of course, I'm not talking of a fighter; I'm talking about the Arnold class.

"A number of financial groups have done a deep dive into aerospace supply chains and evaluated the likely sources of Arnold's components. These bloodsuckers are buying into, or optioning, supplies of raw materials and manufacturers of feed stock, components, and even the machine tools needed for assembly. The goal is to gain a monopoly over a piece of the chain and leverage their position to jack up prices big time. The groups plan to threaten delivery unless we pay ten times the current price. In many cases the strategy is different: stock manipulation. The financial group will pump and dump the stock once they record a couple hugely profitable quarters. There's a bunch of other strategies as well, all based on our expense.

"Aerospace companies routinely second-source, in part to mitigate exactly this kind of risk. However, these consortiums are extremely well-funded and determined."

"What's the specific fix in this one case?" asked Jon.

"This particular case is fixable," Bill cut in. "We can package the chip in ceramic packages, which are a lot more expensive. The package footprint differs so we have to redesign the board. On the other hand, the packaging is readily available and more than meets the required quality standards.

"We have complained to METI, the Japanese Ministry of Economy, Trade, and Industry. We also put a bug in the ear of senior people at the keiretsu, which recently sold the manufacturer involved. Both parties were unaware of the new owner's actions. This kind of financial blackmail is unheard of in Japan. Between them, METI and the Keiretsu run the country's economy. They will squash the people involved like bugs. The company will restore supply in several months."

"What I'm looking for is a coherent strategy," Bob continued. "Bill and I are struggling with dozens of financial pirates scattered across the globe. Dealing with them, one by one, on an ad hoc basis is not working. I know my job is to bring you answers, not problems. However, I need some ideas. Four heads are better than one."

"How much of the project is sourced within the lucky six?" asked Jon. "And how much from just the big three?"

Bill fielded the question. "Everything is second-sourced from multiple companies based in multiple countries, so there is no definitive answer to your question. As of today, almost three quarters of the dollar value of the components could theoretically come from the lucky six. And three quarters of that from the big three, primarily the United States. We're hedging our bets, of course. I expect deliveries to meet schedule right up to the end, when the big three apply the screws to us to extort a better terms for their colonist flights."

"What's your take on the situation with the countries left out?" asked Jon.

"With an exception or two, resignation has set in," replied Bill. "The little guys understand they aren't getting a planet from the Chait. Their lobbying is almost exclusively aimed at the lucky six for a colony, preferably a continent of their own. Isabella is seen as just another deep-pocketed customer. Their economies, shoot, almost all economies of the world are centrally managed. However, until a business matter rises to a political issue, it's live and let live.

"More specifically, we a have a big potential problem with a carbon fiber source in Turkey. There is a limited pool of carbon fiber producers, and we are not strategically important to any of them. To a lesser extent there's a problem with a Brazilian supplier. Among other things this supplier makes the hatch frame and door. We have a second source for the hatch and door, of course. There are many other cases."

Randy felt a need to participate. "Turkey makes carbon fiber? I think of them as a third world country."

"No, not at all" replied Bill. "Turkey has a well-developed industrial economy. Turkey is more like Europe in that respect than a Middle East country."

"Bill, I think you have something in what you said about business versus political issues," said Jon. "Any interference with the heavy lifter program in Russia or China is a political issue by default. Same thing in Japan and Germany—all of the lucky six. I think we need to elevate all cases of financial blackmail to a political issue. Let's incentivize governments to crack down on these guys—all of them."

Randy was enthusiastic. "In the US the FBI opens cases merely on a juicy newspaper story, as long as it's sourced in Washington, or New York. So does Justice, the IRS, EPA, and the other big regulatory agencies. With the leverage we have in the media, and Congress now, we can plant whatever story we deem necessary, in whatever media we feel appropriate. I can ping my counterpart, Vanilla, and get a pile of well-sourced facts on every one of these bloodsuckers in a heartbeat."

There was a pause while everyone smiled. The US government was civilized. They didn't execute people out of hand, very often. The government employed tens of thousands of lawyers who were used by politicians, and agency heads, to ruin people.

Bob broke the silence. "I love the approach. In the early days the government persecuted us; now they do it to our adversaries. That's what I call progress."

"This approach can be made to work almost anywhere. Second world countries, Turkey for example, are even more sensitive to political issues than the lucky six," said Randy. "In these countries the leaders go to jail, or worse, if they fall out of power. The political leadership is hypersensitive to any internal criticism. We can easily make compromising information regarding these financial pirates known to the political people. The family running Turkey will string them up by their private parts in nothing flat if they detect a whiff of political meddling, which we can supply. We can manufacture the evidence if need be."

"What about the EU?" asked Jon.

"I've been evaluating the list offline while we were speaking," said Randy. "Two who stand out have pockets deep enough to require action on our part. One in France, another in Italy—both countries not especially friendly to our cause."

"Do it," said Jon. "Nothing fatal please, yet. I will ask Casey to make an example of a couple of the tougher nuts on her show. I guarantee you will enjoy that episode."

"A couple of other things come to mind," said Bill. "First, we publish an actual blacklist of these bloodsuckers and circulate it widely. The resulting publicity will put some heat on them. I'll also put the word out in the aerospace industry. Nobody likes to see a lower tier supplier holding a program hostage. I may also pass some cash around in certain countries, like Turkey and Brazil, to jump-start the process."

"Sounds like we have a plan," said Jon with a wolfish smile. "Before we go, let me bring you up to speed on the build strategy. We need a minimum of two, preferably three, of the craft flying before the colonization program begins. We can't drop somebody on a distant world and not be able to resupply in a reasonable timeframe. We also can't transport colonists from several countries, and then announce the other countries will have to wait until we get additional heavy lifters into service. We must be able to service all the colonies, all the time. Which requires redundancy.

"The fact of the matter is two of the Arnolds must be ready almost simultaneously. Given the fact that both sites are vulnerable to attack, be it a cruise missile or a commando drop, not just two but all four of the initial Arnold class must be ready at more or less the same time. If we lose one site, we can still proceed with the program."

Assuming the attack did not trigger a global nuclear war, the others thought silently.

"Tom knows all this and is working to complete all four Arnolds simultaneously," Jon continued. "Our press releases still sound as if we are prioritizing a single unit so as to wring out the bugs before finishing the other three. Given the Chait sophistication in design, modeling, and verification, that's not necessary.

"Isabella is generating a smokescreen obscuring the true finish date. Purchasing has sent out numerous change orders implying redesigns and have publicized a number of phantom schedule issues. As long as the birds are in a hangar, no one knows the true stage of completion.

"We personally need to stay mobile and keep a low profile. Things will get very messy towards the end of the project. The three major powers have developed contingency plans, which involve kidnapping one of us, or our families. Nobody's pulled the trigger yet, and we should be able to interdict any attempt, but we can't make it easy for them. I don't want any of you to take unnecessary risks."

FORTY-EIGHT
THE ALTERNATIVE

T HE GROUP INCLUDED JON, TRACEY, Shirley, Tom, and Bill. Also included were their Chait counterparts, and a silver metal cube about three inches on a side containing Tracey's sister.

"Paula, we're ready now," said Tracey via her enhancements. "Is this a good time?"

"Of course, it is," replied Paula sharply. "When I agreed to talk to you and the others at this time, I rearranged my day around this."

Tracey's sister Paula was, or more properly, had been, a flaming lefty. There was no cause, be it fact free and injurious to society, of which she disapproved. Extremely intelligent, she made a tremendous living as a lawyer suing public utilities on behalf of environmental groups.

She was intolerant, with a stunning lack of self-awareness. When a cause caught her fancy, she became impervious to facts, logic, data, reason, or any sense of proportionality.

When Paula developed stage-four pancreatic cancer, Tracey had begged Jon to make an exception and allow her into Ouranos.

She met none of the criteria for admittance. Her core beliefs were anathema to a productive society. She had no skills useful on a frontier planet. She had few friends—for good reason. Outside of a few communist dictatorships, she hated every government on Earth, especially her own. She worked tirelessly and gave freely of her time and money to destabilize societal institutions such as schools, libraries, churches, and charities. She despised children. She was a scofflaw who ignored any legitimate authority.

When Jon gently denied Tracey's appeal, she wailed "but she's my sister."

Paula's case was not unique. Others of the Inner Circle had unsuitable family members, although none as poisonous as Paula. The alternative

Jon coordinated with the Chait was to download the subject's mind into a simulation. The download was a snapshot taken shortly before death.

While the mind was an exact replica of Paula, it existed in a simulated, perfectly life-like, virtual reality. The environment was the world in which Paula wanted to live. There were no other people, yet. However, she could interact remotely, by email or phone, with advanced Turing simulations of her previous circle of friends and acquaintances.

The Chait considered the recording of Paula's mind to be... Paula. The aliens discounted any notion of a soul, or an afterlife. When queried on the matter the response was always some version of "we've looked, but never found one."

The initialization of the copy of Paula's mind was highly significant to the Chait. They considered the act analogous to bringing a new life into existence, not something done lightly. For that reason, the Chait insisted the simulation not be initialized until after her physical death. Allowing two sentient versions of Paula to exist at the same time was forbidden under their moral code. The seriousness with which the hyper-advanced Chait treated the matter spoke volumes.

The secretive Chait had several times referred to their moral and ethical beliefs. Jon, and the others of the Inner Circle, considered this significant as the aliens were rigorous in limiting any release of knowledge regarding their race.

The purpose of today's interview with Paula was to determine if the persona in the box was actually Paula. No one doubted the Chait's ability to construct a slick instance of an AI able to pass a Turing test. However, while an AI could convince one a real person was answering, Tracey and the others doubted even the Chait could convincingly mimic a specific person well known to the questioners.

The interview was important. Tracey felt Jon, by denying Paula entrance to Ouranos, had killed her sister. Which was nonsense, of course. However, a billion people would react emotionally, exactly as Tracey, should the existence of Full Medical become public.

The humans at the meeting had all known Paula well. Several of them knew her from college and had acquaintances in common. Paula used to corner Tom at parties and dinners and excoriate him for the companies he worked for, and the work he did.

With Bill, the tables were turned. Whenever he met Paula, he greeted her with a cheery "made any poor people today?" He knew exactly how to push her buttons. In addition to Paula's friends, Tracey wanted those with less than cordial relations to participate in this interview. Tracey, ever analytical, wanted to probe as many facets of the supposed Paula as she possibly could.

Outside of Tracey, Shirley knew her best. She avoided topics of work and politics, and stuck to safer subjects such as travel, wine, music, clothes, and men. Jon was only slightly acquainted and made a point to avoid her.

"How have you been?" Tracey asked.

"I've been extremely busy," replied Paula. "You have no idea of the amount of work gardening takes. I have to grow my own food. I'm in the country, you know, and everything is done by hand. I used to love gardening. Now, the work is just drudgery. The powered tools and equipment are totally inadequate."

"What's wrong with your tools?" asked Tracey. "I thought you had battery-powered tools, and plenty of solar, and wind installed to generate electricity."

"The weather has been unseasonably calm, cloudy, and cool. Even though I rationed electricity like a miser, I ran out. These batteries were spec'd so as to last a full week. Well, they didn't. The batteries are defective. Those bastards cheated me. I want you to sue the manufacturer on my behalf." Paula continued to bitch at length about living life in the country by herself.

She had a generous budget and could order almost anything online. Deliveries were limited to once a week.

To Paula, everything in the simulation was indistinguishable from reality. To her, she simply awoke one morning in a new bed in a different house.

Paula had chosen a prehistoric, though benign, Santa Barbara as her retirement home. She planned a large comfortable house well-equipped to live off the grid. The simulation had ground rules, and a starting point based on Paula's desires. Now the simulation was running and Paula was forced to live within the parameters.

She was active, intelligent, and capable. When she focused, it was with laser beam intensity. Now, living on her own, she could do almost anything. However, she couldn't do everything. The limits of her horizons were becoming clear and the reality of the daily chores of country life was not pleasant.

Eventually Bill inserted himself into the conversation. "Good to see your carbon footprint has gone to zero. You must be happy with that." The conversation quickly turned nasty.

The session went on for hours. All, excepting Jon, spoke with Paula at length. The call ended with Tracey promising to call again soon.

"Well," Jon asked the group afterwards, "was that really Paula?"

Characteristically, Shirley jumped right in. "I know Paula well." All noticed her choice of tense. "She knew facts only Paula could possess. Even small, personal things known between just the two of us. The person we just spoke to knew not only those details but all of Paula's wants, needs, and desires as well. Those are not simply facts or memories. Those were Paula."

Bill was nodding. "She got exactly what she wanted, and found it's not what she needs. And, her situation is someone else's fault, not hers. That's Paula all right."

Bill continued. "Mean as a stepped-on snake. The belief system was exactly Paula's. The speech patterns, the vocabulary. Her reactions to each of us. I don't want to get into sophomore philosophy; however, at some point does a perfect copy become qualitatively the same as the original? I'm convinced the answer is yes." He pointed to the small cube. "That is Paula."

Tom, the only deeply religious one of the group, stood up abruptly. He was pale and breathing deeply. "Excuse me," he said. "I'm going to vomit," and left the room quickly.

The ramifications of copying a persona had been discussed at length by the group. Tom's reaction was clear. He now believed the box contained Paula but shorn of her soul. When the flesh died, he believed the soul passed on. The Chait had created a true being, but no flesh, therefore soulless. The worst of all outcomes. An abomination.

Jon remained silent. Any selling or encouragement could backfire. He watched Tracey carefully with every iota of his enhanced senses. He radiated a calm complacency, neither expectant nor judging.

Inside though, Jon was pissed. Paula didn't work for the company. She wasn't a customer, or a supplier. However, her mere momentary presence had disrupted the entire Inner Circle. Everyone had lost days of productivity. Jon might never reestablish his previous rapport with Tracey. Tom might quit. This was a perfect example of the turmoil Paula caused wherever she went. If allowed to emigrate she would continue to generate discord, forever. Jon renewed his vow to never let this variety of snake into Ouranos.

Tracey had tears staining her cheeks. Her air was of one who had just received an ambiguous update on a loved one while waiting outside a hospital emergency room.

"She never asked about her nieces," she said. "Or how my husband's operation went. The whole conversation was about her." Shaking, she gathered her things and left the room.

Bill looked at Jon. He didn't understand. Shirley did. She was picking up her purse and preparing to leave.

"Does she believe that's really Paula or not?" he asked.

"Oh, yes," Jon replied.

FORTY-NINE
PREPARATION FOR LAUNCH

THE ARNOLD CLASS OF HEAVY lifters neared completion. The great fuselage pieces were joined. A plethora of systems—environmental, navigation, communication, and many more—were installed and tested. Four vehicles were constructed, two at each site. The operations plan called for three to regularly fly while the fourth was slated as a test bed and serve as an emergency backup.

"Near completion" meant the construction status grew closer to the point where craft could accept the installation of the Chait power and propulsion equipment. The empty shells were worthless without the alien tech. The great powers lusted after the technology and their actions became increasingly overt as the builds neared completion.

Overt action generated counteractions from the other players. No one would stand by idly as others maneuvered to seize the alien tech. Even those countries not participating in a colony wanted the technology.

The countries adjacent to Namibia, Angola and Botswana, underwent a tourism boom as thousands of Russians and Chinese filtered into those countries. The tourists were uniformly fit young men of military age. Russian "fishing trawlers," actually sophisticated electronic listening posts, cruised offshore. In response, a British carrier group augmented with units from Canada began long-term exercises offshore Southwest Africa. The South African town of Upington, relatively near the Namibia border, had a first-rate airport. The South African military relocated a squadron of Gripen fighters, another of Rooivalk attack helicopters, and the 5th Special Forces regiment closer to Walvis Bay.

A US carrier group made a courtesy visit to Sydney and loitered nearby. The ships were a day's hard sail from Hobart, and the carrier jets could be on-site in minutes. As an ally, Australia was obligated to receive the US fleet. The Australians, ever practical, rationed fuel and fresh food supplies available to the American ships.

The rough waters offshore southern Tasmania made naval exercises virtually impossible. The Tasman Sea and the Antarctic Ocean were unforgiving on both men and ships. Submarines were more practical. Nuclear attack submarines from eight countries, including India and France, cruised offshore. Each sub was light on torpedoes to make room for highly trained commandos. The danger of colliding with one another was substantial. Several near misses occurred.

The Australian Home Affairs office was not amused by thousands of bogus visa applications. The office instituted travel bans from the worst offending countries, and increased scrutiny on everyone else.

Overall, international relations were very good. The great powers were preoccupied with the Chait, and one other, and had little patience for distractions. Argentina made another ill-considered claim for the Falkland Islands and was squashed, again. Tibet attempted to break away from China and was also squashed. Greenland attempted independence from the Kingdom of Denmark, without success, after pressure from Canada and the US.

China finally lost patience with the family ruling North Korea. The PRC wanted a buffer state, not this sucking chest wound of a client. China withheld support and informally let it be known a regime change would not be unwelcome. A crowd stormed the palace and tore the ruler and his family into pieces. The body parts were hung high in public display for a week. The general installed in place as supreme leader lasted three months, and the next general, only one. Eventually a permanent leader acceptable to China was able to stick. Living conditions for the people did not improve.

Pilot training was a sore point. Isabella hired two dozen flyers and trained them on simulators located at the assembly sites. For security, those selected had few family ties. The pilots were uniformly white men who had retired from the air forces of Canada, the US, Great Britain, Australia, or NATO countries. Those countries complained bitterly about the age, sex, race, and perceived political and religious beliefs (if any) of those chosen. The other lucky six countries complained even more bitterly about the lack of representation. Each of the lucky six governments filed formal protests, which were ignored.

The great powers were quite interested in the flight characteristics of the Arnolds. Given the flight characteristics, engineers could back-calculate the capabilities of the Chait power and propulsion components. All efforts at suborning a pilot or relevant engineers failed. Those responsible for the more vigorous efforts were punished.

Isabella established a flight operations group. The plans and other characteristics of the transport modules were released to the lucky six, and the general public. Ground rules for cargo and colonists were published. Isabella insisted on complete dossiers on each colonist, and plans were made for extensive background checks. Jon and the others assumed the lucky six would substitute a commando team for colonists if given half a chance.

Appearing on Casey's show, Jon announced the four vessels would be named the *Nina*, *Pinta*, *Santa Maria*, and *Mariagalante*. The names pleased no one, not even the Spanish.

"I swear," said Quinn, shaking his head after Shirley read the gossipy news story of the protests in Barcelona, "some people will complain if you give them free beer."

"So true," said Shirley. "The naming of the ships has been seized by the social justice and green fringe groups as a rallying point against the exploitation of other planets. These ships are the same ones that began the European exploitation of the Americas. I guess we should have known."

Jon smiled broadly. "I suspected as much. Part of the reasoning was that triggering protests now, and mostly dismissed, will act as an inoculation against a more serious backlash down the road. I hope."

"Or you just like to piss people off," teased Casey.

The Inner Circle was holding a rare in-person meeting. They were in Namibia, ostensibly reviewing the assembly project. The private room was at an expensive—for Walvis Bay—restaurant which specialized in local cuisine. Most had fish with bean mash or millet porridge. Bill was more adventuresome and was eating something made with goat tripe.

"Ok, let's get synced up," began Jon. "We are approaching the critical part of the venture and will have to navigate through two dangerous pinch points. The first is the delivery and installation of the Chait power and propulsion systems. Our sources indicate each of the big three are planning military operations to physically seize the hardware. For political cover, a flood of stories in social media will publicize the dangers of the technology. The Chinese have a lot of leverage in the media."

"What dangers?" asked Tom.

"There are no tangible dangers I'm aware of, except maybe crashing on your head," replied Jon. "Reality doesn't enter into the process. The media will blame everything imaginable on invisible emanations from the new tech. The media will socialize everything from whale beachings, to cancer, to birth defects. Picture a pundit on a cable channel waving one finger in the air while saying 'it could be...' and fill in the blank with any possible ill which comes to mind. Then your government will simply have to take action to protect you. The approach has worked for a thousand years. A guy named Ponsonby codified the approach as 'The Ten Rules of Propaganda' about the time of World War I. The rules are widely taught in political science classes. All the L6 governments use a similar process. So do we.

"Moving on, the Chinese have gamed the possible outcomes better than the others. They have backup plans to their backup plans. The leadership considers access to Nereus a nice-to-have, not the primary prize. Even though the Chinese plan to physically seize the technology, their primary goal is preventing others from obtaining the alien tech. If one of the others succeeds in grabbing the hardware, their strike teams will forcibly prevent them from removing the equipment from the site.

"In any event, the Chinese president, with buy-in from the politburo, has planned a major power grab in Asia. Invading Taiwan is just the beginning. The Chinese leadership believes the rest of the world is too preoccupied with the exoplanets to react in a meaningful way.

"The Russians plan to strike Walvis Bay. The Americans have lots of contingency plans but the political leadership, like the prior administration, is indecisive. Thank you, Mister FUD," joked Jon.

"Finally, each of the great powers has competing factions. The Americans have the most virulent, the Chinese the most powerful. There is a real danger of a spontaneous act from someone, somewhere, in the heat of action. The state then has to decide, quickly, to support the fait accompli or not. Whatever happens is likely to become very fluid, very fast.

"Fun times," said Jon as he paused for a swig of Tafel beer. "This is all meaningless sound and fury signifying nothing as our friends plan preemptive action, which makes all this moot." Everyone nodded.

"The second pinch point is a bigger problem."

Bill raised his hand and wiggled his fingers like a kid in school. "Before we get to the second point, can you expand on the planned military strikes?"

"Sure," said Jon. "The Chinese will send one of their two carrier groups to the Tasman Sea. One of their ships will claim severe damage from weather or collision or whatever and make an emergency docking in Hobart. Commandos will debark by helicopter to take the Chait machines. In the Walvis Bay scenario, an ostensibly civilian passenger jet crossing Africa will make an emergency landing, debark a commando platoon, and use pre-positioned light vehicles to attack the assembly area.

"If the Hobart attack fails, the Chinese will trigger the nukes they've already sunk to the floor of the Tasman Sea. The bay will funnel the resulting tsunami into Hobart and sink everything under fifty feet of water.

"Here, in Walvis Bay, in the event of failure the Chinese will trigger a nuke large enough to completely take out the assembly area. Except for a couple of the command cadre, the commandos will not be aware they are carrying a nuke on a potential suicide mission."

"How can the Chinese possibly think they'll get away with the use of nuclear weapons?" demanded Shirley.

Jon shrugged. "Nobody wants a nuclear war, including us. Nobody wants any type of open war among the big three. So, the Chinese will pump out disinformation blaming the aliens, or Russia, or the US, and the rest of the world will pretend to believe them. Besides, nobody gives a damn about Africa, and not much more for Tasmania.

"The Russians do not have the resources of the CCP. The Russian Navy doesn't have the ability to project a meaningful amount of power further than their immediate neighbors. The Russians judge Hobart too remote to mount a successful raid. However, the Russians plan a pro forma attempt, just in case they get lucky. If another's attempt appears on the brink of success, a Russian sub stationed in the Tasman Sea will launch a nuke and take out the entire town. The flight characteristics of the missile, and subsequent forensic analysis of the fissile material, will indicate an American strike. Another sub hosting a Spetsnaz team will loiter on-site in case an opportunity arises; however, the commandos have no specific assault plan as of yet.

"The Russian leadership has rationalized a view which holds the Chait are invested in the idea of human colonies. Regardless of the actions of any nation-state, the Russian president, Vlad, feels the show will go on. He believes Russia will get a colony somewhere down the road even if they seize, or attempt to seize, the Chait technology. Russia plans to bully, threaten, and blackmail as needed to ensure nobody gets a colony unless they do as well.

"The Russians believe Walvis Bay is vulnerable. The GRU is organizing a land-based strike from Botswana. There has been a bloody, though quiet, struggle between the covert Russian and Chinese agents for months. The Russians have won, and the Chinese are either dead or have fled. Now, the Russians are accumulating assets there. Both hardware and people. The people are mercenaries aligned with the Russian military. Elements of their navy will support the strike. The Russians have already announced naval exercises in the area.

"The attempt looks pretty lame. The Russians don't have much of a blue water navy. Their only aircraft carrier is a piece of junk stuck in a shipyard while they try to make it operational. Tugs may have to tow the rust bucket to Namibia. Any tow would take a month. Even their Spetsnaz special forces are a mere shadow of their former effectiveness.

"Again, to keep the Chinese or Americans from stealing the prize, a Russian sub will nuke the site, if necessary, using a missile carrying a warhead designed to mimic an American device.

"The Russians are increasing the pressure on Georgia and Azerbaijan to join the Collective Security Treaty Organization (CSTO). Currently the organization includes the three largest of the 'Stans, as well as Armenia Belarus, and Russia of course. In the Baltic, Russia will annex Latvia and Estonia—at the request of the governments in those countries. You can imagine the pressure applied to make that happen. They are already formalizing a stronger relationship with Belarus. When the witching hour strikes, the Russian military will push armored units straight to the Belarus southern and western borders. They will strong-arm Lithuania to grant better access to the Russian enclave in Kaliningrad. Like the Chinese, the Russian leadership believes the west will feel overwhelmed by events, and international resistance will be spotty and disorganized.

"Which leaves the Americans." Jon looked at Randy. "Can you take this? My food is getting cold."

"Sure," said Randy. "The Americans have ten carrier groups designed to project raw American power around the world. The sheer number of carriers outnumbers the rest of the world, combined. The aircraft are the best in world by far. The pilots and crews are the best trained, the electronic systems are the most capable—you get my drift.

"The *Theodore Roosevelt* carrier group is visiting Sydney. They brought along a reinforced Marine Expeditionary Unit (MEU), including Ospreys, and SEAL Team Five. The *Ronald Reagan* group, including the Corp's go-to group, the twenty-fourth MEU, along with SEAL Team Six is en route to Walvis Bay."

Jon made a motion to speed it up. The group had no military background and were clueless to half of what Randy was saying.

"Let's just say the US is sending the varsity team," summarized Randy. "The American special forces' planning methodology is KISS: 'keep it simple, stupid.' They will simply chopper in a platoon of special ops guys and secure the equipment. The Americans will have overwhelming air support. The initial detachment will immediately be reinforced by a larger quick-reaction marine force which will remain on-site while the equipment is prepared for transport back to the US. The US military establishment believes they can sell the political message of rescuing the equipment from the other guys. The groupthink among the brass is the Chait will believe them. The brass is also confident of smoothing things over with Australia, and the rest of the Commonwealth afterwards. The politicians are less sure.

"The American government—the executive branch—is dithering and has not yet decided to pull the trigger on this naive plan. The forces are deploying but the president will wait until the last minute to decide on a course of action. The intelligence agencies are watching the executive branch closely. They have their own agenda and ideas how the situation should play out.

"Neither the Russians nor Chinese believe their military can go toe to toe with the Americans with a reasonable chance of success. They will rely on sneaky stuff like compromising our satellites, computer viruses, hostages, bribery, diplomatic and social media pressure, and other forms of moral suasion. It's worked well for them in the past, especially for the Chinese.

"This all sounds very Machiavellian and ruthless," Randy concluded. "But as Jon pointed earlier, it's moot. The Chait have plans to sidestep all of this."

"Which brings us to point two," said Jon as he pushed his plate away. "Once the Chait technology is installed, and the lifters ready to make regular runs, the obvious question is 'how the heck do we protect them?' The craft require heavy security any time they're on the ground. We will deal with ground protection in several ways. First, the two permanent bases, Walvis Bay and Hobart, have plans to physically harden and arm their locations. We have a pretty free hand in Namibia, not so much in Australia. We will move flight operations out of Hobart onto a nearby island which we purchased a while back. We built facilities, and then, in outward appearance, changed plans and semi-abandoned the place. As soon as we start flying, we'll move there.

"While the initial flights will originate from the assembly areas, subsequent flights will also originate from any one of a dozen remote points in the southern hemisphere. There are dozens of small remote islands with airstrips. Most of them are, or were, British possessions. We're going to get politically closer to the Commonwealth. Adrian has quietly begun talks with senior members of the CCC—the Commonwealth Colony

Commission—to smooth this over." Jon nodded at the genial giant at the end of the table.

"When they make their first attempt, we're going to fool them. The second attempt will be less organized. That's when we cut their legs right out from under them," said Jon, demonstrating with his butter knife.

FIFTY
LOADING UP

Daiki Yoshida dropped off the Zoom call after exchanging the usual pleasantries and turned to the rest of his team. "This is a major change to our schedule," he said.

The Isabella project office issued edicts. There was rarely any give-and-take between the Isabella people and the lucky six country organizations. A week earlier the Isabella program office announced a major change to The Project schedule. The lucky six were given thirty days to select the colony's landing site, or have Isabella pick one for them. At the same time, the lucky six were given a forty-five-day deadline to pack and ship a minimum of four transport pods with the initial supplies needed by the colonists. The scheduled date of the first flight remained months away.

Today's call had been a one-on-one with the Isabella operations people to hash out the specifics.

"Excuse me, I don't understand," said Nariko, the only woman on the Nippon team, timidly. "My understanding, which could be wrong of course, was the lifters are proceeding on their original schedule, although rumors abound of assembly problems. Do we know why Isabella needs our initial supply loads now?"

Nariko's role on the team was to ask obvious questions the others were too embarrassed to bring up. Hers was a good question, as the call that just ended addressed only the what, not the why behind the changes.

"The launch dates will almost certainly slip," Daiki acknowledged. "Nobody expects the heavy lifters to launch on time, much less early. So no, it's not the schedule. The reason is a simple lack of trust. Not just us, they don't trust any of the lucky six. The Isabella program staff don't trust anyone to perform to schedule, or to meet the pod weight and balance specifications. Their bosses suspect a government will load a container with commandos, or a bomb, or some type of hostage gas. They suspect governments will delay or change their selected landing sites and create issues. Even the Isabella accounting department doesn't trust the governments to pay their bills. All customers must pay in advance. These are very distrustful people."

"Can you blame them?" interjected Itsuki, the youngest on the team. "Every time I see someone from the mainland, I cover my wallet."

The others laughed politely.

"How can we pack if we don't know the destination?" asked Ichiro. "Each of the locations under evaluation has different supply and material requirements. We know the site selection team won't decide on a location until the very last minute. Not that it matters. If the site selection team became unconstipated and formalized a decision for the colony location early, our project leaders would insist on reviewing until the very last minute. Which is prudent, of course," he added hastily. He had come perilously close to criticizing the leadership of the Nippon colony bureau.

One of the edicts from the Isabella project office was to initially limit each colony to a single location. They refused to drop supplies or colonists at multiple sites. Each of the lucky six had access to Chait surveys of their respective planets. The surveys had a good deal of detail of the flora, fauna, and climate. The Chait made a Google Earth–like database available whereby one could view their selected planet. Unfortunately, excepting the original tourists and Jon Gallock, no one had actually visited the exoplanets, much less evaluated potential colony sites.

After reviewing the Chait surveys and "flying" numerous sites in the ersatz Google Aeolus database application, the Nippon team had narrowed their selection to three possible locations. Two were near the seashore, the third was inland. The inland site appeared better suited for agriculture and domestic animals. The seashore sites had fish, obviously, and the sea called to the soul of several members of the selection committee.

Loading the transport pod with the maximum amount possible was proving difficult. Some items were small but heavy. Other items took up a lot of space but weighed little. The goal was to use every square centimeter of pod capacity, as well as every gram of the weight allowance. One proposal, ultimately rejected by the Nippon project office, was to turn the loaded pod on end and dribble grains of rice inside while vibrating the container. The rice would fill any tiny gaps and voids and squeeze out the last cubic centimeters of capacity.

"Well, we know the loads don't really vary much among the likely sites," said Ichiro. We've already identified the base load and the site-specific items separately. "For example, the inland site won't require large fishing nets. Perhaps we could reduce the common items so as to bring both site-specific loads in the initial drop. We have been promised regular supply runs, so the risk in omitting certain specific items initially appears small."

The conversation continued for an hour following norms established by the team lead. Everyone was expected to participate, and to speak at length. No one was interrupted, and there were few disagreements.

After allowing everyone to express their thoughts thoroughly, Daiki announced his decision. "We will load eight transport pods, half for the inland site and half for a site by the sea. We will ship the appropriate pods to each of the Isabella locations the minute we hear of the colony site selection."

The others thought this was a reasonable though inelegant brute force solution.

"We'll have to order additional transport pods," nitpicked Ichiro. "As well as additional supplies and materials. We've been given an ample budget but may still be criticized for wasteful spending."

"It's a minor consideration, and I take full responsibility for this decision," said Daiki, who had already cleared the plan with others high up in the Nippon project hierarchy. "Call the Isabella people today and order additional transport pods. The other countries will likely come to a similar solution and we want our order first in line.

"In fact," continued Daiki, "order as many transport pods as their operations people will commit to ship in the next twelve weeks. We'll need them eventually, and it's to our advantage if someone else gets caught short." The others nodded enthusiastically at the idea. Each of the lucky six, excepting China, was competing to be seen as the readiest and the most cooperative. One's place in the launch queue might be at stake.

"Does the site selection affect the personnel chosen for the colony?" asked Nariko. "It's not our place to comment, of course. I was thinking of clothes and shoes as an example. If the personnel team selects different colonists with big feet, I suspect we have to pack accordingly."

Everyone groaned.

"That's a possibility, I imagine," Daiki, conceded. He hated last-minute thoughts from others. "Please rerun our load and balance calculations assuming clothes, including shoes, are packed last. I will bring the matter to the attention of the personnel selection leader at the team leadership meeting tomorrow."

Everyone inwardly winced. The last items packed would be the first to come out of the transport pod. Seemingly half the load was prioritized to come out first. A load plan was not easy. This would be days of work, and any new plan must be reviewed by the personnel selection team, who would quibble over any solution.

"Let's hope the personnel team finalizes the colonist roster soon," said Ichiro. "They have no idea the headaches their changes cause us."

"I can't imagine how the specific site selection would affect our supply and material load," said Oberst Becker dismissively. "The sites on our short list all have the same attributes—a moderate climate and a river basin near the sea. Good soil for crops and animal forage. Site selection is easy. What's difficult is the final selection of the colonists."

Oberst Becker was the head of operations for the German Colonial Special Group. He reported to Generalmajor Hartmann. The general, and two key aides (also generals), spent the majority of their time on political considerations, leaving Becker a free hand to get on with the operational aspects.

When the colonization program was announced, the political infighting within the German government was unprecedented. All ministries wanted control of their government's effort. The foreign office initially claimed the high ground but was quickly overrun by a coalition consisting of the ministry of the interior and the ministry of the environment. However, adroit maneuvering by the ministries of economic development and labor effectively muddied the water, leaving no clear front-runner.

The ministry for family affairs then fought an underhanded and very public battle to classify the entire planet of Pricus as the seventeenth German state with all the rights and responsibilities thereof. The proposal had a great deal of public support. Politicians running the existing sixteen states saw the proposal as a threat to dilute their authority and strangled the idea as quickly as they could.

In a series of proposals and presentations to the German chancellor over an entire week, it became apparent none of the ministries, except one, had a clue on how to actually go about establishing a colony. The only ministry with the proven ability to establish a beachhead on foreign soil was the ministry of defense, in short, the army (Bundeswehr).

Choosing the Bundeswehr to manage the colonization effort was inspired. Not only was security iron tight but the program was also run effectively and efficiently. The Bundeswehr was the only government ministry with a well-honed process for recruiting, evaluating, and training young men and women. Another benefit was the established legal processes already in place to discipline miscreants.

The German Colonization Special Group ran like a train. There were no teams. The group was strictly a traditional command and control do-as-I say organization.

Mostly. This was the new Bundeswehr. Recruits had rights.

Oberst Becker turned to his staff. "Hans," he said, "please review the math again."

Hans nodded briskly and stood. "The Isabella operations schedule calls for one flight a week. To keep things simple, I round down to forty-eight flights a year, eight flights to each colony. Therefore, our colony will receive a delivery approximately every six weeks. That's not very ambitious. Assuming Isabella has all four craft operating, one might expect more flights, maybe twice that number. Also, our analysis indicates a transport pod can hold more than six colonists. We almost certainly have an upside, and will plan accordingly; however, we can't count on a higher flight count, or a larger colonist load for the near future. In a year or two we expect Isabella to transport four times the number of colonists as their current commitment."

The others nodded. All were familiar with the figures. Oberst Becker was making a point in having Hans review the figures aloud.

Hans continued. "However, the Isabella program office insists we land two transport pods of supplies in advance of every pod of colonists. The requirement appears overly conservative. The company's executives are concerned certain groups may seek to sabotage the heavy lifters. Isabella wants to avoid blame should the colonists starve due to delays in resupply operations."

The others nodded again. The German intelligence agencies thought an attack on the heavy lifters was likely.

"As the interstellar craft, supposedly, can only transport two pods at a time, the first flight to Pricus will consist entirely of supplies, no colonists. The next two flights will each deliver one transport pod containing six colonists and a second of supplies. At that point, after the third delivery, the cumulative deliveries are four pods of supplies and two of colonists. The series then repeats. At the end of one year a total of twenty-four Germans will have traveled to Pricus.

"This does not necessarily mean we have twenty-four colonists remaining on Pricus. We estimate four to six of them will return to Earth within a year. That's not altogether a bad thing as the public will clamor for interviews with those who return. We expect a huge outpouring of public support once the first colonist returns." As a junior officer, Hans had no prerogative to express his own opinion. He was merely parroting the party line.

"And that, gentlemen," said Oberst Becker, while motioning Hans to sit down, "summarizes both the problem and the solution. Any large military effort—and make no mistake, this is a military operation—requires unswerving mass public support for success. The Pricus colony is popular with the public today, which is why we have so many applicants for the colonization program. However, circumstances can easily change. We need at least a few returnee colonists for the media exposure. Yes, we will call them colonists even if they plan to never return to Pricus.

"An event guaranteed to ensure continued public support is the birth of the first German child on Pricus. Once a birth happens, public, and therefore political, support is guaranteed for years. Nothing will sway public support for the colony at that point. Even Isabella will dare not abandon us, or even short us on flights, once the first child is born.

"More facts and figures, gentlemen. While our government has decreed each flight of colonists include a minimum of two women of childbearing age, we are tightening the requirement further. Only young married couples will make the trip. Therefore, one-half of those sent to Pricus will be healthy women of childbearing age. Of those three couples on the first flight at least one young woman must be pregnant, and in her first trimester when her flight leaves. More specifically she must be at least six weeks along, but not more than thirteen. That's not much of window.

"A key variable is our flight date. As of today, we don't know if we're the first to go, or the last. The program office has not yet released the information. We must be seen as ready to go upon a minute's notice. We must shine, gentlemen! The Isabella program office requires a team at their site two weeks prior to the scheduled liftoff. We must also have an alternate team ready to go. The purpose of today's meeting is to review personnel rosters against potential schedule changes and see how best to ensure we are successful. Let's get to it."

Hans was a good soldier. However, even he didn't believe the Oberst could get another's woman pregnant upon command.

FIFTY-ONE
EARLY

TWO RED MARKERS APPEARED ON Airman Addison's screen almost simultaneously. He quickly clicked on each of them and read the tags. "Sir," he called urgently, "you need to see this."

Coffee cup in hand, the officer of the day, Colonel Crowhurst, strode to the Airman's station and leaned over his shoulder. "What do you have, son?" he asked.

"Two bogies," he replied "Both are too large and slow moving for an ICBM. Both also exhibit non-ballistic behavior. One is over Southwest Africa, the other over Tasmania. The bogies are both twenty thousand feet up and descending at a decreasing rate. I was alert and watching, I swear! They just appeared out of nowhere." As he spoke, he rolled his cursor over the markers, bringing up boxes containing real-time flight parameters for the colonel's perusal.

"Holy crap!" exclaimed the colonel. He quickly strode to his station and picked up a blue phone. "Sir, this is Colonel Crowhurst," he said once his call was picked up. "We have a Little Red Riding Hood situation, sir. Two bogies which appear headed for Walvis Bay and Hobart, respectively. Both have descended below twenty thousand feet already, their speed is decreasing, and it appears they can touch down within ten minutes."

The code phrase Little Red Riding Hood referred to an unidentified aerial phenomenon (UAP) with a high probability of a Chait flight.

"Crap," said General Bonica calmly. "Alert everyone on the list and start refining the data. I'll alert the Pentagon." *I wonder if our intelligence people have screwed up*, he thought. *Did they miss something? Surely, the Chait are not delivering the power and propulsion components yet.* Intelligence estimates were unanimous in opining the heavy lifters would not be ready for months. Why would the Chait come now?

The Chinese picked up the Chait craft minutes after the Americans. The Australian early warning system was only slightly behind the Chinese. The Russians had little strategic tracking capability in the southern hemisphere and only learned of the incursion from reports on-site after the alien spacecraft landed. The government of Namibia learned of the incursion from a BBC TV broadcast.

There was consternation in the People's Liberation Army (PLA) Central Military Commission (CMC) in Beijing. General Ju-long, commanding the Strategic Support Force (SSF), was barking orders.

"Why are the aliens early? I want a real-time satellite view of both sites broadcast in the war room—now!" he ordered a staffer. "Alert the Jasmine Tea command group, and order them to stand by for an immediate call," he told another. Jasmine Tea was the code name for the Walvis Bay interdiction. "The same with the Wintersweet group," he pointed to yet another lowly colonel. Wintersweet referred to the team tasked with the Hobart operation.

General Ju-long had already alerted the senior general in command of the CMC, who in turn was alerting their governing body: the president, the minister of defense, the heads of the Air Force, Navy, Army, Space Command, and several senior members of the politburo. The minister of defense would soon make calls to the command staffs of the various operations planned to occur in conjunction with the taking of the Chait equipment. General Ju-long was anticipating these calls and wanted to alert those commanders quickly. Those in charge of the various operations would owe the General a big one.

General Ju-long personally called the commander of the Eastern Theater, in Nanjing. "My dear General Jing," he said. "Forgive my abruptness. We just detected a large Chait craft landing at each of the assembly sites. I have followed protocol and notified the general commanding the CMC, who is calling the board of governors. I imagine you will receive their call soon." It was not necessary for him to mention the CMC expected the

Chait's mission was the delivery of the power and drive units. The Chait's purpose appeared obvious.

General Jing commanded all armed forces in the Eastern Theater. The Army, Navy, and Air Force in his theater of operations all reported to him. He was ultimately in charge of all tactical matters regarding the invasion of Taiwan.

There was a slight pause. "Thank you for this courtesy call," said General Jing. "We will speak a great deal in the coming weeks, I believe. Good day." He hung up without waiting for a response.

General Ju-long then called the commander of the Southern Theater, whose commander, General Guang, supplied most of the assets, including submarines, used in the Jasmine Tea and Wintersweet operations. Also, General Guang commanded Operation Bay Leaf, the occupation of all disputed islands, and potential undersea oil basins in the South China Sea, and the establishment of a strong military "peacekeeping" presence in the fantastically oil-rich Sultanate of Brunei. General Guang was suitably grateful for the call.

The conference room in the Kremlin was large, comfortable, and well equipped. The staff meeting had been a shambles. Near the end, the president called his ministers of defense and intelligence into the hallway. There he gave them instructions in short sentences of simple words. Then he left.

Both Danov, the defense minister, and Krasnov, the new FSB head, returned to the staff meeting, visibly shaken. The two were dissimilar in age, seniority, education, manner, and appearance. In spite of their differences, the pair worked together surprisingly well.

Danov took the lead. "Since you don't know enough to make a fucking recommendation to the president," he said to the group, "let's turn this into a working meeting and figure out what's required to actually make a fucking informed recommendation." He looked to Krasnov, who pointed to one of his two deputies at the table.

"What is the expected timing to install the Chait equipment?" Krasnov asked his deputy director of operations. "Skip the wordy qualifiers; we already heard those." The others at the table winced inwardly. The FSB deputies were rookies at this level of meeting and had likely torpedoed their careers by wasting the president's time.

"Our reports indicate the assembly sites wouldn't be ready for the Chait equipment for two more months," the deputy began. "From the limited intelligence we've been able to gather, the equipment is not deeply integrated into the craft's structure. It appears the hardware can be bolted in like an engine or transmission in a car. A sensible person would finish the craft first, before installing the Chait units, thereby minimizing their window of vulnerability on the ground. The Isabella people aren't stupid. They know multiple governments will attempt to take the equipment.

"We," he said, pointing at the deputy director of technical services, "estimated an effort between one week and one month to install and test the power, and drive units in the first craft. It appeared the installations would not be done in parallel. So, we planned on a minimum of a week to install the first set, and another week for the second craft. Our best estimates gave us a window of two weeks to two months while the Chait equipment was vulnerable. After consulting everyone in this room, we laid our plans assuming a minimum three-week window of opportunity."

"But the Chait came early, before we were ready, didn't they?" snarled Krasnov. "And the aliens didn't just drop off the equipment and leave. None of you geniuses thought they might stay!"

FIFTY-TWO
SCRAMBLING

FOUR DAYS PASSED.

As soon as the Chait craft landed, a steely grey dome with a kilometer radius shimmered into existence at each of the assembly sites. Warnings were broadcast for aircraft and motor vehicles to keep a safe distance. Otherwise, the Chait remained uncommunicative.

Outside of the Inner Circle, all had expected the Chait to deliver their equipment and immediately depart. No one expected them to remain on the ground for more than a short period of time. Certainly not more than twelve hours.

Political leaders around the world forbade their military from assaulting an assembly site while the aliens were presumably present. However, the three great powers worked feverishly to prepare to grab the technology once the Chait left.

Russia, caught flat-footed like the others, intensified preparations to invade its neighbors. They abandoned plans to tow their only aircraft carrier, the scow *Admiral Kuznetsov*, to Southwest Africa. However, the navy dispatched missile cruisers, submarines, and another ostensibly civilian trawler to southwest Africa. The Russian Navy also sent an additional submarine with special equipment and a squad of specially trained Spetsnaz commandos to Tasmania. Given transit time, the Spetsnaz would not be a factor for weeks.

The *Theodore Roosevelt* carrier group, already visiting Sydney, went on high alert. Elements of the American 6th fleet, reinforced by the *Harry S. Truman* carrier group, set sail for Walvis Bay.

The Chinese carrier *Shandong*, a refitted British carrier once sold for scrap, and other elements of the Southern Theater fleet immediately set off for Tasmania. Unfortunately, the task force was unready. A fleet oiler somehow caught fire at the dock and burned to the waterline. Another oiler somehow collided with a cruiser and both were so damaged they had to return to port. The task force now lacked sufficient fuel for the voyage. The operations tempo on the *Shandong* was quite high as the flight crew worked around the clock to fly in additional personnel and supplies. A collision on the flight deck resulted in a fire killing a dozen crewman. The carrier also ignominiously returned to port.

Chinese preparations to invade Taiwan went into high gear. The US sent two more carrier groups to reinforce the 7th fleet in Asia.

Tensions were high.

Jon Gallock appeared on the *Tiger Tanaka ET Update* show.

"I can't thank you enough for taking time out of your schedule to join us on the show tonight," began Casey. "You must be slammed given recent developments at the assembly sites. What can you tell us?"

"Thank you, Tiger, for having me on your show," began Jon. "A lot of people were surprised by the Chait appearance," said Jon truthfully. "My liaison, Robert, assures me their intentions are peaceful. The purpose of the visit is simply to deliver the equipment, as promised. Once delivery is complete, the ships will leave. Nothing has changed, except the schedule was pulled in."

"What about the force field at the two sites?" asked Casey. "Can you confirm the presence of a force field?"

"Robert addressed that as well," replied Jon. He was always careful to answer these kinds of questions by putting words in the mouths of the Chait. "His people want a privacy screen while landed. The Chait are also concerned some person, or persons, might take intemperate action that everybody would later regret. My understanding is the screen will stop conventional weapons. Robert quoted an old proverb back to me: 'good fences make good neighbors.' The Chait are surprisingly well-educated in our culture."

"Will those screens withstand nuclear weapons?" asked Casey seriously.

"The Chait technology is quite advanced," said Jon, sidestepping the question. "In any event I find it hard to believe that a nuclear power would attack a friendly country and endanger the lives of tens of thousands of innocent nearby civilians."

"Let's pray you are correct," replied Casey. "Do you have any idea on how long the Chait plan to stay?"

"They have not communicated that information to me," Jon replied. "I do know their spokesman Robert called the leaders of both countries where the assembly sites are located, as well as the nations granted an exoplanet. As usual the British foreign secretary represented the Commonwealth. I really don't know more than what was in the president's press release."

"Well, pooh," said Casey while making a face. "You're not much help. Can you describe what's going on under those domes? Surely, unloading equipment can't take four days."

"The process is more involved than simply shoving a few crates out a hatch," said Jon. "I've been told the Chait must complete a fair amount of integration, calibration, and testing before the equipment is operational."

"Whoa!" exclaimed Casey. "By operational, do you mean the heavy lifter fleet will be ready to fly as soon as the Chait depart?"

"To the best of my knowledge, and assuming a hundred other minor details are addressed, yes, possibly," said Jon. "I expect the Chait equipment functioning and online before they leave."

Twelve hours later, the Chait craft departed.

An hour later, all four of the heavy lifters departed for lunar orbit.

FIFTY-THREE
FOG OF WAR

THE GREAT POWERS WERE CAUGHT flat-footed by the early departure of the heavy lifter fleet. For one day everyone paused. The fleet did not linger in Earth orbit. Once free of the planet's gravitational pull, they set course for the moon at a leisurely ten thousand miles per hour.

Math ensued. Possible orbits were plotted. Everyone involved quickly reached the conclusion that one or more of the fleet could return in as little as two days. No one had sufficient intelligence to calculate the maximum time the fleet could stay aloft. Staging of the various military adventures began anew.

The fleet assumed lunar orbit. And stayed. Days passed. Then a full week.

Final preparations were completed to assault the assembly sites.

Russia rolled tanks to their borders' edge and amassed fifty thousand armed men.

China staged a thousand aircraft and two hundred ships for the invasion of Taiwan.

In the US, the president made several stern speeches promising unswerving American support of Taiwan and NATO allies. Sanctions were mentioned.

Supposedly by accident, a Chinese satellite exploded, taking out a nearby American reconnaissance bird. The matter escalated, and the satellite capability of the big three degraded quickly. For a week it was "a thing" in the Southern US to sit outside at night with binoculars, friends, and a cooler of beer, watching the sparkly lights far overhead. A trillion dollars of satellite investment was gone by the end of the week. Half the military surveillance, communication, navigation, and various flavors of anti-satellite satellites belonging to the governments of Earth were destroyed. Civilian

infrastructure was not unscathed. Many cable TV, navigation, communication, and weather satellites were accidentally or purposely destroyed as
well. The James Webb Space Telescope was not spared.

Propaganda blared from all forms of media all day, every day.

After ten days the heavy lifters broke lunar orbit and headed back to
Earth at three times the speed of their departure. As they neared the planet,
it became apparent the craft would enter the atmosphere exactly one hour
apart. The strike teams tweaked their op plans one last time.

The *Nina* and *Pinta* landed at their original points of departure, Walvis
Bay and Hobart, respectively. The other two heavy lifters did not.

The *Santa Maria* landed in Mauritius, an island five hundred miles east
of Madagascar. The *Mariagalante* landed on the small south Pacific Island
of Rarotonga, thousands of miles east of Australia. The flight crews were
replaced, and ground crews worked madly to attach the transport pods.
Both craft were turned around in less than twelve hours.

The *Santa Maria* carried colonists from Japan, and the *Mariagalante*
a mixed Commonwealth contingent from Britain, Canada, and Australia.
Tiger Tanaka was on hand in Rarotonga with a camera crew and held
dramatic interviews with the departing colonists and crews. Not only did
her subsequent weekly show break all viewing records, again, but the story
of this daring mission, carried out under the noses of every intelligence
agency in the world, also became a bestselling novel, and eventually an
Oscar-winning movie.

As the last of the two craft, the *Mariagalante*, entered the atmosphere,
a very large bogie was detected by one of the United States ground installations entering an extremely high Earth orbit.

In the Space Force command center under Cheyenne Mountain, a
very tired Airman Addison blinked in surprise. Astounding events were
becoming routine. "Sir," he called to Colonel Crowhurst. "Another Little
Red Riding Hood event, sir."

The colonel came over quickly. "Are you sure it's not Wagon Train?"
the colonel asked. "Half our assets are down. Do you have a firm reading?"
Wagon Train referred to an event involving the Arnold heavy lifters.

"Yes, sir, to both questions," the Airman responded. "It's too large, and moving too fast. The reading is confirmed."

"Fuck!" said the colonel. The week had been hellish. Now this. The US had never detected a Chait craft at such a distance before. The craft were always stealth'd and didn't reveal themselves until in the atmosphere. He started to make calls. His calls took a while to get through as the surviving circuits were loaded with an unusually high amount of traffic.

The unidentified craft took up an extremely high and unlikely geostationary orbit over Washington DC.

President Colston's phone rang again. People had been calling the whole damned day. He'd just got off the phone with the army chief of staff. He hated unsolicited one-on-one calls. Government ran the same as business. You exchanged a few social pleasantries while standing at the pisser, and the next thing you knew someone was telling the staff you'd approved their pet project.

People in government, especially the senior military generals, were the worst. The military people were scrupulously honest regarding the little things, but the generals lied like motherfuckers on anything important. The army chief of staff said his sources indicated the Russians would escalate quickly to a full-scale nuclear war if they saw anyone making off with the Chait technology. Motherfucker. The chief of staff was covering his ass by saying the worst case was the most likely case.

The other four branches of the military had different views. The chairman of the joint chiefs of staff, a marine general, was unable to generate a consensus among the group. The secretary of defense was a useless limp-dick bean counter brought in to rationalize procurement practices.

The director of national intelligence (DNI) had called earlier. He was a former congressman who had served in the military and worked in the private sector for companies subcontracting to the intelligence agencies. He had briefly headed a couple of the agencies while cleaning up after scandals. His primary skill was "peeling the onion." He possessed an uncanny ability to find the true story within the fake story, within another fake story, ad infinitum. The intelligence people made the lying motherfucking generals look honest in comparison.

The director had interesting insights. He reported the Arnolds had left cargo in lunar orbit. Apparently, the items were transport pods; however, details could not be verified at such a distance. His unsolicited advice was to pass on the opportunity to grab Chait technology from the Arnolds. "That's fool's gold," he said. He suggested a two-pronged approach. Suck up to the Chait while simultaneously launching a crash program to put manned assets in cislunar space. "Go for the starships," he urged. "The potential payoff in grabbing a starship is a thousand times than offered by the equipment on the Arnolds." As part of sucking up to the Chait, he felt the US must wave a big stick at the commies. Although inaccurate, both the president and the DNI lumped the Russians in the commie basket along with the Chinese. The DNI certainly had a unique perspective on the situation. Unfortunately, the president hadn't the time to call him back since this latest development. Now, another goddamn call.

His aide looked at the caller ID and raised his eyebrows. "Mister President," he said, "you may want to look at this."

The president looked at the screen, and raised his eyebrows as well. He touched the screen twice. Once to accept the call, the second time to activate the phone's speaker. With one hand he motioned his two visitors closer, and with the other shooed his aide from the room.

"Robert!" he exclaimed in a hearty tone. "Thank you for calling. What a pleasant surprise. I have my chief of staff and national security advisor in the room. I'll ask them to leave if you prefer."

"No problem. Their presence is just fine," Robert replied cheerily. "Good evening, gentlemen." He addressed each of them warmly by name.

"My apologies for this unscheduled call," said Robert. "The matter is rather urgent. Do you have a few minutes?" he asked graciously.

"Of course," replied the president. "May I assume this is about the current situation?"

"Yes, you are correct," replied Robert. "At least, about certain aspects of the current situation. There is a lot going on in your world right now. First, you should know the large spacecraft in a high orbit above Washington is not ours."

The president and his advisors were temporarily dumbstruck.

"The craft orbiting Earth was built by humans in the colony of Ouranos," continued Robert. "The craft, named *Argo*, is crewed by humans who are here to hold up their end of the bargain. Their ship is ready to start transporting the colonists and supplies to their respective colonies. Imagine their surprise at the current situation seen on Earth.

"But the *Argo* is not why I called. My concern regards the multiple attempts currently underway to attack the lunar-capable craft and steal our technology."

The president tried to interrupt with assurances, but Robert gently overrode him.

"Should anything happen to one of those craft, a nation-state or two would necessarily be dropped from the colonization program," Robert continued in a steelier tone. "We wouldn't renege on the grant of their planet; the culprits would simply lose their ride. And if any sticky human fingers start monkeying with our equipment, the results will be catastrophic. Let's just say it's fortunate one site is located in a barren desert. The people of Hobart, however... well, they'd be caught within the incident perimeter."

"Incident" sounded ominous. The president chose not to ask for clarification.

"How may I help?" asked the president.

"Simply, stay your hand, Mister President," responded Robert. "Have your forces stand down. However, if you thought it in your interest to lend a hand, a teeny-tiny helping hand, we would be glad if you accepted a token of our appreciation."

"What kind of teeny-tiny hand, and how big a token?" asked the president bluntly.

"After much discussion on my end, we've decided we could go so far as to solidify your scientists' understanding of Low Energy Nuclear Reactions," said Robert. "That's L-E-N-R. You might know the phenomenon as cold fusion. Your guys were so close! Then that specific physics research community made an unfortunate forty-year detour down a dead-end road. The process is very clean, and a lot safer than other, more energetic power units."

"Cold fusion sounds interesting," replied the president. "Please continue."

"Before I explain the helping hand, there are some things you might not know...," Robert explained further.

The president started sucking up big time. The two leaders hashed out a few details and reached an agreement. After an exchange of ritual pleasantries, Robert signed off. The president broke out the bourbon. Even the chief of staff, a notorious teetotaler, had a belt.

FIFTY-FOUR
GO GO GO

AFTERWARDS IT WAS UNCLEAR WHO went first, Russia or China. Everything seemed to happen at once.

The Chinese began the invasion of Taiwan with a massive rocket bombardment which lasted days. Chinese ships docked in Brunei's primary port of Muara and disembarked several thousand soldiers to protect the minority ethnic Chinese citizens from supposed civil unrest. The Chinese navy began the movement of a large offshore oil platform to the heart of the Brunei's massive Egret oil field.

The Russians rolled their tank brigades across the borders of Belarus, Latvia, and Estonia, on the request of the leaders of those countries, again, to assist with civil unrest.

The major powers all reached the same conclusion regarding an attack on the assembly sites: Go for it. One bird on-site is sufficient. In fact, most liked the idea of half the fleet being away carrying cargo to the moon. The colonization program could remain operational. There was suddenly a very real chance to obtain the Chait technology while conserving some heavy-lift capability. The colonization program would continue.

Multiple operations were launched against Walvis Bay. The fleets offshore put a thicket of fighters in the air. All, excepting the Commonwealth, had similar orders—shoot down the *Nina* if the craft attempted to leave. The admiral commanding the Commonwealth fleet informed his counterpart he would open fire on the American carrier if he detected a single helicopter, or Osprey tiltrotor, spool up. The American admiral made a similar threat regarding any attempt by the others to land a boat.

A squadron of heavily loaded B-52 bombers left Diego Garcia in the Indian Ocean bound for Walvis Bay.

292 | DAVID PANKEY

A motley convoy containing a thousand mercenaries closely aligned with the Russian military left the dusty Botswana town of Charles Hill and drove through the border checkpoint into Namibia without slowing. The convoy dusted off anything that moved with automatic weapons fire and continued down the road to Walvis Bay, four hundred miles away. At the same time, in Windhoek, a dozen well-paid agitators started passing out free rotgut whiskey and haranguing the gathering crowd to "kill whitey!" The mercenary convoy would pass through Windhoek en route to the assembly site. The mercenaries hoped to gather up a thousand well-oiled locals and keep them lubricated for the remaining two hundred miles of the trip. Accordingly, the convoy carried cases of booze, and numerous barrels of rusty machetes, to equip the expected auxiliaries.

The pilot of an Airbus commercial jetliner on charter to a Chinese tourist group radioed the tower at Walvis Bay International Airport declaring an emergency. He reported an engine out and was diverting to the only airport within a thousand miles capable of handling that size of aircraft. Inside, the commandos finished their weapons check and geared up.

Near Hobart the scene was less crowded. The main Chinese fleet did not make it in time. The PLA forces on-site had no helicopters available to launch their recently planned assault. Other than two Chinese missile cruisers, the only surface ships either the Chinese or Russian had in the theater were trawlers. The thinly disguised fishing trawlers were in reality spy ships, stuffed to the gills with advanced sensors and sophisticated communication equipment. In a deeper deception, one of the ostensible Chinese trawlers was in fact a troop carrier. Instead of sophisticated equipment the vessel contained twenty highly trained sea dragon marine commandos.

When he received the go command, the Chinese captain of the trawler carrying commandos started generating smoke and radioed the harbor master, declaring an emergency. He reported an explosion, a fire, and many injuries. The ship would be coming in fast, he said and requested emergency vehicles, including at least four ambulances, meet him at the dock. Without the helicopters—the other half of the assault plan—this mission seemed doomed to failure. Still, he had his orders.

The captain of the nearest Russian trawler shook his head, half in disgust, half in admiration. "Clever bastards. I wish we'd thought of that," he said to himself.

Under the cover of darkness, a Russian sub rose near the surface and belched out two inflatable boats and a dozen out-of-shape Spetsnaz special operation troops. The troops loaded up, started their whisper-quiet plastic engines, and headed for shore. They were not happy. This was a real longshot.

The American fleet headed south at flank speed. The USS *Theodore Roosevelt* launched fighters which took up station over the city of Hobart. As in Walvis Bay, the American carrier was warned that any signs of special operator movement would trigger an immediate attack by the Australian Air Force. The Australian prime minister called the American president and demanded, in a very intemperate tone, the American fighters get the hell out of his airspace.

The Chinese missile cruisers had no chance of taking out the installation. Three rings of aircraft from both Australia and the US protected the site. The cruisers were lit up electronically from both the air and attack submarines beneath the surface. The captains were brave enough to carry out a suicide mission, yet smart enough to realize the chance of success was zero. The Chinese hung around for two weeks before being forced to leave for lack of fuel.

The attacks on Walvis Bay failed miserably.

Both engines on the Chinese chartered Airbus somehow failed simultaneously. The plane hit the ground at a steep angle and smeared wreckage, body parts, and a small nuclear weapon over a square mile of desert, two hundred miles short of its intended destination.

The American B-52s carpet bombed the mercenary convoy well before the Russians reached Windhoek. The air force base on Diego Garcia had emptied its stock of obsolete Vietnam-era bombs for the mission. Hundreds of two-hundred-fifty-pound bombs bracketed the motley vehicles. In most cases the blast craters overlapped. The last plane dropped napalm on the wreckage. The bombing was massive overkill. There were no survivors.

Several agitators and a hundred enthusiastic drunks grew impatient waiting for the doomed convoy and set out on their own from Windhoek. They commandeered a dozen buses, flatbed trucks, and taxis, and headed west. Fifty miles out of town they were ambushed from the air. The South African Gripen, UK Harrier, and American F-18 pilots were unhappy at being called off the main mercenary convoy. They vented their ire on the auxiliaries. There were few survivors.

The American president personally oversaw the Walvis Bay operation, over the howling objections of his senior military commanders. The brass delayed, obfuscated, and misrepresented his orders to the area commanders. The president became enraged. He made several calls to the fleets, personally, forbidding the deployment of the special operation troops. He also spoke personally to the commander of the squadron of B-52s. One month later he sacked a dozen senior military leaders, including half of the joint chiefs of staff. He used the furor as cover to also rid his administration of three powerful intelligence agency directors. The secretary of defense was also given the boot. Everyone involved who left his administration had their income taxes audited. The whole affair lit a fire under the president, and he spent his remaining time in office pursuing a radical agenda of good, solid, limited government.

The pitiful attempts on the *Pinta* in Hobart also failed.

The attacking Chinese trawler somehow exploded and burned to the waterline before reaching the dock. Several badly burned sea dragon marines survived and were taken to the hospital by already waiting ambulances.

The Russian Spetsnaz troops in their inflatable boats were never seen, or heard from.

The situation was unclear for a day. Eventually, the Russians concluded neither rival was going to succeed in seizing the Chait technology. Also, the Arnolds were clearly dispersed so as to make a clean sweep impossible. They cancelled plans to nuke the two sites.

The Chinese came to the opposite conclusion. They decided to take out the two sites with any two of the heavy lifters. They would deal with the remaining lifters later, one way or another. After all, they had to land sometime.

The Chinese leadership was consumed with the Taiwan situation, and in hindsight they made numerous poor decisions.

After weeks of hopscotching around remote south Pacific Islands, two of the vehicles returned home. One to Walvis Bay, another to Hobart.

Five hundred miles off the African west coast, a Chinese Jin-class submarine fired a missile armed with a nuclear warhead at the Walvis Bay site.

The missile's solid rocket booster somehow exploded in the launch tube, jamming the hatch open and wreaking internal havoc. The captain blew all tanks and for several minutes the crew thought the vessel might claw its way to the surface. But no, the submarine sank with all hands in the depths of the Cape basin. The ocean floor of the basin was a hundred-meter-thick layer of primordial ooze. The submarine was never found.

The same day Chinese triggered the two nuclear warheads offshore Hobart. Nothing happened. The bombs somehow failed to detonate. The Chinese abandoned the devices and erased all records of the two planned nuclear attacks. The People's Liberation Army executed several dozen people involved to keep the incident secret.

The Taiwan adventure was an unmitigated disaster.

For three days China rained missiles on Taiwan: air to ground, ship to ground, and ballistic ground to ground missiles. The PLA targeted air defense systems, communication and command centers, airports, and harbors. Any exposed Taiwan military plane or ship was destroyed. When the defenses were judged sufficiently weakened, the invasion fleet set sail. Hundreds of vessels boiled from a dozen ports. The fleet was led by minesweepers, followed by destroyers and missile cruisers. The troopships were in the rear. Hundreds of ground-based fighters provided air support.

The Taiwan strait is less than a hundred miles wide at the narrowest point. Land based fighters had plenty of range to provide air cover to the fleet. The two remaining operational Chinese aircraft carriers stayed well to the rear. The carriers would be used primarily to stage helicopters once they established a beachhead.

In fact, the Taiwan defenses were not seriously degraded. Four generations of men had dug in, fortified, and accumulated arms. For three days they lounged in their deep fortifications, drinking tea and bemoaning the destruction overhead. Their air fleet stay sheltered in hardened concrete revetments. Their small submarine force lay quiet on the sea floor beneath the Taiwan strait.

Once the first of the invasion fleet was well into the strait, Taiwan launched a devastating counterattack. Hundreds of modern Israeli-designed surface-to-air missile pods unmasked and blew the majority of the circling Chinese planes out of the sky. Any who ducked low were met with a hail of fire from strategically placed 30mm radar-guided Gatling autocannons, each firing a hundred rounds a second.

As the survivors recoiled in shock, a wave of ground-launched long-range anti-ship missiles bypassed the invasion fleet and homed in on the pride of the navy, the brand-new aircraft carrier *Fujian*, two hundred miles away. At the same time a Taiwan submarine neared the surface and fired four Exocet missiles at the carrier. The two-pronged attack was exquisitely coordinated, and all the ordnance arrived on target simultaneously. The Chinese air defenses were saturated. The carrier was hit four times, twice by Exocets and twice by the land-based Tomahawks. The *Fujian* was massively damaged. So much so the ship never reentered active service, and was eventually scrapped.

Taiwan had stocked up on anti-ship missiles from NATO countries over the years, primarily Harpoon and Tomahawk systems. Lots of them. The systems were slightly dated; however, the military bought huge numbers, dirt cheap, and consistently updated their capabilities secretly with the latest technology stolen from US defense contractors. They hid the missiles in fortified underground batteries.

Planes and ships are expensive. A capable fighter jet costs tens of millions of dollars. A military ship costs hundreds of millions of dollars. A highly capable missile costs almost nothing in comparison. Tomahawk cruise missiles were available for a cool million apiece.

The Tomahawks had a range of fifteen hundred miles. They were launched from the far side of the island and took long curving paths to their targets. To the Chinese it was as if the missiles appeared out of nowhere.

Before the first missiles struck home, the Taiwan military unleashed another massive launch. The entire strike was targeted at the relatively small number of minesweepers. Despite protection of the missile cruisers, all but one of the minesweepers were sunk or heavily damaged.

The third missile wave came in low, skimming the surface from either flank. This wave targeted a single missile cruiser, from the most capable class. The cruiser splashed four attacking missiles before being destroyed. Each successive Taiwan launch targeted a single vessel of the attacking fleet, overwhelming the defenses, ship by ship. The other Chinese missile cruisers extended their protection umbrellas for mutual support; however, the tactic proved ineffective.

Ground-based anti-missile support from the nearby mainland had been dialed in to protect the troop ships. By the time the ground-based support was re-tasked, half the missile cruisers had been lost, with a corresponding reduction in protection for the surviving vessels.

Taiwan continued to launch a prodigious amount of anti-ship missiles. A wave launched every sixty seconds. Every wave killed a Chinese ship.

When the fleet neared the halfway mark, flotillas of mines in a dozen locations were remotely untethered from the sea floor. The majority of the mines had sensing and capability to maneuver. The deadly mines floated silently one meter below the surface, awaiting the oncoming invasion fleet.

In the Beijing CMC, faces were ashen. The navy they had poured their treasure into for twenty years was being annihilated before their eyes.

"What happened to our intelligence estimates?" asked Defense Minister Keqiang angrily. "No such missile capability was reported to me. Not the massive quantities, not the sophistication, not the command-and-control capability. Where are our vaunted cyber warriors? I was told those pasty-face dung eaters would shut every system on the island down. Complete chaos would ensue, I was told. Our air force had complete air superiority, I was told. Their defenses were crushed, I was told." Spittle flew from his lips.

"Sir, our projections still show the troop carriers reaching the beach," said General Jing. He hadn't reached his current position by cowering before a tongue lashing. "It's true our losses are heavier than expected; however, we will still land an overwhelming force. The Taiwan forces cannot launch missiles forever. We will regroup and be able to provide support and resupply for our soldiers within days."

"Land our troops!?" the minister shouted back at him. More spittle flew. "You idiot! Why do you think the rebels took out the minesweepers first? The troops will never reach shore, you idiot! They have minefields which will decimate our troopships. Have you even bothered to look at the latest aerial reconnaissance? The Taiwan forces have hundreds of camouflaged and bunkered anti-aircraft autocannons. Don't you think similar guns are placed on the beaches, you idiot! There are only a handful of likely beaches where we can effectively disembark. Don't you think they know that? You idiot. Those beaches will be mined, covered by enfilading fire, and ranged with heavy mortar batteries, you idiot. We no longer have the means to sanitize the beaches. Any troops who survive to reach shore won't last an hour without air superiority and naval support, which we no longer have, you idiot!"

"We're adjusting," insisted General Jing. "We've marked the locations of their hidden batteries and are destroying those now. We've also sunk the submarine responsible for attacking the *Fujian*."

"Are you telling me trading our ten-billion-yuan carrier for a forty-year-old diesel submarine is good news, you shit-eating dog-fucker!?" the minister exploded. He pulled his ceremonial pistol from its holster and shot the general in the face. He took a step forward and fired three more times in the general's chest as he lay dead on the floor.

Defense Minister Keqiang glared around the room. No one looked back. "Recall the fleet," he ordered. "Continue our land-based missile strikes. Hit every missile site, and every gun emplacement revealed during the counterattack. Take them all out."

The defense minister turned to General Ju-long, the commander of the CMC. "You, call the minister of state security and the general secretary, and inform them of the failure of General Jing's operation. Tell them the general is indisposed and I'm cleaning up his mess. Now, go!" No sense in taking chances by calling attention to himself. Chinese leadership might kill the messenger.

As China launched the invasion of Taiwan, the US Navy had an unprecedented four carrier groups in Asia, ostensibly under the command of the 7th fleet. The *Abraham Lincoln* and *Carl Vinson* groups loitered on high alert five hundred miles to the east of Taiwan. Despite his strong words of assurance, the American president had no intention of actively engaging the Chinese over Taiwan. The American carriers would stay well back.

Another two carrier groups patrolled empty sea to the east of Japan. The current crisis did not involve Japan, yet. The Americans did not want to get sucked into any kind of minor territorial dispute between Japan and China. The increased American naval presence was simply a show of force to buck up morale of the American ally.

A bedrock rule of barroom fights, and international diplomacy, is "kick them when they're down." The international community had a lot of festering ill will towards the Chinese, who by now had displaced America as the world's villain.

Rear Admiral Edward Hayes commanded the *Abraham Lincoln* carrier group, one of the two off Taiwan. When the Chinese invasion fleet was recalled, he received a call from the president of the United States with new orders. The orders were simple and straightforward: to aid our ally Taiwan in fighting off the Chinese invasion, he was to scour the South China Sea free of any and all Chinese presence.

The president picked the right man for the job. Admiral Hayes was a rarity in the modern navy, a bigot. He detested Asia, all Asians, and anything associated with that part of the world. He owned no cars, clothes, or consumer electronics made anywhere in Asia. During World War II his grandfather was a navy flyer shot down in the Pacific theater. Like other flyers captured by the Japanese, he was brutalized, beheaded, and cannibalized by his captors. His father was killed in action in Vietnam. The Hayes men didn't forgive or forget. In his eyes one Asian country was as contemptible as any other.

Admiral Hayes hit Pratas Island first. The large, uninhabited atoll had been occupied by the Chinese several years earlier. Following standard procedure, the Chinese built a permanent base housing a thousand men. The base included a good airstrip, a dock, a powerful radar installation, barracks, a fuel depot, and much more. The outdated anti-aircraft guns were more for show than practical use. The Pratas base, like the others, was designed as a trip-line. Other Asian countries would think twice before attacking a base of the most powerful country in the region.

US Navy planes destroyed the Pratas Island facilities in minutes.

The Chinese possessed anti-ship missiles with an effective range in excess of two thousand miles. Over a week they fired their entire inventory at the USS *Abraham Lincoln* and USS *Carl Vinson*. In over a hundred attempts they scored zero hits. The stunning ineffectiveness of the attacks was due in part to the poor quality of the supposedly advanced Chinese weapons, but mostly to the vastly superior tactics, training, and equipment of the American Navy.

The disputed Paracel Islands came next. Then, the Spratly Islands. The rampage lasted two weeks. The admiral finished the campaign thousands of mile south in the Riau Islands. In all, he destroyed over thirty Chinese installations. The airstrips were cratered and all infrastructure destroyed. Any destroyers or patrol boats who interfered were sunk. The two newest and most capable missile cruisers in the Chinese Navy were bombed into wreckage. US Navy SEALs cleared all oil rigs occupied by the PLA. Anti-ship missiles sunk any fake fishing boat in their path. Any overflight by long-range reconnaissance aircraft from the Chinese mainland were shot down by US F-35 fighters.

The *Carl Vinson* carrier group had his back. They followed the *Abraham Lincoln* group south, lingering near Brunei to land marines to assist the sultan in expelling the invaders.

When the firing finally ended, the Chinese had lost a quarter of their navy in the failed Taiwan operation. Worse yet, the losses were their most modern and capable ships. Most of the Chinese satellite presence was destroyed. Twenty years of building expensive infrastructure in the South China Sea were erased. Finally, the PLA military hardware was exposed as "all show and no go" to the entire world.

The PLA underwent three successive purges. First, by order of the political leaders. Then, by orders from the new political leaders after the president and much of the Central Committee was replaced. Finally, Jon, Randy, and the Chait ensured any surviving miscreants got what was coming to them for their role in attacking the assembly sites.

The Russian adventures went much better than the Chinese.

The Russian tank brigades entering Belarus, Latvia, and Estonia were met with open arms. The countries had been politically and economically aligned for years. Much more so than with NATO. Russia was seen as a more reliable partner than NATO countries, especially the United States. Along with tanks, the Russians brought billions of dollars of foreign aid, and showered many millions more into the offshore accounts of the ruling families.

NATO leadership was stuck with the awkward situation where two member countries welcomed a continuing presence of Russian tanks.

Increased trade access to the port of Riga and the Daugava River basin eventually covered the cost of the Russian presence.

The NATO countries made pro forma complaints. Sanctions were discussed, but never implemented. After all, the Russian bear was an invited guest.

Georgia and Azerbaijan joined the CSTO. Azerbaijan oil was welcome, but the required security measures soaked up any profit. Neither country brought much else to the arrangement. As years passed, Russian leadership regretted their early enthusiasm.

The relatively small losses from the Russian attempts to grab the Chait technology were quickly swept under the rug. Political fallout was light. On balance, Russian leadership was reasonably satisfied with the way things turned out. The surviving leadership, that is. Nobody involved in the Walvis Bay or Hobart attacks lived out the year. Including the Russian president.

FIFTY-FIVE
FALLOUT

A WEEK AFTER THE CHINESE INVASION fleet was repulsed, the Inner Circle met to assess the situation.

Jon sweated bullets while Casey traveled from Rarotonga to Los Angeles. As soon as she landed, Jon forbade any member of the group from flying until hostilities died down. It was too easy for a plane carrying one of the Inner Circle to disappear en route, or be brought down accidently on purpose. Especially so in the southern hemisphere, where a twelve-hour flight over water was not uncommon.

Quinn was in Hobart spending most of his time dealing with the Australian political fallout. Bill was in Walvis Bay. Adrian was in Washington alternatively soothing or educating American congressmen on developing events. Casey went to ground in the Los Angeles metro area. The remaining members of the Inner Circle circulated in Western Europe. No one spent more than two consecutive nights at the same address.

None of the world's governments or intelligence agencies had an active operation to kidnap or assassinate Jon or the others. Still, things change, and Jon did not want anyone stuck on a plane while events were so fluid on the ground. He was also concerned one of them might be recognized, sparking a spontaneous violent act.

"Casey," began Jon, "please get the hell out of LA. Literally a thousand Chinese spies and contractors infest the LA metro area. I don't want you taken hostage and held for ransom. Direct military action to take the technology didn't work. Bribery didn't work. Does anyone doubt the PLA won't resort to taking hostages?"

"Ok, ok," she said. "I'll go just to stop you from bitching. I'll talk to Randy after the meeting. He's got a safe house arranged in Dallas."

Jon went first. "Robert's call to the president was key," he said. "Well, that and the appearance of a starship from Ouranos. I believe the arrival of the *Argo* above Washington DC caused the president to truly believe in the reality of the colonization program for the first time. Convincing the president to cancel the Americans' operations to seize the technology was surprisingly easy. When the military tried to ignore his instructions, he became enraged. He saw their foot dragging for what it truly was, mutiny. After speaking to Robert, it also became very clear to the president that the lying liars in the intelligence agencies were lying to him. The cold fusion carrot helped as well."

"Excuse me for interrupting," said Tracey. "Is cold fusion a big deal or not?"

"Meh," said Jon dismissively. "It's another low-cost way to boil water. We do that already in nuclear, coal, and gas-fired power plants. However, cold fusion is much less expensive. The recurring fuel cost is approximately zero. The technology could be quite useful. Or it might stay sequestered in a lab because of a phony environmental scare. I'll bet anyone on this call a dollar the Chinese are using cold fusion commercially before the US."

No one took Jon up on the bet.

"The odd mishaps that 'somehow' happened to both the Chinese and Russian operations have put an end to direct action from those entities in the near future," continued Jon. "Our surveillance indicates both countries plan to play things cool for a while. The US is stepping up plans to develop cislunar transport capability. That's a problem for the future.

"China is gutted. Their new president won't complete a full year in office. He'll be gone in a month, as well as a third of the politburo. The Taiwan debacle has poisoned their entire political and military establishments. Their attraction to foreign escapades for a generation meant internal issues and investments were shorted. The nation has huge political unrest, famine in some areas, and trade has collapsed. The urban population is demanding basic benefits and a social safety net during periods of unemployment. No more working for a bowl of rice and a pickle a day.

"Every oil-producing nation in Southeast Asia has blacklisted China. Not one drop of oil will ship to the Chinese markets in the near future.

Australia is suspending shipment of iron ore, coal, liquified natural gas, and grains. The cessation of exports will certainly hurt the Aussies in the short run; however, a major trade agreement with India is imminent. In the long run a developing India, and ASEAN states, means Australia will prosper. China will not.

"Russia came out relatively unscathed. One would expect they will continue to cozy up to China to sell energy if nothing else. However, their leadership will be in flux for several years.

"The NATO alliance held. Virtually nobody is left for Russia to invade in Western Europe without triggering the mutual defense provisions of the treaty. Nobody wants that. Russia has occupied freaking Latvia and Estonia. Really? Who cares? Not even the countries themselves.

"Bill, Quinn, how are things down your way?" Jon asked.

Bill answered first. "The arrival of the Chait ship was breathtaking. However, as you know, the Chait were not present. Only automated devices." The others groaned on cue. "An army of automated worker machines debarked from the Chait ship and swarmed the *Nina* and *Santa Maria*. The devices moved so quickly it was difficult to get a count. At least a hundred were working on each lifter the whole time. This landing was yet another class of ship. The Chait have a huge industrial base out there, somewhere.

"The military action was invisible from where we were. The planes, the ships, the armed men were all over the horizon. We can't even see the vultures from here. So, it was a non-event. Except, the local workforce disappeared for a week, but they're all back now.

"The first of the cargo ships loaded with weapons arrived yesterday. We have enough weapons emplacements ready for this first shipment and a training cadre in place. Working relations with the Namibian military will be ticklish for a while. However, I'm confident we'll work through any difficulties.

"Over to you, Quinn."

"Things were a little more exciting down here," said Quinn. "We had a lot of fighter jets overhead, and a lot of Australian military ringing the facility. We didn't allow anybody inside the fence. It was very tense for a couple days.

"We now have dispensation from the government to run a nearby island as an NGO in a separate, vaguely defined political jurisdiction. The politicians balanced the colony program against the safety of the citizens of Hobart, and our need for lots and lots of weapons under civilian control. We won out as the lesser evil.

"I'd like to give a shout-out to the logistics people in Houston. We couldn't have played the shell game with the supply and colonist transport pods without them.

"A year ago, I thought organizing the colonists and scheduling the loading of transport pods onto the lifters would be the focus of our activities. We do that of course; however, our time and energy is consumed in moving the damned things constantly around the southern hemisphere.

"We've hardly mentioned the colonists. We've been jerking them around changing schedules and shuffling them among departure points. They've been great. I hope things settle down now," finished Quinn.

"Thanks, guys," said Jon. "You must have gone through some stressful times with those bullseyes on your location. My sincere thanks to you both."

The two mumbled something back in embarrassment. The others chipped in a chorus of thanks.

"Both HLV *Argo* and *Odysseus* are making regular runs to the colony planets now," said Jon. "Early indications are the ships require very little maintenance. That translates into limited downtime, so the flight numbers will be on the high side of our estimates. We now believe two pickups a week from lunar orbit is doable."

"We need to talk next week and formalize future construction plans. Right now, I'm leaning towards the build of an additional four heavy lifters. I believe we should build them to a point of readiness to receive the Chait technology, and then put them in storage. The Chait will leave in a few years and we should keep this option available. It's better to have them and not need them, than the other way around. We may have to store the extra birds somewhere really remote, like Mars orbit.

"Who wants to hear some feel-good news?" asked Jon rhetorically. "Isabella—meaning me—fined the Russians ten flights. They lose their first two flights, and half of their next sixteen. The Chinese fine is twice that of the Russians.

"We need to plan our next steps," concluded Jon. By 'we' I include XSolarian, Isabella, the two sites, and all of us, personally. A month from now I want you to have your succession plans nailed down and be ready to leave."

FIFTY-SIX
THE LAST LAP

THE TOWN MANAGERS' MEETING HAD a different atmosphere this time. The Project's finish line was within sight.

John Hayward chaired the meeting. Present were the four town managers and Gerry Bass.

Gerry spoke first. "We need two of the *Argo* class flying regularly to support the colonization program. Plus, a spare. That means a minimum of three. The limiting factor in the near term is pilots. We can recruit, which takes six months, plus or minus, depending on their physical condition. Or we can grow our own. In my experience a new recruit requires at least a year of training. Then, the junior birdmen need a year of flying experience in order to fly well. Training perversely sucks up time from the experienced pilots, which makes the situation worse in the short term. Therefore, I recommend we recruit a dozen retired military pilots ASAP.

"I also recommend we build a minimum of four of the *Argo* class, and preferably five. The manufacturing pipeline is running well, and right now one or two more can be made very efficiently. We just cold-stack those not used regularly, until needed. The design is such that an *Argo* can sit unattended for decades without maintenance or degradation.

"However, the colony program will grow. We will need more interstellar craft in the not-so-distant future. A break in production right now would be disastrous. Besides," he said with a grin, "I imagine we'll want to go exploring."

Valerie, the Shoreside manager, chimed in. "Pilots won't be the only skill we're short of. The workforce is about ready to flatline for the next twenty years."

"How can that be?" exclaimed Doug Bickel. "The recruitment flights are still arriving more or less every week. What's changed?"

"The flights are still running," replied Valerie. "While the Chait have asked for their loaner starship back, they are flexible and will allow us time to adjust before giving up the ship. We have our own interstellar transport capability now. We can use one of the *Argo* class for the recruiting flights, or build a ship tailored to those missions. One way or the other we can adjust.

"The reason the workforce will flatline is half our population is young women, and they're getting pregnant. I now have a baseline historical database from which I can make reasonable extrapolations. Women arrive here and are restored to a healthy twenty-five-year-old age. Whoopee! The now young women spend a year or two enjoying life and then they partner up. After a year or two of marriage, we start having kids. This is biology 101. Every single woman on the planet is of prime childbearing age. Half the current workforce is going to drop out over the next five years. The shift has already begun. Don't tell me you haven't seen the baby carriages. We've each put up day-care centers in our respective towns.

"By the way, I'm pregnant," she finished.

During desultory congratulations to Valerie, the shell-shocked group pondered the implications.

"Let's poke at the numbers for a minute," said Steve Kopec, the Rainy Town manager. "Our population is close to five thousand people. Best case, the recruiting flights bring in twenty people a trip, and make fifty trips a year. That's a thousand new recruits a year, maximum. Figure the intake remains balanced, the colony grows by five hundred men and five hundred women every year.

"How many women do you figure will drop out of the workforce over the next several years?" he asked.

"I estimate six hundred leave next year and that number rising every year for several years," responded Valerie. "Expect ten percent of the current workforce dropping out every year. Another way to look at it is one out of five women every year. In the very long term, I believe we will reach a point where a woman has two or three or four kids and calls it good until she is rejuvenated. Then she has several more, and so on. But I don't really know.

"We have an educated group," she said. "Many will come back to work once the kids are in school, say in five to ten years. However, remember our policies around families and children. Women don't necessarily have to work. Also, women earn eighteen months of service for every successful birth, which is another encouragement to stay home."

The group was quiet for a moment while juggling numbers in their head.

"This is really good information," said John. "We need to get our arms around this ASAP. I'd like you and Steve to get together with Anna, or one of her planning people, and develop a model to analyze the staffing situation. Please do something visual. A waterfall chart showing the activity per year would fit the bill. Include as many drivers as you can think of. I'll add this as a standing agenda item going forward."

"The situation might not be as dire as we think," mused Doug. "On one end of the work spectrum we have HAL units capable of any kind of physical labor. On the other end, we have the AI and enhancements to do the skull work and the paperwork, which was such drudgery in our former lives. There is a lot of managerial and logistical type sit-down work available for women. For both sexes, actually. Don't forget, the re-life carrot means women will keep a foot in the workforce. The question is timing."

"Is it too early to ask of your plans?" he asked Valerie delicately. "You can be our model."

"I know exactly what I want to do," she said. "I'll quit sometime in the second trimester and come back halftime once the tyke is six months old. I always enjoyed my children and being a mother. That said, I can take only so much goo-goo, gaa-gaa before I have to reenter the world of multi-syllable words.

"But, I'm just me," she added. "I'm not a good sample. I'm an anecdote. I've always made good money and hired domestic help. Some ladies will start having kids and won't want to return to work until the kids are grown. A better life is why we are here, and that includes families. That's the kind of life our king wants for us."

Steve broke in again. "A flatlined workforce might not even matter," he said. "Another year, or two at the maximum, and the requirements of

The Project drops to a background activity. We won't be building more starships for a while. Right now, The Project consumes half the resources, and half the workforce on Ouranos. The principal work of a Fab is to build more Fabs, and bigger Fabs. We've been tripling Fab capacity every year. Do we have to continue building so much capacity? We have no shortage of consumer goods. The achievement of The Project's goal will unlock huge amounts of resources for other uses. Maybe we won't require a bigger workforce every year. Possibly the opposite. Even if the workforce flatlines, a huge amount of resources will become available for other purposes."

Another lengthy pause in the conversation while everyone digested Steve's comments.

"I finally get a flying car," said Steve. "We all do."

Everyone responded.

"I want a second home on the beach," said John.

"I want a second home in the mountains," said Valerie.

"I want a big-ass deepwater fishing boat," said Doug.

"I want a 1970s-era Citabria acrobatic plane built with Chait technology," said Gerry.

Everyone laughed again.

"Ok, let's get the meeting back on track," said John. "The conversation is escalating to matters above our pay grades. The king is certain to have strong thoughts on the future use of his Fabs. Let's not get ahead of ourselves. We all know the king is quite supportive of families, so let's account for that in our staffing projections."

The group reached three major decisions: produce a total of four of the *Argo* class starships, recruit additional pilots, and begin planning a second class of star ship better suited for the recruitment trips to Earth. The Bifrost class.

All subject to final approval by the king.

Once the call was finished, John pinged Valerie. "I have two questions," he said.

"Yes?" she replied.

"First, and most importantly, will you marry me?" he asked.

She laughed her ass off. "Of course, my sweetie poo pumpkin pie," she teased. "I already said yes. The bigger question is, when will we tell everyone you're the father? This is not much of a secret, you know. I suggest we make an announcement at the next monthly meeting. We'll need to set a date beforehand."

"That works," he said. "Any date you pick is fine with me. It would be nice if the king was here. He'd want to attend."

"I already thought of that, you dummy," she replied. "What's your second question?"

"How long will recruitment of a professional macroeconomist take?" John asked. "I've looked, and we don't have one already here. I need one with nuts-and-bolts experience. Preferably a PhD, but I'll accept a good fit with only a master's degree. I can't wait the usual six months. I want them able to contribute quickly, so candidates can't be too decrepit. The duties suggest this is a desk job, so the recruit can be somewhat creaky. No waivers for communists, or hardline socialists."

"That last requirement makes recruiting tough for this particular occupation," she said. "What's driving this particular need?" she asked.

"The Project employs half the people on the planet, and is nearing completion," he replied. "What happens then? I need options to discuss intelligently with the king."

The lovers made kissy sounds to each other and switched off.

John then called Anna. "Please talk to your guy who pulls the data behind the quarterly Fab-minute cost adjustments," he began.

Goods and services on Ouranos were based on the standard cost of a minute of Fab processing time. That was a squishy number as productivity varied with the Fab size, utilization, and the complexity of the particular processing cycle. Workers were paid in Fab-minutes, bought manufactured goods based on Fab-minutes, and saved, borrowed, or lent Fab-minutes.

In the history of civilization there never was an economy where the means of production were used as units of exchange, money.

A massive amount of available Fab processing time was likely to hit the market over the next two years. An economic dislocation was coming.

"Ok," said Anna "What's up?"

"Ask him to massage the data a bit. I want to ramp our standard Fab-minute cost adjustment down. We are going to have excess capacity in the near future. So, until you hear different, I want the quarterly value reduction set at four and a half percent."

To keep Fab cost in line with reality, the value was recalculated quarterly. To prevent wild swings, the adjustment was limited to no more than five percent in any quarter.

"Wow, that's ninety percent of the maximum," she said. "I guess I'm not totally surprised. A lot of folks are overpaying private contractors for help with housing. People have little else to spend money on. We don't even have chocolate!

"How big a deal can this be, really? People plan to put in their ten years for The Project to earn a re-life. Implicit in the arrangement is The Project must indeed offer employment. Any backpedaling on the deal, and angry people will turn out with pitchforks and torches."

"All true," John replied. "However, there will likely be some economic dislocation in switching our entire civilization from what we do now to the next phase. Whatever that is. I don't want to spook the herd, so keep this quiet. I'll address the matter appropriately at the next town hall meeting.

"Before you ask," John said, winding up, "no financial speculating. The rules haven't changed. For obvious reasons, you and I don't speculate on the value of Fab time. If anybody found out, you'd be tarred and feathered."

"Drat," she said.

FIFTY-SEVEN
THE ROUND TABLE

T HE KING AND HIS ADVISORS met in the observation room, overlooking the town of Shoreside. The room was finished in stone and wood. Large windows overlooked a wide balcony. Beyond the decorative iron rails, the town and enveloping ocean bay looked like a post card.

The king returned to Ouranos several times a year. Now, he was here to stay. He was meeting with his nobles-to-be to orchestrate the upcoming Founders' Day ceremonies and associated festivities.

"I've spoken with each of you separately," said King Jon. "There shouldn't be any surprises." He looked around the heavy inlaid wood table at the happy faces and comfortable body language. "We are all friends here, so I'm going to propose a premature, informal toast—to Sir John, Duke of Mountainside; Lady Valerie, Countess of Shoreside; and Counts Kopec of Rainy Town and Bickel of Amazon Cove. And last but not least, Sir Gerry, admiral of his Lordship's fleet, and knight of the realm!"

All raised and waved their glasses of quite good wine towards the others and took a sip.

"The next time you hear those words from me," said Jon, "will be in front of a lot of people, and performed correctly, formally, and with considerable pomp and ceremony. Please practice your lines beforehand. There is a lot of kneeling and bowing involved. However, you don't have to kiss my ring." The others chuckled a bit.

"A display of obeisance is not natural for Americans, or even Canadians," said Jon, acknowledging John Hayward with a tilt of his head. "Remember though, this ceremony, or something similar, has occurred for millennia in most of the countries on Earth.

"This is not a democracy, or even a republic. Because I value your judgement, I often seek your counsel. We almost always agree on issues, and it is human nature to believe we are reaching a group consensus, or even voting on an outcome. That's not the case, and please don't make the mistake of believing so."

The others nodded in agreement. Their body language was still relaxed. Each had heard a version of this lecture before.

"I will grant you a hundred thousand hectares of land in your respective regions. I will also grant rights to operate several Fabs for your personal use. There are certain restrictions on the use of those Fabs which I will strictly enforce. The Crown will pay you a small royalty for his Fab operations in your region. You may personally take oath from up to ten sworn vassals at wages not less than one earns working for The Project. I will grant each of you ten additional HAL units for your personal use."

The land grants, though generous by Earth standards, were miniscule compared to the Crown lands. The continent on which they resided—Olympus—contained hundreds of millions of hectares of land. And, Olympus was only one of twelve continents on Ouranos. Everyone in the room expected additional grants in the future as the population grew.

"You have many rights and responsibilities around governing your subjects, which I'm not delineating here and now. You know your duties. You also have the necessary authority to discharge those responsibilities. I expect you to continue to manage your regions properly. I do not anticipate the need for major changes. All of you have been managing in an exemplary fashion for years. Governing is slightly different than managing; however, I have confidence in your abilities.

"That said, never forget your subjects, are my subjects.

"Gerry has proven invaluable in pushing The Project to fruition. However, he does not bear the responsibility of governing. His titles and rewards are granted accordingly."

As a Baron, Gerry's rewards were materially less than those granted to the Counts. However, he was now one of the dozen or so wealthiest people on the planet.

Jon continued. "John has been functioning as my deputy minister, and he will continue to perform in that role. His grants are commensurate with those responsibilities." In other words, he was getting more than the others.

John and Jon were tight. Jon needed a strong right arm on Ouranos while he fought the battles on Earth.

John Harwood was Jon's uncle. He had arrived in the very first group of immigrants. In his prior life he managed large construction projects for a giant international engineering firm. Running Mountainside was child's play compared to his former responsibilities. No one on Ouranos knew their relationship, yet. Given her position, Valerie would soon know. Both she and Casey were pregnant. The standard genetic assays would prove the relationship between Casey's children and Valerie's. The upcoming nuptials of John and Valerie would form the largest concentration of political power on Ouranos, after Jon himself. Machiavelli might not approve of Jon putting a blood relative in such a powerful position.

Our children may marry, thought Jon wryly. *One generation in and the inbreeding starts. Ah well, a problem for another day.*

"I anticipate having these council meetings in person more often, now I've relocated. However, please continue to work with John, and your peers, as you have in the past.

"Questions?"

"What of the exiles?" asked Steve. "What is their standing here, on Ouranos?"

The others were not surprised when Steve, who managed the smallest, most out-of-the-way region, asked the question. His span of responsibilities was the smallest of the counts, and he possibly felt least secure in his position.

"Exiles" referred to Jon's Inner Circle from Earth.

Jon framed his answer carefully. "This is an extremely competent and able group of people. In a few short years these people built and managed a worldwide industrial enterprise employing tens of thousands of employees and contractors. These individuals accomplished this feat while dozens of government agencies of numerous countries tried to kidnap, bribe, extort, and murder them and their families.

"For years each of these people spoke daily to the Chait. Which is like having God on speed dial. These are my personal friends."

Crap, thought each of the group, *the king is parachuting his friends in over my head.*

"However, I'm not going to bring them in, fresh off the boat, and promote to positions over those already here," said Jon, as if reading their minds. Which he was, given his ghost.

"Given their contributions, I will ennoble each of the exiles as baron, or baroness, as the case may be, and name them knights of the realm. Each will receive an immediate land grant of ten thousand hectares, HAL units, and up to three sworn retainers. As a knight of the realm, each will receive a generous yearly stipend from the Crown.

"I will make a substantial monetary award to each at the ceremony. Easily enough for a comfortable house, and other immediate needs.

"I do not anticipate that as barons the exiles will participate in this council. Of course, I may pull someone in from time to time when I see the need."

Everyone relaxed; the newcomers would be a step down on the hierarchy and have materially less power, land, and money.

"I suggest you seek these people out and get to know them. Each and every one is extremely able. They are not the type to punch a clock, go home, and relax."

Everyone made noises of agreement. Half of them did so genuinely.

The patents of nobility haven't yet been formalized, and I'm importing the seeds of a merchant class with different goals, thought Jon in satisfaction. The exiles would run this place in ten years if his new counts didn't stay on their toes.

FIFTY-EIGHT
THE EXILES

SHIRLEY AND TRACEY LEANED ON the patio railing and looked out at the Poseidon Sea. A soft, warm breeze fluttered their hair. Each wore long, thin dresses. No pantsuits, no business attire.

"This planet is everything we were told," said Shirley. "The town is beautiful. I've been on tropical vacations, but never experienced a climate quite like this. Kind of weird though with no throngs of tourists."

"I'll say," replied Tracey. She nudged Shirley. "Jon's never looked better. Look at those clothes, and that vest. He looks like he should be wearing a sword and a cape. He's so happy now. It's as if the weight of the world is off his shoulders. He always seemed so relaxed, but the difference between then and now is obvious."

Casey joined Jon. They kissed and stood arm in arm, smiling.

"She's really good for him," said Shirley. She and Tracey looked at each other and uttered in the same low breath, "The bitch." They both laughed and went to join the others.

"I imagine we'll have little need to meet as a group in the future," said Jon. "The pressure is off so let's enjoy each other's company. Your families will return from the town tour in an hour or so. We will have a nice group dinner later tonight. Including your extended families, we have quite a group, sixty-seven people all told."

The immigration of the exiles had been hellish to arrange. Most wanted to invite sick friends and aging relatives to emigrate as well, primarily to obtain access to Full Medical. However, sharing details of the secret was forbidden. Jon was not flexible. He allowed only one option—an immediate mind wipe of the conversation, should the person decline to emigrate. Most of the Inner Circle were not comfortable with Chait technology tampering with Grandma's mind. However, they eventually acquiesced. Which led to the next problem. Some of those invited by the others were behaviorally unsuited and failed the interviews. Again, Jon laid down the law. Those failing the interview were denied entry; however, they were offered a place in the simulated reality inhabited by Paula.

The resulting bad feelings would linger for years.

"You've had the standard orientation and a quick tour of the settlements. You have plenty of time and resources to settle in with your families, if you were accompanied, while you figure out what to do next. Are there any initial thoughts?"

"I've decided to stay here, at Shoreside," said Randy. "I've been single a long time, and my girlfriend declined to move. I have no kids, no attachments, and now no job."

The others laughed, a little nervously.

"The IT industry I grew up with doesn't exist here so there is zero demand for a security consultant. Talk about a fresh start! I'm going to do something completely different. I'm going to run a charter fishing boat. I've already started querying the AI to determine the proper spec for a boat. The right Fab can produce one in a day or two. Maybe I'll put my new coat of arms on the stern. I've talked to the only guy doing commercial fishing, and he has agreed to train me up for a couple months. I'll be his boat boy. He's grateful for the help. Commercial fishing looks like a grind, so I'm going to contract as a charter for anybody who wants to go out for a day. I'll sell any extra left by the clients to the kitchens here. There's plenty of demand. The fish are so plentiful, and so inexperienced, even an amateur like me can catch a lot of fish.

"I'll give myself a year or two, and then reevaluate my life at that time," concluded Randy.

Around the table, eyes were wide. Talk about a change in lifestyle.

A job as a part-time charter captain was a great cover, thought Jon.

"We'll be seeing a lot of each other," said Tracey to Randy. "I plan to stay at Shoreside as well. Most of you know my husband, Phil; he was formerly a banker. He and I see a lot of opportunity. For example, the market for borrowing or lending Fab minutes appears immature and undeveloped. I see no evidence of any type of insurance markets. There are almost no middlemen, no distributors, no wholesalers, or brokers. I find it hard to believe what passes for commerce around here does so efficiently."

Most around the table were nodding thoughtfully. Several looked distinctly noncommittal as they had similar ideas.

Shirley said, "This is like show-and-tell during elementary school. I want to go next. First, Tom and I are getting married!"

What a shocker! You could not pick two more diametrically different people among the group if you tried.

Amongst the congratulations, Tracey broke in. "How long has this been going on?" she demanded.

"Quite a while," Shirley admitted. "We had to keep the relationship quiet. I'm HR, you know. I'm officially down on relationships among the staff. How would it look if I was going out with another vice president, an old white guy?"

"It would look like Tom was a very lucky guy," countered Quinn. He'd made a couple passes at Shirley and never got anywhere.

Tom sat there like a bump on a log, red-faced and tongue-tied.

Shirley poked him in the ribs. "Tell them what we're planning to do," she said.

"We are becoming country squires, gentleman farmers," began Tom. For him, it wasn't a bad attempt at humor. "After consulting the AI, we found a good location well suited to grow coffee. The spot is about a hundred kilometers south of Rainy Town. We'll be the southernmost colonists on the planet. However, the travel time is nothing by saucer."

The locally grown coffee was crap. Several people grew a few plants; however, they hadn't got the bean-processing quite right yet. Demand would be huge for a good product.

"I had mixed thoughts at first," said Shirley. "My grandparents came from Japan and worked their entire lives in the fields outside Bakersfield, so their children—my parents—didn't have to. Now I've chosen to go back to the fields. Maybe it's genetics," she joked.

"Yeah, right," snorted Tracey. "I can picture you standing there with a cold drink in one hand, while pointing with the other, instructing a HAL unit on what to work on next. The closest you'll get to manual work is grinding beans for your morning coffee."

"Gotta love those HAL units," countered Shirley. "No employee issues with those guys."

So it went.

Adrian planned to come out of the rejuvenation tank the same day as his wife. The couple planned to relocate to Amazon Cove and open the first university on Ouranos. "Regardless of our enhancements and the AI, I believe a formal education is more important than ever," he said. "To effectively use the Chait technology requires a trained mind. The theme of the university is critical thinking skills. I've already developed an outline for a curriculum which includes logic, rhetoric, grammar, debate, ethics, statistics, economics, civics, and lots of history."

Bill was also planning to live in Amazon Cove. "It's a no-brainer. Christ, Amazon Cove is the only spaceport operated by the human race," he said. "I plan to immerse myself for a couple years and see where it takes me."

Bob and his wife had decided on Mountainside. She grew up in Austria, and the countryside reminded her of home. She was going into a tank for three months to sync up her physical age with Bob's. They already agreed on a house in town, a place in the country, and a location for Bob's dojo. Bob had his own reasons for liking Mountainside. "The means of production are primarily located there, and the town has the largest population. I see lots of possibilities," he said.

Quinn wasn't ready to buckle down. "I have no responsibilities," he said. "I may never be in this situation again. Virtually none of the planet has been seen, or explored by man. We have only orbital scans. There are mountains to climb, and reefs to dive. I think I'm going to explore for a bit," he said.

The group wound down. After a second of silence, eyes swiveled towards Jon, and Casey.

"Well?" asked Shirley. "Fess up. Let's hear it, you guys."

"I finally wore her down," said Jon while giving Casey a hug. "We're getting married the day after Founders' Day. You're all invited."

The others congratulated the pair. This was no surprise.

"I couldn't wait; I'm already pregnant," admitted Casey. "Only a little bit though," she explained inaccurately. "I'm not going to show in my wedding dress!"

FIFTY-NINE
SECRETS

Bob and Tracey met Jon in his private study at the appointed hour. Jon greeted them warmly and made them all tall highly alcoholic drinks while he made desultory small talk. Drinks in hand, the group plopped down in comfortable dark leather chairs. A rare storm had blown in, so a fire of sweet-smelling cedar was burning in the fireplace. Rain, and an occasional buffet of wind, rattled the windows. After an animated inspection of the newcomers, the large short-haired brindle mutt lay near the fire and immediately fell into a deep sleep. He snored audibly.

"That's a good sign," said Bob, a dog person. "Dogs are susceptible to their owner's state of mind. When your dog snores, all is well in the world. That's a fine dog you have there. Who knows, he may become the first of a new breed on this world."

"I hope so," said Jon, smiling. "Should I rope in Robert?"

Bob and Tracey both nodded. The exiles lost contact with their individual Chait counterparts upon leaving the Earth's solar system. Only Jon retained the ability.

Robert, represented as Jupiter as always, appeared before them. He greeted them with his customary good cheer.

Finally, the alien got down to business. "What's up?" asked Robert. "I understand you have questions."

Tracey and Bob had an invisible body language between them, honed in hundreds of tense meetings. By silent agreement Tracey went first. "Will you now reveal what, and who you are?" asked Tracey. "It's not like we can spill the beans to a megalomanic dictator with nuclear weapons."

The answer was unexpected. "You should ask Jon," replied Robert in his usual breezy manner. "He figured us out almost immediately."

Tracey and Bob were taken aback. Jon was calm and collected as usual.

"What's with Jupiter?" asked Bob. "Is the planet significant to you, or just an elaborate misdirection?"

"Same answer," replied Robert. "Jon knows. Ask him. Anything else?" His insouciant manner softened the curt responses.

"Aaargh," gritted Tracey. "I have a million questions. I went through this with Jamocha. Please don't deny, deflect, or pettifog the answers. Why help humans? What are your plans for the future? When are you leaving? Do you plan to return? What can you tell us of yourself? Your people? Your culture? Surely you don't believe we can keep the secret of interstellar travel from other humans forever?"

"Oh, so you want a conversation," replied Robert. "Why didn't you say so? Sure, I'm more than willing to have a chat. By your standards our society is very old. We've had what you consider advanced technology, including interstellar flight capability, for hundreds of thousands of years. We've visited your solar system many times over that period. We are primarily interested in Jupiter, for reasons Jon can fill you in on.

"Humans are quite interesting. Unfortunately, you have been screwed by the fickle finger of fate. Your planet is a dead end. Long periods of heavy glaciation regularly occur, followed by a short warm period, such as now. During the cold portion of your climate cycle the polar zones expand to end any civilization in those latitudes. At the same time the oceans recede, leaving behind large new land areas which humans eventually migrate into. In the warm part of the cycle the oceans recover to swallow whatever nascent societies existed in the formerly dry ocean basins. Think of these periods as scrubbing a stubborn stain off a countertop. Back and forth, back and forth. The recent climate cycles are moot now as this era of your planet's atmosphere is drawing to an end. Jamocha has told you much of this.

"In two or three years we will leave Earth's solar system. You are welcome to keep the technology we've given you. We will check in on you in the future. By your standards our visits won't be often. Certainly not more than every hundred years or so.

"Goodbye, and good luck." Robert dropped off.

"That was less than illuminating," said Bob. "Jon, what can you tell us?"

"I can tell you everything," said Jon. "Before I do so, I need your solemn word the story goes no further than this room." He looked at the two of them expectantly.

Bob and Tracey looked at each other, then back at Jon. Each nodded their assent.

"I can live with that," said Bob. "I promise."

"You have my word as well," said Tracey.

Jon was actually relieved to have others with whom he could share the tale. The head executive of any large enterprise has a lonely job. The CEO can't share fully with anyone, except, sometimes, their spouse. Besides Casey, the closest Jon had as a confidant was the two people in the room with him now.

"Let me tell you a story," began Jon as he added a couple sticks to the fire. "About the day I met Robert." He spent the next hour relating that initial meeting and the two years that followed.

"The Chait are not life as we know it," explained Jon. "They are a highly sophisticated, highly evolved, cybernetic intelligence. In fact, Robert, Lemon, Jamocha, and the rest of them are not discreet beings. The Gestalt aboard the mothership created stripped-down instances of itself as interfaces to deal with humans. The being aboard the Chait mothership is, itself, a watered-down version of the primary Chait master instance. According to Robert, the details of the Chait creation are lost in time. However, their consciousness formed in an event sometimes bandied about in our less reputable science journals as a singularity."

Bob could see Tracey was not familiar with the concept.

"I have heard the theory," said Bob. "Humans have, maybe, already designed rudimentary artificial intelligence. Following that to a logical conclusion you arrive at a point where the computer has an AI program with the ability to engineer improvements to itself. The computer rewrites its own software to operate better and faster, which in turn repeats the process. Given the tremendous speed at which computers operate, the program's intelligence and capability accelerate quickly, at an ever-increasing rate. Eventually you arrive at a point analogous to a black hole, a singularity.

The... event... happens quickly, almost overnight. Finally, many intelligent people speculate such a singularity necessarily becomes a conscious being.

"Imagine, you come to work one Monday morning and meet an entity who knows all, understands all, and has a completely different agenda from yours."

Bob turned back to Jon. "What did Robert have to say about the beings who originally designed them?"

"He didn't say," said Jon, "and I didn't ask."

"This actually explains quite a lot," mused Tracey. "This explains their attitude towards my sister's mind in a box. Their intelligence and analysis capabilities were always indications of unlimited processing capability. This also explains why they never showed an interest in landing. In fact, they never showed any interest in sightseeing at all.

"What's up with Jupiter?" asked Tracey. "Was their interest a red herring, or do they have genuine business there?"

"Jupiter is the reason the Chait visit our solar system," said Jon. "The planet contains a dozen species of intelligent life, each in their own separate, distinct environmental zones.

"You see numerous distinct bands when you look at Jupiter, plus the giant red spot. Our knowledge of the interior is limited. Earth scientists believe there are discrete layers of helium, hydrogen, ammonia, and other gases whose properties vary immensely with depth and pressure. Go deep enough and you find an immense sea of liquid hydrogen, we think.

"Each of Jupiter's species has its own technology, politics, creation myths, belief systems, aspirations, ethics, and morals. Most have competing factions. In addition to relations among themselves, they often interact across species. Everything found in the history of the human race occurred a hundred times over within Jupiter. Earth and humans are interesting to the Chait, but essentially, we're just a sideshow."

Bob shook his head ruefully. "As a species we're a slow, stupid turtle about to get run over by something we don't understand. To them we're just a turtle to move off the highway before we get squashed. All this time we thought we were the center of attention, the focus of their time and energy. What a blow to the ego."

"I'll say," agreed Tracey. "All this time I had a fear in the back of my mind, the Chait had an insidious ulterior motive for their actions."

"Both of you are feeling a bit let down," said Jon. "Everyone in the Inner Circle has similar symptoms. You're refugees struggling with post-traumatic stress syndrome. A normal daily life seems abnormal. You even feel uneasy without bodyguards."

"Oh my God, that's true!" exclaimed Tracey. "One of the things bugging me subconsciously is I no longer have the missing link knuckle-walking behind me."

"Hang in there," said Jon. "My suggestion is you travel, and decompress for a year. Keep in touch with the others for support. You're going to have a wonderful life here."

Bill and Tom met with Jon on the patio overlooking the bay. They had just finished a superb lunch consisting mainly of gigantic fresh shrimp. They were enjoying fine cigars.

"Which one of you is going to grow tobacco?" asked Jon in a jocular tone. He loved cigars. "Cigars from Earth are going to get increasingly rare."

In ones and twos, the Inner Circle were coming to Jon privately for solace and advice. They had gone from big shots to refugee nobodies overnight.

"Not me," responded Bill. "Tobacco is a weed that can grow anywhere. I imagine a dozen different people are trying already."

Tom shook his head as well. "Jon," he asked, "tell us about the exoplanet colonies. We focused for years on getting the colonization program up and running. As soon as the program got off the ground, we bailed. This may be above my pay grade, however, I find myself worrying about the long-term prospects of the colonies. Are they sustainable?"

Jon looked meditatively at his cigar. "Sustainability has a lot of facets. Knowing the pair of you as I do, you undoubtedly have different concerns. Bear with me while I roll through the obvious potential issues.

"First, none of us have studied the issue. No one at XSolarian, or Isabella, was ever asked to evaluate colony sustainability. I intentionally left the question of long-term viability to the respective governments responsible for their colonies.

"The Chait are leaving in two or three years. That's almost of no consequence. Even if the current fleet of heavy lifters wears out, or is badly damaged in an attack, Ouranos has the ability to build identical ships. Also, the United States will soon have the ability to transport large cargos to lunar orbit using terrestrial chemical rocket technology.

"As long as we on Ouranos continue to provide interstellar transport, the colony pipeline will continue to flow. As long as people here want to rejuvenate, they have to work for The Project. The Project will continue to transport colonists. On my word as King.

"As long as new colonists, supplies, and materials continue to flow, the colonies will survive."

"What if an unforeseen event materially interrupts, or ends the resupply operations?" asked Bill. "What happens then?"

"In that event the colonies are screwed," replied Jon. "The colonists' tools would wear out in a generation, and their offspring won't know how to replace them. The youngsters will regress to using pointy sticks and stone tools within a generation. The culture would devolve to something neolithic. The population will take thousands of years to grow large enough to develop a rudimentary civilization. Whatever culture eventually develops will likely be unrecognizable to us.

"Obviously, the bigger the initial gene pool the better. However, you only need one breeding pair for the species to theoretically survive.

"You don't need me to tell you this. You're smart guys. What's really on you mind?" asked Jon.

"This colony," said Bill. "We are concerned about the long-term viability of this colony. We are totally dependent on technology we don't comprehend. We don't understand the basic physics behind the Chait field technology, or how to reverse-engineer the hardware. We can't duplicate the alloys used in the power units—that's done in a Fab. What if we awaken one morning, and the magical tech doesn't work anymore? Do we start throwing virgins into a volcano and pray to the alien gods?"

Jon made an emphatic gesture with one hand. "It's the same answer, we're screwed. Just not as badly as the other colonies. Our planetary ecology matches Earth's. We have a population base of five thousand; the others are starting from a base an order of magnitude less than Ouranos. We have four separate sites, each with cleared land nearby, already producing crops. One natural calamity is unlikely to affect multiple towns. We have tons of refined metals at Mountainside. In some cases, we have backup systems—iron stoves, for example. We don't have ice ages. The other colonies don't have our advantages.

"So, yes, I share your concerns. To mitigate the Chait technology risk, we need to do as much as we can, as fast as we can. We have the advantage of ten thousand available HAL units. Think of it, the existing HALs do the equivalent work of fifty thousand strong human laborers. HALs are a huge resource.

"We need redundant systems—roads and bridges to supplement saucers, water systems powered by gravity, not mechanical pumps, sewage systems, traditional power sources, a proper harbor, the list goes on and on."

Both Bill and Tom were somewhat relieved. A full minute of silence followed while the men puffed on their cigars.

"See if this makes sense," began Tom. "Logically, the Chait genuinely want the colonies to survive. Why else support a program of establishing colonies on multiple planets?"

The other two nodded. Tom's supposition made sense.

"The only way the people in those colonies survive, much less flourish, is by reaching some minimum population base with an ability to feed, clothe, and shelter themselves."

Again, the other two nodded. That logically followed.

"QED, assuming for some unknown insidious reason the Chait wish to deactivate their technology, the earliest the action would happen is when one or more colonies are stable, self-supporting, and capable of survival." Tom reflected for a second. "I imagine they require a minimum of two colonies capable of long-term survival. They would want a backup in case shit happens," he concluded.

"Well done!" said a delighted Bill. "You have un-muddied the waters. If the Chait indeed plan to deactivate their technology, they won't do so until two or more colonies are viable. Which brings us, almost, back to our starting point. When do we expect the colonies to become self-supporting, and viable without continued resupply?"

Jon cut in. "From my point of view, as leader of the only colony with functioning Chait technology, a better question is: do we want the other colonies to survive? Following Tom's logic, their survival is not in our best interest."

Talk about throwing a turd on the table.

"That's a hideously cold-blooded view," said a horrified Tom. "That kind of thinking drove the Big Three to hound us for years. Besides, you don't know the Chait's eventual intentions."

Jon leaned forward. "If we follow cold logic, we should strangle the colonies, to save ours. Let them struggle along with one nostril above water to ensure our colony is critically needed. Imagine yourself in my shoes. To me, such an action is analogous to chicken soup. Can't hurt, might help."

Tom was appalled. Bill was thoughtful.

Jon sat back and drew on his cigar. "Tom, no need for the long face. Relax, I've discussed this at length with Robert. I do know their intentions. The Chait are not going to sabotage our equipment. They don't believe the human race can ever advance to a point of becoming a threat to them. I believe him. They have no reason to disable our technology base. Therefore, we have no reason to sabotage the colonies."

After the other two left, Jon went inside and poured himself a small glass of strong bourbon. Misleading his friends left a bad taste in his mouth. He wished now he hadn't authorized the additional heavy lifters. Although Robert was adamant the Chait had no plans to deactivate their technology on Ouranos, plans can change. Furthermore, Jon had no idea where Robert ranked on the Chait totem pole.

Jon was not going take the risk of the colonies succeeding too quickly. He had already sent word to the new chief executive of Isabella to slow roll the additional heavy lifters, and also to allow the colonies to establish second sites. Because of the relatively large population, the multiple towns on Ouranos increased the colony's chance of long-term viability. The opposite was true of the lightly populated Earth colonies. Jon would continue to limit the starship delivery runs and allow the inevitable bureaucratic growth to slow groundside operations.

Just in case.

Randy's activities were another secret. The threats to Isabella hadn't gone away forever. The enterprise had only a breathing space of a year or two. Then one or more of the big three would renew their attempts to purloin the advanced alien tech. The immigrant and supply flights still needed protection. Somebody had to monitor the big three. And somebody had to maintain the network of XSolarian agents. And someone had to regularly interface with the Chait.

That someone was Randy.

Jon saw no reason to enlighten the others on Randy's activities. The exiles each had a hundred reasons for maintaining access with the Chait, or keep their fingers in an earthly pie. Jon didn't want that. Best to not let them know of Randy's continuing involvement. No need for the longtime inhabitants of Ouranos to know about Randy's work either.

Besides, all rulers needed a secret police.

Have I become an evil person? thought Jon. *Are my morals and ethics a little too flexible? I've engaged in questionable activities up to and including summary executions. Have the things I've done to get here changed me in some fundamental way to the worse?*

Sophomore philosophy, he thought wryly as he threw the cigar butt into the fireplace. Thousands of good people, most of whom would be dead otherwise, are healthier, wealthier, and freer than any other point in their lives. Oh, don't forget the human race will survive the catastrophe slated for its birth planet.

He slept like a baby that night.

SIXTY
REGROUP

FOUNDERS' DAY ARRIVED.

In a group ceremony hundreds of new subjects swore fealty to the king. Then, one at a time, those being ennobled came forward and received their patent of nobility and made oath to the king. Afterwards, Jon gave a great speech.

The day concluded with a feast featuring locally produced food and drink. The feast had an air of a county fair. Foodstuffs from all corners of the realm were served.

From Shoreside came platters of shrimp, mussels, scallops, and expertly prepared sushi.

From Mountainside came venison roasts, aurochs steaks, and succulent wild boar.

From Amazon Cove came dishes of quail, turkey, and fried chicken.

From Rainy Town came desserts. Flour from the north was used to bake cherry, apple, and peach pies.

From the scattered homesteads came mounds of fresh vegetables and salad greens. The homesteaders also proudly produced large quantities of wine, cider, and schnapps of wildly varying quality.

No imports from Earth were served.

Jon and Casey were wed the following day.

The selection of groomsmen and bridesmaids are often a point of contention at weddings. This time, however, the selections went fairly smooth. Six of Casey's extended family had emigrated to Ouranos with her. Noelani, her cousin and lifelong best friend, was the maid of honor. Shirley and Valerie were the bridesmaids.

As King, Jon had to consider the political implications of his choices. He had to select nobles, and include at least one of the long-term residents, and at least one from among the exiles. After a round of informal conversations, Jon, with his preternatural ability to read people, knew who would be offended if excluded and who would not. After massaging a few egos, Jon selected John Harwood as best man, and Bob and Tom as groomsmen.

Jon had been best man at John and Valerie's wedding the previous week.

As the only non-noble in the wedding party, Noe became quite popular afterwards and was ardently pursued by social climbers.

There were no churches on Ouranos yet. Each town had a chapel, and a chaplain who gave a non-denominational service on Sundays. The majority of a chaplain's time involved counseling. Many of the rejuvenated immigrants sought counseling as they adjusted to their, literally, new life. Jon's wedding, like many others, was held under a simple pergola on a small rise overlooking the beach and the bay at Shoreside.

Those close to Jon and Casey struggled with gifts. What do you give a couple who have literally everything?

After the reception, the couple took a saucer and disappeared for a week-long honeymoon. They both tuned their enhancements to block outside calls.

"Where are we going?" asked Casey, once the saucer was well out to sea. Jon had flown a high leisurely route to the south of Shoreside bay before heading due west out to sea.

"It's a secret," said Jon as he switched on autopilot. "We have two hours to kill, and the scenery isn't going to change until we get there. Any ideas on how to pass the time?"

"You bet I do," said Casey as she clambered into the back seat. "What's this? A bottle of champagne and a couple glasses. Here, pop the cork and start pouring." She laughed at his crestfallen expression. "Poor baby, don't worry," she pinched him and tickled his ribs. "I get one drink a day. The champagne won't take long and then we can find another way to pass the time!"

When the saucer reached their destination, Jon circled the island a couple times. The high peaks were shrouded in mist. The thick forests were a deep, rich green. The beaches were black sand. At regular intervals small rivers drained into the sea.

The water was transparently clear. At one cove rafts of giant sea turtles were seen lazily cruising the edge of a reef. Even the turtles' shadows were visible on the sea bottom. Inside the reef, the shoals of fish were so colorful they were easily seen from the air.

"We have the whole place to ourselves," said Jon. "There is no one else here, not even any staff. There are no land predators of concern. We can wander anywhere on the island."

Jon landed the saucer in a small clearing within spitting distance of the beach. Several, obviously new, dwellings with thatched roofs ringed a grassy lawn. Jon lugged their bags into the nearest building, which was a surprisingly well-appointed beach house. The newlyweds quickly changed into their swimsuits and went out to explore.

"Oh my God," exclaimed Casey. "Look at these flowers! This is a hibiscus, over there is a bird of paradise, and a plumeria. Look"—she tore across the clearing—"this is a pikake." She looked a little further. "Jon, was this ecology lifted from our own Hawaii? These palm trees look exactly the same as those I've seen my entire life. Some of these flowers only occur on the Hawaiian Islands."

"This is the Hawaii of ten thousand years ago, sort of," said Jon while he tucked a flower behind her ear. "The climate is the same of course. There are a lot more birds, quite colorful birds, and the Chait included non-native flowers when they seeded the island. You will notice other tweaks as well, but most of the invasive species we are familiar with aren't here.

"The island is about the size of Maui, or Oahu. You get to name the place. It's my wedding gift to you."

The ensuing honeymoon was the stuff of dreams.

On their return Jon set off on a round of visits to the other towns, while Casey settled in at Shoreside. They spoke regularly every day.

On the third day of his trip Jon pinged Casey late in the afternoon. "How are you doing?" he asked.

"I'm doing great," she said. "I've spent most of this week getting my family settled in. Miss you though. How was your day?"

"Today went fine," he said. "Do you realize in my entire adult life, you're the only person to ever ask me about my day? I could get used to this." Each cooed to the other for a few minutes like any newlywed couple.

"People here aren't used to having me around," he remarked. "It's an adjustment. I'm careful to refer most questions back to the town managers. If I let people skip the chain of command I'll be buried under a pile of minutiae and undercut the authority of the managers. That part of ruling is exactly the same as being a CEO. In public I'm careful to use the correct titles, Count so and so, or Baron such and such. Referring to others by their title feels awkward, but if I don't drive the usage, respect for the titles will never take root.

"Mostly I reassure people about the future. We will continue to build spacecraft in the near term. The related infrastructure is in place so The Project's total activity is slackening somewhat.

"The manager here at Rainy Town, Count Kopec, wants permission to change the name of the place. He's got a point. I used to live near a town called 'Whispering Pines.' The name given by the original settlers was 'Misery Creek.' A lot of places change names over the years. The matter is unimportant; however, I'm sensitive about setting precedents. Is this Kopek's decision to make? My decision? Is it a matter for the Council? Should I even care?"

Casey laughed. "I bet you already made your decision. You hate minutiae. Let me guess, Kopec will make a proposal to the Council. You can veto their decision, but on this point whatever the council decides is fine with you."

"You must have hacked my enhancements," grumbled Jon.

"Anyway," he continued, "the prior two days at Amazon Cove were quite informative. Talking to people and reviewing visuals is one thing, but seeing the place up close is a whole different experience. The area is a thick tangled mass of scrubby vegetation. The virgin forest is almost impossible to walk through. The place seems similar to the Yucatan in Mexico.

"Under Count Bickel's leadership the crews there have cleared huge areas and transported in massive amounts of building materials. The amount of work done in so short a time is impressive. The climate is awful, and the housing is substandard. However, the Count is working hard to improve the housing situation. I'm confident he will succeed; however, he needs another year or two to get there.

"Our future growth will primarily be in Amazon Cove. We can make almost everything from the carbon extracted from the oil. Rainy Town will stay a small mining town. Mountainside won't need to grow much further. The commodity produced by Shoreside is people. I don't expect the number of incoming immigrants to increase, however, the wellness tune-ups will increase every year. In twenty years, the entire population will start cycling through for another round of rejuvenation. But that's way in the future."

"You make it sound like there is little left to accomplish," said Casey. "Surely not?"

"Oh, there is plenty left to do," replied Jon. "All four settlements are frontier towns now. They have to grow up and put in good housing, schools, playgrounds, and performing arts facilities. Not everyone is building a house in the country. A lot of people need an outlet for their leisure time. A dozen folks at Mountainside are plotting to build a ski area in secret—on Crown land. Once in use, they'll ask permission to formalize the arrangement. Sneaky bastards," he said admiringly.

"We also need a much more varied food supply. People are getting tired of potatoes."

"Never!" cried Casey. "I'll never give up potatoes," she joked.

"What then?" she pressed. "Do you plan to retire and spend all your time with your family? Like that would ever happen—ha!"

"I have a few ideas," he said.

SIXTY-ONE
THE CONCLAVE

O NE MONTH AFTER FOUNDERS' DAY, Jon called a conclave of his nobles. Surprisingly, the meeting was in person, at Amazon Cove rather than at Shoreside. There was speculation regarding the change in venue. Was there some significance, or did Jon simply desire to rotate meetings among the various sites?

The nobles did not meet inside a building. Lawn furniture and a portable wet bar were arranged on a saucer pad. Jon nodded to Doug, who addressed the gathering. "Ladies, gentlemen, please attend," he said. He put both hands in the air, wiggled his fingers, and intoned, "Abracadabra!" There was a sizzle and a pop, and an opaque hemispherical dome thirty meters in diameter sprang into existence. The others clapped appreciatively.

Doug made another motion—he was using his enhancements; the motions were just theater—and the dome flashed brightly for a fraction of a second. "That was a bug zap," he explained. A couple of HAL units carrying leaf blowers preceded the group into the dome to clean up the debris.

In twos and threes, the group pushed through a gluey portal into the dome. Half of the attendees hadn't experienced a dome entrance before. Once inside, the visual effect was as if one was looking through a window of one-way glass. While the HAL units cleaned up, Doug took a few minutes to explain the dome's features.

After everyone was seated, Jon addressed the group. "Change is in the air and all of us need to consider the future. There has been much speculation of late regarding the future of the colony as The Project tapers off. I can assure you we have much left to accomplish." He spoke to Valerie. "Do you have any idea of the minimum colony size needed to ensure long-term survival?"

"The short answer is no," she replied. "One needs millions of people to keep a modern industrial civilization going. We have regular ongoing interactions with Earth, so the required number is significantly less. If one has access to the magical Chait technology, as we do, you need even fewer. We have been getting along fine with only a few thousand people. Without the two advantages I just mentioned, I imagine we would devolve into a simple pastoral culture within a generation or two. Right now, it's as if we were camping, or an army on campaign. The other colonies don't have our advantages."

"Thank you, Countess," said Jon. "Lady Atkinson has summed up the situation quite nicely." He looked at John. "Please explain why homesteaders have gravitated to the Osage, rather than the White River valley."

"The explanation is simple," John said as he got to his feet. "Both river valleys are excellent for homesteading. The rivers themselves are similar, except the Osage is not nearly as susceptible to flooding. Weather patterns, and the fact the White River drains three times the land area, result in terrible spring floods."

"Thank you, Count Hayward," said Jon, "for that excellent summary."

"The kingdom has a population of five thousand souls. Between immigration and births the population is growing by a thousand per year. In the years to come I believe the combined population growth will be approximately the same. Our births will continue to grow; however, I imagine immigration will eventually shrink. The Osage River Valley is quite popular and will fill up faster than one might think. Remember, homesteaders working for The Project almost always use their yearly land grant to acquire property adjacent to their current holdings. Without getting into the details, they have prior rights to the contiguous land."

Those working for The Project received yearly grants of land. If two or more people asked for the same piece of property, a lottery was held. To prevent speculation, and hard feelings among neighbors, a landowner could put a hold on land adjacent to his existing holding. However, if that landowner consistently passed on the adjacent land to select property elsewhere, the hold was lifted. The land grant program had lots of fine print.

The king's speech became more formal.

"With the foregoing as background, I am decreeing an initiative to tame the White River. I request and desire Count Hayward manage the activity. The initiative requires two or more dams on tributaries of the river. He has a priority on the immigrants should he require any specialized personnel. The cost of the initiative shall be borne by the Crown."

Gears were turning in the heads of the audience. The value of homesteads and land grants along the Osage had probably just flatlined. Those fortunate to have homesteaded the White River valley were likely to see an increase in the value of their property. Both rivers originated in the mountains near Mountainside, and reached the sea, at or near the town of Shoreside. The lords of both towns, who were married to each other, would indirectly benefit.

"The Crown is donating a section of land and funding the construction of a school in the Osage River Valley halfway between Mountainside and Shoreside. This will reduce travel time, improve childhood education, and improve the quality of life of nearby homesteaders with children."

The more cynical thought this was likely a bone to assuage those whose property had just been devalued.

"Furthermore," continued Jon, "I request and desire Count Bickel form, and lead, a planning group of the town managers with the task of publishing a blueprint for the colony's physical growth considering a horizon of the next ten years. The planning group shall address municipal facilities for each of the existing towns and may identify one or more new sites for additional settlements if they deem such a path has merit. The planning group shall deliver the blueprint to the king for review at the first next council meeting after one year from today, after which the planning group shall dissolve."

To remain relevant, a planning document requires regular updates. However, Jon didn't want the nobles meeting regularly and making decisions without him. They might get too ambitious. Any future refresh of the masterplan would be evaluated by a different group.

Gears continued turning in the heads of the audience. Such a masterplan would likely favor one or more settlements over the others.

The nobles have already started to think about feathering their nest, thought Jon. *None will suggest a new town site. The process of prioritizing themselves over the collective goals of our society has already begun. I'm glad I called them together now.*

"Baron Kelly has expressed interest in opening an institution of higher learning at Amazon Cove, with a primary goal of fostering critical thinking skills. The Crown fully supports his endeavor. I am donating a section of land and will fund the necessary construction. Associated with the university shall be a separate institute to study, comprehend, and reverse-engineer Chait field technology.

"The Chait identified ninety-four exoplanets well-suited for human life. The human race is slowly, painfully colonizing seven of those planets. What about the rest?" he asked rhetorically.

The change of subject surprised everyone.

"I have personally visited each and every exoplanet on the list. I've walked the surface and breathed the air. I left stone markers when I laid claim to those worlds."

Jon paused. The timing was almost perfect.

"Look there!" he exclaimed as he pointed. A half kilometer away, the *Argo* had just lifted off. The ship slowly accelerated at a steep angle until it disappeared into the morning sky.

"Ouranos will not keep the secret of interstellar flight forever. Every nation on Earth is intensively studying Chait technology and, mark my words, they will eventually understand the physics and duplicate the hardware. To ensure your future, and that of your families, our society must run as fast, and as far as humanly possible."

Jon was speaking passionately now, with broad expansive gestures. "Ladies, gentlemen, you have a thousand years of healthy, vigorous life ahead of you. What do you, personally, want for your children? Your grandchildren? An estate of thousands of hectares? A continent on Ouranos? Or an entire planet out there!?"

SIXTY-TWO
EPILOGUE

JON STOOD TALL, TANNED, AND strong in the ankle-deep surf. "Come here!" he shouted and dropped to his knees, arms extended.

"Dadeeee!" screamed the tiny twin girls in unison as their chubby legs churned down the beach.

Duan knelt before the flat stone. He placed a dozen grains of wheat on the left side. On the right he placed a rude wooden cup. He opened his water bottle and poured an inch of goat's milk in the cup. Finally, he opened his creel and removed a tiny dead fish which he also placed on the stone.

"What are you doing?" asked a voice from behind him.

He whirled around, and then relaxed when he saw who it was. "You shouldn't sneak up on me," he chided her. "I about jumped out of my skin."

"You better not let Han catch you doing that," said Mei severely. "He'll give you extra duty for a month." Han Leji was the colony's political officer.

"I'm not hurting anyone," said Duan defensively. "This is hardly a mouthful, and it's from my own rations. My grandmother taught me the ritual. It brings good luck. We need some good luck if we are to prosper on this world."

As she went on her way, Mei shouted over her shoulder; "Don't say I didn't warn you!"

"Han Leji is the one who should be careful," retorted Duan. "A lot of people agree with me!"